CHRIS RYAN

- CREDENTIALS -

Joined the SAS in 1984, serving in military hot zones across the world.

Expert in overt and covert operations in global theatres of war including Northern Ireland, Africa, the Middle East and other classified territories.

Commander of the Sniper squad within the anti-terrorist team.

Part of an eight man patrol on the Bravo Two Zero Gulf War mission in Iraq. The mission was compromised, resulting in the deaths of three fellow soldiers and the capture of four more as POWs. Ryan was the only person to defy his adversaries, escaping to Syria on foot over a distance of 300 kilometres under heavy pursuit.

His ordeal made history as the longest escape and evasion by an SAS trooper, for which he was awarded the Military Medal.

Informed by his direct knowledge of covert operations, military strategy and the battlefields of today, Chris Ryan's books deliver an authentic reading experience, providing a fierce snapshot of life on the front-lines – and beyond.

He is the author of 13 bestselling military thrillers alongside the true-life account of his death-defying Gulf War mission, *The One That Got Away*.

His books are dedicated to the men and women who risk their lives fighting for the armed forces.

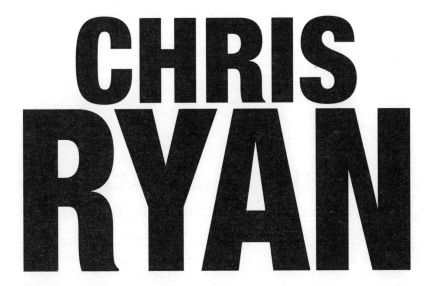

CHRIS RYAN

Who Dares Wins

Century · London

Published by Century in 2009

2 4 6 8 10 9 7 5 3 1

First published in the United Kingdom in 2009 by
Century
Random House, 20 Vauxhall Bridge Road,
London SW1V 2SA

www.randomhouse.co.uk

Addresses for companies within The Random House Group Limited can be found at:
www.randomhouse.co.uk

The Random House Group Limited Reg. No. 954009

A CIP catalogue record for this book
is available from the British Library

Hardback ISBN 9781846053276
Trade paperback ISBN 9781846053283

The Random House Group Limited supports The Forest Stewardship Council
(FSC), the leading international forest certification. All our titles that are printed on
Greenpeace approved FSC certified paper carry the FSC logo.
Our paper procurement policy can be found at:
www.rbooks.co.uk/environment

Mixed Sources
Product group from well-managed
forests and other controlled sources
www.fsc.org   Cert no. TT-COC-2139
© 1996 Forest Stewardship Council
FSC

Typeset by SX Composing DTP, Rayleigh, Essex
Printed in Great Britain by
Clays Limited, St Ives plc

ACKNOWLEDGEMENTS

To my agent Barbara Levy, editor Mark Booth, Charlotte Haycock, Charlotte Bush and the rest of the team at Century.

Also by Chris Ryan

'Everyone is like a moon, and has a dark side which he never shows to anybody.'

Mark Twain

PROLOGUE

Iraq. 2003.
Baghdad had fallen.

The streets were filled with troops, panic and fear. Sam Redman could taste it. The newswires buzzed with scenes of jubilation, with images of the grotesque statue of a hated dictator being toppled by the newly liberated citizens. But that was only half the story. The cobra's head might have been cut off, but its body was still flailing dangerously. There was talk of killing squads of former Iraqi Republican Guards tearing through the streets on white trucks, brandishing AK-47s and settling old scores. Earlier they'd come across a dismembered torso lying in an alleyway. The legs, arms and head were missing and the rest was covered in flies. A witness had seen the man, a Western security guard, get pinned down during an ambush. His captors showed no mercy. In full view of the street they forced him to the ground and hacked off his limbs with a machete. The witness told them that the captors had made a mess of it; the blade wasn't sharp enough and it took two men several minutes to hack through the bone and gristle. When they were down they peeled off his skin and beat his torso with his own limbs. Nearly an hour after they had captured him, the killing squad put a bullet through his forehead. One of the guys had filmed it on a camera; no doubt the footage was being uploaded on some dodgy Arabic website at that very minute. It was a sign of the way the country was

1

headed: to hell in a fucking hand-cart. Only the presence of the Coalition forces held it still. If they were to leave now the city – the whole country – would be held to ransom by the looters, the rioters and the profiteers. By people like the man who sat in front of Sam now, sweat shining on his dark-skinned face and a nauseating stench of halitosis drifting from his gap-toothed mouth.

'*Miaat elf doolaar Amreekee*,' he said, before spitting on the floor and then setting his lips into an oily smile.

Sam turned to his brother. Jacob's command of Arabic was better than anyone's in the Regiment. He'd been over the Iraqi border more times than he could count in the past few years and he knew how to play it with these people.

'A thousand American dollars,' he translated flatly.

Mac Howden, the third man in their unit, sneered. His left hand wandered up to his right ear, half of which was missing – a scar from a firefight in Borneo. An inch to the left and it would have been a different story. 'I could do with a thousand Yankee dollars myself. Difference is, this greasy little fucker'll probably just go straight out and spend it on an RPG. He'll be taking potshots at Chinooks in two hours.'

The Iraqi tout had said his name was Sadiq. None of them believed him, but in a situation like this one name was as good as another. Whether he knew that Sam, Jacob and Mac were SAS – or what the SAS even was – was anybody's guess. Beyond doubt, however, he knew the value of the information he carried. Sadiq's face remained fixed in that unpleasant smile as the three of them talked. *Discuss it among yourselves*, his expression said. *I'm in no hurry.*

'And anyway,' Mac continued, 'rule of engagement number one: never trust a fucking raghead. How do we know he's telling the truth?'

'We don't,' Sam growled. He didn't care about the money – it wasn't like it was his – but he cared deeply about this guy pulling a fast one on them.

Jacob sniffed and his eyes narrowed slightly. Sam knew his brother well enough to realise he was about to do something. But with Jacob, you could never quite tell what. His brother took a step towards the straight-backed chair where Sadiq was sitting. They'd put him there, in the middle of this gloomy basement on the outskirts of Baghdad, so that he would feel intimidated while the three of them loomed over him. He didn't appear to be intimidated at all, however. As a beam of the morning sun shone on to his face through the air vent at the top of the outside wall – the only source of light available to them – he looked quite at ease. As if he had the upper hand.

That look of smug satisfaction did not change as Jacob approached; but it soon fizzled away as Sam's brother wrapped his big hand around Sadiq's neck. The tout looked angry first, then frightened as Jacob pulled a handgun from his belt and crushed it against the Iraqi's skull. There was a moment of silence, broken only by the faint gasping sound as Sadiq struggled to breathe, before Jacob spoke.

'I know you speak better English than you're letting on,' he hissed.

Jacob's fingers twitched as he squeezed Sadiq's bulging neck a little harder. A croaking sound came from the Iraqi's throat.

'*Please,*' he croaked. '*You hurt me . . .*'

At first it looked as if Jacob hadn't heard. He just kept his fingers firmly in place. Then, with a sudden explosion of force, he thrust his arm forward. Sadiq's chair toppled backwards. As he fell he hit his head against the stone floor, crying out with pain. Like a rodent that has been suddenly disturbed, he scurried on all fours towards the back wall, then pushed himself up to his feet.

Jacob had been watching him dispassionately. Now that Sadiq was standing again he advanced. He put the butt of the handgun flat against the tout's forehead and looked directly into his frightened eyes.

'I'm going to speak very slowly and very clearly so that there's no risk that you don't understand what I'm saying.' Jacob's voice was calm and insistent. Sadiq nodded to indicate his agreement.

'Good,' Jacob whispered. 'Now it's very simple. You're going to show us where he's hiding. We'll give you something to leave outside his house as a signal. After that we never want to see you again.'

Sadiq nodded even more enthusiastically.

'But if we find that you're lying to us,' Jacob continued, as though talking to a child, 'we'll come looking for you. And you know what will happen then, don't you?' He tapped the end of his gun against Sadiq's head to reinforce his threat. He was a sweaty, shady little prick. Jacob would slot the fucker given half a chance, and from the look in Sadiq's eyes the Iraqi understood. He started to breathe heavily. 'What about my money?' he asked in awkward, stilted English.

'You'll get your money,' Jacob replied. 'You'd better just make sure we get what *we* want, otherwise it could end up being an expensive day for you.' He rapped the end of the gun against the Iraqi's sweaty forehead.

'Please,' Sadiq whimpered, jolting as though he had just received an electric shock. '*Please.* I do as you ask . . .' His knees buckled.

Jacob nodded slowly, then lowered his gun. As he turned, the light from the air vent caught his face. He winked quickly at Sam, who did his best to stop himself from smiling. If everything went according to plan, this had the makings of a very good day.

'Let's get ready,' Jacob announced. 'We'll get on to the Farm, request air support. Strike at midday when our friend is sheltering from the heat.'

Sam looked at his watch. 10.00 hrs. Two hours to go.

'Where's the house?' Mac demanded of Sadiq.

The tout sniffed, apparently relieved to be talking to someone other than Jacob.

'Al-Mansour district,' he said.

Sam consulted his mental map of Baghdad. 'It's the other side of town,' he noted. 'We'd better get moving.'

★

'Slow down!'

Sadiq drove them in his beaten-up old Toyota and he was driving them too quickly. Jacob sat up front with Sam and Mac in the back. He poked his handgun into the tout's ribs. 'I said, slow down.'

The tout hit the brakes.

'Just take it easy,' Jacob instructed. 'We don't want to be pulled over.' Sadiq didn't reply. He just kept looking in his mirrors, both at the other cars in the broad, tree-lined road and at the grim-faced SAS men sitting in the back.

It was already very hot – air conditioning was a luxury Sadiq evidently couldn't afford. The heat made Sam's six-week old beard itch and he noticed the others were scratching at their faces too. The SAS men were all dressed as Arabs in dishdash, traditional robes that were grubby and sweat-stained. Underneath the robes, however, was a different story. The three soldiers were packing ops waist-coats filled with all the tools of their trade: covert radios, Sig 226 9 mm pistols, fragmentation grenades, flashbangs and ammo. At Sam's feet was a rolled up piece of carpet. Walk down the street with it and nobody would raise an eyebrow, but that was because they didn't know he had a Diemaco C8 secreted inside, complete with a C79 optical sight, a Heckler & Koch 40 mm grenade launcher and a Surefire torch. He had applied green and black camouflage paint to the weapon and wrapped black plumber's tape around the pistol grip to stop it slipping in the hot, sweaty conditions he knew he

5

could expect. A bungee cord was fastened to the butt, ready to be slung round each shoulder, forming an X shape across his back.

The other two were similarly tooled up, Mac carrying his main weapon in a bag on his lap, Jacob having strapped his to the side of his body. A barely visible comms earpiece was fitted snugly inside his ear, but for now the unit's comms were switched off.

The Al-Mansour district bore the scars of the invasion: shop fronts had been reduced to rubble, cars were burned out. The US Air Force boys had done a right number on this place. The air was still shit hot and when Sam breathed in his lungs felt like they were on fire. Everywhere stank of cordite. Amid the rubble of an obliterated two-level house, a grey-haired man was on his knees. His white shirt was torn and smudged with black streaks, and on his lap lay a lifeless body of a girl no older than eight or nine, her face pebble-dashed with shrapnel. Despite the chaos, it was clearly an affluent part of the city. The houses were grander, the shops classier. Their target was the Commander of Saddam's Special Republican Guard. The Yanks were baying for his blood – he was high up on the Personality Identification Playing Cards, the deck issued to the American army to help them identify the leading members of the Ba'ath Party. It was difficult for these people to leave Baghdad and it made a certain kind of sense that he'd be holed up somewhere with a few luxuries. After years of power, these guys wouldn't want to hide out in some hole where they couldn't even piss in comfort. More likely that he'd have surrounded himself with a miniature army in a large house. Sadiq claimed this was what he'd done.

There was a manic air about the district, even now. Despite the heat many of the streets were teeming with people – Iraqi citizens and Coalition troops – which made it difficult to find a place to stop where they wouldn't be interrupted or overlooked. They eventually stopped in a side street that smelt of rotting vegetables and urine. Sam checked his watch. 11.30. There was a moment of silence as the engine died. Jacob placed his canvas bag on his lap and unzipped it. From inside he carefully removed a battered fizzy drinks can, artfully dented in places. Not Coca-Cola, but some red and white Iraqi equivalent. Sadiq looked at him as if he was mad.

'Take it,' Jacob instructed. He placed the can in Sadiq's reluctantly outstretched hand. The tout weighed it up, clearly surprised that it was heavier than he expected.

'It contains a tracking device,' Jacob explained. 'Chances are the house is being watched. If we follow you, they might clock us. All you need to do is put this can outside the gates of the house then get the fuck out of there. Walk, Sadiq. Don't run. If they see you running someone will get suspicious. And remember – we know how to find you and your family. Pull a fucking fast one and we'll be knocking on your door.'

Sadiq looked fearfully at the drinks can and then back at Jacob. It was clear he was having second thoughts. The expression on his face changed, however, when Jacob pulled out a stash of American dollars. The tout grabbed them quickly, stuffed them into his pocket then licked his dry lips. 'Okay,' he said, sounding like he was psyching himself up. 'I will do it now.' He looked at each of the SAS men in turn, as though waiting for a friendly goodbye. All he received, however, were stern, unresponsive looks. His face twitched and, still clutching the drinks can, he opened the car door and stepped outside.

None of them spoke until he was out of sight. Then Mac let out a burst of breath, half-amused, half-relieved. 'Fucking hell, J.,' he said. 'I thought he was going to piss himself there and then.'

'You said it yourself,' Jacob replied, leaning over to look

7

at them in the back with a twinkle in his grey eyes. 'Never trust a raghead. Especially a raghead tout. Much better to put the shits up him before he starts deciding to play silly buggers.'

Sam allowed himself a smile. It was classic Jacob – the tout was now so scared of his brother that he'd do anything he was told. 'Not much chance of that,' he murmured as he pulled his Iridium mobile sat phone from his ops waistcoat and dialled a number. 'HQ,' he stated, 'this is Yankee Delta Three. Our man's heading towards the target. Over.'

A brief, crackly pause and then a voice. 'Yankee Delta Three, we have the signal. Await further instruction.'

'Roger that.' And then to the others, 'They've got him.'

Back at the base, Sam knew, Sadiq the tout would be a green blip moving its way along a map displayed on a GPS receiver. They sat in silence, waiting for confirmation that the tracking device had stopped. It seemed to be taking a long time, but maybe that was just the heat. Sam's mouth and lips were burning dry. He pictured Sadiq, half-walking, half-running, his face still covered with that inexhaustible supply of sweat. The smell of the Iraqi's bad breath lingered in the car.

And then, from nowhere, the sat phone crackled into life again. 'Yankee Delta Three, we have a location.'

Sam nodded at Jacob who pulled out a battered GPS screen of his own, fiddled momentarily with it, then handed the device round. It showed a map of the area and a small dot which indicated where the fizzy-drink can had come to rest. From where the car was parked they had to head east, turn left then third right. The can would be outside the house they were to hit. They memorised the position. No one said a word. They didn't need to. The unit was operating almost on autopilot.

Sam spoke into the sat phone again. 'This is Yankee Delta Three. We're going for a stroll.'

'Enjoy the countryside, Sam,' the voice came back. 'Air support turning and burning, ready on your order.' Reassuring words. It meant that back at base, an American-flown Black Hawk was already in a holding pattern, preparing to fly to their location the second they received word that hostages had been secured. A minute to get here, a minute to extract. Those choppers were every soldier's favourite asset.

They climbed out of the car, each of them switching on their comms as they did so. 'I'll go first,' Jacob announced. 'I'll stake out the front. Sam, take the rear. Mac, the street. RV back here in fifteen minutes.'

'Roger that.'

They left at thirty-second intervals – Jacob first, then Mac and finally Sam, his dishdash flapping around his legs and his carpet-wrapped Diemaco C8 held nonchalantly under his arm – to avoid attracting unwanted attention. Sam followed his mental map and in less than a minute he was turning into a broad, tree-lined street. The houses here were grand, some with ornate columns on either side of the door that wouldn't have been out of place in Mayfair. But there were other things you wouldn't see in London: as Sam walked down the street he noticed bullet marks along one of the walls. AK rounds, he thought to himself. Maybe a scar of the invasion; or maybe they had been there before. In Baghdad, everyone had a gun. There were plenty of people in the street, but they all walked in a hushed, hurried manner, avoiding each other's eyes.

Sam had walked about thirty metres when he saw the drinks can carelessly discarded in the street. Nobody paid it any attention – it was just one of any number of bits of litter. He glanced up at the house outside which it was lying. It was a big place, more like a compound, with a large whitewashed wall surrounding it and a vaulted gate with iron spikes at the top and a heavy padlock. As he sauntered past, Sam collated all the information he could about the place. There was a large courtyard at the front. The main door looked like it was made of heavy, thick wood – difficult to force down with the limited weaponry at their command. The roof was flat, with plain little turrets at each corner. As he glanced up Sam couldn't see anybody on it, but he had no doubt that if Sadiq was right and this place really did house the man the unit was after, they would be there. There were two low, shuttered windows on the ground floor, but none further up. His eyes flickered around looking for Jacob. He saw him fifteen metres away, leaning against a tree. They acted as if they didn't know each other.

The house occupied a corner plot and Sam turned into the small road that went alongside it. On this side of the house there were first floor windows, three of them, but he could not see any further down because of the high external wall. At the back of the house was a smaller street, on the opposite side of which was another dwelling place. This house was much less grand; indeed it looked deserted, as if it had been the scene of fighting in recent days or weeks. Sam slipped into the house and up the stairs onto the roof. The fierce sun beat down on him as he kept his head low and approached the front wall. Here there was a lattice of holes in the brickwork, allowing him to look through and onto the roof of the other house.

It didn't take him long to see movement. Two people keeping guard over the back of the house; no doubt there were at least two more on the other side. Below them was a garden of sorts – palm trees and even a patch of rough grass and some flowers, a strange sight in the middle of a war-torn city. The back wall had a wooden door. It was flimsier than the one at the front, easier to break down; but he wouldn't want to do that while it was overlooked. Still, that was their most likely point of entry. All they had to do was make sure there wouldn't be a welcoming party when they came knocking.

Sam looked at his watch. Nine minutes had passed; RV in six. He slipped back downstairs, out into the street and round the other side of the house. As he walked back to the car he could see Mac up ahead. He controlled his natural urge to catch up with his friend; keeping his head down, he wove his way through the people in the street and a minute or so later was back at the RV point. The Toyota had gone – no doubt Sadiq had picked up his car and got the hell out of there – but Jacob and Mac stood where it had been. The three of them took shelter in the doorway of a closed-down shop.

'Front gate covered from the roof,' Jacob stated, his voice brisk and businesslike. 'Three of them at least, maybe four. Two snipers in the front yard.'

'I clocked two more on the roof at the back. Good point of entry. Wooden door. Flimsy.'

The two brothers looked at Mac. 'No obvious lookouts in the street,' he said.

'Good,' Jacob replied. 'We need that chopper to extract us the moment we've apprehended the target.' His eyes flashed. 'It'll be Yankee scran for our man tonight.'

'Fuck of a sight better than the filthy Iraqi stuff he's used to,' Mac observed. 'We're practically doing the bastard a favour . . .'

'*Shut up!*' Sam barked.

The other two looked at him in surprise. Sam was holding his palm out towards them, indicating that they should keep quiet. He had dialled HQ on the sat phone and there was a noise of confusion at the other end. Panic at the Farm. Clearly something was going wrong.

And then the instruction came. '*Yankee Delta Three, hold your mission! Repeat, hold your mission! Do you read?*

'Yeah,' Sam snapped, 'I fucking heard you. What's the problem?'

'Black Hawk down,' came the curt reply. 'Small arms fire. Fucking Iraqis. All helicrews diverted to assist. Sorry, Sam. This is going to have to wait for another day. You're ordered back to base.'

A crackle and then silence.

'*Shit!*' Sam hissed, thumping his hand against the wall.

'What is it?'

'Chopper down. We've got no support. They're scrubbing us.'

'How many we lose?' Jacob demanded.

'Didn't stay. Still, they're not going to be queuing up for sticking plasters, are they?'

Jacob and Mac both turned away, silently cursing. Sam felt himself sneering as a hot surge of anger ran through his veins. The Regiment had taken a hit. He was damned if they were going to return to the Farm with nothing to show for it.

'Let's do it,' he said.

The others looked round at him.

'What do you mean?' Mac demanded. 'If we can't . . .'

'Listen – the moment the Yanks know we've got this bastard, you can bet your boots they'll have someone along to extract him. And if they don't . . . fuck it, he's only one guy. We just have to make sure everyone surrounding him goes down.' Somewhere deep inside, Sam knew he was being reckless. But he also knew they had a chance. He looked at Jacob. His brother's dark eyes were unreadable. 'We just need a distraction, J. Something to draw everyone out.'

The two brothers stared at each other. Jacob's eyes narrowed as he considered the suggestion. 'We've got our own distraction,' he said finally. He inclined his head slightly before dipping once more into his bag. He fished out a small device, about the size of a mobile phone. Just a black box with a small switch. 'I gave the Coke can a bit of extra sugar.'

Sam could sense Mac tensing up next to him. 'What the fuck are you talking about? I thought it was just the tracker.'

Jacob nodded. 'The tracker, yes. And a bit of plastic explosive, just in case. Enough to get our friends running to the front of the house when it blows to see what's going on.' His demeanour became instantly more serious. 'Sam, you and Mac take the back. I'll fire a few rounds to disperse the civilians, then explode the device and start picking the guards off when they come to check out the fireworks. Reckon it'll give you enough time to gain entry?'

Sam gazed at his brother. Mac was right to be pissed: if Jacob had this planned, he should have shared it with them. But his brother always did like to pull the cat out of the bag. Or in this case, the C-4 military-grade explosive out of the tin.

'Yeah,' Sam replied grimly. 'It'll give us time.' He looked at Mac. 'You good with that?'

Mac clenched his jaw – a momentary expression of his disapproval – before tugging at his half ear again.

Jacob flashed him a smile. 'You're a long time looking at the lid, mate,' he said.

It didn't take long for professionalism to overcome Mac's irritation.

'Bring it on,' he said.

★

Sweat trickled down the side of Sam's face next to the unfurled bit of carpet he had used to conceal his weapon. The midday sun scorched the back of his neck as he lay flat on the roof facing the back of their target's house. Mac lay five metres away, his Diemaco C8 loaded and at the ready. Through the brickwork lattice they could see the guards on the opposite roof – a distance, Sam estimated, of thirty metres. One of them was smoking a cigarette; the other was fiddling with his weapon.

Sam checked his watch.

'Contact in sixty seconds,' Jacob's voice came over their comms earpiece.

'Roger that.'

They waited.

The hard, angular contents of his ops waistcoat dug into his ribcage.

Thirty seconds.

Fifteen.

The distinctive crack of rounds being fired. The smoker dropped his cigarette and sprang to his feet, immediately rushing to the front and out of sight. Sam and Mac waited for the second man to disappear. Moments later he did.

Sam steeled himself for the noise of the explosion.

When it came, it sent a brief shock through his body. Sam's experience had taught him to judge the size of any explosion he heard, and it sounded big. It didn't stop him from moving, though. He got to his feet while Mac stayed in the firing position, ready to cover him. Instantly, however, there was a shout. '*Sam! Get down!*'

He immediately fell back to the ground. The second sniper had reappeared, ten metres to the right of the first. His AK-47 was ready to fire and he had noticed Sam. Two rounds hit the top of the roof in quick succession.

They were the last two rounds the Iraqi guard would ever fire.

Mac's aim was unerring. As he pressed down on the trigger, Sam could tell that his friend was totally in the zone. He could almost visualise the cartridge stirring to life in the chamber, the propellant gases expanding and exerting pressure on the bolt, creating a calculated delay that permits the projectile to exit the barrel, the gas pressure dropping again once the projectile has been released.

The MP5 round hit the guard straight in the face. There was a flash of red before the sniper fell to the ground and out of sight.

'*Go!*' Mac urged.

Sam sprinted, knowing he was covered. It took him no more than fifteen seconds to hurtle down the stairs and across the ten–metre-wide street before firing several rounds at the handle of the door. The wood splintered and broke – one good kick and it was open. He scanned the back garden for hostiles, his eye zeroed in on the sights and his finger resting lightly on the trigger. Convinced that it was clear, he looked up at the roof where Mac was covering him. 'I'm in,' he stated over the comms, giving his friend the thumbs-up sign, then directing his gun once more into the back garden of the house.

Mac was there within seconds. They nodded at each other as Mac covered the entrance, allowing Sam to push on inside. There was no one here – it looked like Jacob's strategy was working.

It was less than a minute after the initial explosion that the two of them gained entry into the house. Out front they could hear the sound of shots, a distinctive loud, sharp crack, then the rounds nicking against the walls and ricocheting into the ground. Sam steeled himself against the image of his brother being fired at. His instinct wanted him to join in the firefight, but Jacob was a big boy. Older than Sam and more experienced. He could take care of himself. But just to reassure himself he asked the question. 'You okay, J.?'

'Walk in the park,' came the reply, followed by another round of fire.

Sam and Mac swept the ground floor in under a minute. Empty. Mac took the lead up the stairs. These were pressed up against one wall with a solid banister on the other side. They led up to a balcony-style landing with a metre-high wall looking over the ground floor. Sam covered Mac from below. His friend disappeared from sight. There was the sudden, brutal sound of two rounds in quick succession: Mac had double-tapped someone. Sam sprinted up the stairs in time to see an Iraqi with half his head missing slide down the whitewashed wall, leaving a brushstroke of red where the fatal wound scraped against it.

They were in a corridor–cum–landing. To Sam's right the low wall overlooking the ground floor. There was a door at either end and one in the middle. It was this door that the Iraqi had been guarding, so they immediately took their positions on either side of it. Sam plunged one hand down the top of his dishdash and pulled a flashbang from his ops waistcoat, then nodded at Mac who held up three fingers, then two, then one. Mac kicked the door in, before aiming his weapon into the room and allowing Sam to rip the pin from the tennis-ball sized grenade and hurl it inside. As soon as it was in, Sam braced himself, clenching his eyes slightly and waiting for the explosion.

One second.

Two seconds.

Impact.

The moment the sonic boom arrived, Sam and Mac appeared in the doorway to take stock of the situation.

It was smoky and dusty, but not so much that they couldn't see to work. There were four men inside. They were all suffering temporary blindness from the grenade; one of them had a thin streak of blood seeping from his ear. Three men were clutching their AK-47s, waving them dangerously around the room despite the fact that they were totally disorientated. The fourth, an older man with a face Sam thought he recognised, cowered in the corner. That was him, he thought to himself. The target. It had to be. And even if it wasn't, their next move was clear. The Iraqis carrying the weapons needed to be plugged before they blindly opened fire and got lucky.

16

Three shots. Three direct hits. Each round produced a satisfying whump as it crashed into human flesh, hot lead burning a neat, perfectly round hole into the body, the round then ricocheting off bone and muscle, ripping through organs and severely fucking up the target. The men fell dead to the floor, with bits of bone and thick clumps of brain around them.

Sam entered the room. The fourth man – massively fat and with a scraggly beard – was groping blindly. As Sam grabbed him he started shouting, his voice harsh and full of authority. What he was saying, Sam had no idea. He just used one hand to pull his Iraqi hostage out of the room, his other hand outstretched and pointing the Diemaco in front of him. The man stumbled as Sam dragged him into the corridor. He continued to bark harshly in Arabic.

'Target attained,' he said curtly into the comms. No reply. 'Repeat, target attained. I've got him. Over.' Still nothing. He cursed. The fucking comms were down. Sam looked up at Mac whose nod told him he was experiencing the same problem.

They needed to get this guy out of the house as quickly as possible. A quick look at the stairs, however, told him that getting out was going to be a problem.

There were four of them, positioned at intervals along the staircase. Their AK-47s were raised and although Sam could tell at a glance from the way they held their weapons that they were not well trained, he also knew that he and Mac were in a world of trouble. In an instant he grabbed his hostage and used his body as a shield before aiming the Diemaco directly at his head. From the corner of his eye he saw Mac hit the floor. His friend was shielded now by the low internal wall that looked over the ground floor. Sam followed suit, pulling his hostage with him.

The two SAS men were breathing heavily. Mac took up position, crouched down on one knee, the butt of his gun pressed hard into his shoulder as he aimed towards the top of the stairs.

Stalemate. The Iraqis knew they couldn't advance; neither could Sam and Mac leave the protection of the wall while the enemy were on the stairs. The first person to put their head above the parapet would get it. There was a tense silence.

'What the fuck now?' Mac asked under his breath.

Sam sensed that his hostage's sight was returning. He was looking at Mac with an animal snarl and had started to struggle. Sam dug his weapon into the fleshy part of the man's neck and felt his muscles freeze.

A figure suddenly appeared at the top of the stairs. He was stepping sideways, facing Mac and Sam, his gun already pointing in their direction. Mac didn't hesitate. His first bullet hit the guard in the chest, knocking him backwards.

'Take that, you cunt.'

The Iraqi's AK–47 discharged a round harmlessly into the air above them before Mac's second shot hit him in the head. He slumped heavily to the ground. Sam's hostage looked in horror at the sight of the shattered bone and brain matter that had burst from the dead man's head. His limbs started to tremble.

Another silence.

And then it was broken. Not by the guards this time, but by something quite different. A voice, down below. Urgent and bellowing.

Jacob.

Sam pictured him on the ground floor below, just by the back entrance with his weapon pointed across the hallway up towards the stairs.

'*Sam!*' he shouted. '*Mac! Flashbang!*'

Sam braced himself – and just in time.

The bang from Jacob's grenade was close by and deafening. Even with his eyes shut Sam could see the flash illuminating the red of his clamped-shut eyelids. In the confusion, he heard three shots and then his brother shouted out again.

'*Clear!*'

Sam opened his eyes. Mac was crawling forwards. He carefully peered round the corner at the top of the stairs, then slowly got to his feet, his weapon still at the ready. Having taken stock of the situation, he turned round and nodded to Sam.

The terrified hostage was like a dead weight as Sam pulled him to his feet. When he saw the sight that greeted them, he started trembling even more than before. It was a bloodbath. The three remaining guards had slumped to the bottom of the pale stone stairs, leaving trails of blood along the steps. Their bodies were in a crumpled pile, their limbs distorted. The only sign of life was the blood still pumping from their wounds. Sam forced his hostage down the stairs and over the pile of bodies. And while Mac covered the entrances to the hallway where they stood, Jacob directed his gaze towards the Iraqi. He then pulled something out of his ops waistcoat.

It was a playing card, one of the ones issued by the Americans. Printed on the front was a man in military uniform. He wore a black beret, sported a bushy moustache and had an aloof smile of self-satisfaction. He didn't look a whole lot different to Saddam Hussein himself.

Their hostage looked a good deal less smug in real life than he did in the picture. His beard had several days' growth, his hair was dishevelled and there were dark rings under his eyes.

There was no doubting, however, that it was the same man.

Jacob held the playing card up to the hostage's face.

'Snap,' he said.

★

The processing centre was not far away. Before the invasion it had been an interrogation centre for Al-Mukhabarat, the Iraqi Intelligence Service – not a place you wanted to end up. Sam wasn't so green not to realise, however, that little had changed in that respect since the Americans had taken over the facility. Al-Mukhabarat were not known for the gentleness of their interrogation techniques; but then, neither were the CIA.

They drove in a three-vehicle convoy, one truck containing the SAS unit, their hostage, and a driver, the other two flanking them on either side. Their driver, a beefy American in shades and a combat helmet, had a bad case of the verbal runs and wasn't put off by the fact that Sam, Jacob and Mac were sitting in stony silence. 'Processing centre's overrun,' he observed loudly. 'They're pulling every last fuckin' Iraqi in they can lay their hands on, Ba'ath Party or not. Course, a lot of them get sent home again, but not before they get interrogated.' The driver barked, a brutish, ugly sound. 'Interrogated? Jeez, they're getting medieval on them in there. Good thing too if you want my opinion.'

He glanced in the mirror, perhaps waiting for some kind of agreement. When it wasn't forthcoming he carried on. 'Reckon they'll find a cell for this one, though. High up on the list. How d'you boys find him?'

It was only the fact that they were arriving at their destination that stopped the driver asking again.

From outside it would be impossible to guess what went on behind the concrete façade of this bland building. Only the military presence – unusually heavy even for Baghdad – gave any outward sign that this place was anything more than a standard administrative building. There were ten men, perhaps more, wearing US combats, Interceptor body armour and brandishing standard service rifles. As the military convoy pulled up it aroused a good deal of interest in the soldiers standing guard outside the facility. And when

Jacob, Sam and Mac emerged into the sweltering heat with their bedraggled, terrified hostage, there was a palpable sense of excitement. Since the invasion, people had been dragged into this place from all over Baghdad, but they didn't usually have this kind of escort.

'Welcome to the Baghdad Hilton, shit-for-brains,' an American voice called out. A few others laughed as their hostage stared at the US troops in bewilderment. Word of his arrival had evidently preceded him.

'Looks like you got Delta Force showing you to your room,' someone else shouted. 'Don't forget to tip them!'

Sam, Jacob and Mac remained stony faced. Typical of the Yanks to assume it was their boys who brought this guy in, Sam thought, but none of the unit were about to correct them. That wasn't the Regiment style. Sam pulled their hostage by his upper arm towards the main entrance. The fat Iraqi was sweating like a pig and he'd gone limp. In fact Sam almost had the impression that he wanted to stay close to the unit and away from these scornful American soldiers. Better the devil you know, he supposed, even if they have just eliminated your thirteen guards in under two minutes.

They crossed the threshold into the processing centre. There was a dark reception room, mercifully cool thanks to the stark concrete walls. On the far side were a series of three arches looking on to a courtyard about the size of a large swimming pool. There the resemblance ended, however: the courtyard was parched and dry, a layer of dust covering it. The high building cast sharp black shadows over it from the blazing afternoon sun. Soldiers milled around the shaded areas, but those parts of the courtyard that were in full sun were deserted. No one wanted to be in this kind of heat unless they had to.

Two men awaited them. They too wore American combats, but no body armour. Sam could tell instantly that there would be no banter from these two.

21

'Hand him over,' the taller of the two men said, addressing the unit like they were little more than servants. 'You'll have to wait here for a debrief.'

'How long?' Jacob demanded.

The tall man raised an eyebrow as though he were speaking to a kid who had just answered back. 'As long as it takes, soldier. Why? You got something better to do?'

Jacob gave him a dark look, but said nothing. Beyond him, from the corner of his eye, Sam noticed a couple of soldiers escorting a young Iraqi lad – no more than a teenager – across the courtyard. The kid looked frightened.

'You,' the tall one continued, nodding at their hostage. 'Come with us.' There was no attempt to speak to him in his native language, but the Iraqi understood what was being said to him well enough. He followed the two soldiers across the courtyard, disappearing with them through another archway on the opposite side.

'Have a nice day,' Mac muttered in a sarcastic American accent.

The three of them stood there in silence – a rare moment of rest. It was good to be out of the heat just for a few minutes. 'Won't be long before he's crying for his mummy,' Mac observed, breaking the silence. 'Those CIA boys won't fuck around.'

Jacob and Sam nodded curtly in unison. Sam's blood was boiling at the way they'd been spoken to and he could sense the annoyance radiating from Jacob too.

Whenever Sam Redman looked back at the events of the next few minutes, they would always have the hazy, detached quality of a dream. There was something hazy about them as they happened, too. Perhaps it was because his ears were still numb from the flashbangs; perhaps it was the heat. Whatever the truth, he felt like an outsider looking in as the main entrance door slammed open. He squinted slightly at the sudden influx of light, then saw three soldiers

22

enter. They had a kind of swagger that instantly set Sam's teeth on edge. If they noticed the three of them dressed in blood-spattered dishdash, they made no attempt to acknowledge them; their attention was firmly fixed on the people they were bringing in.

There were three of them: a grey-haired man, a woman and a young boy. A family? Sam didn't know, but they could well have been. What was obvious from the first glance, however, was that they were scared. With good reason. The soldiers had them at gunpoint and were manhandling them roughly into the courtyard. One of the uniformed men even elbowed into Sam. 'Fuck's sake,' the newcomer muttered without even looking at him. 'Get out the way. We got hostages.'

'Yeah,' Sam murmured. 'They look like a dangerous bunch, too.'

Only then did the solder pay any attention to Sam. He looked him up and down, clearly unimpressed by his dirty dishdash, then spat at his feet before joining his mates. Sam caught Mac's glance. It said it all.

As the troops spilled out into the courtyard, the three SAS men closed ranks, like a thick curtain being drawn. They stood in the shadow of the arches and watched in silence. The Iraqi man had been thrown to the floor. He was a pitiful figure as he sat in the dust looking up and watching one of the soldiers grab his wife by the face and squeeze his fingers into the hollow of her cheeks.

'Easy, mate,' one of the soldiers called. Sam was surprised to discern a Birmingham accent – this lot were British army. 'I don't think you're in there!'

The others laughed, just as the young boy hurled himself at them. His arms and legs were bony; they flailed inexpertly and inefficiently as he tried to attack the soldiers. Of course, he was no match for them. One solid blow to the stomach and he was bent double in pain, gasping for breath. The

23

soldier who had hit him grabbed a clump of his hair and dragged him across the courtyard, dropping him in the dust just as one of the others landed a brutal and quite gratuitous kick in the stomach of the older man.

The soldiers turned their attention back to the woman. She had started to sob, but that only seemed to amuse them more. 'Please . . .' she said in faltering English. '*Please . . .*'

'Look at that,' one of the soldiers announced brutishly. 'She's begging for it. You've got her fucking *begging* for it, mate!'

The soldiers laughed again.

It could have been any of them who stepped in to stop it happening. Sam had no doubt that they all felt equally sickened by what was unfolding before their eyes. It just happened to be Jacob. He strode out into the sunlight and grabbed the wrist of the soldier who was still clutching the woman's face.

'Enough,' he said, his voice perfectly calm, but braced with authority.

Sam felt himself tensing up like a tightly coiled spring, ready to pounce; he could sense Mac breathing steadily, meaningfully beside him.

The soldier who was dragging the boy stopped and turned. Everyone else was like a statue. Jacob pulled his man's wrist away from the woman's face. There was clearly some resistance, but Jacob was the stronger of the two.

'I said, enough,' he repeated.

A brief pause. A flurry of movement as the three Iraqis ran to each other and huddled up, while the two other soldiers went to the defence of their mate.

'Who the fuck do you think you are?' one of them called. He was broad shouldered and his lip curled in derision. 'Robin fucking Hood?' As he walked forcefully towards Jacob he stretched out his arms, his palms flat outwards, ready to push him away.

He never got the chance.

Jacob's reactions were cheetah-like. He yanked the wrist of the man he was holding, pulling it behind his back in a nelson hold that made his the soldier cry out in pain, before throwing him at the advancing man. The two of them tumbled to the floor. Sam and Mac stepped forward, ready to help him if necessary. At the same time, the third soldier who had been kicking the older Iraqi man advanced. He swung his big fist in the direction of Jacob's jaw.

He missed. Jacob grabbed him and, with a sudden, brutal force, swung him round in the direction of Sam and Mac.

The soldier almost flew through the air. Sam had to step sideways to avoid a collision, but he was still the closest to the soldier when it happened. The man's head cracked against the corner of the concrete archway – a vicious, sickening slam that made everyone in the vicinity freeze.

He crumpled.

As he fell, his head landed against the corner of the concrete step that separated the room from the courtyard. This time there was blood. A lot. The guy was hurt. Badly.

After the sudden burst of violence, everyone was silent – even Jacob, who looked uncharacteristically worried at what had just happened. Sam hurried to the fallen man, who was lying face-downwards in the dust, a small trickle of blood seeping from his ear and forming a dark, dry puddle next to him. He rolled the guy over, then briefly closed his eyes.

The soldier didn't look good. Not good at all.

Then Jacob and Mac were there, towering above him. Sam looked up at his brother. Neither of them spoke.

From behind Jacob came a voice – it was one of the soldiers, the one with the Brummie accent. 'You fucking psycho . . .' he said.

None of them acknowledged him. Sam placed two fingers on the fallen soldier's neck then pressed lightly.

Nothing.

He looked up at his brother.

'What?' Jacob demanded, his face red. 'Fucking *what?*'

Sam drew a deep breath. 'He's dead,' he replied.

Jacob stared at him, his lips receding in anger. Sam tried to think of something to say, but there was nothing. His brother had just killed a British army soldier. He didn't need Sam to point out to him the implications of that . . .

A hunted look passed over Jacob's face. He spun round to stare at the other soldiers, all of whom took a wary step backwards. Then he turned again and looked desperately at Mac and then Sam, both of whom were struck into silence.

And then he looked at the corpse of his victim. His eyes flashed and in a sudden outburst he kicked the dead man in the stomach before stepping over him and disappearing into the shadow of the reception room. Sam heard the door slamming, then exchanged a glance with Mac. Their look said one thing and it was Mac who articulated it.

'Jesus, Sam,' he whispered. 'What's he done?' And then, shaking his head in disbelief at the sight of the British army soldier lying dead at his feet, he repeated himself quite unnecessarily.

'What the *hell* has he done?'

PART ONE

ONE

Shepherd's Bush, London. Six years later.

It was a cold May evening – no longer winter but not yet summer – and the traffic along the eastern end of the Uxbridge Road was sluggish. The many pedestrians on either side of the street moved more quickly than the cars and buses whose headlights illuminated them as they trudged home from work. The air was filled with traffic noises, fumes and the smell of food being cooked in Middle Eastern fast-food joints.

One man moved more slowly than the others, partly because he felt no need to hurry, but also because he was not built for speed. He wore a large woollen overcoat that went some way to disguising his generous stomach. His head was covered with an old-fashioned Trilby hat which, although seldom seen in this – or any – part of London, did not look out of place. In one of his gloved hands he carried a briefcase, the sort a doctor might have, its leather worn and soft; and he surveyed the world through a pair of glasses – square, thick rimmed and outmoded.

He found this part of London rather distasteful. In the past he had listened to his students assure him that it was vibrant and colourful, but to him it always looked dirty and ramshackle. He passed a bus stop where a teenage girl listened to something appalling over the speaker of her mobile phone; the people around her either didn't mind or were too timid to ask her to turn it off. Further along the street there was a grocery stall. The vegetables – some of which he did not recognise – were neatly and abundantly displayed. As he passed, however, he felt the hostile eyes of the shopkeeper – arms crossed as he stood in the doorway – on him. It still did not make him hurry, but it did nothing to change his opinion about this part of town.

A few doors down there was a newsagent's. He entered. It was almost empty, just a middle-aged woman buying cigarettes. His eyes wandered to the top shelf of the magazine rack and he selected three pornographic magazines at random. With a bit of luck he wouldn't need them, but they were a necessary insurance policy. He paid for them without embarrassment, slipped them into his briefcase and left the shop.

He had examined the map carefully, so he knew when to turn left. There was a pub on the street corner, an unfashionable place only half full. By the time he had passed it, the noise of the main road was already receding. There were far fewer people in this side road, which made him feel more conspicuous. It was easy to get lost in a crowd, but in a less populated residential road where everyone was familiar with the sight of their neighbours, one was more likely to stand out. He pulled the brim of his hat further down and bowed his head as he walked.

He found the house he was looking for soon enough. He didn't stop, though. Instead he kept walking a few metres, crossed the road and examined the place from a short distance. It was one of a row of terraced houses – a couple of storeys high and mostly, he assumed, divided into flats. The flat with which he was concerned was in the basement. There was a metal gate at street level and a small garden, unkempt and overgrown. That was good. It obscured the front window from the gaze of passers-by. Parked outside was an ancient Ford Escort – nothing expensive, but it had been souped up with a spoiler and go-faster stripes.

The man looked at his watch. A quarter past seven. He felt inside the jacket of his overcoat. It was there, he reassured himself. Ready to be used. He crossed the road again and approached his destination. The metal gate creaked slightly as he opened it, but that was okay. He descended the steps inelegantly on account of his girth, stopped at the front door and used his free hand to ring the bell.

It took almost a minute for the door to be answered by a tall young man. He had cropped brown hair, a slightly hooked nose and a protruding Adam's apple. He wore a tracksuit and no shoes, and he exuded a certain shiftiness as his eyes moved up and down, sizing up the newcomer.

'Yeah?' he demanded, one hand still clutching the half-open door, the other pressed flat against the wall.

The newcomer took care not to let any expression show on his face. 'Good evening,' he said quietly. His voice bore the trace of a foreign accent. He had been in the UK for many years, however, and was sure that nobody would be able to place his nationality with any confidence.

The young man continued to look surly and impatient. 'What do you want?'

'I'm here on . . .' He cleared his throat and allowed himself a small, nasty smile. 'I'm here on *agency* business.'

That certainly grabbed the young man's attention. His eyes narrowed slightly, as though he were judging whether or not to believe the newcomer, then he licked his lips and looked briefly up towards the street. Nervousness? The newcomer thought so. A little excitement? Possibly.

The young man opened the door a bit further, allowing him to enter. He nodded as he did so, muttering a brief 'Thank you'. The older man noticed with satisfaction that the younger man's tracksuit trousers were made of a thin, flowing material. Ahead of him was a narrow kitchen; to his right a door that led into the main room of this small flat. It was about what he expected. A large television screen hung on the wall. The sound was down, but it was filled with images – extreme skiing of some kind. Just the sort of thing he *would* be interested in. On the floor in front of it was a tangled mesh of wires connected to a video console. In the middle of the room was a coffee table, covered with the accumulated debris of more than one day's worth of ready-meal packaging. There were, he noticed, no books on the shelves. That didn't surprise him. He knew enough about this young man – and others like him – to realise that the slow pleasures of reading would be unlikely to appear high on the list of his priorities.

He stood in the middle of the room, placed his briefcase on the floor and slowly slid his leather gloves off his hands.

'Thought you lot had forgotten me,' the young man's voice said from behind him. He made no attempt to hide the dissatisfaction in his voice.

'Oh no,' the newcomer replied mildly. 'We haven't forgotten you.' He placed his bare hand back into the pocket of his coat just as the young man walked past him to turn off the television.

In all his years of doing this kind of thing, he had learned that it is best to grab your opportunities when they arise. For that reason, as the young man faced the television with his back to him, the newcomer moved swiftly. From his pocket he pulled a hypodermic syringe and instantly removed the plastic cap that covered the protruding needle.

He stepped forward.

The area around the centre of the buttocks was, he knew, the best location. It was fleshier for a start. Easier to puncture. And the mark that the needle would undoubtedly leave would be somewhat hidden around that area of the body.

He jabbed his arm forward and his aim was true. He squeezed the syringe.

'What the f . . .?' the young man started to say. By the

time he had turned to look at the newcomer, however, the needle had been removed.

The two men stared at each other, one of them holding the needle and making no attempt now to hide it, the other gazing at it in a mixture of confusion and horror.

The young man took a step forward. His attacker did not flinch. He knew it would only be seconds before his victim was completely incapacitated.

Sure enough, as the young man tried to take a second step, he appeared to have difficulty moving his leg, as though he had suddenly been frozen. The young man looked down at the ground, then up again at the newcomer.

And then he collapsed. His attacker caught him as he fell – it wouldn't do for his body to be too bruised – then laid him out on the floor. By the time he had finished doing this he was red-faced and out of breath.

The newcomer surveyed the scene. The young man's eyes were still open, still seeing; his limbs, however, were completely paralysed. The injection had done its work. It was a useful compound, suxamethonium chloride – a muscle relaxant that had the effect of completely paralysing the body while leaving the mind aware and remaining difficult to detect in the bloodstream. He did not have the opportunity to use it often, but for this particular job it was just right.

He opened his briefcase, dropped the syringe inside and then put his gloves back on. Walking into the kitchen he searched through the drawers, taking good care to put everything back in its proper place. He grunted with contentment when he found a roll of large, clear polythene bags. He'd brought some with him, of course, but much better for his purposes to use what was already here. He tore off a bag – it shimmied a little under the soft touch of his gloves – left the roll artfully on the cluttered work surface, then returned to the main room.

It was not entirely straightforward to remove the young

man's clothes, but he managed it and dumped them in a pile by the coffee table. Returning to his naked body, he slipped the plastic bag over his victim's head. He pinched the open end around his neck before inclining his head slightly and looking directly into the young man's eyes.

It was very hard to read any expression there, but his victim would know he was being suffocated. It was curious to witness the young man making no attempt to struggle. The plastic bag formed a concave hollow around his mouth which popped out and then in again. Over a period of about a minute the movement became gradually weaker until it stopped completely.

The young man was dead, but his assassin's work wasn't finished. Not yet. Letting go of the plastic bag his eyes fell upon another door at the opposite side of the room. He went through it to find the young man's bedroom. It was stark: a chest of drawers, a cupboard and a large, unmade bed in the middle; an iPod left carelessly on the floor and a laptop computer next to it. The man took the laptop and switched it on. Opening the Internet browser he searched through the history of recently visited websites. They were largely what he expected: links to details of fast cars and gadgets, information on handguns and other weaponry, military websites and of course a good deal of pornography. He smiled. It looked like he wouldn't be needing those magazines after all. Using the wireless connection that the laptop had automatically picked up he navigated to what looked like the young man's favourite – it was nothing too specialist, he noted as he started to play a long video. He did, however, allow himself a few guilty seconds to watch the three naked, entwined bodies before placing the laptop on the coffee table.

Only then did he step back to admire his handiwork. It pleased him.

Auto–erotic asphyxiation. The young man had a history of

it. For a moment the fat man wondered what pleasure anyone could possibly derive from the act of bringing oneself almost to the point of suffocation in order to achieve sexual gratification. Then he shrugged. People such as the young man he had just killed derived pleasure from all manner of pursuits that he himself would never consider. Foolish pursuits. Dangerous pursuits. In a strange kind of way it made them easier to eliminate. No doubt some girlfriend from the past would be found to confirm the young man's penchant for such activities. He felt confident, from his considerable experience of these things, that his death would be put down to a tragic – if unsavoury – accident.

It wouldn't do to stay here much longer. The man closed up his briefcase, glanced momentarily and with satisfaction at his little production, then let himself out of the flat. He closed the door silently before ascending the stairs, turning right and walking calmly back to the Uxbridge Road.

This really was quite the most unpleasant part of London, he decided. He would be very glad to get back home.

★

Much like the portly man who even now was making his way back up the Uxbridge Road, the car that travelled round the raised, curved slip road and into an almost diametrically opposite part of London was not built for speed. But it was being driven very quickly anyway.

It was a Renault, small and neat. The interior was immaculately tidy and faintly perfumed. It would be easy to mistake this car for one that had just been driven out of the showroom, but in fact it was a couple of years old. It just happened to have been very well looked after. The owner, Kelly Larkin, sat in the passenger seat. Her hair, which she had spent so much time on that morning, was mussed and unruly – at least by her standards. The scream of the small engine roared in her ears and, not for the first time, she found herself shouting. 'For God's sake, Jamie! Just slow down!'

No more than fifteen metres ahead, a car heading towards them moved into their lane to avoid a parked motorbike. Kelly clamped her eyes shut as her boyfriend slammed the engine into fifth gear and swerved sharply to avoid it. The angry sound of a horn filled her ears before fading quickly away. When she dared to open her eyes again the car had completely left the motorway and was on a wide, three-laned thoroughfare that would take them past Walthamstow and into that unfashionable slab of north-east London where she lived.

Jamie had a grin on his face. He was a good-looking guy, there was no doubt about that, but at the moment he looked like a psycho. He chewed on an imaginary piece of gum and held the steering wheel with a single finger. When he glanced into the rear-view mirror it was to admire himself.

At twenty-six, Jamie Spillane dressed like a teenager in his Converse boots and hooded tops. Kelly found herself with him quite against her better judgement; but at her age, thirty-three, she found herself being less and less picky in her desire not to end up on the shelf. She glanced at the speedometer. Ninety-six. 'Please, Jamie,' she begged as her left hand clutched the passenger door even more tightly. Perhaps pleading would have a better effect than shouting. '*Please* just slow down.'

Jamie turned to look at her. Instantly she wished she'd kept her mouth shut, because it meant his eyes were off the road. He had a neatly shaved goatee beard, which actually made him appear almost childlike because it looked so inappropriate. It was that look that had first attracted her to him, but right now she wished he would just grow up. He winked at her. Either he was totally oblivious to her fear, or it thrilled him. Whatever, he didn't slow down. Kelly just closed her eyes again and tried to master the cold sickness that left her body weak. She would have liked to start crying, but somehow she was too scared even for that.

As they entered the outskirts of Walthamstow, Jamie reduced his speed. Not by much, though. He ran two red lights – they were just the ones Kelly counted when her eyes were open – and as he turned into the top of Acacia Street the speedometer was still wobbling around fifty. The tyres screeched as he took the corner; Kelly screamed at the sight of a couple of kids running across the road ahead. But at the last minute he swerved again and by some act of God managed to miss them. Outside her flat he swung the car to the side of the road. One tyre pulled up on to the kerb as he came to a halt, but he didn't bother to rectify his inexact parking. He flamboyantly turned off the ignition, flung his arm into the air and turned once more to look at Kelly. His grin was still there and he was out of breath, as though he had run all the way from the M11, rather than driven.

Kelly opened the car door and stormed out. The air was cold, but she was too furious to take her coat from the back seat. As her heels clattered along the pavement she found that her mind was bubbling with angry words. Kelly was not the type to have a stand-up argument in the street, but, knowing that if she stopped now she wouldn't have much choice, she hurried to her front door. If Jamie thought he was coming in after *that* little display, he had another think coming.

As she approached the door, Kelly fumbled in her handbag for her house keys, then frowned as she realised Jamie had them. She breathed out huffily and, feeling her muscles tense with anticipation of the impending row, turned around.

Jamie was at the end of the little pathway that led up to the front door of her flat. He held the keys up and jingled them as he sashayed towards her. When he was less than a metre away, Kelly tried to grab them, but she was too slow: he jerked his hands out of the way.

'Just give me the fucking keys, Jamie.'

'Touchy, touchy . . .' he replied.

'You're an idiot, Jamie. You could have killed us.' She made another swipe at the keys; this time Jamie grabbed her wrist. He pushed her up against the door, pressed his body against hers and went in for the kiss. Kelly turned her head to one side to make her lips inaccessible. She wasn't the type to snog in public any more than she was the type to argue. 'Just open the bloody door,' she hissed. 'It's freezing.'

They tumbled inside. Kelly stopped to pick up her mail – what looked like a gas bill nestled among a flurry of pizza delivery leaflets – while Jamie opened the main door to the flat, looking for all the world like he owned the place. It wound Kelly up even more – she'd only been seeing the guy for six weeks and he was practically living there, eating her food and channel hopping her television with his feet up on the coffee table. He said he had his own place, but Kelly had never seen it and was beginning to wonder.

'That's the last time you use my car,' she stated as she slammed the door shut, more to make it clear that she was still pissed off than anything else. Jamie was helping himself to a beer from the fridge in the kitchenette area that formed part of the main room. She noticed that the surfaces were considerably less tidy than they had been when she left for work that morning. Jamie had clearly been there for most of the day and hadn't bothered to do much cleaning up after him. Kelly put her large, fashionable handbag down on the cheap blue sofa and turned to face him. 'I said, that's the last time you use my car, Jamie. I'm sick of you driving it like bloody Lewis Hamilton.'

Jamie took a pull from his beer. 'Thought you *liked* me picking you up from work.'

Kelly bristled. Now was hardly the time to admit it, but

she did like the way the other secretaries at the law firm where she worked would congregate not very subtly in the foyer whenever she happened to mention that Jamie was meeting her at home time. He was several years younger than her – than any of them, in fact – and was, by all appearances, a Good Catch. Of course, she had kept quiet about the down side of being with Jamie: the constant sponging. Kelly even found that she would fool herself, whenever her purse was light, that it was down to her own scattiness. But Kelly wasn't scatty by nature. She was methodical and thrifty. If she thought there were two twenty-pound notes in her purse, there *should* be two. Not one. Deep down she knew that, but she chose to ignore it. She chose to ignore, too, the time when she had searched through his jacket while he was in the bath. Kelly's intention had been to flick through the messages on his mobile phone, but instead she had found something else: a thick wad of notes – two or three hundred pounds by the look of it. A lot of money for a young man who was 'between jobs'.

'Anyway,' Jamie continued as he walked louchely up to her, 'what would you rather be doing? Putting on a nice pair of slippers like all those other boring old cows you work with?' He hooked his free arm around her waist and lightly kissed her neck. 'Watching *Gardener's World*?' He said it in a mock high-pitched voice that made Kelly smile despite herself.

'No,' she breathed, her voice still a bit surly. And then, 'You just scared me, Jamie.'

'Don't you like being scared?' he asked.

He kissed her on the neck once more. This time it sent a little shiver of pleasure down her spine. Her boyfriend pulled away, then looked at her with an obviously fake little-boy-lost look. 'I'm sorry,' he said with an irresistible half smile. 'I'll *never* do it again.'

'Liar,' she whispered.

And then he kissed her again, on the lips this time as his free hand formed an arc around the curve of her buttocks. It was a serious kind of kiss and she could not help but close her eyes. Her tense body became softer, more compliant. Though their mouths were still locked in a kiss, she heard herself gasp.

Jamie was far from gentle as he removed her clothes, but for some reason she didn't mind that. It took almost no time at all for her trouser suit, blouse and underwear to be relegated to a crumpled pile on the floor. She kept her fashionable glasses on, as well as her bead necklace, because she knew he liked that.

Jamie took a step back and surveyed Kelly's body. It flashed through her mind that she had gone from utter fury to absolute desire in minutes; a small corner of her brain wondered how Jamie had done that, or what she should think of herself for being so easy. But she didn't really care that much. She liked the way her young lover looked at her. She liked being desired. She liked the way she could now pretend to be in control.

She gave him a steady, cool stare, then turned and walked into the bedroom, making very sure to sway her naked hips seductively as she went.

TWO

An unmarked white minibus stopped at the entrance to RAF Credenhill. The MOD policeman on duty spoke briefly with the driver, glanced into the vehicle, then nodded and allowed the barrier to open. The bus drove into SAS headquarters and came to a halt. Eight men spilled out.

They crossed the courtyard to the main building, each of them carrying a heavy bergen and walking with the slow gait of soldiers who had been in the field for a long time. Their calves were beasted, their clothes baggy from the muscle mass they had lost on op. Sam Redman was at the back of that little group, his friend Mac alongside him. Both men had deep tans, their skin weathered by several weeks of harsh sunshine. Their beards were bushy – almost comically so – and Sam was looking forward to shaving his off. They'd had twelve hours at Bastion, during which time he'd been able to clean up a bit and wolf down a few platefuls of nosh – hardly Gordon Ramsay, but better than the biscuits brown and Panda Colas they got with their ration packs. Now he needed scalding hot water, rough soap and a proper fry-up from his favourite greasy spoon in Hereford. And after that, come evening, a few beers. Quite a few. It had been a rough two months.

One of the lads in front of them, a young Cockney boy new to the Regiment, turned his head. 'Keep up, you two,' he called. 'They'll be pensioning you off if they think you can't keep up with the young 'uns.'

'Don't you ladies worry about us,' Mac replied quickly. 'We've got all the energy in the world. Just ask your mum. It were only last week we were taking turns giving her a Bombay Roll. Gave her a right good fucking seeing to. Tell her I said hello, won't you?'

A few of the guys laughed. Mac just looked at Sam and rolled his eyes before looking around at the bleak, utilitarian surroundings of Credenhill. After the bright blue skies, golden desert and lush vegetation of Afghanistan, it was drab and grey, this featureless compound under a Tupperware sky. 'Nice to be home,' he observed without a trace of sarcasm.

'Too right,' Sam replied. Unlovely though it was, it was a hell of a sight better than being in the green zone of Helmand Province, not having to worry about some black-robed, bearded bastard taking potshots at you or your mates. 'Too damn right,' he repeated.

An hour later, Sam had finished the process of dumping his kit in his single-bunked room and checking his weapons back in. There were no messages for him in the squadron office and he was looking forward to getting to the ground-floor flat on the outskirts of Hereford that he called home. Passing through the mess room, however, he saw Mac again. Unlike Sam, Mac was already cleaned up and shaved. Like many of the troopers they'd just returned with, Mac was bunking down at Credenhill. For the rookies it was because they were relatively new to the Regiment and had not yet bought themselves a place in the town; for Mac it was because his missus had kicked him out of the house for the umpteenth time. Some indiscretion with a Regiment groupie, no doubt – Sam had long since given up asking.

His friend was sitting alone at a table with a broadsheet newspaper spread out in front of him. Sam sat heavily opposite him. 'What do you think you are?' he asked, flicking the newspaper with his forefinger. 'A fucking intellectual?'

Mac ignored him. 'Listen to this,' he said before reading from the paper in a mock-posh voice. '"Questions are being asked as to how long the SAS can continue operating at such an intense level. 'There is concern in the Regiment that if they keep going at this high tempo it won't be long before they suffer a big loss,' one source said."'

'One source?'

'Yeah,' Mac scoffed. 'Your mum probably.' Then, realising what he had said, he looked up. 'Sorry, mate,' he said quietly. 'I didn't mean . . .'

'Forget it,' Sam replied, reaching to another table and grabbing a tabloid paper. It was the usual stuff, none of which interested him much. His eyes lingered briefly on the topless model on one of the inside pages; he read a report about the war in Afghanistan which used phrases like 'brave heroes' and 'our boys' – phrases that would never be uttered within the confines of Credenhill, or any other regimental barracks for that matter. His attention was caught by the story of some kid who'd been found dead in his London flat with a plastic bag over his head and a laptop full of porn. Death by misadventure, the coroner had said.

'Dirty fucker,' Sam mumbled.

'What?'

Sam folded up the paper and tossed it on to another table. 'Nothing,' he said. He stood up. 'I'm out of here. Catch you later, yeah?'

'Yeah,' Mac replied. 'Later.'

Sam was about to walk away from the table when someone else entered the mess room. No one could say that Mark Porteus, the burly CO of 22 SAS was a particularly friendly man, but there weren't many who held that against him. He wasn't supposed to be likeable. His cropped hair was almost completely grey, his face deeply lined. He had a scar on the left of his chin where the skin was completely white – a souvenir from Northern Ireland – but somehow

43

his features wouldn't be complete without it. A Sandhurst graduate, Porteus was a career soldier from the tip of his boots to the top of his head and was held in respect by every man in the Regiment – and in awe by quite a few of the younger ones. He was wearing combats – Sam couldn't remember when he'd last seen the CO out of them.

'Boss,' Sam greeted him across the room. He liked Porteus. He'd known him for years.

Porteus appeared to see him for the first time. His eyes narrowed and, for a brief moment, he looked distinctly uncomfortable. 'Sam,' he nodded in their direction. 'Mac.'

And then he turned, leaving the mess as suddenly as he had entered it.

Sam's brow furrowed and he looked over at Mac. 'What's wrong with him?' he demanded. Normally Porteus would always stop to talk.

Mac shrugged. 'It's the beard,' he replied. 'Makes you look a bit dodgy. I don't know if anyone's told you, but the Mullah Omar look's not really that hot right now.'

Sam looked back over towards the entrance to the mess room, his eyes narrowed. 'If I want fashion tips,' he said vaguely, 'I'll buy *Cosmo*. I'm off.' He gave his friend a smile and walked out of the mess. Tempting though it was to stay and shoot the shit with Mac, he had a job to do. And putting it off wasn't going to make it any easier.

★

Kelly Larkin glanced up at the clock. Twelve thirty. A bit early for lunch but what the hell. She was still bleary eyed and could do with getting out of the office. All morning her mind kept flitting back to the previous night: the stupid car journey, making love before getting drunk and making love again. She blushed. The boy had stamina, there was no doubt about that. Kelly pushed back her chair, grabbed her bag and headed out of the little typing pool she shared with four other secretaries.

She was waiting for the lift when one of her colleagues – a dark-haired girl from up east with a voice like a thousand cigarettes – hurried after her, her coat only half on. Her name was Elaine and she was good fun – Kelly had even shared a few drunken confidences with her in the past. 'Going for lunch?' she gabbed. 'Mind if I come?'

Kelly inclined her head. 'Sure,' she replied. 'I'm not much company today, though.'

Elaine gave her a sly look. 'Yeah, you look a bit peaky. Keeping you up all night, is he?'

Kelly opened her mouth to reply, but at that moment the lift arrived with three of the law firm's suited partners inside. The two secretaries clamped their mouths shut and Kelly could sense they were both doing their best not to laugh as they all silently took the lift to the ground floor and spilled out into the foyer. Elaine lit up the moment they were outside; by the time they had walked thirty metres down Chancery Lane to the sandwich bar where they regularly went she had smoked the whole cigarette and stamped it out on the pavement.

The sandwich bar wasn't busy yet. Kelly wasn't hungry either, but she ordered a panini anyway from the camp Italian who called all his female clients *belissima*. She and Elaine sat quietly for a minute or two, munching mouse-like at their lunch. It was Elaine who broke the silence. 'So . . .' she began, her gravelly voice cheeky and inquisitive. 'What *did* you get up to last night?' It was an innocent enough question, but the piercing look she gave Kelly made it quite clear she was after some juicy gossip.

Kelly shrugged. 'Not much,' she replied. 'Just stayed in with Jamie.'

Elaine raised an eyebrow and nodded, not taking her gaze from Kelly, who felt herself blushing again. 'You know what they say, darling,' Elaine observed. 'You're as old as the man you feel. He must be taking a good ten years off you.'

Kelly thought of the car journey. 'Yeah,' she replied. 'Or putting it on.'

'What's that supposed to mean, then?'

Kelly's brow furrowed. 'Oh, I don't know,' she said. 'There's just something . . . something a bit *shifty* about him. I never meet any of his friends and he doesn't even mention his family. He *says* he's got a place of his own, but he never seems to go there. He's been living with me practically since we met. He hasn't got a job or anything . . .'

'What does he do for money?'

Kelly shrugged and avoided her colleague's eye.

'Fucking hell, love,' Elaine retorted to Kelly's silence. 'Don't tell me you're bankrolling him and all.'

'Not much,' she said. 'Just now and then.' She didn't mention the missing twenties from her purse, or the wad of cash she had once found, or her suspicion that Jamie might even be involved in dealing drugs. But even so she realised how foolish she must sound.

Elaine's demeanour had changed, from gossipy girlfriend to resolute ally. 'Just don't let the bastard take you for a ride, all right love? Sounds like he's stitching you up like a kipper.'

Kelly smarted and it must have shown in her face, because Elaine clearly felt the need to justify her comment. 'Well,' she continued forcibly, 'you hear about it, don't you? Young men giving older women what they want in the sack . . .'

'I'm not that old!' Kelly protested.

'. . . telling them all sorts of rubbish to keep their interest up,' Elaine continued as though she hadn't heard. Her eyes widened mischievously. 'What's he been telling you?' she teased. 'Let me guess – his dad's a squillionaire and he's going to inherit as soon as the old boy pops it!'

'*Elaine!*'

'I know, I know!' She was warming to her subject now. 'He's on the run from . . .' She looked around the room, as though it would give her some sort of inspiration, her eyes finally settling on the Italian behind the counter. 'The Mafia!' she decided. 'He can't go back to his house because Al Pacino's sitting there waiting for him with a – oh, I don't know, name a kind of gun . . .'

With that, the two women dissolved into giggles. 'Seriously though, love,' Elaine said when their laughter had subsided. 'Don't let the geezer take you for a ride. You know what men are like. Bone idle, most of them. He should be taking you out a bit, treating you right. And I'm not just talking between the sheets.'

Kelly blushed for a third time. She eyed Elaine over the brow of the cup. Her friend was right. Jamie Spillane had some explaining to do. She wasn't going to be taken advantage of. Not by him, or by anyone.

She would bring it up with him, Kelly Larkin decided, that very night.

★

For the first time in weeks, Sam felt clean. The second he'd got back home he had stripped off and walked straight into the shower. The Afghan dust seemed to have soaked into the very pores of his skin and a once-a-day wash with a few baby wipes in the field hadn't made any difference. There was black shit under his fingernails and his hair was matted in thick clumps, glued together with blood and sweat. *Fuck Afghanistan*, Sam thought. *I won't be going back there on holiday any time soon.* He scrubbed himself vigorously, but no amount of soap would get rid of the dirt of his latest operation. Only when the water started to run cold did he step out. The mirror in his small bathroom was clouded over. He wiped away the condensation, then smeared shaving gel over his dishevelled beard and started to hack away at it. It took a good half-hour for his face to become smooth-skinned again. Looking in the mirror as he shaved he was surprised to see a tightness around his eyes. In his mind, Sam was still the fresh-faced kid who had signed up at seventeen at his brother's insistence, more to keep him on the straight and narrow than anything else. But that was a long time ago and the mirror didn't lie: Sam looked a lot older than the mental picture he had of himself.

Looking down at his torso, he saw that it was cut and bruised. Out in the field you never noticed stuff like that. It was only when you got home that the scars of a mission became apparent. He slung the razor into the sink, grabbed a towel and used it to wipe his face, before stepping back into his bedroom and finding a clean shirt and a pair of jeans. Only when he'd put these fresh clothes on did he really feel like he was home.

His car keys were just where he'd left them before he'd gone out to Afghanistan – in a little wooden box in the front room. The room itself was largely bare – a sofa, a TV, a few shelves with nick-nacks on them. It was the space of a person who didn't spend much time there. A space that lacked the softening touches of a female influence. It wasn't that Sam's flat hadn't played host to plenty of women. It had. They just hadn't been given the opportunity to stay around long enough to get stuck into the soft furnishings. As Sam took the keys from their box his attention was caught by a photograph. His brother looked young in the picture. To his side was the black Labrador that had been his constant companion whenever he was at home. More than once he'd heard people wonder out loud if Jacob preferred dogs to people. Sam hadn't seen him for six years and the photo had been taken some time before that. It seemed like a lifetime ago. Sam missed his brother, but he was angry with him too. Not a word for all these years, nowhere to be found – and

Sam had certainly tried. For all he knew, Jacob could be dead.

Sam suppressed a shudder at that thought. Clutching the car keys he turned and left.

Sam's flat might have been small and barely furnished, but he had not applied the same restraint to his choice of car. The black Audi was parked up outside his front door, gleaming and immaculate. He clicked the doors open, climbed inside and drove off without bothering about the seatbelt. Normally he'd drive hard, but today he was in no hurry. Far from it. He had been dreading this little trip ever since they touched down at Brize Norton. Out on ops, he could forget about what he had left back home; back on British soil he knew what his duty was, even though it was a chore to have to fulfil it. It took twenty minutes to reach the institutional building he was headed for – even the slowest old granny in a Robin Reliant could have made it in fifteen.

It didn't matter what part of the world Sam had been to or for how long; nor did it matter what had happened while he'd been away. This place never changed. The red brick of the building was always immaculate; there was always a fair smattering of cars in the car park that surrounded it; and as he walked into the main reception there was always that faint, hospital-like smell of antiseptic.

This wasn't a hospital, however. At least not quite. It called itself a residential care home and the brochure made it look like a place of great luxury; the reality, however, was quite different. With places like these, Sam had found out, you get what you pay for. And on a military pension with precious few savings, Sam's father couldn't afford much.

The nurse sitting behind the wooden reception desk recognised Sam as he entered. 'He'll be looking forward to seeing you,' she said pointedly. 'It's been a while.'

Sam grunted and hurried on, down the institutional

corridor and up the stairs which clattered and echoed as he climbed them. He walked past the emergency exit, doing his best to ignore the old lady who tottered along with the aid of a frame. The very fact of her presence there made him scowl. It just brought home to him the reality of the place where his father was forced to live. The reality of his condition.

The door to his father's room was closed. He knocked, but didn't wait for a reply before opening it and stepping inside.

Very little had changed since his last visit. His father lay in a hospital bed with high sides staring blankly at the television. His pyjamas hung loosely from his body. Sam remembered, when they were growing up, thinking his dad was the strongest, most muscular man in the world and he probably wasn't far wrong. Now he looked like a scarecrow that had been dressed up in clothes too big for him. Hanging to the side of a bed was a colostomy bag, half filled with deep brown liquid.

The small room smelled of the uneaten lunch that sat on a tray by his bed: a perfect sphere of mashed potato and a pool of brown stew. It was bland and barely furnished, with just one threadbare armchair for visitors and a small table for the kettle and tea-making facilities that were checked every morning by unenthusiastic care workers. Not that they had to replenish the supplies very often. Dad never had visitors. Just Sam. He'd lost count of the times his doctors had said that visitors would do him good, help keep him alert; but Sam knew his father better than that, and he accepted that the last thing the old man wanted was for anyone to see him like this.

'Hi, Dad,' he announced as brightly as his glum mood would allow. 'It's me, Sam.'

Ever so slowly, his father turned his head. 'I might be a fucking cripple,' he replied, 'but I'm not blind.'

Nobody who knew Max Redman in the old days would ever have been able to imagine him in this state. A giant of a man with a personality to match, there was a time when he filled the room with his personality and his stories of a life in the Regiment. He had travelled the world and seen things only a soldier could see and his name still came up in conversation among some of the older guys back at base.

'No, Dad,' Sam replied, trying to keep his voice level. 'I know you're not blind.'

'Well that's something, I suppose.' Max weakly turned his head back to the television.

'You should eat some lunch.' Sam dug a teaspoon into the mashed potato on his father's plate. It had a dry crust around it – Sam started to raise the spoon to Max's mouth, but his father raised a bony wrist and pushed it away.

'I'm not a fucking kid, either.'

Sam let the spoon fall back on to the plate.

Father and son sat in awkward silence.

'Where've you been?' Max asked finally.

'The Stan,' Sam replied quickly, grateful that the silence had been punctured. And then, more quietly, 'You knew that.'

Max remained expressionless.

'Nasty,' Sam continued. 'Taliban crawling all over the place like ants. Nail one of them and another two pop up in his place. We could have used Jacob out there.'

At the mention of his other son's name, Max's eyes closed briefly. In his private moments, Sam wondered whether it was Jacob's disappearance that had sparked all this off. The doctors had said no – it was a purely physical condition, a gradual wastage of the muscles that would eventually leave him too weak to breathe. But Sam had seen it happen. When Jacob had left the country it had hit both their parents hard. Their mother had died two years later; by that time

51

Max was already having difficulty walking. His subsequent decline was sudden and steep.

'Jacob was a real soldier,' Max muttered.

Sam didn't say what came into his head – that if Max had only told Jacob that, just once after he'd been kicked out of the Regiment, his brother might never have done a runner. Instead he took a deep, steady breath. 'We're all real soldiers, Dad.'

'Not like him. None of you.' Max turned to look at his younger son again. 'Especially not you, Samuel Redman. If it wasn't for your brother, God knows where you'd have ended up, so you can stop talking about him like that for a start.'

Like what? Sam wanted to say, but he knew better than to carry on with this childish argument. Jacob had always been Dad's favourite. Since his disappearance, he'd achieved almost mythical status in the old man's eyes. 'Look, Dad. I just wanted to see how you were, but you'd obviously prefer it if I wasn't here . . .'

'Don't be so fucking touchy, Sam. Pass me a ciggie.'

By Max's bedside there was an opened packet of cigarettes. His habit of smoking in the room infuriated the nurses, but they had learned not to complain too heavily. Sam placed a cigarette in his father's mouth and lit it using the orange lighter stashed away in the packet. Max took several deep drags and appeared to relax a little. With difficulty he lifted his arm and waved the burning cigarette in the direction of a photograph in a tarnished silver frame that sat by the TV at the end of the bed.

'Pass me that,' he instructed. Ash fell on the sheets.

Sam did as he was told.

Max was in the middle, flanked by his two boys who stood on either side of him. Jacob and Sam looked younger there. Sam's unruly blond hair was a little longer than it was now – this was taken before his Regiment days – and there was a heaviness around his face. Puppy fat, some people might call it. His eyes twinkled and he looked like he was not taking the whole thing entirely seriously.

Jacob was a different matter. His features were quite different to Sam's, even though anyone would be able to tell that they were brothers. Jacob's hair was jet black, his eyes gun-metal grey. His eyebrows were dark and heavy and he had a dimple in his chin that made him look not cheeky but intense.

'Remember when this was taken?' Max asked.

'Of course,' Sam replied. It was the day he'd passed selection for the Paras. It had been Jacob's suggestion. 'You'll like them,' he'd said archly. 'Bunch of fucking lunatics, like you.'

'He always looked out for you, Sam.' For once, Max's voice did not sound accusatory.

'You talk about him like he's dead.'

Max turned to look at his son. His tired eyes narrowed and they were suddenly piercing. 'He probably is dead.'

'Why?'

Max's cigarette had burned to a stub. He awkwardly waved it in the air, not knowing where to extinguish it. Sam took it from his father's shaking hands, stubbed it on the bottom of his shoe and threw it into the waste paper bin. 'Why do you think Jacob's dead, Dad?'

Max's thin face hardened. 'You know what those bastards are like,' he replied cryptically. 'Jacob was an embarrassment to them. We both know how easy it is to get rid of people who are an embarrassment.'

Sam closed his eyes. 'Come on, Dad,' he said softly. 'Why would they bother? Jacob took the rap. He wasn't going to blurt anything to anyone. None of us were.' He paused. 'You hurt him, Dad. You and mum. More than you think. When they kicked him out of the Regiment you refused to even see him.'

'Shut up, Sam. You don't know what you're talking about. So we argued. Happens all the time. We're arguing now – doesn't mean you'll never come and see me again.' His breathing was weak and shaky. 'If your brother was still alive, what's the one thing he'd do if he knew I was cooped up in this shit hole, pissing into a pipe and wasting away to a fucking skeleton? What's the one thing he'd do?'

Sam looked at the floor. He knew the answer, of course – argument or no argument, Jacob would come to his father's bedside. Nothing would stop him. But he couldn't quite bring himself to say it, because then he'd have to come to the same conclusion Max had arrived at. The conclusion which, in his darkest hours, had always nagged at the edge of his mind. Jacob dead? That didn't bear thinking about. It would leave a hole in their life too big to be endured.

The silence was strained and uncomfortable. Max stared at the photograph in his hands and for a moment Sam felt as though his father had forgotten he was there.

'I'd better be going, Dad,' he muttered quietly. 'I'm back for a bit. I'll come again soon.'

Max didn't answer. He was still looking at the photograph as Sam left the room and closed the door quietly behind him.

THREE

'You never talk about your family.'

Kelly was fired up, ready for an argument. She'd been acting it out in her head all the way home on the Tube and before that – ever since lunch with Elaine. Ask him all the questions she wanted answers to and if he got shirty, confront him about the missing money from her purse.

'Nothing to say.'

Jamie was sitting in his preferred position, lounging on the sofa with his feet up on the coffee table. The TV was on with the sound down and he was fiddling with his iPod.

'For God's sake, Jamie, there must be *something* to say.' Kelly stood in the kitchenette area of the room throwing together some supper. She wasn't a very good cook, but Jamie didn't appear to mind. He ate anything. 'What about your mum and dad? Am I ever going to meet them?'

'Might be a bit difficult, that.' Jamie avoided her gaze. She noticed, though, that his eyes twitched slightly.

'Why?'

'They're dead.'

He said it quietly, his attention firmly on the screen of his iPod. To Kelly, he looked like someone who was doing his best not to let his emotions show. She let the salad servers fall to the side and hurried over to the sofa where she sat down next to him and put a hand on his shoulder. This wasn't what she had expected – all of a sudden the road plan of her argument had taken a turn for the worse. 'I'm sorry,' she whispered.

Jamie shrugged.

'Do you want to talk about it?'

'Told you. Nothing to say.'

They sat there in silence for a moment. Kelly felt a creeping sense of guilt about the light-hearted conversation she'd had that lunchtime. She had the urge to be more sensitive now. 'What did they die of?' she asked quietly.

'Mum, cancer.'

'What sort?'

Still Jamie wouldn't look her in the eye. But she saw his face twitch as he spoke. Heard the catch in his voice. 'At the end,' he said, 'everywhere. Started in the lungs. Spread to the . . . Oh, I don't know. Ask a fucking doctor.'

Kelly's wide eyes blinked; she felt herself holding back tears. She squeezed his shoulders gently, not knowing quite what to say. Only then did Jamie look at her. Kelly could see the hurt in his eyes.

'Took her about six months to die. Painful. They put her in one of those places for the last couple of weeks . . .'

'A hospice?'

'Yeah,' he replied. 'A hospice. Gave her liquid horse on a drip.'

'You mean morphine?'

'Same thing. She had this button, you know, to give herself more if she wanted it.'

They sat in silence and for a moment Kelly felt closer to him than she ever had. She too had seen a loved one die in this way – an aunt. She knew something of what he was feeling.

'How old were you?' she asked.

Jamie looked down. 'Seventeen,' he said.

Seventeen. Barely a man. It all sounded so terribly sad.

'What about your dad?' she asked.

Jamie sniffed. 'Army.' He stood up, leaving Kelly's hand to fall to her side. 'Actually, special forces.'

'What,' Kelly asked, 'like . . .'

'SAS,' he interrupted. He pulled gently on the lobe of one ear. 'Never really talk about it,' he added. 'Dad didn't. Just got on with the job. Know what I mean?'

Kelly didn't know, but she nodded anyway.

'How old were you when he . . .?'

'Thirteen.' He spoke quickly, as though he were trying to get it over with. 'Out on operations. Northern Ireland. They never told us exactly where or how.'

'Jamie, that's awful.'

Jamie shrugged for a second time. 'It's the life, isn't it?' he said, as though he were talking to someone who had undergone the same experiences. 'You know the risks when you take it on.'

'But you were just thirteen. A little boy.'

'No point crying about it.' All of a sudden he seemed to have closed up. Kelly stood and stepped towards her boy-friend, wanting to give him a hug. But as she approached, Jamie walked into the bedroom. When he returned he was carrying his coat. 'Where are you going?' Kelly asked with concern.

'Out.'

'What, now?'

'Yeah,' Jamie replied. 'Now.'

'Oh, Jamie. I didn't mean to upset you.'

'I'm not upset. Just want to be by myself.'

'But I'm cooking dinner.'

'Not hungry.' He headed towards the door.

'Don't go out, Jamie. Please. I want to talk.'

Jamie Spillane turned to look at her. 'Yeah,' he replied. 'Well I don't. I'll be back later, all right?'

Kelly looked at him, her eyes full of sympathy and confusion. 'All right,' she replied weakly.

And with that, Jamie walked out of the flat. Kelly sat on the sofa for a good long while after that, staring blandly at the silent TV screen. The supper she was cooking went uneaten; all she could do was think about what Jamie had told her.

His mum.

His dad.

And how alone he really was.

★

The Lamb and Flag had an old-fashioned pub sign swinging outside. That was its only concession to tradition, however. Inside it lacked any of the trappings of comfort to be expected from a more appealing hostelry: this was a place designed for drinking, not socialising, and the few punters were mostly on their own doing just that. There was a bar with three pumps of lager – one weak, one strong and one cheap – and five optics of spirits on the wall behind it. You'd need to drink the lot, Sam reflected as he approached the bar, in order to start harbouring romantic thoughts about the barmaid. She had a thicker neck than most of the boys back at base and a smile that made the Taliban look like Blue Peter presenters. The best that could be said of her was that she didn't share the fanatics' taste in facial hair.

Sam tapped one of the beer pumps at random. 'Pint,' he said shortly.

The barmaid poured his drink wordlessly and unenthusiastically, before accepting his twenty-pound note in a chubby hand and plonking the change back down on the beer-stained bar. Sam drank half the pint in two gulps, closing his eyes as the warmth of the alcohol immediately seemed to radiate from his chest. After drinking warm water out of a pouch for the best part of two months he enjoyed a proper drink. He finished the whole pint in less than a minute and, having ordered another one, carried it to a corner table by a window that had a scenic view on to the car park. That way he could keep an eye on his black Audi – the smartest car out there by a pretty large margin and no doubt an object of envy for the shitkickers who frequented this place.

The Lamb and Flag was out of the way and that was why Sam had chosen it. The guys would have converged on one of the regular Regiment haunts in the middle of Hereford, but at the moment he didn't feel like joining them. They'd be drinking themselves into post-mission raucousness. Good on them. If he hadn't spent time in the company of his father that afternoon, he'd be doing the same, but now he wasn't in the mood. He'd even ignored the two messages that had come through on his mobile phone. Both from girls he'd been with before he left for Helmand. Normally on his return from an operation, he'd be pretty much indiscriminate about who he took to bed. The sex was all that mattered and the well-used springs of his double bed would take another battering. But not tonight. He took another large gulp of his pint and ignored the curious looks of the locals.

Sam couldn't remember a time when he hadn't known that Jacob was the favourite. Growing up it hadn't seemed a problem. He had admired his older brother just as much as his mum and dad had. But looking back he couldn't help wondering if he'd been such a waster as a kid precisely because he knew he could never live up to Jacob's example. When his brother was a smart young recruit in a neatly pressed uniform, Sam was hanging on street corners and enjoying petty theft. By the time he was fifteen he'd lost count of the occasions he'd been collared for playing truant, hotwiring cars and joyriding. There were never less than three girlfriends on the go, simply for the thrill. There were brushes with the law, of course; the occasional night in the local police cells. Some of them he kept a secret from his family; some he couldn't. Everyone knew what he was up to, though. He was, as his dad had told him a million times, 'on a hiding to nothing'.

It had all stopped on one particular day. Sam remembered it as clearly as if it were a week ago. He was in with a bad crowd. Not criminals exactly. Just chancers. Chancers with a plan to mug some office worker. His mates had been watching the guy for a week, making note of what time he left the office with his bag full of cash. On the day in question they were to hold him at knife point. Sam's job was to borrow his dad's car for the afternoon and wait on the street corner to pick him up. The hapless victim probably wasn't carrying more than a few hundred pounds, but Sam's mates had spoken of the winnings they hoped to receive as if it were all the riches in the world. Sam himself wasn't that interested in the money. It sounded exciting, that was all. It made his mouth dry to think about it. His blood warm.

To this day Sam didn't know how Jacob had got wind of it. Maybe he'd seen him take his father's motor and followed him; maybe it was just fluke. All he did know was that as he was sitting in the car waiting for the job to go off, his brother had climbed into the passenger seat.

'Fuck off, Jacob,' Sam had said.

Jacob shook his head. 'No,' he replied, his dark eyes more intense than Sam had ever seen them. 'Don't think I'll be doing that.'

There was a silence. A silence that Sam remembered well. It put him on edge and caused a hotness at the back of his neck. Embarrassment.

'I think you should drive home, Sam,' Jacob said. 'Now.'

Sam looked into the rear-view mirror. No sign of his mates. Not yet.

'You think you're the big man. You think you're the brave mister soldier. You think I'm too yellow to do this.'

Jacob's expression barely changed. If he was insulted by Sam's words, it didn't show.

'I don't think you're too yellow to do it,' he replied calmly.

They sat there in silence for a moment. Jacob did not take his gaze away from Sam's eyes.

And then Sam had started the car. As he pulled out into the traffic he saw his mates arrive, but he didn't stop. He drove home with his brother, neither of them saying a word.

It was months later that Sam heard what happened to his accomplices. Three years, each of them. Out in eighteen months if they were lucky. But by then, Sam's life had changed. On Jacob's insistence he had already been recruited into the Paras; by the time his mates were back on the streets, Sam had his sights set on the Regiment. As his brother was so fond of saying, you're a long time looking at the lid.

He drained his pint and walked back up to the bar. The barmaid's face spread fatly into a toad-like smile. Jesus, Sam thought to himself. Is she giving me the come-on? It was enough to put him off his beer. For a split second he considered fleeing to another pub, but that thought was interrupted by his mobile phone buzzing in the pocket of his jeans. He pulled it out and looked at the screen. Number withheld. His instinct was to leave it: it was probably one of the girls calling to give him his welcome-home present. But as his eyes flickered up again at the barmaid, the prospect suddenly didn't seem so bad. He flicked the phone open and walked out of the pub to answer the call.

'Yeah?' he said.

'Evening, Sam,' a voice replied. 'Jack Whitely.'

Sam's brow furrowed. Jack Whitely was the Ops Officer back at base. What the hell was he doing calling him now?

'What is it, Jack?' He knew he didn't sound very friendly, and he didn't much care.

'You're called in. Squadron briefing. 07.00.'

'What are you talking about? We only got back this morning. We're not standby squadron.'

'07.00, Sam. CO's orders. I'm calling in the rest of the squadron now.'

'Good luck,' Sam snapped. 'It'll go down like a pork chop at a fucking bar mitzvah.'

'They'll get over it. Go and get your beauty sleep, Sam. Or sleep with whichever beauty you've got lined up. I'll see you in the morning.'

There was a click as the Ops Officer hung up.

Sam stood for a moment looking out into the darkness, with the phone still pressed to his ear. When he finally clicked it shut, it was with a sigh of pure irritation. After eight long, dry weeks in the field the beer was going to his head. He was knackered and he needed to lay up for a bit. A squadron briefing first thing in the morning was the last thing in the world he wanted. He glanced over his shoulder through the frosted glass window of the pub door. There was a warm glow from inside that belied the spit-and-sawdust nature of the place and he wanted to go back in. Then he looked back out towards the car park.

'Fucking hell,' he whispered to himself as he stuffed the phone back into his pocket, pulled out his keys, walked to the car and headed for home.

★

It was midnight and the pubs were chucking out. Jamie Spillane had tried to get drunk, but without much success. It wasn't lack of money – earlier on he had withdrawn cash on the card Kelly kept hidden at the back of one of her dressing-table drawers; it was just that the booze wasn't doing its job. He wasn't feeling woozy and pleasant; he was feeling lairy and on-edge. The bar staff had lowered the lights in a last attempt to get the punters out, but Jamie was sitting in the corner, his half-drunk pint on the table in front of him.

'Drink up please now, sir.'

Jamie looked up. The guy standing in front of him wore a suit and tie, had a shiny, shaved head and was built like a brick shithouse. Jamie vaguely recognised him as one of the bouncers that had let him into this place a couple of hours earlier.

'Now, please, sir,' the bouncer repeated.

Jamie picked up his glass. Slowly he put it to his lips and took the most minute of sips before placing it down on the table. He looked up at the bouncer and gave him a smug smile.

'All right, sunshine,' the bouncer growled. 'Out you get.'

Jamie stayed where he was, his chin jutting out with arrogance. He felt a frisson of excitement at the confrontation to come and took a perverse pleasure in sipping once more from his drink.

The bouncer looked over his shoulder and gestured at his colleague. A second man approached. He was taller, his bright blue eyes small and aggressive, his nose long and aquiline. 'Playing silly buggers, is he?' the man asked in a quiet Cockney accent.

The broad-shouldered man nodded.

'Look, son,' the new arrival continued. 'Piss off home, eh? We've had a nice quiet night and I don't want to spoil my lovely manicure on your jaw.'

Jamie took another sip. 'Tell you what,' he replied. 'Why don't you two homos go back to the gents where you belong and . . .'

He never finished the sentence. With a flick of his big hand the broad-shouldered man swiped Jamie's pint away then leaned over and grabbed him by the scruff of the neck, before pulling him over the table towards him. Jamie was thrown to the floor at the feet of the two men. He shook his

63

head in an attempt to clear it, then pushed himself upright again.

The tall man was standing in front of him now, the broad-shouldered one behind him. Jamie staggered from one foot to the other, a leering smile obstinately on his face, then held up both hands palm outwards.

'All right!' he said. '*All right!* I'm going.'

The tall man physically relaxed. His shoulders lowered and his jaw loosened. It was then that Jamie made his move. With a sharp, upward movement he jerked his knee sharply into the man's bollocks. Instantly he doubled over with a groan like a collapsed lung, giving Jamie the opportunity to hit him round the side of his face with a clenched fist. It stung his knuckles and barely seemed to make his victim move, but his smile broadened as he did it anyway.

He was half-expecting to be walloped from behind, so when it came it was no surprise. It knocked the wind out of him, though, so that he was bent double. And when the tall man returned the punch, it was with interest. Jamie felt his neck cricking and a spatter of blood spray from his nose. Seconds later he was lifted from his feet, taken to the pub door and unceremoniously flung on to the pavement.

A group of lads on the other side of the road jeered as Jamie scrambled to his feet, flicked a V sign at the bouncers still standing threateningly at the doorway to the pub and stumbled off into the Soho night.

As he walked, Jamie used the back of his hand to wipe away the blood that oozed from his nose. People were glancing at him and he quite liked that; and even though his face hurt, he was flushed from the excitement of the encounter. He wandered aimlessly for a few minutes, waiting for the blood to stop flowing and his head to stop ringing. When finally it did, he stopped and looked around. Soho was still busy at this late hour. Cafés were open, so were clubs; and on the other side of the road was a seedy-looking entrance with a fat, overly made-up woman behind a counter and a neon sign over the top. It flashed its message in big, bright letters: GIRLS.

Jamie smiled and almost instinctively moved his hand into the back pocket of his trousers. His fingertips felt money there. Notes. He looked up at the woman. The stare with which she returned his gaze was dismissive and unfriendly, but Jamie didn't care.

Stage two of his impromptu night out had just been decided on.

But at that exact moment he was interrupted by the ringing of his mobile phone. He cursed and pulled it out. Sleek and thin. The latest model. No number flashed up on the screen and he almost didn't answer. The truth was, though, that Jamie Spillane was not the kind of young man to ignore a phone call. His curiosity always got the better of him. If it was someone he didn't want to speak to, he could always pretend not to hear them. He accepted the call and put the handset to his ear.

'Yeah?'

Jamie recognised the voice, of course. The slurring, shouting, barely articulate female voice at the other end, a sound he remembered from his earliest childhood. He sighed and looked up at the neon light in front of him, all enthusiasm for his next adventure instantly dissolving into nothing.

When he spoke, it was with the stuttering hesitation of someone trying to get a word in edgeways.

'Jesus, Mum,' he said. 'What do you want? I told you not to call me. What do you *want* . . . ?'

FOUR

Sam spent a restless night, knowing he had to wake early. He was up with the sun and, his fridge being bare, ate breakfast at a café before heading back to base. He arrived there fifteen minutes before the agreed RV, in time to see the rest of the squadron arriving. To a man, they looked unshaven, hungover and above all thoroughly pissed off to be called in so early.

He found Mac outside the squadron office. 'They told you what all this is about?' Sam demanded. As a troop sergeant, Mac would normally have been pulled in early, had the mission explained to him and the plans presented. But he looked more like he'd spent the evening with a bottle of JD than the Ops Officer and he shook his head.

'Got the call when I was in the boozer.'

'Yeah,' Sam observed. 'You look like shit.'

'The good ladies of Hereford didn't agree with you,' Mac replied with a wink.

Sam shook his head. 'It's no wonder your missus won't let you back in the house,' he said. 'Other women would've stuck a knife in your back by now. We'd be reading about it in the *News of the World*.'

'Who dares wins, mate,' Mac said.

Sam couldn't help smiling. 'You know where the briefing is?'

'Kremlin.'

He nodded and together they started walking towards the

briefing room. As they walked they chatted. 'Been to see the old man?' Mac asked.

'Yeah.'

'How is he?'

'Fine,' Sam lied. 'Terror of the fucking nurses.' He said it with a note of finality. Mac took the hint and didn't say any more.

The Kremlin was located deep inside the main HQ building, near the records room and the CO's office. The two men walked in silence. When they entered the briefing room itself, they saw about twenty of the guys already there. Major Jack Whitely was up front: a short, squat man in camouflage gear, with a shock of ginger hair and sharp green eyes. He stood at a lectern, rifling through some notes. As Sam and Mac took a seat at the front row he nodded a greeting to them and then went back to what he was doing.

Over the next couple of minutes a further ten men arrived and at 07.00 hrs precisely Jack Whitely cleared his throat. 'Okay,' he said. 'Let's get started.' He flicked a switch on his lectern and the lights dimmed. An overhead projector at the back of the room beamed light onto a white screen behind him. Jack picked up a small remote and pressed a button. A map of Central Asia appeared behind him.

'At 12.00 hrs on Thursday you'll be bussed to Brize Norton,' Whitely announced. Today was Tuesday. They had about forty-eight hours. 'From there you'll be taking an all-expenses-paid flight to Bagram Airbase, northern Afghanistan.'

Several of the men in the room groaned noisily. Sam felt like joining them and so, from the look his friend gave him, did Mac. 'What was the fucking point in coming back?' Sam whispered.

'All right, guys,' Whitely said firmly. 'Listen up.' He flicked the button on his remote again. A new map appeared on the screen.

'We have a training camp in southern Kazakhstan,' Whitely continued. 'An area called the Chu Valley. We're expecting there to be about twenty individuals there. Our orders are to make sure they don't wake up in the morning.'

The men were silent now. Listening hard.

'Mode of insertion,' Whitely announced, 'HALO. Air troop, this is your gig. Rest of the squadron to remain on alert at Bagram in case of problems.'

All of sudden, Sam was in the groove. He'd been in hundreds of briefings like this before and any tiredness or annoyance he had felt when he first arrived had been shed. He listened keenly, his senses alert, knowing that he had to be on the ball. Air troop was his. He needed to be on top of things.

'There'll be a further briefing at Bagram,' continued Whitely. 'We have spooks on the ground who'll give you more detail on the geography. But first off, you need to be made aware of something.'

Whitely looked out over the briefing room. In the dim light Sam could see that the Major's face had suddenly gone serious, as though he were judging the mood of the men.

'MI6 have supplied us with pictures of the targets we expect to find there.' He pressed the button on the remote for the third time.

It was not in the nature of Regiment men to express surprise. They'd been asked to do enough morally ambiguous things in their time to be largely shock-proof. But Sam knew, as the image beamed out by the overhead projector changed, they would be taken aback by what had just appeared. On the screen in front of them were twenty grainy photographs. They varied in their quality. Some looked like passport photos, taken in cheap booths; others looked like they had been cut and pasted from bigger pictures. But they all had one thing in common. White skin.

Caucasian features. The squadron wasn't being presented with the usual brown skin, beards or turbans.

'Your targets,' Whitely announced firmly, 'are British citizens. They'll be speaking English. That shouldn't distract you from the job in hand.'

There was a brief silence before a voice called from the back of the room. 'What's the story, Boss? Who are they?'

'That, I'm afraid,' Whitely replied, 'is for our masters in the Firm to know, and for us not to find out. It's an in-an-out job and is strictly under the radar. The UK's relationship with Kazakhstan is good, but fragile. Any whiff that this is our doing and we'll be giving the suits in Whitehall a right headache, and I know how upset you'd all be if that happened.'

There was a smattering of cynical laughter.

Sam didn't join in.

He had barely heard what Whitely was saying, and laughter was the last thing on his mind.

His attention had been grabbed by something else.

Something on the screen.

Sam Redman had a good eye. A mind for detail. As soon as the photographs had appeared on the screen he had methodically and meticulously studied each one for a few seconds. His gaze fell on one picture. It was halfway down the group of images, no bigger than the others, no less indistinct. And yet when he saw that photograph, his blood turned to ice in his veins. The man had dark hair and a beard, flecked with grey, that covered most of his face. There was a bruise to one side of his forehead. It was the eyes that gave him away, though. Dark eyes, with shadowy rings dug underneath them and thick-set eyebrows.

Sam would know those eyes anywhere, because they belonged to his brother.

It was like a dream – a dream in which he urgently had to do something, but couldn't force his body into action. This

69

was a mistake. It had to be. Sam looked over his shoulder at the guys congregated in the room around him. Their faces glowed in the dim light of the OHP, but their expressions registered no surprise as they gazed at the screen. Sam's eyes darted from one face to another. None of them, he realised, would recognise Jacob even if they saw him. They were either too young or never knew him.

All of them, he realised, except one person.

Sam faced forward again and glanced to his right where Mac was sitting. His friend looked up at the screen. There was no twinge of recognition in his face.

And then the room was plunged into darkness as the OHP was switched off. 'All right, guys,' Whitely announced brightly as he turned the main lights on again. 'RV back here 09.00 on Thursday. Rest up before then. Tell your missus to keep her hands off you – everything goes right you'll be back for tea and blow jobs Sunday lunchtime.' He straightened his papers on the lectern and headed for the door.

There was a hubbub in the room as the assembled squadron rose to their feet and started chatting. Sam didn't move. There was a sickness in his stomach, a kind of breathlessness. If he opened his mouth to speak, he wasn't quite sure what would come out. Everything was confused in his head. Perhaps he'd made a mistake. Perhaps it wasn't Jacob, just someone who looked like him. That would make more sense. The bearded figure in the picture looked rough and worn. Jacob had always taken care of what he looked like.

He tried to persuade himself in the few moments that he sat there that he had indeed made an error; but deep down he knew he hadn't. It was Jacob.

Sam closed his eyes, took a deep breath and turned to look at Mac. But his friend wasn't there. He was already walking out of the room, deep in conversation with one of the younger guys. Almost before Sam knew it, he was alone.

The sudden burst of anger came from nowhere and was beyond his control. With a swipe of his hand he hurled the chair on which Mac had been sitting on to its side, then stood and kicked it a good couple of metres. It was stupid, pointless, and didn't make him feel any better. He left the chair on its side, though, and, cursing under his breath, stormed towards the door. There was a suspicion at the back of his mind that someone was playing games with him. He didn't like it. He wanted it to stop. Now.

The drab, flat corridors of the Kremlin were unpopulated at this hour. Sam stormed through them, a thousand questions bursting from his brain. When he came to Mark Porteus's office he barely stopped to draw breath before knocking on the door: not a polite rap, but a solid thump with a clenched fist.

No answer.

'Boss!' he shouted, banging again on the door. But still nothing. '*Boss!*'

'Everything all right, Sam?'

He turned. It was Jack Whitely. The Ops Officer's green eyes were narrowed. Sam clenched his jaw and gave him an unfriendly stare. Whitely was an old hand. Several tours with the Regiment. He was organising this mission – surely he knew what was going on. Damn it: if Porteus couldn't tell Sam what the hell was happening, Whitely was the next best thing.

'What's . . .?' he started to say.

And then he stopped.

Amid the confusion in his head, one single thought began to crystallise.

What if Whitely *hadn't* recognised his brother? Or Porteus. Or even Mac. What then? If he alerted them to it, Sam would be instantly pulled from the op.

Whitely blinked, then raised an eyebrow. 'Yes, Sam?'

He drew a deep breath.

'Nothing,' he said. And then, because Whitely was still looking strangely at him, '09.00 on Thursday.'

Whitely nodded. Sam walked away. He could feel the Ops Officer's eyes burning into his back. It took everything he had to keep his pace steady and his mind calm.

★

Kelly Larkin awoke, bleary eyed. The room was dark and in her drowsiness she thought it must still be the middle of the night. It was a lovely feeling, splintered only when she saw the orange glow from her bedside alarm clock. Seven-thirty.

'*Shit!*' she hissed, suddenly awake. She clambered naked out of bed and hurried to the underwear drawer of her dressing table, pulling on some knickers and awkwardly hitching her bra behind her back, before she finally remembered the revelations of the previous evening. Jamie's confession; the way he had stormed out of the flat; how she had stayed up waiting for him until sleep finally overcame her. And now, she realised as she turned round to look at her bed, there he was. Asleep. She breathed a sigh of relief.

Quietly Kelly walked round to his side of the bed and perched on the edge. His head was covered with the duvet, his breathing regular and heavy. Kelly gently uncovered his head to look at his slumbering face.

What she saw made her catch a breath.

His upper lip was smeared with blood, dark brown and flaking at the edges. The smear itself extended up on to his right cheek before streaking gradually away. The blood, though, was not the most distressing thing. His skin was purple, bruised and mottled; his right eye was blackened and closed up. Jamie looked like he'd been in the boxing ring.

Kelly shook him by the shoulder – not forcefully, but tenderly and with concern.

72

'Jamie,' she whispered. 'Jamie, wake up.'

He didn't stir, so she shook him again. This time he started. His eyes opened and he looked around without moving his body, as though he didn't know where he was. When his eyes fell on Kelly, he shut them again for a moment before pushing himself up on his elbows.

Kelly touched his face lightly with her fingertips. 'What happened?' she breathed. 'What time did you get back?' The pungent smell of last night's alcohol wafted under her nose.

'Late,' Jamie replied non-committally.

'I know it was late, Jamie,' Kelly retorted a bit more sharply than she had intended. 'What happened to your face?'

'It's all right,' he said. 'Nothing I can't cope with.' He smiled at her – a peculiarly gruesome expression given the state of his face – then stretched out his hand towards her breasts.

She shrugged him away and stood up. 'I'm late for work,' she said. With her back turned to Jamie she walked to her wardrobe and pulled out a charcoal grey two-piece suit and cream blouse; still with her back turned to him she put it on. Tears were coming. She didn't know if she'd be able to stop them and she didn't want him to see.

Her eyes were hot now as she finished getting dressed. She felt a riot of emotions all trying to burst out. Confusion; anger; sympathy. Almost on an impulse she turned round, the first tears dripping from her eyes. He was still sitting there, eyeing her up with that self-satisfied look on his face. 'For God's sake, Jamie,' she railed. 'I just don't know what to think.'

His expression changed to one of wariness.

'All I want to do,' she wept dramatically, 'is get close to you.' She knew she was sounding dramatic, but she couldn't help it. Rushing to his bedside she sat down again and grabbed his hands.

'Those things you told me last night,' she continued. 'It meant so much that you opened up to me.'

Jamie looked down at the duvet.

'You don't have to be embarrassed,' Kelly insisted. 'I know you've been drinking. I can smell it on you. But please just tell me, what happened last night?'

There was a pause. Jamie took a deep breath and when he gazed back up at her, his forehead was creased. He looked for all the world to Kelly like a confused little boy.

'I can't,' he said quietly.

'Why not?'

'I just . . . I can't,' he replied. 'There's things I can't tell you about me. Things it's best you don't know. That you wouldn't believe.'

She squeezed his hand a bit harder. 'I *would* believe you, Jamie. Just *trust* me.'

Another pause. Jamie's eyes flickered away from her. He looked like he was trying to make a decision.

'All right,' he said finally. He got out of bed, approached the window wearing nothing but his boxer shorts and gently parted the curtains with one finger. He looked outside, let the curtain fall closed and then turned to look at her. He wavered slightly, as though drunk. 'This is going to sound stupid,' he said.

Kelly shook her head. 'No it isn't.'

He shrugged. 'All right then. There's things I can't tell you because I'm . . .' He faltered. 'I don't know what the proper word is. I'm an agent.'

Kelly blinked. 'A what?'

'An *agent*.'

'What . . .?' she hesitated. 'Like an estate agent?'

Jamie closed his eyes in frustration. 'No,' he replied, exasperation in his voice. 'A *secret* agent. A spy.'

She blinked again. There were no tears now. They had instantly dried up.

'A spy,' she repeated.

Jamie nodded.

All the anger Kelly Larkin had felt a couple of minutes ago disappeared. She smoothed the legs of her trouser suit, stood up and turned to face Jamie. He looked so ridiculous there, semi-naked in her bedroom.

'And your dad was in the SAS?' she asked. 'And your mum died of cancer?'

Jamie nodded.

'And you thought that if I believed all that it would make it okay for you to steal money from my purse?'

Jamie's lips parted slightly, but he didn't say anything.

Kelly walked up to him as coolly as she was able. She came to a halt right in front of him.

She smiled.

And then, with all the force she could muster, she slapped him hard round the side of the face.

'Ow!' he shouted, but she was already talking over him, her voice a low, menacing hiss.

'Get out of my house, Jamie Spillane,' she spat. 'And don't come back. I've had enough of you, your sponging and your stupid, insulting lies. I never, *ever* want to see you again. You've got five minutes.'

With that, she turned her back on him, walked out of the bedroom and into the bathroom. She locked herself in and listened at the door, waiting to hear the sound of her ex-boyfriend leaving the flat.

★

Sam floored it home. He barely saw anyone else on the road, not because there weren't any cars, but because he was blind to them. He blocked out the angry sound of horns as he cut up the other road users; he ignored red lights and pedestrian crossings. After his encounter with Jack Whitely outside the

75

CO's office, Sam had walked straight out of the Kremlin and left the base as quickly as possible. He didn't stop and speak to anyone. He just had to get out of there. And now, as he sped round the roads of Hereford, there was one thought in his mind. *Get home. Get away from everyone else. Then you can try to work out what the hell is going on.*

Coming to a halt outside his flat, Sam parked badly, one wheel on the pavement, the back of the car jutting out into the road. He didn't care. He just leapt from the vehicle, ran into the house and – for some reason he couldn't quite put his finger on – locked himself inside. He drew several deep breaths before going into the kitchen and opening one of the cupboards. It was empty apart from a half-drunk bottle of Scotch. He poured himself a glass and downed it in one, before pouring another and waiting for the alcohol to do its work on his nervous system.

Jacob had changed. There was no doubt about that. He looked older, more weather-beaten. It probably wasn't so surprising that Mac hadn't recognised him. Sam's brother had just been one of a number of faces and the photos were of poor quality. He sipped at his whisky, closed his eyes and tried to get his thoughts straight. *It made no sense.* Why would the Regiment be sending out a troop to kill a bunch of British citizens; why would they be eliminating one of their own?

As that thought crossed his mind, he stopped. He gently placed his drink on the kitchen worktop and closed his eyes. Sam thought back to the previous day. He was in his father's room. The old man had said something. What was it? Sam's brow furrowed as he tried to remember the exact words.

You know what those bastards are like. Jacob was an embarrassment to them. We both know how easy it is to get rid of people who are an embarrassment.

He shook his head. His father's words were nothing, just grief-induced paranoia, the delusions of an old man with time on his hands coming up with reasons to explain his favourite son's absence.

Weren't they?

'Damn it!' he shouted, kicking the kitchen unit so that it rattled. Sam downed the Scotch, then started prowling around the flat like a caged animal. He needed answers, but there was nowhere he could get them – if Sam alerted anyone to what was going on, there was no doubt about what would happen. He'd be pulled from the op and a team of trained SAS killers would fly to Kazakhstan to eliminate his brother, without Sam being able to do anything about it.

Morning passed into afternoon. The effects of the alcohol wore off, leaving only an uncomfortable, nagging sensation in the pit of Sam's stomach. His phone rang several times; he ignored it.

Afternoon melted into evening. Sam felt like a prisoner in his own home, as though even stepping over the threshold would somehow reveal his suspicions to everyone, like an escaping convict walking into the beam of a searchlight. As the light outside began to fail, so it grew darker in his bare front room. He sat on the old sofa and allowed the gloom to surround him. From where he sat he could see out into the road. His badly parked Audi was just outside; occasional passers-by sauntered across his field of vision.

Evening became night. The streetlamps flickered on outside. Still Sam didn't move. He had no idea what time it was and he didn't bother to check. Before long he was sitting in darkness.

By the time he noticed the figure on the other side of the street, Sam couldn't have said how long it had been there. It was faceless, the head covered with a hood, the kind worn by kids. If this was a kid, though, it was an unusually tall, stocky one. He stood leaning against a lamppost; and although Sam could not see his face, he had the sudden, unnerving sensation that this person was looking straight through the window of the flat and into Sam's front room.

The unnerving sensation that he was some shadowy sentinel, keeping watch.

Sam froze.

The figure was in the light; Sam was in the dark. Chances were this guy couldn't see him. Slowly, he slid down the sofa on his back and on to the floor. On all fours he crawled out of the front room and into the corridor. It was very dark in his flat, he used the tried and tested Blade method of not looking directly at objects, but looking around them, using his periphery vision, which is better attuned to seeing in the dark. He made his way confidently to the bathroom without switching on any lights. Once in there, he fumbled towards the toilet. Sam lifted the lid of the cistern and carefully groped inside.

The handgun was there, a fully loaded Beretta 92 9 mm, carefully perched on the mechanical intestines of the cistern. He picked it up gingerly to stop it from falling into the water; but once it was in his hand, he gripped it firmly.

He felt a whole lot better with the reassuring weight of a weapon in his fist.

Chances were it was just some guy waiting for his girlfriend, or his dealer, or who just happened to be standing outside Sam's house. But there was no doubt that Sam felt a cold, bristling uncertainty, a kind of sixth sense that experience had taught him never to ignore. He checked the weapon quickly before leaving the bathroom and walking back down the corridor, the shallow, steady sound of his breath the only noise in his ears.

He stopped at the door to the front room, pressed his back against the wall and, squinting his eyes slightly, peered across the room and out of the window. Sam gripped the weapon a little bit more firmly when he realised the figure under the lamppost was no longer there.

Out of the blue, a motorbike roared down the street. It

made Sam start momentarily, but more than that it messed with his hearing, which had been carefully tuned to the quiet. The noise of the motor took a while to fade; only when it had finally disappeared could Sam readjust his ears to the thick silence of his flat.

But silence wasn't what he heard.

It was faint, but it was there: the sound of footsteps. They were brisk and they were getting louder.

Sam felt his jaw setting solid. The handgun was pointed out in front of him now as he backed up and headed towards the front door.

The top panel was made of frosted glass. He stood several metres from it and held the gun at arm's length towards the door. Head height. His eyes twitched slightly as he watched the blurred silhouette of a figure come into view. It was easy to determine the curved outline of the man's hooded top, the broad shape of his shoulders.

It would take two shots, he calculated, to kill him. One to shatter the glass, one to finish him off. And Sam was ready to do it; ready to defend himself at the first sign of danger.

The figure remained perfectly still. In some part of his brain that was not concentrating on keeping the guy in his sights, Sam wondered if the hooded figure knew he was there.

Movement.

Sam's trigger finger twitched.

A noise.

It was the sound of the letter box opening. Sam watched as an envelope slowly glided through the hole in his door. Instinctively he threw his back to the wall, not knowing whether that envelope was concealing something else; but it fell harmlessly to the floor. Almost immediately, the silhouette melted away and Sam heard once more the sound of footsteps, getting quieter this time. He ran to the front room window just in time to see the unknown delivery boy disappear round the corner of the street.

Only then did he shake his head. Jesus, he thought to himself. And you thought Dad was paranoid. He felt stupid. He felt angry with himself. But why, then, did he still not want to turn on the lights?

Why did he still not want to illuminate himself?

Why did he still feel safer with the gun in his hand?

He stepped away from the window and returned to the front door. The envelope was still lying there.

Sam Redman bent down and picked it up.

FIVE

It was a plain, brown A4 envelope. There was no writing on the front and the seal had been Sellotaped down. It crossed Sam's mind as he opened it up that the lack of saliva on the seal would make it difficult for anyone to discover who this envelope had come from, if they were of a mind to do so.

Inside there was a thin sheaf of papers stapled together at one corner. In the darkness of the hallway Sam was unable to read what they said; he made his way back to the bathroom, closed the door and switched on the light above the shaving mirror. Only then, as he sat perched on the edge of the bath, did he start to read.

The document consisted of four pages. It was barely legible, however, because large chunks of the text had been blacked out. At the top of the front page was an official stamp.

MINISTRY OF DEFENCE
SUPPRESSED UNDER DA–NOTICE 05 (UNITED KINGDOM
SECURITY & INTELLIGENCE SERVICES & SPECIAL
SERVICES)

Sam read those bits of the text that remained: '. . . *a car park of a service station on the M4 . . . cold day . . . seemed agitated . . . second meeting in a country pub . . .*' It was meaningless to Sam. He held the paper up to the light, hoping to read what was underneath. Nothing doing.

Whatever this was, it had been heavily censored. Someone had wanted to make sure that it was incomprehensible. They'd done a good job.

But there was something else.

On the top page, scrawled in blue biro and roughly circled, was a name – Clare Corbett – and next to it a telephone number. A mobile.

Sam looked at the number for a good long while. He even went so far as to punch it into his phone. But something stopped him from dialling. He closed his eyes and tried to clear his head. Everything was so muddled, so confusing. Who was this Clare Corbett? Did the document he held in his hand come from her? What was the point of him seeing it if he couldn't understand a word that was written?

No. This wasn't right. He saved the number to his phone, but didn't dial. He had a another idea.

Sam glanced at his watch. Ten thirty. He couldn't believe that the day had passed – it seemed like only a few minutes ago that he was in the briefing back at HQ. It was late, but that didn't matter. He sniffed and then searched for another number on his phone. Nodding with satisfaction when it appeared on his screen, he allowed his thumb to hover over the dial button.

He stopped again, then shook his head. No. He knew that it was too easy for someone to listen in on his phone calls and until he knew what the hell this was all about, that wasn't a risk he was going to take. He switched off the light, allowed his eyes to get used to the darkness, then moved to his bedroom.

Sam's leather jacket was slung over the back of his chair. He put it on, secreted the handgun in the inside pocket, then returned to the front door. Moments later he was on the pavement, walking almost at random until he found a public phone box.

Only then did he make his call.

Detective Inspector Nicola Ledbury of the Metropolitan Police had endured, even by her standards, an extremely shitty day. The trial she'd been working on for three months solid had gone tits up on a technicality, prompting a bollocking from the judge and her DCI – no doubt there would be more to come in the morning, if she ever made it in. She dumped her bag in the hallway and went to the kitchen to pour herself a large glass of wine. As she did so, she looked at the clock on the oven. Ten-thirty and she was just getting in. No wonder her personal life was such a disaster.

She took two deep gulps of wine before going into her small bathroom. As she always did, she glanced in the mirror. Nicola knew she was quite pretty on a good day, but today wasn't one of them. Her blonde hair was a disaster and she had bags under her eyes. The kind of clothes that she had to wear on the job flattened out her slim, curvy figure and she couldn't wait to get out of them. So, running the bath, she started to strip. Her clothes stank of London fumes – it was disgusting and all she wanted to do was wash away the grime of the city. Her blouse dropped to the floor, then her bra. As she was undoing her trousers, however, she felt her mobile phone buzz against her skin. Nicola's heart sank. Who the hell was calling her at this hour? She pulled out the phone and looked at it. Number withheld.

The DI sighed. It was probably the office. Wearily she switched off the bath taps and took the call.

'Yeah?' she intoned, making no attempt to hide the reluctance in her voice.

'Nicola?' A man's voice. Quite deep. She recognised it, but couldn't place it.

'Who's this?'

'Sam,' came the reply. 'Sam Redman.'

A pause as a little smile played across her lips.

'Hello, Sam,' she replied, her voice all of a sudden kittenish and full of intonation. She quickly stepped half-dressed out of the echoing bathroom, touching her hand to her hair even though there was nobody to see. 'Long time no speak.'

'I've been away,' came the reply.

'Anywhere fun?'

'Not really.'

Sam's voice was curt, almost businesslike – a far cry from his boyish fair hair and mischievous eyes – but that didn't bother her. It was just the way he was. In the couple of weeks they'd worked together while he and his SAS mates were body-guarding a witness, she'd grown used to it. Fond of it, even – fond enough, at least, for them to indulge in a bit of extra-curricular activity. Nicola blushed slightly to think about it.

'So,' she said lightly, 'you thought you'd phone me to arrange a . . .'

'Listen, Nicola,' he interrupted. 'I need a favour.'

She hesitated. There was something in his voice. He sounded tense.

'What's the matter, Sam? Everything all right?'

'Fine.' He sounded like he was simply brushing away the question. 'Listen, I've got a mobile number. I need a billing address. Can you get it for me?'

As he spoke, Nicola felt deflated and she couldn't prevent it from sounding in her voice. 'I suppose so,' she replied. 'What's it for?'

'Mate of mine,' Sam replied blandly. 'Getting funny phone calls. Wants to put a stop to them.'

He was lying. Nicola could tell that easily enough, but she couldn't be bothered to make a thing of it.

'All right, Sam,' she sighed. 'It'll take me twenty-four hours. Give me the number and call me tom . . .'

'I haven't got twenty-four hours,' Sam said. 'I need it now.'

84

A pause. 'Sounds like your friend really wants to put a stop to these calls,' Nicola remarked lightly.

'Can you do it?' Brusque, businesslike.

'It's half-past ten at night, Sam.'

'Can you do it?'

Nicola sighed again, heavily this time. 'All right, Sam. I'll see what I can do.'

'Good.' He gave her the number, then said, 'I'll call you in half an hour.'

Without another word, the phone clicked off.

Nicola looked at the silent handset, then longingly back at the half-run bath. Then, muttering under her breath, she went to find herself a dressing gown.

Sometimes, she thought to herself, she was just too obliging for her own good.

★

Sam replaced the phone on its cradle, then immediately walked away from the booth.

He was just outside a parade of shops, most of them shut apart from a kebab shop half full of pissed-up kids. Sam was hungry, but something stopped him from wanting contact with anyone else, so he walked purposefully away. The half-hour passed slowly. He found a second pay phone in about ten minutes, then spent the rest of the time hanging around waiting to call his contact again. He didn't really know what he was going to do if he found out an address for this woman – it rather depended on where she lived – but at the moment he didn't know what else to do. It was just gone eleven when he made the call.

'It's me.'

'Somehow I thought it would be.' Nicola sounded annoyed.

'Did you get the address?'

'Yeah, I got it. You didn't tell me it was a woman.'

'I didn't know,' he lied.

A disbelieving silence. 'Look, Sam,' Nicola said finally, 'I don't know what this is all about, but I've got enough trouble at work as it is. This isn't going to put me any deeper in the shit, is it?'

Sam sniffed. 'It's nothing to worry about,' he lied. 'I promise. It's just personal.'

He breathed steadily as he waited for Nicola to reply.

'All right,' she said, her voice heavy with resignation. 'You got a pen?'

'I can remember it.'

'Fine. Ground Floor Flat, 31 Addington Gardens, W3. Hope your *friend* likes Acton, Sam. Personally, I think it's a dump.'

Acton, London. At this time of night he could make it in a couple of hours.

'Thank you, Nicola. I owe you one.'

'As far as I can remember,' she replied, a hint of archness returning to her voice, 'you already did.'

For the first time that day, Sam smiled. 'Don't let the bed bugs bite,' he told her quietly, but there was no reply. Nicola had already hung up.

Fifteen minutes later, Sam was in the car, one finger on the steering wheel as he hurtled out of Hereford down the A road that would lead him to London. The screen of his SatNav illuminated the route, but he barely glanced at it. He knew the way well enough. The lights of the cars ahead of him were nothing but a blur – not only because the speedo was constantly tipping a hundred, but also because his mind wasn't really on the road. The events of the day churned over in his head, a series of disjointed visions; but the more he thought about them, the more confused he became. Sam didn't even know who he was going to find at Addington Gardens. Clare Corbett, whoever the hell she was? Or someone else? He glanced down at the passenger seat. The handle of his handgun was peeping out from under the document in its envelope. There were enough rounds in there for him to keep himself safe; he couldn't shake the feeling that he would be discharging some of them before the sun was up.

It was gone one in the morning by the time Sam approached London. The roads were practically empty and he burned up the tarmac, slowing down only when the time came to pull off the motorway. The female voice on the SatNav was irritatingly calm as it guided the speeding Audi through the West London suburbs and by a quarter past one he was nearing Addington Gardens. It was an ordinary residential road with a long line of terraced houses on either side. Sam didn't turn into it, deciding instead to park several streets along. Once he'd come to a standstill, he took his jacket from the back seat, secreted the handgun and the document inside then climbed out of the car. The locking lights illuminated the dark street as he walked towards his destination.

There was nobody about – just an urban fox further down the pavement who stared at him with glinting eyes for a few seconds before turning tail and disappearing. In the background Sam could hear the vague hum of traffic on the main road, but here all was still. At the end of Addington Street he loitered, his narrowed eyes surveying the scene. He didn't really know what he was looking for, but he'd recognise it if he saw it. There was no sign of anybody at this time, and none of the vehicles looked suspicious.

Except one.

It was a white van, old, well used. Counting down the house numbers from the end of the street, Sam calculated that it was parked outside number 75. Too close to the address he was visiting for his liking. He decided to investigate further.

Sam walked casually along the pavement. As he passed the white van he saw there was nobody in the front seats. But there was a panel blocking off the rear of the vehicle, so he couldn't see inside. On the back doors there were blacked-out windows and a little sticker: NO TOOLS ARE KEPT IN THIS VEHICLE OVERNIGHT.

With his right hand, he gripped the gun inside his jacket. He approached the back of the vehicle along the pavement side and then, with a sudden sharp jerk of the elbow on his left arm, he shattered the window, then immediately pulled out his gun and aimed it into the body of the van.

Nothing. Empty. Sam drew a deep breath and withdrew his gun from inside the window. Somebody would be cursing the vandals first thing in the morning, but he wouldn't be losing too much sleep over that. He turned his attention to the house numbers. Number 31 was only a few paces away.

There was nothing to distinguish it from the other terraced houses along this street. It had a small front garden that had been concreted over and was now home to only a couple of wheelie bins and a few old crisp packets that had been blown in. The ground-floor flat had a large bay window at the front, blocked with wooden slatted blinds. On the wall just above the window the cover of a security alarm blinked in the night. As Sam opened the metal gate it creaked quietly, so he didn't close it before walking up to the bright blue front door.

By the side of the door was a video intercom with two buttons, one for the ground-floor flat, the other for the first floor. Next to each button was a scrawled name tag. The tag for the ground floor was simply marked 'CC'. Clare Corbett.

Sam took the envelope from his pocket and removed the document. Then, with one hand over the lens of the intercom camera, he pressed the button, holding it down for several seconds without releasing his finger.

And then he waited.

There was no reply.

Sam cursed under his breath. He hadn't really considered the possibility that there wouldn't be anybody here. His hand still covering the camera, he rang the intercom again.

Again he waited.

This time, his patience was rewarded.

The woman's voice that came over the loudspeaker was groggy and throaty, as though its owner had just woken up. But it was wary too.

'Who's that?' it demanded.

Sam put his mouth to the intercom. 'Clare Corbett?' he asked.

'Who's that?' the voice repeated. Tense. 'Who is it? Why can't I see you?'

He let his hand fall from the camera and replaced it with the document. 'I need to talk to you about this.'

A pause.

'What about it?'

'I've got some more information,' Sam improvised. 'You need to hear it.'

A scratchy sound came over the intercom, the sound of movement. 'All right,' the voice said finally. Reluctantly. 'Wait there. I'll get dressed and let you in.'

Sam put his hand back over the camera. He didn't know quite why he wanted his face to remain anonymous, but he did, and there was nothing to stop whoever was inside the flat from looking out even when they weren't speaking. Secreting the document back in his jacket, he used his free hand to grip the gun. He had no idea who was going to answer the door and he wanted to be prepared for any eventuality.

A minute passed.

Two.

Sam looked over his shoulder, then back down at the intercom.

Why had nobody opened the door yet?

He rang the bell again, but this time he didn't wait for an answer. Something told him there wasn't going to be one.

Hurrying back on to the pavement he looked from one end of the road to the other. Had there been an alleyway leading behind the houses when he turned into Addington Street? He thought there had. Sam glanced back at the front door. Nothing. Not even a light. Whoever he had just spoken to was taking too long to answer the door. There was something else going on.

He thundered to the end of the road. Sure enough, a pokey alley led down the side of the end-of-terrace house. Sam sprinted down it, turning a corner at the end. He knocked a dustbin as he ran; it clattered over and spilled its putrid contents on the ground. In the darkness he could see movement up ahead. He didn't shout: he just upped his speed.

There was an open door, a wooden one leading from the garden of one of the terraces. And beyond it, running towards him, a woman. She had blonde hair – shoulder length – and wore a chunky, knee-length cardigan. When she saw Sam bearing down on her she immediately turned and ran in the other direction. Sam easily caught up and grabbed her. The woman flipped and fought, like a fish that has just been pulled from the water. She kicked Sam hard in the shin, in the groin. It hurt, but he just held her, firmly, until it became perfectly clear that she wasn't getting way. It took about a minute for the fight to go out of her, for her limbs to stop flailing and go limp. Only then did Sam realise how badly she was shaking.

He turned her round and looked at her face. The silver moon illuminated her features. The skin was white apart from where Sam's hand had been, where it was a mottled red. A sob escaped the woman's lips and her eyes were suddenly filled with an unmistakable look of total, abject fear.

'Please,' she whispered. '*Please!* I haven't told anyone. I've done what you said. *I haven't told anyone!*'

She hid her face in her hands.

'Please!' her voice was muffled now. Filled with brutal, racking sobs of terror. 'Please, don't kill me.'

SIX

Sam held the woman in silence for a moment, while she continued to cry. Beneath the tears he could tell she was attractive. She smelled of perfume. But she was a pitiful sight with her raw eyes and streaked mascara.

'Who else is in the house?' he demanded.

'Nobody,' she breathed. Sam heard a trace of a Northern Irish accent in her voice.

He waited a couple of seconds and then, with a sudden movement, pulled out his handgun and held it to the side of her head.

'*Who else is in the house?*'

'Oh, God . . .' The woman's knees buckled. 'Nobody. I swear. Oh, sweet Jesus, I swear . . .'

Sam narrowed his eyes. She was telling the truth. 'All right,' he said. 'Get back in there. I'll be right behind you. If you shout for help, I'll shoot. Do you understand?'

No reply. Just a trembling wreck of a human being.

'I said, do you understand?'

'Yes,' she whispered.

He nodded at her and stepped aside. With shaky, nervous steps the woman moved into her garden. The back door to her house was still open, but there were no lights on inside. Sam followed her in, closing the door behind him. He was in a kitchen. Behind him were wide French doors with slatted blinds above them. Sam stepped further into the room. 'Put the blinds down,' he instructed.

The woman did as she was told, slowly and clumsily. Sam found himself growing impatient. But the woman was scared. Telling her to hurry up wouldn't have done any good. When the blinds were finally lowered, she turned to look at him.

'Turn the lights on,' he told her.

She edged round him, her eyes constantly glancing at the gun. By the main door was a light switch. She flicked it on and illuminated the room. Sam looked around. The kitchen was immaculately tidy, nothing out of place on the work surfaces. There was art on the walls and cookbooks on the shelves. It was a pleasant, comfortable, ordinary place. In the middle of the room was a pine table with four chairs neatly tucked underneath. The woman still trembled as she stood by the door.

'Are you Clare Corbett?' he asked.

She nodded her head.

He pointed his gun at one of the chairs round the table. 'Sit down,' he told her.

Clare didn't move. 'Are you going to kill me?' she asked.

'Sit down.'

The woman stepped fearfully towards the table, pulled out a chair and sat. Her wide eyes looked up at Sam, who tucked the gun back into his jacket.

'If I was going to kill you,' he said, 'you'd already be dead and I'd be halfway out of London by now.'

Clare closed her eyes. 'Is that supposed to make me feel better?' Her breathing was a little steadier now, however. She appeared fractionally less frightened.

Sam pulled out the document and dropped it on the table in front of her. 'This fell through my door a couple of hours ago. Care to tell me what it is and why it's got your name scrawled on it?'

The woman looked down at the papers in front of her. For a moment she didn't reply, but just gazed at the document.

'Who are you?' she asked finally. 'How did you find out where I live?'

'You're not asking the questions, sweetheart. I am. What do you know about that document?'

Clare looked up at him again. 'I can't tell you,' she replied weakly. 'You don't know what they're like. You don't know what they'd do to me.'

Sam didn't take his gaze from her. 'You're right,' he replied. 'I don't even know who *they* are. But I'll tell you what. Why don't we pretend that I make *them* look like Mother fucking Theresa?' He pulled the weapon from his jacket again. 'What is it?' he demanded.

Clare looked nervously at the gun. When she spoke, her voice was cracked and timid. 'It's an article,' she whispered. 'I wrote it. It got spiked.'

'Spiked?'

'Pulled. Withdrawn.'

'Why?'

Clare took a deep breath, as though steadying her nerves. 'Reasons of national security,' she replied. 'At least that was the phrase they used.'

'You keep saying "they". Who are you talking about?'

'They said they were from the Government. They took my laptop and all my notes.' Words started to tumble from Clare's mouth. 'I'm a journalist. I contacted the Foreign Office for a quote and an hour later they were here. Three of them. One of them sat at this table. He told me . . . he told me that I should forget about my story. That if I didn't, people would die. That I wouldn't be safe . . .'

She started to cry again, wiping the tears away from her face with the back of her cheek.

Sam lowered his weapon. This woman, whoever she was, was a mess. But she was also a mess who had information he needed, and now that she had started to speak, threatening her wasn't going to be the best way of making her open up even more. He pulled out a chair and sat opposite.

'You thought I was one of them?' he asked.

'Aren't you?'

'No.'

'Then who are you?'

'What was your story?'

She shook her head. 'I can't,' she breathed. 'They meant what they said.'

Sam allowed a silence to fall between them. When he spoke, his voice was softer. Calmer. 'Is your front door locked?' he asked.

She nodded.

'What about the burglar alarm?'

Clare shook her head. 'It's a dummy.'

'All right then. Listen to me carefully. I'm in the military. As long as I'm here I can make sure nothing happens. You believe me, don't you?'

She nodded again.

'Good. Listen, Clare, I'm sorry if I frightened you out there. Truth is, I'm not quite sure what's going on or who I can trust. I think I can trust you, but you've got to tell me what you know. Will you do that?'

Still she looked at him timidly. 'All right.' She smiled, a scared little smile. Her breath came in long, slow sighs, as though she were psyching herself up to speak.

And then she did. Slowly. Nervously.

'About a month ago, this guy got in touch. He'd read one of my articles – I can't remember which one – and said he wanted to talk.'

'What about?'

'He didn't say. To be honest, I thought he was a nutter. Refused to meet anywhere there might have been CCTV. I kept trying to put him off – thought he sounded like the type to do a Jill Dando on me – but he kept calling till I agreed to meet him just to shut him up.'

95

'Where did you meet?'

'To start with, out of town. He wanted to go somewhere deserted, but I wouldn't do that, so we met in the car park of a service station on the M4. He was scared shitless.' Clare looked down. 'I know I'm not one to talk.'

'Carry on.'

'He said his name was Bill. Cockney lad. I didn't believe him, but I don't think he expected me to. He was . . .' She shrugged. 'Mid-twenties? A bit younger maybe. Bolshie. Would've come across as a bit of a wide boy if he wasn't so frightened.'

Clare started to chew on her thumbnail, clearly perturbed by the memories.

'What was he frightened of?'

She paused and breathed heavily, steadying herself. 'I didn't believe him at first,' she said. 'It just sounded like . . . I don't know . . . just rubbish. Thought he was a timewaster. He said he'd been recruited by MI5 as some kind of operative. Someone to do their dirty work.'

'MI5 already have people to do their dirty work,' Sam stated.

Clare looked sharply at him before carrying on. 'He said he'd been taken to some kind of training camp, a place where they were trained up in certain techniques. Weapons training, surveillance, things like that. The camp was in . . .'

'. . . Kazakhstan,' Sam completed her sentence under his breath.

Her eyes narrowed at him as she nodded. 'Like I said, I thought it was all bullshit. Bill could tell I wanted to get away so he stopped talking. He just made me promise to call him if I wanted to know more.'

'And did you?'

'I didn't want to. I just tried to ignore it for a couple of days. But I couldn't. I kept thinking about it. The story was far-fetched, but he sounded convincing. At least, he sounded

96

as though he had convinced himself. So I called him back. Arranged to meet again, somewhere we could talk more privately this time. He asked me for some money – a couple of hundred pounds.'

'Didn't that make you suspicious?'

'Not really,' Clare replied. 'Everyone thinks their story's worth something and most people think it's a lot more than that. I also got the impression that he really needed the money. We arranged to meet at a country pub, out in the sticks somewhere. That's where he told me everything he knew.' She tapped her finger on the document. 'Everything that ended up in there. Look, could I have a glass of water?'

Sam nodded. 'Go ahead.'

The woman stood up and turned her back to him. As she took a glass from a kitchen cabinet and filled it with water, she spoke. 'So are you going to tell me your name?' she asked, clearly trying to sound bold, but unable to hide the tremor in her voice.

'Sam,' he replied.

'And what part of the military are you in, Sam?'

She turned to face him and drank deeply.

Sam didn't reply. Clare nodded, as though his silence had confirmed a suspicion of hers, then took her seat once more.

'In the article,' she resumed, 'I call them "red-light runners". In fact, that's what Bill called them.'

'Who?'

'People like himself. People MI5 are targeting. From what he said, they've been on the lookout for thrill-seekers. Danger merchants. The kind of young men who would run a red light without a second thought. Long story short: Bill told me that MI5 have ways of identifying people like this. It's amazing really, the kind of information they have on all of us. The red-light runners, they all fit some kind of . . .' She searched around for a phrase. 'Psychological profile. They look at the obvious things, of course. Criminal records, employment history. But smaller stuff, too. Speeding fines to judge their attitude to risk, supermarket club-card points to draw a picture of their lifestyle. Air miles – the kind of person they're looking for is more likely to have visited Ibiza than Vienna, if you know what I mean. They use all this information to draw up a profile of people willing to take risks. And willing to be groomed.'

There was a noise. Clare's head shot round to see what it was.

'It's nothing,' Sam told her. 'Just the house creaking. Carry on.'

Clare took a moment to compose herself. 'Bill was terrified,' she continued. 'He kept referring to a job, something the security services wanted him to do. He never told me what it was, but it was enough to give him second thoughts about working for them. He was on the run, hiding from them.'

'If he'd gone dark,' Sam asked dubiously, 'what was he doing talking to you?'

Clare shook her head slightly. 'That's what I couldn't work out. At first I thought it was just the money. I mean, the kid had to eat, you know what I mean? But then maybe I thought it was more than that. I think perhaps he was gambling that if he spilled the beans and it appeared in the national press, it would embarrass MI5 into shutting the operation down.'

'The guys from Five,' Sam muttered, 'don't really do embarrassment.'

The woman shrugged. 'Whatever,' she replied. 'It was difficult for me to back any of this up. It was all down to Bill's word and I wasn't even sure how much I believed him. The only thing I knew for sure was that he was very, very frightened of being found out. That led me to believe that there was at least something in what he was saying. And whatever it was that the security services were asking him to do, it was something bad.' She looked straight into Sam's eyes. 'Something one of these red-light runners would baulk at.'

For some reason, the stare she gave him made Sam feel deeply uncomfortable.

'Go on,' he told her.

'That was the last time I saw Bill. We spoke on the phone once or twice, when I wanted to ask him a question or check a fact. I wrote my article sitting at this table. I didn't show it to anyone. I didn't even *mention* it to anyone. To be honest with you, I didn't even think it would see the light of day. I thought it would be laughed at.'

'So why did you carry on writing it?'

Clare stuck her neck out slightly. 'Because *I* believed it,' she said. 'I believed, at least, that some of it was true. My plan was to show it to the powers that be, to gauge their reaction to what I had written.'

'And did you?'

'Oh, yes,' Clare replied, her Irish accent suddenly light and dancing. 'I did that all right.' She stared into the middle distance, as though remembering something that left her numb. 'I did that all right,' she repeated.

'And what happened?'

Clare frowned. 'It sounds a bit stupid, doesn't it? Giving everything you've got to the enemy, I mean. But actually I wasn't being all that dumb. The way I figured it, they could do one of three things. If it was all a load of rubbish, they'd just ignore it. I'd have been stymied if they'd done that, to be sure. If it was true, they could either deny it – that's what I was hoping for – or slap a DA notice on it.'

A DA notice. Sam stretched out and picked up the document. He read the front page again.

'So that's what they did.'

'Sure,' Clare told him. 'That's what they did. With bells on. I don't know how much you know about DA notices,

99

Sam. The MOD uses them to suppress information that might compromise national security. It's a voluntary code, not the sort of thing they can actually enforce. Not legally, anyway. But my editor would never print something that had been suppressed under a DA notice. It's just the way it works.'

Sam dropped the document back down on the table.

Clare closed her eyes and pinched her forehead. 'It happened about a week ago. I sent my article to the Home Office for them to comment on it first thing in the morning. About four hours later there was a knock on my door.' She smiled faintly. 'Well,' she said, 'a ring on my bell, I suppose. But you know what I mean. I answered it. There were two men there. They said they were from the Government and asked if they could come in.'

She paused before continuing weakly. 'I should have asked them for identification,' she said. 'But I didn't. I don't know why. Suppose I thought I was probably on to something. I let them in and we came back in here. That's when I realised something was wrong.'

'Why?'

'Because there was another man standing by the back door. They didn't seem surprised to see him, so he was obviously one of them. The damn door was locked when I answered the bell, I'm sure of it. So I don't know how he got in.'

Any number of ways, Sam thought, but he kept that to himself.

'There was one man who was older than the others,' Clare carried on. 'He wore a big black raincoat, even though it was a fine day outside. Looked like someone's granddad. Well . . .' She hesitated. 'Not my granddad, anyway, but someone's. Sort of posh. Polite. I didn't like it. He sat down where you're sitting now. The other two just stood by the doors. The old man didn't tell me his name. None of them did. But he sure as hell knew mine. He told me that they were going to search my house, take away my computer, any notes I had. And then he told me to forget everything I had heard about this . . .' She raised her fingers in the air to indicate quotation marks. 'This "red–light runner nonsense".'

Clare's words were tumbling from her mouth now. Sam had the impression that she felt somehow relieved to be unloading them.

'I'm afraid I didn't really take it lying down. Occupational hazard, I suppose. If it was such nonsense, I asked him, why was he coming to my house to intimidate me? He didn't say anything, not at first. He just handed me a picture.'

Clare passed her hand across her face. The memory of that picture, whatever it was, was clearly traumatic.

'It was Bill,' she whispered. 'Although I could only just recognise him. He was lying on the ground. He was dead. His legs were pointing in different directions and one side of his face was all mashed up. There was blood all around.'

She sobbed suddenly, loudly. 'It was awful.'

Sam let the woman take her time.

'The old man held the picture in front of me for a long time,' Clare continued. 'A minute at least, maybe two, before he spoke. I'll never forget what he said, not as long as I live. "A terrible accident, Clare. It could happen to anyone, and it would be a dreadful shame if it happened to you. Do you understand what I'm saying?" Then he told me again to forget everything about what I'd written. And he told me that if I ever saw him again, it would mean I was in a whole load of trouble.'

A silence fell on the room, and a coldness. Clare pulled her cardigan more tightly around her shoulders.

'I've barely left the flat since it happened. Only to buy food. I keep seeing things from the corner of my eye. I keep imagining I'm being followed. And now you turn up on my doorstep. Holy Mother, are you surprised I'm so frightened?'

Sam looked steadily at her. 'No,' he said quietly. 'I'm not surprised at all.' He glanced beyond Clare to the kitchen door. 'You said you keep seeing things from the corner of your eye. Is that you, or do you think they're really there? Do you think you're really being watched?'

Clare shook her head. 'I don't know. I just don't know.'

Sam considered that for a moment. Then, without a word, he stood up and headed out of the kitchen.

'Don't go!' Clare shouted. He turned to look at her. 'Don't leave me alone,' she added weakly.

'I'm not going anywhere,' Sam told her. 'Just wait there.'

He explored the flat in the darkness. Towards the front, off the main corridor, there was a lounge. This was the room he'd seen from outside with wooden blinds. He edged towards them, lifting a gap in them with one finger, and peered out. All was quiet on the street. No movement. No people. He let the blind fall closed again and allowed himself a moment in the darkness.

Who the hell had posted this article through his letterbox? And was Clare telling him the truth? The only way he could be sure was by forcing it out of her, but the woman seemed so brittle she could snap. In any case, forcing things out of frightened women wasn't what he'd signed up for. And whatever the truth, Clare was certainly frightened. She certainly believed at least some of what she was saying. He decided to give her the benefit of the doubt. At least for now.

Sam walked back down the corridor, passing Clare's bedroom on the right-hand side. Even in the gloom he could see the unmade bed that had been left in a hurry, the nightclothes strewn on the floor. Back in the kitchen, Clare was weeping again, her head buried in her hands. Sam walked round her, checked through the blinds of the back door, then spoke again.

'Who else knows about this?'

It took a moment for Clare to stop sobbing. 'No one.'

'I mean it, Clare. Friends. Family. Boyfriend. Someone you called because you were scared.'

She shook her head. 'On my mother's life. I didn't want anyone else to be in danger. Jesus, I wish I'd never started any of this. They weren't messing with me, Sam. You know how you can tell, when someone's stringing you along. That old man, he'll have me killed if he thinks I've told anyone about this. I know he will. You've got to keep it a secret – you can't let anyone know you've been here.'

Sam walked up to her. He perched himself on the table and put a hand on her slim shoulder. 'Remember what I told you?' he asked. 'That if I wanted to kill you, you'd already be dead. Well the same goes for them. If they wanted you out of the way, they wouldn't bother playing with you first.' And then, quietly, 'Look at your friend Bill.'

She looked up at him with wide, scared eyes. 'Do you know who they were?'

Sam paused before answering. 'I think they were MI5.'

A silence.

'Think about it,' Sam continued. 'Your man was on the run. You alerted the security services to his whereabouts and a few hours later he was dead.'

'But . . .' Clare looked shocked. 'I never told them. I never once said where he was.'

'You didn't need to.' He walked to the table and pointed at the telephone number scrawled on the document. 'Did you speak to him on that phone number?'

She nodded mutely.

'Five would have had your phone records up in about ten seconds flat,' Sam told him. 'As soon as they narrowed down the possible numbers for your man, they'd have kept tabs on them. The minute he made a call, his phone became a tracking device. All he had to do was dial out for a pizza and the spooks would have had his location. Easiest thing in the world.' He didn't add that he'd done it himself before now.

Clare was shaking her head. 'You mean . . . you mean it's *my* fault.'

'You didn't kill the guy,' Sam said.

'But I . . .' She became breathless. 'I . . .'

'You didn't know.'

'But . . . you're really telling me that the British government murdered Bill?'

He stared at her. As he sat there on the edge of the table in this strange flat with a woman he'd never met before, the memory of the previous day's briefing filled his mind. The rough, grainy photographs of the targets. The picture of his brother. And the Ops Officer's stark warning. *Your targets are British citizens. They'll be speaking English. That shouldn't distract you from the job in hand.*

A silence. Sam stood up and looked again through the blinds.

'Why are you here, Sam?' Clare asked suddenly. 'Who gave you this copy of my article?'

Sam sniffed. 'I wish I knew.'

'You said you were in the military. Care to elaborate?'

'Not really.'

'But you knew about the training camp. The one in Kazakhstan.'

Sam nodded.

'And you seem to know more about how MI5 work than the average joe.'

'You need to stop thinking so hard, Clare.'

Out of the blue, she slammed her hand down on the table. 'I need to know what's going on!' she announced with sudden spirit. 'Holy Mother, half an hour ago I thought you were going to kill me. I think I deserve an explanation, don't you?' She paused and caught her breath. 'I'm not stupid, you know. You're in the military and you deal with

MI5. In my book that makes you special forces. Right? *Right?*'

Sam stayed quiet.

'Damn it!' she exploded. There was a fire in her now that he hadn't expected. All of a sudden she was no longer the frightened woman who had wept uncontrollably. She stood, then strode over to him, her arms raised and her fists clenched. 'Tell me what's going on!' Sam blinked, then realised she was actually going to try to hit him in the chest in fury.

He grabbed her slender wrists. Her eyes flashing, Clare struggled, but without success. Sam kept hold of her and for the second time he smelt her perfume. He pulled her towards him and felt her breasts pressing lightly against his torso. She was warm. Almost comforting.

The struggle stopped and they stared at each other. Clare was blushing faintly. Maybe it was the anger; or maybe, Sam thought, it was something else. Her breathing trembled. Sam knew what it meant. He knew how easily some women would give themselves up to a man they thought could protect them.

He knew, even as he spoke, that he should keep his mouth shut. That sharing what he knew could lead to trouble for both of them. But his natural caution had been replaced by other emotions. 'I'm SAS,' he said. Calm. In control. 'An operation has just been ordered. We're to deploy to the training camp in Kazakhstan and neutralise all the British citizens there. Looks to me like you've opened up a can of worms. Five have got a covert network across the country. It's started to spring a leak so they're shutting it down. Permanently.'

Clare drew away slightly. 'Neutralise?' she asked. 'You mean . . . kill?'

'Yeah,' Sam said. 'Kill.'

'Oh my God,' she whispered. 'How many of them are there?'

'Twenty.' He felt his face tensing up as the image of Jacob, bearded and rough, passed into his head. 'Maybe more.'

Clare breathed deeply as she assimilated the information. Sam noticed that she didn't pull her wrists away from his hands.

'I still don't know why you're here,' she whispered. 'I still don't know what this is all about.'

'It's about someone trying to warn me.'

'What of?'

Sam knew he shouldn't tell her. He knew he should keep it to himself. But he could feel her warm breath and could sense that she was looking at him through different eyes. And anyway, maybe she was right. Maybe he did owe her some sort of explanation.

'One of the targets,' he said quietly, 'is my brother. And if anyone thinks I'm going to go out there to put a bullet in his head, they can think again.'

*

She had stopped asking him questions soon after that. She'd stopped crying too. But she hadn't stopped looking at him, that look which was a mixture of apprehension and something else. It was edging towards morning when Clare slipped into her bedroom, leaving Sam sitting at the table, the lights dimmed almost to nothingness, the document and his gun laid out in front of him. She wanted to be alone, she said. She wanted to think. That was fine by Sam: he knew she wouldn't want to be by herself for long.

It was a Regiment tradition to laugh at Five, to take the piss out of the suited goons who turned up at HQ with a slew of orders and an unwillingness to get their own hands dirty. Civil serpents, they were called. Fags. Tossers. And a lot more besides. But beneath all that, away from the bravado and everything that went with it, there was at least some sort of respect. The Security Service was secretive; it was difficult to understand; it had sent the Regiment on operations that most people would find morally dubious. But nobody doubted that they were on the same side.

At least that was what Sam had always thought. In the last few hours, though, he had become less sure. He didn't know whose side he was on, nor even what the sides were. All he knew was that somewhere, in some god-forsaken shit hole in central Asia, his brother was a target. He didn't know why and he didn't know how; all he knew was that Jacob had been shat on by the Government once before. He was damned if he was going to let it happen again.

A noise. His hand grabbed the gun at lightning speed.

It was only Clare. She stood in the doorway, her pretty features softened by the dim light. She was wearing a nightdress that fell to just above her knees. One of the straps had slipped slightly down her shoulder, but she made no attempt to adjust it. They stared at each other for what seemed like an age.

Sam stood up. Almost absent-mindedly he brought the gun with him. As he stepped towards Clare, he saw her lips part slightly. She was several inches shorter than him; as he grew closer she raised her head.

His gun hand was pressed into the small of her back now. The nightdress was satiny and so thin it might as well not have been there. Her body felt warm, but she was trembling.

'Stay with me,' she whispered.

Sam nodded, then pressed his lips against hers.

She kissed him nervously at first, as though she shouldn't be doing it. But that timid kiss soon turned into something else. Something more passionate. Gently Sam slid the straps of her nightdress from her shoulders. The garment fell to a silent, gossamer heap on the floor, leaving Clare naked. She pulled her lips away and opened her eyes. There was still a look of anxiety on her face. No smiles. That was good. Sam didn't feel like returning one.

She turned and walked to the bedroom. Sam followed, laying his gun on a small table by the doorway. Clare was standing by the bed. The bright moon shone through her bedroom window illuminating her body. His eyes followed the line of her hips, the curve of her breasts. He placed the gun on a chest of drawers and stepped towards her.

Clare's breath was heavy. Shaking. She stretched out a nervous hand and slid it between the buttons of Sam's shirt. He started to undo them and as he felt her hand wander over his torso, he felt at least some of the tension of the past twenty-four hours ease away. He pulled Clare towards him and kissed her again, before gently but firmly pushing her onto the bed. She gazed up at him as he removed his shirt.

'Don't go,' she whispered.

Sam gave her a serious kind of look. 'I'm not going anywhere.'

He lay on the bed, softly ran his hands over her breasts and then kissed her again.

'Not yet,' he said.

SEVEN

The same moon that shone into the West London bedroom of Clare Corbett shone into an attic room on the other side of the city. It was a good deal less comfortable – a single bed, a rickety wooden table and a chair. It smelt a bit – not just of the fast-food packaging on the floor, but also of the neglect that is particular to a certain type of rented accommodation – and it only contained one person. Jamie Spillane lay on the bed and gazed through the skylight. He wished sleep would come, but he knew it wouldn't.

Jamie felt stupid. He must have still been drunk the previous morning when he came clean to Kelly. Either that or just desperate to tell someone. But that had been the one thing they'd told him not to do. He remembered their words. 'It's not called the Secret Service for nothing. If you tell anyone, you won't only blow your cover, you put them in danger as well. So remember that, and keep your fucking mouths shut.'

In the darkness his own stupidity hit him yet again.

At least she hadn't believed him. That was something. Kelly wouldn't go blurting it out to anyone. She'd just bitch about him to her friends, tell them what a useless bastard he was. He didn't mind that.

Or did he? Truth was that the idea made him feel a bit uncomfortable. If he was honest with himself, he'd have to say that he liked Kelly. It wasn't just the sex, although that was good; he liked the way that she just . . . looked after him a bit. He felt bad now about taking the money from her, bad that she knew about it and had something else to chalk up against him. The few weeks he'd spent with Kelly had been all right. He'd been kicked out by girlfriends before now, of course he had. But he felt particularly gloomy about this one.

Not least because he had nowhere to go. Home wasn't an option, obviously. Jamie had decided he was never going back there. His mum and dad were the last people in the world he wanted to be with. He felt embarrassed that he had made that stuff up about them, but Jamie wasn't so naïve about himself that he couldn't admit that these were little fantasies about his parents that he'd had since he was a child. That his dad was, well, *someone*. Not just a pathetic, pissed-up waste of space. And his mum? He sneered in the darkness. Jamie didn't even want to think about her.

Maybe he had tried to tell Kelly his secret because he knew he could never tell his parents. They always thought he was worthless. As a kid, when he'd gone off the rails, it hadn't made them pay more attention to him. It had just reinforced their opinion. When he'd spent three months in a young offenders' institute for joyriding and smashing up someone's motor, they had seemed totally unsurprised. They didn't visit him once. When he got out, the petty crime had continued. He got a buzz out of it. And some-where deep down he wanted his parents to take notice. They never did.

Which was why he was here. A cheap, faceless bedsit. Rooms rented by the week. When he had been targeted by the Security Service and told he'd be put on a retainer of a few hundred pounds a month, paid directly and anony-mously into a bank account, it had sounded like a deal too good to be true. But a few hundred pounds, he soon realised, doesn't get you very far. He wouldn't mind if they'd just give him something to do – *anything* to do – but since he'd got back from the training camp, there'd been nothing. Silence.

He'd been warned that this would be the case. 'You won't hear from us,' he'd been told. 'Not until the time comes for you to be activated. When that happens, we'll find you. Just carry on as normal. Live your life. And remember: *don't tell anyone.*'

This wasn't living his life, though. Nothing like. He wanted some excitement. He was hungry for it. And he wanted something to do.

Jamie wouldn't be able to tell his parents about it. He knew that. But he would know. He would know that he wasn't the useless kid his mum and dad saw.

The moon continued to shine into the attic. Jamie continued to lie awake, waiting for morning, whatever it might bring.

★

A podgy man with square, thick-rimmed spectacles sat in the leather driving seat of his large, comfortable car. The coldest hour, he thought to himself, was always just before sunrise. He was glad of his coat and glad, too, that sunrise was just around the corner. He had spent too much time for his liking in this bland estate on the outskirts of the monstrosity that was Milton Keynes and he was looking forward to this particular engagement being over. That would happen – if everything went according to plan – very soon.

The Americans called what he was about to do the Boston Brakes Technique. Trust the Americans, he thought to himself, to claim the credit for everything. The technique in question, or course, had been used all over the world, not just in Boston. He himself had performed it five times and though he was not one for conspiracy theories, it did not take a genius to understand that the famous car crash under the Pont de l'Alma in Paris bore all the hallmarks of what he was about to do.

Car crashes, he found, were so *satisfactory*. They were commonplace, for a start. How many of them happened around the world every day? He did not know the exact statistic, but it was many, certainly. The cynic in him suspected that a small but significant number of these accidents were in fact carried out by the security services of various countries for precisely the reason he favoured them. Nobody would suspect foul play. And nobody would examine in any detail the crushed, crumpled shell of a wrecked motor vehicle; certainly they would not look close enough to find the small electronic device attached to the car's steering column – if, indeed, the device itself had survived the crash.

He looked a little further down the residential street in which his car was parked. The vehicle he had targeted was on the other side of the road about twenty metres down. He couldn't see it in the darkness, but as the sky gradually started to move from black to steely grey, the vehicle came into his field of vision. Only two nights previously, in the small hours of the morning, he had broken into it with some ease. It had taken only a few minutes to remove the panel below the steering wheel, attach the device – no bigger than the smallest mobile phone – and walk briskly away, though not before locking the car carefully once again.

It was pathetically easy to kill people sometimes.

He looked at his watch. A quarter-past five. In one hour and thirty minutes, the door of the house outside which the vehicle was parked would open. A louche youngster in his mid-twenties would walk out, approach the car and slouch into the driver's seat. Until then, he just had to wait. He would have liked to listen to something – there was a cassette of sacred choral music slotted into the dashboard – but if he did that he risked attracting attention. So he just sat there in silence.

A quarter to seven. The house door opened and a figure appeared. He wore sunglasses, quite unnecessarily, and a T-shirt with the logo of a pop group that the man didn't recognise. No doubt his target's musical tastes were buried somewhere in the details that had been supplied to him – the man's employers were extraordinarily thorough – but he had not retained them. It wasn't necessary for what was to happen today.

The car – an old silver Ford with shiny alloy wheels and certain other modifications intended to make it look like a much more desirable object than it actually was – pulled out into the road. The man didn't follow. Not yet. Instead, he switched on a small visual display unit that was gummed to the front windscreen. It looked like a satellite navigation unit; indeed that's what it was. It just wasn't the kind that anyone could buy in the high street.

A map appeared, and on it two green dots. One did not move. The other, which was flashing, did. At the side of the screen a digital display showed some constantly changing numbers: the other car's increasing speed. The man waited for the vehicle in the road to disappear from sight. And then he followed, using the tracking screen to stay behind his target, but at a distance.

He knew where the young man was likely to go, of course. On to the motorway and then north towards the service station where he had worked for precisely seven months and two weeks. His take-home pay was £180 a week, £130 of which was spent on rent. He bought his food from the local Tesco – the cheapest brands of everything except, it seemed, cigarettes. No doubt he found the extra money – the retainer, paid into his bank account anonymously – immensely useful. However, as was so often the way with these people, he squandered it on trinkets for his car, expensive evenings in nightclubs and, more than once, prostitutes. Whether his target had ever been activated, the man didn't know. That was information which was neither useful to him, nor supplied.

He drove slowly. Safely. If his target forged too far ahead he didn't worry. It was not his intention to stay close, after all. At least, not just yet. The early morning traffic had not built up and it didn't take long for the flashing green light on his screen to reach the blue map line that indicated the motorway. As soon as it did, the speed indicator started to blur. In the space of about ten seconds, it went from a steady 35 mph into the decidedly unsteady nineties.

The man's own car stayed well within the speed limit. Even when he himself reached the motorway he stayed in the slow lane at under 50 mph, allowing more impatient drivers to overtake him.

On the passenger seat lay a little black box. Had a child seen it, they might have thought it was the control unit for a radio-controlled car. In fact it wasn't far off. Keeping one hand on the steering wheel, the man stretched out the other one and picked it up. He glanced back at the screen: his target's car was doing nearly 100 mph now. That would be just right. He flicked his thumb on to the switch; it moved with very little resistance. Then he carefully put the unit back on the passenger seat, his free hand back on the steering wheel, and continued his slow, steady journey.

The green light continued to flicker. That was as it should be. The man pictured what was happening inside his target's car. The steering column would have been disabled, as would the brakes, and at that precise moment the driver would be struggling with the newfound realisation that he was unable to control his car.

The man watched the screen intently. Ten seconds passed.

Fifteen.

And then, without so much as a blip, the green light disappeared.

He smiled. About two miles, he calculated, between himself and the place where the accident had happened. In about a minute the traffic would start slowing, almost to a standstill. He had no desire to get caught up in that, so when he saw an exit signposted up ahead, he switched on his indicators and prepared to leave the motorway.

The traffic started to slow. By the time he bore left it was grinding to a halt. He drove his car up the slip road at the top of which there was a roundabout, one exit of which led to a bridge passing back over the motorway. He took that exit, and as he passed over the road he looked out to his left. There, scattered across the motorway, was the result of his morning's work.

He continued to drive, but as soon as he could he pulled off the main road and into a lay-by before leaving the car and walking back to the bridge. It was a weakness, he knew, something he really ought to master; but he couldn't resist examining exactly what he had achieved. He stood at the side of the bridge, peering through his square glasses onto the devastation below.

There were three cars involved in the crash, as far as he could tell. It was difficult to determine exactly, because they no longer resembled cars so much as smouldering chunks of scrap metal. He ran through the crash in his mind. The car would have slammed directly into the back of the other two motors; he imagined the target jolting forward in his seat at the moment of impact, the sudden jerk of the neck and then the contorted metal of the second car's chassis plunging through the windshield and driving through the skull. He could see something shiny, red and sticky, lying on the road. Lumps of brain matter, perhaps, or the bowels of one of the other victims. A few members of the public had left their own cars and were approaching the wreckage. It was clear, though, that there was nothing they could do. It was clear that the occupants of all three cars would be dead. So much the better. If anything was likely to dilute people's attention away from one death, it was the occurrence of several others at the same time.

He imagined what the eye witnesses would have to say. *The nutter in the Ford was driving like a lunatic. A hundred miles an hour, easy. It was his fault. Stupid bloody idiot.*

Everything had gone very well. He could return home now knowing that his job had been successful. The man allowed himself a brief smile as he wandered back to his own car, put the key in the ignition and, unnoticed by anyone or anything, drove smoothly away.

★

Sam didn't know where he was. A corridor. Cement walls. There was nobody else around. He was on his own. It was dark. He could only see because of the NV, which cast a sinister greenish hue all around. There was a weapon in his fist. A submachine gun. Heckler & Koch, MP5 — he could tell from the view through the weapon's aperture sight as he stealthily continued down the corridor.

There should be other people here. Other guys backing him up. But he knew there was none. He felt out of control, but all he could do was continue down the corridor. All he could do was wait and see.

He could hear his breath and his footsteps on the hard, cold floor. But nothing else.

A door. It seemed out of place, here at the end of this corridor. Through the NV he couldn't tell what colour it was, but it appeared wooden and panelled. The kind of door you'd see in someone's house. There was a burnished doorknob and no keyhole, which suggested it couldn't be locked. He stood there for a moment, looking at this door. It seemed familiar, somehow, but Sam couldn't quite place it.

His weapon at the ready, he prepared to kick it open. But just as he raised one foot, the door swung inwards.

Everything happened in a second. Sam's eyes focussed on a figure in the room beyond. It was a man whose back was turned to him. Firing the weapon was like a reflex action; Sam's aim was precise. There was a flash in his NV as the round burst from the barrel of the MP5; he knew that his aim was true and that he had hit the figure directly in the back of the head.

A silence. No movement. From this range, and with this weapon, the figure's head should have been decimated. But it remained whole.

Sam paused. Then, not knowing quite why, he removed the NV goggles from his face. There was enough light to see. As he did so, the figure turned around. It was with a sickening feeling that he realised the person ahead of him was not, as he had previously appeared to be, a grown man. He was just a boy. It was only when the two of them were facing each other that he saw who it was.

Jacob couldn't have been more than thirteen, though he had always looked old for his age. His dark hair was scruffy and boyish; his gaze – those dark, intense eyes – was confused. He opened his mouth to speak, but no words came. Just a choking, coughing sound. And then blood, overflowing from his mouth and dribbling over his chin.

Only then did the rest of the room come into focus. Only then did Sam recognise it. It was a room from his childhood, the lounge of the house where he had grown up. Jacob was standing in front of the three-bar electric fire that had stood for as long as he could remember in the grate. With a jolt he realised that to one side, sitting in a comfortable armchair,

117

was his father – younger, more vigorous. And on the other side, one hand squeezing the other in an expression of undisguised despair was his mum

Sam didn't understand. His mum was dead.

'What have you done, Sam?' she whispered, and he realised that up till now he had forgotten what her voice sounded like.

Both parents looked at him, and then at Jacob. His thirteen-year-old brother's face was pale now. When he collapsed it was almost in slow motion. A pool of blood spread unrealistically around his head. Sam couldn't tell whether he had taken a few seconds to die, or an hour.

He looked back up towards his mother, but she was no longer there. He opened his mouth to call her name, but before he could do so his father was suddenly in front of him. Max looked young and strong. He stretched out his arms and grabbed the barrel of Sam's gun and pulled it into the flesh of his lean stomach.

'Kill me!' he hissed.

Sam shook his head.

'Kill me now!' insisted his father. 'You might as well.'

Sam tried to pull the weapon away, but his father was too strong for him. Far too strong. The older man held the weapon firmly against him and, staring Sam straight in the eye, used his other hand to fumble for the trigger.

'I didn't mean it . . .' Sam heard himself saying. 'I didn't know it was him . . .'

But by then, it was too late.

It was the sound of the dreamlike rounds discharging into his father's spectral body that woke Sam. He sat bolt upright and as the bright morning sun beamed through the windows it took a moment for him to work out where the hell he was. Then he remembered. He looked to his side: there was no one else in the bed. Climbing out, he pulled on his clothes and only then did Clare appear in the doorway.

'I got up early,' she said. 'Before you could sneak out.' She smiled to show that it was a joke, but they both knew it wasn't.

She too was dressed, in the same clothes that she wore last night. Leaning against the frame of the doorway it was clear to Sam that she was trying to look cool. Unsuccessfully. The worry lines in her face were still all too evident.

'I have to go,' Sam said shortly.

Clare nodded, unable to hide her disappointment.

'You'll be okay,' he told her. 'I told you last night, if they wanted to . . .' He chose his words carefully. 'To get rid of you, they'd have done it already. Those spooks that came here, you'll probably never see them again.'

Clare didn't look convinced, but she didn't say so.

'Can I call you?' she asked. She looked momentarily surprised that she had blurted out the question. 'I mean, look, don't worry. I know what last night was. I'm not going to ask you to marry me or anything. I just mean, can I call you, you know, if I need to? I won't make a nuisance of myself.'

Sam pushed gently past her, doing his best not to catch her eye. 'I don't think you should,' he said.

'Why not?' Clare replied weakly.

'It's too easy for them to track your calls. Mine too. You want my advice? Forget you ever saw me. And don't mention anything of this to anybody. Ever.' They were in the kitchen now. Sam turned to took at her. Clare had her arms wrapped around her, embracing herself as though no one else would.

'I won't see you again, will I?' she asked quietly.

Sam narrowed his eyes. 'No,' he replied. There wasn't any point stringing the girl along.

She nodded with the expression of a child coming to

119

terms with something difficult to understand. 'You sure know how to make a girl feel special, Sam.' She tried to make light of it, but when she spoke again her voice was little more than a whisper.

'Those people,' she said. 'At the training camp. Are you . . . Are you really going to kill them, Sam? After everything I've told you, is that really what you're going to do?'

The question hung in the air. Sam looked darkly at her. Any number of responses came into his head, but he knew none of them would be appropriate. He looked towards the back door. He would leave that way. Just in case.

He walked up to Clare and lightly touched his fingers to her cheek. The skin was soft and warm.

'Please,' he said. 'Don't tell anybody I was here. I have to know I can trust you.'

She looked steadily into his eyes. For a moment she didn't respond. When she did, her question came out of the blue.

'Why's your brother there, Sam? What's he doing?'

Sam refused to allow any emotion to show on his face. Clare was making him address things he was trying not to think about. What did Jacob's presence at the training camp mean? It was an MI5 facility. Was he being held captive? Was he being forced into something? Once more, his father's conspiracy theories flashed through his mind. He did what he could to subdue them. They made no difference to what he had to do.

'I have to know I can trust you.' He ignored Clare's question and repeated his own.

'You can trust me,' she said quietly.

He nodded. Somehow he knew she was telling the truth.

'I have to go,' he said, and without another word he raised the blinds, unlocked the door and slipped back out into the garden.

★

Jamie Spillane looked at his watch. Midday. Maybe he had slept or maybe he hadn't. In any case he was still lying on the bed wearing the same clothes from last night. The rumbling in his stomach was telling him it was time to eat. He pushed himself heavily on to his feet and surveyed the debris of fast-food packaging on the floor around him. Jesus. He'd only been here twenty-four hours and it already looked like a shit hole. Smelt like a shit hole, too. He probably wasn't too fresh himself, but the thought of taking a shower in the grubby communal bathroom wasn't very appealing.

He grabbed his wallet and stuffed it into the pocket of his baggy jeans, then left the room, taking care to lock the door behind him. There were other people staying here, as well as a nosy landlady, and he could tell that they would rifle through his room without a second thought if they reckoned they could get away with it. He knew, because he would do the same. Fortunately, though, he didn't bump into any of them as he descended the three storeys of uncarpeted stairway, opened the main door to the faceless mid-terrace which housed the room he was renting and stepped out into the street. The sun was bright today. It made him wince, like an insect on an upturned brick. Instinctively, he pulled his hood over his head. It didn't keep the sun out of his eyes, but it did make him feel more comfortable as he tramped down the pavement.

It took a while to find a supermarket. There were plenty of shops in this run-down area of North London, but they mostly sold cheap booze and cut-price phone cards. By the time he saw the familiar blue logo, he'd been walking for a good twenty minutes and was, he realised, a bit lost. He shrugged. He'd soon find his way back again. It wasn't like there was anything else in the diary, after all.

The shop was almost empty; the few customers were

elderly, pushing or carrying almost empty baskets of ready meals and cheap teabags. Jamie wandered the aisles aimlessly. He put chocolate milk and sandwiches in his basket before approaching the checkouts. There were only two of them open and so, despite the relatively few customers, each till had a queue. He joined the shortest and waited.

There was only one customer ahead of him when his mobile phone rang. Jamie pulled it out and looked at the screen. No number was displayed; to his surprise he noticed a little lurch in his stomach as he wondered if it might, just possibly, be Kelly. He placed his basket at the end of the counter and started to offload his purchases onto the moving belt with one hand. With the other, he answered the phone.

'Yeah?' he said. Cool. He didn't want to give anything away.

A crackly kind of pause.

'Hello?' Jamie bellowed in the way only people talking into mobiles can. Briefly he considered hanging up, but at that moment a voice spoke.

'Jamie Spillane?' it asked.

Jamie couldn't place the voice. 'Who's this?' he demanded.

Another pause. 'You know who it is.'

Jamie blinked. The checkout girl had scanned his items and was looking up at him with a bored, impatient expression. 'Four pounds eighty-six,' she said, a bit too loudly, as though she were saying it for a second time. Jamie hardly heard her. He left his lunch languishing by the plastic bags and hurried away from the checkout and out the shop.

'I thought you'd forgotten I existed,' he said under his breath. Silence. He was on the street now. The traffic was noisy. '*Hello?*'

'You knew it could be some time.' The more the voice spoke, the more Jamie recognised it. 'The company is activating you.'

The company. Jamie knew what that meant. He knew that nobody would ever use the phrase 'MI5'.

'I'm listening,' he replied. He had a finger shoved into his other ear to keep out the noise and it crossed his mind that this wasn't quite how he had imagined things would happen. 'Are you there?' he asked when there was no reply.

'I'm here.'

'What do you want me to do?'

Again a pause.

'Have you told anyone, Jamie?'

He was glad nobody was there to see his face. 'Of course not,' he replied. No hint of a lie in his voice. A bus had come to a halt just in front of him. Passengers spilled out and one of them caught his eye. Jamie started walking, speaking as he went. 'Don't worry about it, mate. It's all cool.'

He carried on walking. His mouth felt dry. Jamie was frightened of the man at the other end of the phone. But he had to keep silent. He didn't want to get Kelly involved in this stuff.

Silence. He continued to walk briskly. Randomly. He was getting a bit out of breath now – through exercise or excitement, he wasn't quite sure which – so he came to a halt on the corner of a residential street. It was quieter here.

'So,' he said. 'What do I need to do? What's the job?'

He held his breath as he waited for the answer.

'The job,' the voice replied, 'is difficult. But it's important, Jamie. Lives depend on it. We're asking you because you showed more aptitude than the others. Can we count on you?'

Jamie's face twitched. 'Yeah,' he said. 'Yeah, you can.'

'Good. You need to listen carefully, Jamie. If you don't understand something, ask me to repeat it. Do you understand?'

Jamie looked around. The residential street was practically deserted; certainly nobody was paying him any attention.

That was good. He pulled himself up to his full height. All of a sudden, he felt tall again. Excited. Useful. The row with Kelly, the shitty bedsit – all that disappeared from his mind.

'Yeah,' he announced into the receiver. 'I understand. Go ahead. I'm listening . . .'

EIGHT

Sam's dream had stayed with him, a shadow that haunted him for the rest of the day, just as it had haunted his night. Other things haunted him too. Clare's story; the anonymous package. Who had given it to him? No matter how hard he thought about it, he just couldn't make things add up. Driving back from London he could barely keep his car straight, let alone his thoughts. But as he approached the outskirts of Hereford, he realised he had come to a decision. And if he was going to pull it off, he had to pretend that everything was normal.

He headed straight for Credenhill. There were things that needed to be done before the op. The last thing Sam wanted to do at the moment was see any of the guys, but he had to make sure he was prepared. *Pretend nothing's wrong*, he told himself. *Pretend it's just an ordinary op*. If he didn't put in an appearance, people might start to ask questions.

It was midday by the time he approached the weapons store and it was with relief, as he stepped inside, that he saw it was just him and the armourer. He was a tall man with short, spiky hair. Sam didn't know his name. He hoped there'd be no wisecracks from him, no inappropriate questions about what use the weapons he dished out were going to be put to.

'Didn't think I'd be seeing your lot so soon,' he observed drily.

A little voice in Sam's head told him to act naturally. *If you can't keep it up in the armoury*, he told himself, *you'll have no chance in the field*. 'Gluttons for fucking punishment,' he replied before flashing a forced, rueful smile.

'Diemaco?'

Sam nodded. 'And the Sig.'

Each man's weapon was particular to him. The rifle and handgun that Sam would be taking to Kazakhstan were the same ones that had kept him alive in Helmand Province; the same ones that had claimed more Taliban scalps in the previous few weeks than Sam could frankly remember. The armourer kept the weapons separate, safe and ordered in this locked, secure building. But it was up to Sam to test fire his guns on the range in preparation for the op, to make sure that they were still zeroed in to his eye. It took the armourer less than a minute silently to locate his Diemaco C8 and place it carefully on the counter along with a small box of 45 mm rounds. The Sig followed, a P226 with a 9 mm chamber and an extended twenty-round magazine. A box of rounds for the handgun and Sam was good to go. The armourer listed what Sam was checking out, then handed over the slip of paper for him to sign. He scrawled his illegible signature at the bottom of the paper, nodded curtly at the armourer and gathered up his weapons.

There were two guys at the range already, both from Sam's troop. Jack Craven and Luke Tyler had been out with him in the Stan. Good lads. Young. Up for it. The sort of troopers who would be down the range whether there was an operation in the offing or not. Sam stood back and watched their practice rounds. They were both firing their Diemacos and their aims were both true. By the time they had finished shooting, the body-shaped targets at the end of the range were punctured in all the right places. They lowered their weapons, then turned round.

'What you gawking at, Granddad?' Craven called good-naturedly. He was a Geordie and thought that gave him a licence to take the piss out of everyone.

Sam winked it at him, then turned to look through the window of the small hut that overlooked the range. He couldn't quite see who was in charge, but whoever it was gave him a thumbs up. Sam sniffed and approached one of the firing alleys. He carefully laid the Sig on the ground behind him, before loading the Diemaco, pressing the butt of the weapon into his shoulder and taking aim.

He had lost count of the number of times he had stood at this range, firing the same weapon at the same target. It was routine. Comfortable. The sort of thing he could do in his sleep. But as Sam stood there, the two younger troopers looking on, he found himself shaking. Anger, he realised. And frustration. His lips were curled, his face set; and as he lined up the sights to the target, he noticed that it felt good to have this gun in his fist. It made him feel in control. He discharged the weapon in a single, brutal burst. His aim was perfect: each round thundered into the head of his target; by the time he had finished, his cardboard enemy was fully decapitated. Swapping one weapon for the other, he loaded the Sig and, discharging it at arm's length, gave the target a bellyful of lead. And with each shot he felt better. Not less angry. Just better. The cloak-and-dagger letters, the spooks with secret agendas – they weren't what Sam was built for. This was. It felt good to be a soldier again.

He lowered his weapon, then turned back to the other two. They were watching him, arms folded and with grins of appreciation on their faces. 'Like fish in a fuckin' barrel!' Craven shouted as Sam walked up to join them. The younger man clapped a big hand on Sam's shoulder. 'Shame it weren't our bearded mates from Now Zad at the end of the alley.'

Sam smiled. 'I'd have fuckin' RPG'd them if it was,' he replied.

'What's the gossip, then?' Tyler asked out of the blue. He was a broad-shouldered Cockney with a rugby-player's nose and a werewolf's eyebrows. 'How come we're being sent straight back out?'

Sam shrugged. 'No gossip,' he said quietly. 'Least, if there is, I haven't heard it.'

'Fuckin' out of order if you ask me,' Craven announced, ignoring the fact that nobody had. Sam couldn't help feeling, though, that despite his words he didn't sound all that offended. '"B" Squadron on standby,' he continued. 'Bunch of fuckin' lard-arses that lot. Probably want to send some real shooters out, make sure the job gets done proper.' He started singing his own words, rather tune-lessly, to a song Sam half recognised. '*You say HALO, I say goodbye . . .*'

The three of them smiled at Craven's remarks. No one really thought that badly about the other squadrons, but slagging them off was a common enough way to pass the time. Back at the armoury they signed their weapons back in. 'Everything as it should be, gentlemen?' the armourer asked.

'We'll sign them out again in the morning,' said Sam. He nodded at Craven and Tyler, then left the armoury without another word. In the morning he would return well before the RV time to assemble his weapons and pack his kit, but until then he wanted to be out of there.

Back home he paced the flat throughout the afternoon. He ate dinner in a café, then returned to pacing into the small hours, playing over the events of the last couple of days, trying to make sense of them, without success. His head was a jumble of images: Jacob's picture; the faceless figure at his door; Clare's terrified face and the tempting curve of her body in the moonlit room; her story. Even now he didn't know which bits of it to believe. He tried to sleep, his handgun resting by his side. But sleep wasn't going to come. Not tonight. And as the grey light of morning appeared once more, Sam felt almost as if he were in a dream. There was something unreal about what he was about to do. For years he had followed orders without question. It was hard-wired into him. Second nature. Even after Jacob had been expelled from the Regiment; even after Sam and Mac had been told, in no uncertain terms, that if they ever leaked what had happened that day to anyone they would be facing court martial; even then, with all the anger that came with it, he had stayed loyal. He hated the authorities that had belittled and humiliated his brother; but he had never been fighting for them. He had been fighting for the men who stood alongside him, the men he risked his lives with. That was what it was all about.

Only now everything had changed.

Now, he wasn't fighting with the men in his troop. He was fighting against them. And they didn't even know it. As Sam prepared to return to HQ, he knew that his objective was different to everyone else's. If his brother was at the camp, there was no way Sam would let him come to harm.

It made Sam sick to the stomach to acknowledge it, but if that meant putting the operation at risk, then that was the way it had to be.

★

Credenhill. 07.00. Sam walked into his single-bunk room. The kit he had dumped in here only a couple of days before was still lying on the floor. Vaguely aware of the bustle and noise of the other guys in his corridor doing the same thing, he upturned the bergen so that everything fell out, then carefully went about the business of repacking. It was reassuring to be performing this familiar, repetitive process. It made him feel calmer. More focussed. His sleeping bag was filled with thick Afghan dust. He shook it out before rolling it back up and stashing it with his Goretex bivvy bag. It was an in-and-out job, and if everything went as it should he wouldn't require either item, but he needed to be prepared. He checked his bright halogen torch and then his small med pack. Sleeping tablets, aspirin, swabs. The patrol medic would have the big stuff – drips, morphine and all the rest of it – so that the rest of the guys could travel a bit lighter. At the squadron stores there was already a buzz of activity. Sam kept himself to himself, speaking only when he was spoken to, as he took a handful of unappetising ration packs to stash away with his kit. Boil-in-the-bag chicken curry with powered soup starter, a packet of crisps and a chocolate bar. All made by some mysterious, unheard-of manufacturer based up in Scotland. There was also something that he understood to be a biscuit, but looked more like a large, circular piece of mould. The boiled sweets were the only item that wouldn't taste of shit. The Americans got to have gourmet packs made by designer chefs, and the Regiment got meals that some Jock had probably shat directly into. Fucking nice to be appreciated. At the signal store he signed out his sat phones and comms kit, returning to his bunk to stow them carefully away before going back to the armoury to get himself tooled up.

The Diemaco was waiting for him, of course, along with a matt black device that looked like a camera but was in fact a thermal imaging sight for the carbine. Sam signed out his Sig along with the ammo he needed, as well as a stash of flashbangs, white phosphorous and fragmentation grenades. They would be hitting the camp at night, so the 4th generation NV sights were essential. Back at his bunk, Sam removed the jeans, shirt and jacket that he'd been wearing for a couple of days. He caught a glimpse of himself in the mirror on the wall. His face was unshaven; there were dark rings under his eyes. For a fraction of a second he saw his brother staring back. Sam took a sharp intake of breath and looked away.

His camouflage gear was packed up in his metal locker. The digital camouflage was made up of tiny squares, like a pixelated image in the familiar browns, greens and khakis. Sam was relieved to pull it on.

08.50. The kit was packed and double checked. RV in the briefing room in ten minutes. As he walked across the courtyard he saw two unmarked white minibuses parked up. Craven and a couple of other guys loaded heavy flight cases into the back of one of them. Away from Credenhill you wouldn't give these vehicles a second look. If you did, you'd probably think they were transporting a school football team. But the flight cases didn't contain sports gear. Far from it. These were the support weapons – a light machine gun, most probably; perhaps a mortar.

Unlike last time he had been here, the corridors of the Kremlin were now buzzing with activity. There were perhaps twenty-five guys in the briefing room and there was a low murmur of voices. Not rowdy, but not subdued either. The first thing Sam did was seek out Mac. The troop sergeant was up front with Jack Whitely, a sheet of plans in front of them. When he saw Sam enter, Mac raised a hand in greeting; Sam returned the gesture, but made a point of sitting at the back. Was it just Sam, or had Mac given him a penetrating kind of look? Ordinarily he would have told himself to stop being so paranoid; but just at the moment, paranoia seemed to be the sensible option. Someone knew more about his operation than they were letting on. Someone had tipped him off by posting that letter. Was it someone currently within the confines of RAF Credenhill?

09.00 precisely. Whitely did a head count. 'All right,' he said with brisk, military authority. The buzz of conversation immediately died down. 'Looks like you all made it out of bed. Transport leaves in twenty minutes. No further briefing till you reach your forward mount position. Let's get moving.'

The sound of scraping chairs as everyone in the room stood up. Sam led the way, walking decisively to his bunk to pick up the gear, then heading to where the buses were parked up. On the tarmac several hessian sleeves were laid out. Sam was the first to place his Diemaco on the sleeve – the others behind him did the same. When there were enough weapons on the hessian, it would be tied up into a bundle ready for transportation. Sam left it for someone else to do that, though. Next to the weapons bundles were the parachute rigs, straight from the para store – chutes, oxygen, goggles, helmets, straps. Sam had done enough high-altitude jumps in his time, but you never got blasé about making them and he felt a little surge – somewhere between apprehension and excitement – at the sight of the gear. He placed his tightly packed bergen in a pile ready to be loaded, and was first into one of the buses, taking a seat up front.

Tyler sat next to him. 'Nothing like an away break,' he commented as he settled into his seat.

'Yeah,' Sam replied, looking over his shoulder to see that the bus was full and the back doors were being secured. No sign of Mac. He must have got into a different bus.

'Yeah,' he repeated, his voice a bit distant. 'Nothing like.'

★

Brize Norton. 12.00.

As they arrived, it was clear that the squadron was coinciding with another movement of troops. The airbase was full of soldiers. Soldiers leaving, soldiers coming back. Sam watched them from the window of the white van as it drove up to the bland terminal building. Some of them

132

would have just landed in the UK for their R and R package in the middle of their tours. They were the ones with smiles on their faces. The glum, serious-looking ones would be returning by the same flight, most likely to one of the war zones of the Middle East. Kandahar, maybe, or Baghdad. No wonder they looked so fed up.

The squadron's convoy of white vans pulled up outside the terminal and the men de-bussed. Once they were all out, the vans drove away. They would be approaching the special forces jet that was flying them to Bagram so that the gear could be swiftly loaded without having to go through the regular check-in process. Like a swarm of camouflaged bees, the Regiment men headed into the terminal. From the looks they were attracting from the uniformed squaddies all around, it was clear that everyone could tell they were not regular soldiers. And it was true: there was an aloofness about the SAS guys. Everyone in that echoing terminal building was on the same side, but that didn't prevent a feeling of 'them and us'. Sam just kept his eyes front and ignored the looks he was getting. The sooner they got on the flight to Bagram, he thought to himself, the better.

He queued to check in behind Craven, Tyler and another air troop member, a hard-nut little Scot called Cullen. Nobody knew his first name, or if they did they had long forgotten it, because Cullen was the only name he answered to. Cullen curtly answered the routine questions of the RAF soldier at the check-in desk before flashing his military ID and moving through to the lounge. Craven and Tyler did the same as Sam fished into his pocket for his own ID. It was a small, battered card, about the size of a driving licence, with a grainy, somewhat out-of-date picture of Sam and the few details that were deemed necessary for someone in his line of work. Name: Redman, Sam. Rank: Sergeant. Blood Group: AB. Religion: C of E. Sam snorted slightly as he read it for the millionth time. If he came home in a body bag they could say whatever prayers they liked. It made no difference to him.

There weren't many people in the departure lounge, but they were all in camouflage gear, idling on the uncomfortable chairs and staring up at the departure screens and televisions dotted around the place. Out of one of the windows Sam saw pallets of cargo being loaded into the belly of an aging Tristar. That elderly war horse of an aircraft was for the regular troops or for their supplies. The Regiment guys knew they could expect something else – a C-17 – manned by special forces crew; but until its departure was announced, Sam would be staying here. He bought scalding hot, tasteless coffee in a plastic cup from a machine and stared blankly up at a news programme on one of the television screens. The hawk-like face of the Russian prime minister beamed the smile of a politician.

Sam found a deserted corner of the lounge and settled down to wait.

★

The cabin smelt of that mixture of grubby upholstery and air conditioning that clings to aircraft the world over; the engines were already humming. The squadron spread themselves out – there was plenty of room to do so. Almost immediately several of the guys started pulling hammocks from their bags and pinning them to the side of the cabin. Once take-off had been completed, they would knock back a sleeping pill and use the seven-hour flight to get some shut-eye. Along one side of the cabin there was a double line of stretcher beds. The first time Sam had ever been on a military flight – years ago, now – the sight of these beds had been more than a little unnerving. Now they were just part of the furniture, despite the fact that he'd seen plenty of guys unconscious, dripped up and full of morphine on those things. Some of them had survived; some of them hadn't. You didn't think of the ones who never made it when you were preparing to go out into the field. Do that and you'd never go anywhere, or do anything.

He chose a window seat over the wing and buckled himself in as soon as he sat down. He turned to look out of the window, but almost immediately he became aware of somebody taking a place in his row of seats. Sam turned to look. It was Mac. His friend was eyeing him a little suspiciously.

'You all right?' he asked.

Sam sniffed and looked away. 'Course,' he replied, aware how disagreeable he sounded. 'Shouldn't I be?'

He sensed Mac shrugging. 'Dunno, mate. Just look like you've been sucking a lemon all day, that's all.'

'Just tired of schlepping to and from . . .'

'Me too,' Mac interrupted.

They sat in awkward silence.

The noise of the engines increased slightly and the aircraft gradually edged into movement. Sam could feel Mac's gaze on him, but he stubbornly refused to return it. Normally in this situation he'd feel a sense of camaraderie. He'd *want* to talk to the guys, to feel comfortable with them. It was important. It would help grease the wheels in the field. But Sam felt totally unable to do it. He felt as alien to the squadron as they felt to the squaddies queuing up in the terminal building. With the others he could pretend. But with Mac . . . no. The man sitting next to him knew him too well. Mac would be able to see through any forced smiles or half-arsed banter.

The calm voice of the captain came over the loudspeaker. Sam barely heard it. He continued to stare out of the window as the aircraft turned on to the runway, accelerated sharply and smoothly rose into the air. The plane juddered as it hit the cloud line; Sam remained as still as a statue. Only when it was levelling off did he allow himself to turn back to Mac.

His friend was still looking at him. A thoughtful look. He opened his mouth as though about to say something and Sam felt his stomach lurch slightly. But Mac said nothing, having clearly thought better of it. When he did finally speak, it was not in the conversational tones of a friend. It was as a troop sergeant talking to one of his unit.

'I'm going to do the rounds,' he said. 'Talk to the guys. We're going in tonight. There won't be much time at Bagram to rest up. You should get some sleep.'

Sam nodded, then looked away again. Mac didn't move, though, so he turned back with one eyebrow raised enquiringly. His friend's lips were pursed, his eyebrows narrow. He held out his hand and offered Sam a small white pill. Zaleplon – half the squadron would be taking them to blank out the boredom of the flight. 'I mean it, Sam,' he said quietly. 'Get some sleep.'

Sam took the pill. He rolled it around thoughtfully in his fingertips. Mac was suspicious of something, that much was clear. Did he know? Did he suspect? Sam couldn't tell. What was more, he was never going to find out while they were 30,000 feet up and surrounded by the rest of the squadron. And it was true. He *could* use some sleep.

'Thanks, Mac,' he said. He popped the pill in his mouth, swallowed it and pushed his chair back.

Unlike most people, Sam could sleep easily in an aircraft seat and that was exactly what he intended to do.

★

It was the pilot's voice that woke him. He roused himself quickly from his deep, dreamless sleep. The Zaleplon had knocked him out, but also ensured that he woke up feeling alert. Outside it was dark and he could feel that the aircraft was beginning to lose height. Looking around, he saw that the rest of the guys were getting ready for landing, removing their hammocks and settling down in their seats. There was quiet in the cabin – the quiet of anticipation, broken only by the noise of the engines and now by the pilot's announcement.

'Gentlemen, we'll soon be landing at Bagram. To conform with the current night-landing regulations in this operational theatre, we'll be turning off all lights both inside and outside the aircraft. Please ensure your seatbelts are fastened and your luggage is safely stowed.'

As it always did, it struck Sam as faintly ridiculous that this instruction should be given to a bunch of guys who, only a few hours from now, would be hurling themselves from the back of a plane. But he checked his belt nevertheless.

The lights were switched off soon after that, plunging the cabin into pitch darkness. Looking out the window Sam saw that even the small wing lights were no longer flashing. Down below he could make out an occasional fire, evidence of a settlement in the arid expanse of northern Afghanistan. How many Taliban were out there, he wondered idly, mortars at the ready in the hope that they might see an ISAF forces aircraft in the sky and get lucky with a potshot? If that happened, they'd get to fall from a plane a bit earlier than they expected, so Sam was more than happy to go through the procedure of a blind landing.

Cloaked in that precarious blackness, with only the whining sound of the jet engines for company, Sam felt at once vulnerable and strangely comforted. Darkness suited him. Hid him. As a Blade he'd been taught to live and hide in the shadows, out on patrols, making himself unseen, always being the grey man. That was the drill – disguise yourself whenever possible, then close in on your target and neutralise it. That was really all he knew.

He heard the pilot's voice, as calm and reassuring as if he

had just delivered a planeload of holiday makers to the Costa del Sol.

'Welcome to Afghanistan,' he announced, as the plane turned from the runway and trundled towards the main terminal building of Bagram Airbase.

NINE

It was only Sam's second visit to Bagram. Most of his previous ops in Afghanistan had been in Helmand Province, which meant a flight to Kandahar in the south before connecting to Camp Bastion a bit further west. But in the summer of 2006 he and three others had been assigned to a job guarding an Afghan politician with an unpronounceable name who, on the instruction of President Hamid Karzai, was making an under-the-radar deputation to a warlord in Parvan Province. He was an unlikeable man who treated the Regiment unit like his own personal servants. At least, he had on the way there. They had left Kabul in an armoured vehicle and as they approached the warlord's village they had driven straight into an ambush. The unit had fought their way out of it and hotfooted back to Kabul, noses bloodied but no lives lost. The politician had wet himself in the middle of the firefight, though. He was a lot less bolshie on the return journey. The secret talks, of course, were never held.

Having been here once before, then, Sam knew what to expect. The large runway was surrounded by three big aircraft hangars. Various other support buildings – originally built by the Soviets during their occupation – provided a pretty basic level of facilities to the troops at the base, though lots of them were little more than empty shells, having been destroyed by warring Afghan factions over the years. The airfield itself was surrounded by the enormous, craggy, snow-topped mountains that characterised this part of the world, but these were obscured by the darkness as Sam and the rest of the squadron disembarked into the warm, dry air. Instead, all they could see were the bright lights and bustle of the airfield at work. The loadies had already started to unload their pallets of equipment and forklift them on to a truck, while the guys themselves were directed towards one of the hangars, outside which an American A-10 Thunderbolt was parked. The aircraft had a mouthful of shark-like teeth painted on its nose, from which protruded a 30 mm gun. Even though it was 11 p.m. and still swelteringly hot, a technician was hard at work on the undercarriage – he barely glanced at the men who, almost deafened by the roar of their own aircraft's engines, walked past him and into the hangar.

It was a huge, cavernous space the size of a couple of football pitches. There were three aircraft housed in there, but hardly any people: just a British Army representative who ushered them in towards the right where an area had been walled off with some temporary partitions. Waiting for them was a man in regular civvies. He wore square glasses with titanium rims and had a tanned face that was beginning to show signs of age. His hair was black, though, with no sign of grey: it was impossible to tell how old this man was and his expression was similarly inscrutable. Sam remembered Whitely saying that a representative from the Security Service would be waiting for them. The moment he saw him, one word went though Sam's head: 'wanker'. The very sight of him filled Sam with a sudden, burning anger.

Once the squadron was assembled, the man spoke – the clear, confident voice of someone used to talking in public. 'Don't get too comfortable, gentlemen,' he announced. 'You'll be going in tonight.' He looked around. 'Air troop sergeant?'

Mac stepped forward.

The spook nodded. 'Get your lads together. The rest of you, remain on standby.'

The British Army representative spoke up. 'You can get food at the PX,' he announced. 'And I'll show you where you can bunk down.' He walked back towards the entrance of the hangar. There was a brief moment of camaraderie among the men – those who were remaining on standby briefly shaking hands with those going on the op. Nothing over the top. Nothing showy. Nobody said 'good luck'; nobody said anything at all, really.

The others quickly melted away, leaving the eight members of air troop alone with the spook. There was Sam and Mac, Craven, Tyler and Cullen; and three others. Matt Andrews was the troop medic. He was black-skinned with short, cropped hair and a quiet, serious manner. Steve Davenport was one of the regiment's parachute instructors. He'd done more HALOs than most of the guys had had hot dinners; he'd taught half of them everything they knew and it was always good to have him along during an airborne insertion. And finally there was Hill Webb. Real name Hillary, but call him that and you'd be given a pretty swift demonstration of the Regiment's more advanced fighting skills. Sam had always found him to be a testy little fucker, but sometimes that was exactly what you wanted.

'You've been briefed on the basic nature of the operation?' the spook asked when they were all alone. It was only half a question, though, and didn't require an answer. He turned and led them to a corner of the partitioned room where a large whiteboard had been erected. Two maps were pinned to the board, both of them a couple of metres square. One was an aerial view of a piece of land, crystal clear. It looked like it had been photographed from only a hundred metres up, but in fact it was a satellite image. Next to it was a simple map, a line drawing showing the salient areas of the region in more detail.

'Your objective is here,' the spook told them, without preamble. He pointed to three long, rectangular-shaped buildings, set at right angles to each other in a horseshoe arrangement with a small, separate building, not much bigger than a shed, at the north-west corner. Arcing round from the south of the training camp to the west was a thin band of forest. Sam glanced at the scale and estimated it to be about two hundred metres deep. North of the camp and the forest, running west to east was a perfectly straight road. Still further east, stretching further than the boundary of the maps, was what looked like agricultural land. The spook pointed at it. 'Hemp plants,' he told them shortly. 'This area is known as the Chu Valley. It's a major centre for marijuana production. There are no major settlements close by, but you need to be aware of the possibility of hemp farmers moving their product up and down this road under cover of night.'

The man moved his attention to the area south-west of the band of forest. 'You're aiming to HALO into this area here,' he said. 'The trees should give you some cover from which to make your assault. We expect most of the targets to be in the southernmost building, but we can't guarantee that. All the buildings need to be cleared before you call in air to pick you up. We don't expect there to be any resistance and there's no intelligence of anything in the way of an armed guard. Once the targets have been taken out, we'll need photographs for identification purposes.'

'Aye, well,' Craven piped up. 'Tyler can do that. Fucking takes enough pictures of the showers, don't he?' He accompanied his joke with a wanking motion to make sure everyone got the message.

'All right, all right,' the spook interrupted. 'Estimated time of insertion: 03.00 hrs. Daylight at 04.27. You need to be well out of there by then. No more than an hour on the ground. Have you got any questions?'

Silence.

'Good.' The spook looked solemnly at them. 'For gentleman of your abilities, it should be a walk in the park.'

Cullen snorted. 'If it's going to be so damn easy,' he muttered in his thick Scottish brogue, 'maybe you'd like to come along?'

The spook made some reply, but Sam didn't hear it. He was too busy staring at the maps for a final time, recording the lie of the land, committing it to memory as he knew his patrol mates would be doing. It was a simple set-up, on the face of it. Their unit would be inside the buildings before anyone even knew they were there. The fact that there were only four buildings to clear made it even more straightforward.

Unless, of course, your objective wasn't what it appeared to be.

As Sam examined the plans, he tried to work out where his brother might be; but it was impossible to tell. Any of these buildings could house him, and when they hit the compound he would be as much at a disadvantage as any of them. If Jacob was going to get away, he needed to be warned of their approach; but Sam couldn't think of any way to do that without making it clear to his unit that he had compromised the mission.

Nor did he have time to give it much more thought. 'You've got half an hour,' the spook told them. 'The aircraft are waiting. Flight time to your insertion point, about two hours.' He looked them all individually in the eye. 'Good luck, gentlemen,' he said briskly. 'I'll be here when you get back.'

★

Three and a half thousand miles away, night was falling over London. The windows of the MI6 building on the Albert

143

Embankment started to twinkle in the half-light and workers started to spill from its main entrance and hurry towards the Tube station.

Inside the building, though, plenty of people remained. Their jobs involved parts of the world in very different time zones to London, after all, so the usual boundaries of the average working day meant nothing to them. Among those offices that were still inhabited was one, high up, that overlooked the river. It was a spectacular view, with the bridges all lit up, and the occupant of that office knew he would never tire of it. He stood at the window in a well-cut suit, his tie an immaculate Windsor knot and his hands behind his back, gazing out. He was an elderly man – older, at least, than most of the people who worked for the Firm and were happy to take their retirement at sixty-five and forget all about the complexities of their working lives. Not so Gabriel Bland. Some of the younger members of Her Majesty's Secret Intelligence Service joked that the only way he'd leave was in a box. Bland had heard the jibes and didn't mind them. They were probably true. Others joked that he had the kind of icy demeanour that indicated he was – that he absolutely *had* to be – some kind of sexual pervert. These rumours were *not* true, but again Bland ignored them, remaining perfectly polite even to those members of the service that he knew to be the most enthusiastic champions of such gossip.

On the desk behind him there was a computer – something Bland really could not get used to – and a small pile of files. There was work to be done on them, but really he knew he would be unable to concentrate on such things. Not tonight. He looked at his watch. Nearly seven o'clock. That would make it almost midnight in Afghanistan where a covert unit were preparing to undergo a mission on his orders. Godwilling they would be successful. If not, things could become exceedingly uncomfortable . . .

A knock on the door. 'Come!' Bland called without turning.

He watched the door open in the reflection of the window. A much younger man walked in. He too wore a suit and had hair that was neatly parted to one side and flattened down with some shiny product. It was a curiously old-fashioned look for someone only in their mid-thirties. 'Yes, Toby?' Bland intoned.

Toby Brookes. Of late, MI6 had taken to encouraging all manner of people into the service. Brookes, however, reminded Bland of himself as a younger man. A little too eager to please, perhaps. But a good worker. Conscientious. Able to see the bigger picture. Heaven knows, Bland thought to himself, in these troubled times that was an important attribute.

'Something's been flagged up, sir,' Brookes said efficiently. 'Clare Corbett. I thought you'd want to see it.'

Bland sniffed. He allowed himself one final glance at the river, then turned to face his young assistant. 'Be so good,' he asked mildly, 'as to shut the door, would you Toby?'

Brookes did as he was asked before speaking again. 'It might be nothing,' he said in his slightly nasal tone of voice. 'But I thought I'd bring it to your attention.'

'That's most kind of you, Toby,' Bland murmured.

'The Met carried out a search,' Brookes continued. 'A billing address for a mobile phone number registered in her name.'

Bland remained silent.

'Like I say,' Brookes continued, suddenly sounding a little less sure of himself. 'It's probably nothing.'

'When was this request processed, Toby?'

The younger man examined a piece of paper in his hand. 'Tuesday night,' he said. 'Forty-eight hours ago. I guess it took a while to come through the system.'

Bland turned once more to look out of the window. 'Do

you know who the police officer in question is who requested this information?' He watched Brookes's reflection as he once more looked at his sheet.

'A DI Nicola Ledbury.'

'I see.' Bland furrowed his hairy, eagle-like eyebrows. 'I wonder, Toby, if I might ask you to invite Miss Ledbury to come and have a brief word with us.'

'Of course.'

He turned again and allowed a friendly smile to spread across his lips. 'Tonight, Toby. If it wouldn't be too much trouble.'

Brookes nodded and gave his superior a look that showed he understood.

'Thank you, Toby,' he said quietly. And as the young man slipped out of the room, he returned to his place at the window, surveying the splendour of that scene as he calmly slotted this new piece of information into the jigsaw of his mind. It worried him that he could not yet see the whole picture.

★

Bagram airbase. Midnight.

Before the off, the unit spent every spare moment checking and rechecking their rigs. There was no banter; there was hardly any conversation at all as they went about the business of getting kitted out. Sam approached the runway knowing that his freefall rig was firmly strapped to his body. He had checked the chute several times and strapped his weapon to his side. As he carried his rucksack and helmet away from the aircraft hangar in the company of the rest of the unit, he couldn't help but feel the familiar sense of tension that always preceded a HALO jump.

It was the little things that could go wrong. At thirty thousand feet there was very little oxygen and the temperature was freezing. Any slight malfunction of the rig and you'd pass out. Problems like that you could predict and prepare for; others you couldn't. During a high-altitude jump over the Syrian Desert, his mate had hit Sam's rucksack from one side as they dived from the aircraft. The rucksack had shifted, changing Sam's centre of balance. He'd started to spin; and once the spinning started, it didn't stop. Freefalling at one hundred and fifty miles per hour it hadn't taken him long to black out. He'd have been a goner if it weren't for the HALO rig's automatic opening device that kicked in at four thousand feet. When he regained consciousness, the capillaries in the whites of his eyes had burst, his inner ears were fucked and he was too dizzy even to walk, let alone continue the operation. He put that thought from his mind. Burst capillaries or not, nothing was going to stop him from completing what he had to do on *this* op. Nothing at all.

'We need to talk.'

Mac had started walking alongside him. His friend put a firm hand on Sam's arm and forced him to a halt, while the others carried on walking. Sam's body tensed up.

'What do you mean?'

Mac stared straight into his eyes. 'You think I didn't recognise him?' he murmured.

Sam felt suddenly trapped.

'I don't know what you're talking about,' he spat. But even as he spoke, he felt his hand move almost involuntarily to his weapon.

Mac glanced down at Sam's gun hand. 'Christ's sake, mate,' he hissed. 'If I was going to stop you, do you think I'd have waited till now?'

The noise of the airfield around him retreated. In that moment there was only Sam and Mac.

'I couldn't tell you before, Sam. Not till we were here.'

'Why the hell not?' Sam was suddenly angry with his old

friend. He didn't know why. He just couldn't control his emotions.

'Think about it, Sam. Something about this whole operation stinks. The Regiment sent out to kill one of their own? And fuck knows what sort of surveillance we're all under. You and me start having cosy little confabs, it's going to send up warning signals for someone, isn't it?'

Sam thought about that. He realised that of all the people he couldn't trust, Mac was the most trustworthy.

'I don't think Five know he's there,' Sam said quietly. And then, in response to Mac's sharp look, 'Or whoever it is who's behind this. If they did, they'd hardly be sending you and me on the op.' He took a deep breath, quickly wondering whether he should tell Mac everything he'd learned – the letter, Clare, the red-light runners, what they were *really* being sent to Kazakhstan to do – and just as quickly deciding not to. It didn't change anything. It didn't change what he had to do. 'I'm not going to let anyone kill him, Mac. I don't care about the other targets, but I'm not going to let anyone kill my brother.'

'And you think *I* am? Jesus, Sam, he was my friend. God knows what he's got himself mixed up in, but . . .'

A shout from up ahead – Tyler, his Cockney voice rising above the noise of the airfield. 'Havin' a mass debate, you two?' he barked lewdly.

Sam and Mac looked towards him, then started to follow the rest of the unit, but slowly.

'Maybe we should tell the others?'

Mac shook his head. 'You can't, Sam. You'll only get them all a stretch in the nick for disobeying orders. You know J. better than anyone – you think he'd want us to do that on his account?'

Mac was right. There was one thing Jacob had always insisted on, and that was fighting his own battles. 'So how we going to play it?' he demanded.

148

Mac walked silently for a moment. 'When we get to the camp,' he said finally, 'We'll need to make some noise, let J. know someone's coming . . .' He let the sentence trail off, clearly aware that it wasn't much of a plan.

'What if Jacob comes out shooting?' Sam asked.

But Mac didn't answer. They had caught up with the rest of the unit.

'Nice of you to join us,' Cullen said darkly.

Mac smiled at him. 'Well,' he said, his voice suddenly much brighter than it had been only seconds ago, 'we didn't really want to miss the party.'

There were two C-130 Hercules aircraft waiting for them up ahead; a refuelling lorry was just driving away. The two aircraft would fly in convoy over a commercial airline route until they reached the insertion point. Once the unit had jumped, one of the Hercules would refuel the other in mid-air before returning to base. The remaining plane, its fuel stores replenished, would circle at a high altitude until they received the radio signal from the guys on the ground that they were ready to be picked up.

But the moment when that was to happen, Sam thought – the planes' engines roaring in his ears as the unit boarded their aircraft – seemed a very, very long way off. Mac's sudden admission had been a shock; Sam didn't know whether he felt better or worse.

They sat in the belly of the Hercules, four to a bench, facing each other. For now their rucksacks and helmets were on the floor in front of them, but when the time came to make the jump, that would change. Around them a loadie checked the plane's apparatus and made it ready for flight. Sam sat opposite Mac. The two of them did their best not to catch each other's eye, but it was difficult and every time it happened, Sam felt a little surge in his stomach. It wasn't the usual pre-HALO butterflies. It was something else.

It was deafeningly loud in there, but Craven managed to make his voice heard above the noise. 'Nothing like a nice quiet evening in,' he shouted. A light-hearted comment, but delivered in a deadpan way. Craven clearly didn't expect a response; nor did he get one.

At that moment the tailgate of the Hercules closed and the lights of the airfield disappeared from sight. A sudden lurch as the aircraft juddered into motion. Any minute now and they would be airborne.

And then?

Sam kept his breathing steady as he prepared for the ordeal ahead of him.

★

The telephone on Gabriel Bland's desk rang three times before he picked it up.

'Bland,' he answered it shortly but not impolitely.

'It's me, sir. Toby. I've brought Nicola Ledbury in. Interview room three. Would you like me to start asking questions?'

'Ah . . .' Bland made a pretence of considering the suggestion. 'Perhaps I'll come down and lend a hand,' he said finally. 'I'll be with you shortly.'

He replaced the phone on its cradle and left the room with a swiftness that belied his advancing years. He took the lift to the basement of the building and stepped briskly along a corridor until he found the room in question. It was sparse and unfurnished. Just a table and a two chairs. Toby was sitting in one of them, and opposite him a woman. She was pretty, with blonde hair and a long, smooth neck. But she looked frightened.

They *always* looked frightened.

Toby stood up the moment Bland walked into the room, immediately offering him his chair. 'Thank you, Toby,' he murmured before sitting down and smiling impassively at the woman in front of him. 'Detective Inspecter Ledbury,' he said calmly. 'How kind of you to come and see us.'

The woman's frightened eyes flickered up towards Toby and her lips grew a little thinner.

Bland feigned concern. 'I do hope Toby wasn't brusque with you.'

'He was bloody brusque,' she replied hotly. 'I'm a police officer, you know . . .'

Gabriel Bland continued as if she hadn't even spoken. 'I wonder, Miss Ledbury, if I might just ask you a few questions.' He paused briefly, waiting for a response that was not forthcoming, before continuing. 'Two nights ago, you requested a billing address for a mobile phone number belonging to a Miss Clare Corbett. Am I right?'

The woman's expression changed. Wariness. 'Should I have a solicitor here?' she asked.

Bland raised an eyebrow. 'Toby,' he said, quite calmly, 'be so good as to lock the door, would you?'

Toby did as he was told; the woman shuffled uncomfortably in her seat.

'Shall I repeat the question, Miss Ledbury? Or would you just like to answer it now?'

The woman hesitated, but only briefly. 'It's common practice,' she said uncertainly. 'An easy way to find some-one. I've done it a lot. Hundreds of times.'

Bland nodded. 'I'm sure you're a very conscientious officer, Miss Ledbury.' His voice sounded a lot less encouraging than his words. 'I'm not much interested in the hundreds of times. I'm interested in this time.'

Silence.

'I want my solicitor.'

Bland suppressed a sudden surge of frustration. 'Miss Ledbury,' he intoned, 'you're not at Paddington Green now.' He stared at her. Gabriel Bland knew that not many people could withstand that stare. Nicola Ledbury was no exception.

'Yes,' she said quietly. 'I asked for the billing address.'

'I see. Would you care to tell me why?'

The woman glanced at the floor. 'It was a favour,' she said. 'For a friend.'

Instantly the atmosphere in the room grew tense. Bland's eyes narrowed slightly. 'Which friend?' He pronounced each word slowly and forcefully.

She closed her eyes. 'His name is Sam Redman.'

'I see. And what can you tell me about Sam Redman?'

'He's . . .'

'Yes, Miss Ledbury.'

'He's military. SAS.' She looked up at him, eyes appealing. 'It was *just* a favour.'

But Bland no longer appeared interested in her. He did his best to look unmoved, but in truth a sinister knot had just tied its way round his stomach.

Bland got to his feet. 'Keep her here,' he instructed Toby. 'Have somebody watch her. No phone calls. Then I think you and I need to pay Miss Corbett another visit.'

Ten minutes later Bland, Toby and a third man – an Asian by the name of Amir – were in a black cab. At least, it *looked* like a black cab, but the driver, an employee of the Firm, wouldn't be stopping to pick up any fares. When, half an hour later, they parked in the quiet residential street in Acton where Clare Corbett lived, the driver pulled out a newspaper and started to read: the perfect image of a cabbie on his break. Bland and Toby approached the front door, while Amir headed round the back alleyway to the rear of the house. Bland looked at his watch: 10 p.m. He stretched out a gloved hand and rang the intercom.

They waited. A crackling noise came over the loud-speaker. Someone had picked it up, but they were declining to speak.

152

'Please open the door, Miss Corbett,' Bland replied. 'Immediately.'

A pause. He spoke again. 'We have somebody at the back entrance, Miss Corbett. I suggest you cooperate.' Beside him, he was aware of Toby handling his firearm.

A buzz from the door. Toby went in first. Bland followed closely.

Clare Corbett stood framed in the entrance to her flat. Her face was white and Bland noticed her hand trembling. 'May we come in?' he asked.

'Do I have much choice?' she asked weakly.

He looked her in the eye. 'We all have choices, Miss Corbett.' She stepped aside and allowed them to enter. 'I'm hoping that you've been making the right ones.'

In the kitchen, Bland indicated to the terrified woman that she should sit down. He remained standing, as did Toby Brookes who hovered threateningly by the kitchen door, making no attempt to hide his firearm.

'I had hoped,' he said smoothly, 'not to have to burden you with our presence again, Miss Corbett.'

'Yeah,' she replied, avoiding his eye. 'Me too.'

Bland sniffed. He waited a moment, then took the direct approach. 'Tell me everything you know about Sam Redman.'

He watched her carefully, looking for the signs. 'I've never heard of him,' she said, but he could immediately tell she was lying. The lack of eye contact. The way she stiffly touched her hand to her right ear.

A thick silence fell on the room. The woman's face began to redden. He looked over at Brookes and nodded shortly. Brookes didn't hesitate. He stepped over to where she was sitting and, with his free hand, grabbed a clump of her hair, twisting it tight so that she gasped with the sudden pain of it. With his other hand he pressed the butt of his firearm deeply into the soft flesh of her cheek. She looked faintly ridiculous, her eyes wide and short breaths of fear escaping from the O of her mouth. Ridiculous, but terrified.

Bland took a seat at the table opposite her. He placed his hands palm downwards on the top and looked straight at her. She wasn't avoiding his stare any more.

'He came here,' she gasped. 'I don't know how he found me. I didn't tell him anything.'

Bland glanced up at Toby; the younger man yanked her hair suddenly and pressed the gun further into her face.

'*Oh God!*' Clare breathed. '*Please, don't! I'll tell you. Please, don't hurt me!*'

Bland nodded at Toby, who immediately let go of the woman. Her body seemed to crumple as she hid her face in her hands. For a moment the room was filled with the desolate sound of her heavy, petrified sobs.

'He just turned up,' she wailed. Her words started to tumble out, as though if she said it all quickly it wouldn't make it so bad. 'He knew about the article. He had a copy – it was all, you know, blacked out, censored. But he made me tell him. He said he was special forces, I don't know which one. And that he was being sent to a training camp . . .'

At this point she removed the hands from her face. Her eyes were red and what little make-up she had been wearing was now streaked over her cheeks.

'Carry on,' Bland said.

'He said his brother was there. And that he wasn't going to let anyone kill him.'

Clare Corbett stared, wide-eyed. She appeared horrified that she had blurted out all these things. Bland barely noticed. He had pushed his chair back and was standing up. 'Make the call,' he told Brookes, his mind suddenly racing. 'Tell them to pull the mission.'

Brookes hesitated, blinking at his boss.

'NOW!' Bland roared.

The man scurried away, leaving Bland and Clare in the room. Not a word was spoken. He didn't even look at her. The only sound was of Brookes in the corridor, talking urgently into his mobile phone. When he reappeared, his expression was dark.

'What?' Bland demanded.

Brooke shook his head. 'The unit's been inserted,' he replied. 'They've already gone in. I'm sorry, sir. It's too late.'

TEN

When you're waiting to perform a HALO jump, two hours seem like two minutes. As the Hercules cruised northwards, Sam and the rest of the unit checked and rechecked their rigs more times than they could count, ensuring everything was packed correctly, nothing was frayed and the oxygen gear had been properly serviced. There was occasional banter above the noise of the engines. When Craven tugged at the straps of his pack for what must have been the twentieth time, Tyler was quick to pounce. 'What's wrong, Jack? Ain't learned to fall stable yet?'

Craven looked up, one eyebrow raised. 'Yeah,' he replied. 'I fall stable on your missus every Friday night.'

The company laughed, but soon they all went back to checking and rechecking their gear. Nobody wanted to leave anything to chance.

The loadmaster approached them. 'Ten minutes!' he shouted over the noise of the engines, holding up the gloved fingers of both hands so that there was no confusion.

The men started to get ready. Sam's chute and weapon were already firmly strapped to his body, as was his GPS unit, but the rucksack was on the floor in front of him. He hooked his legs over it, then scraped it towards him so that it was under the bench. Once it was in position, he clipped the bag to the back of his legs and wound the straps round to his front, pulling them so they were firmly tightened. It would make walking to the tailgate difficult when the time came, but the bag needed to be attached to the back of his legs to balance his weight properly. He then turned his attention to the digital screen of his automatic opening device. Four thousand feet. If all went well they would open the chutes at four thousand five hundred; but if there was a problem the AOD would save his life.

'Five minutes!'

Sam fitted the oxygen mask and helmet to his face. Up until now they had been breathing the oxygen from the aircraft's mainframe, but now they needed to make sure their breathing apparatus was fully operational. As soon as he attached his oxygen mask, Sam's breathing sounded much louder in his ears. It heightened his senses somewhat, even though the toughened black plastic of his mask had plunged the area around the tailgate into a deeper shade of darkness. The men around him looked more like cosmonauts now than soldiers. He breathed steadily and deeply. Everything was as it should be. The air was coming through. He got to his feet, as did the other seven members of his troop. The loadmaster approached to help them to the back of the plane.

Steve Davenport and Matt Andrews went first. Behind them were Tyler and Craven, then Webb and Cullen. Sam and Mac took the rear. In front of them a red light shone in the gloom of the Hercules's belly. When it turned green, that would be the signal for the off.

A sudden rush of noise and with it a judder of turbulence. The tailgate was opening.

Sam was running on pure adrenaline now. Everything else that had been preoccupying him – Jacob, Mac and what the hell was going to happen when they hit land – took second place. Every cell in his brain was concentrating on the jump. Outside it was pitch black: from where he was standing he had the impression that he was about to dive into nothingness.

157

The loadmaster touched one hand to his headphones then held up a single finger. One minute. Sam and Mac looked at each other, but through their equipment the expressions on their faces were unknowable. They both faced forward again.

Green light.

There was no order. No hesitation. Davenport and Andrews jumped to the edge of the tailgate and fell out, their bodies arched and their arms spread out as though they were about to embrace the empty air. Tyler and Craven followed immediately.

A pause. Webb and Cullen waited for perhaps thirty seconds before they jumped. An eight-man unit freefalling in close proximity to each other could cause a splash on a radar; two four-man units were less likely to. Once Webb and Cullen had disappeared, Sam and Mac shuffled behind them. And then, the moment they reached the edge of the tailgate, they toppled forwards.

The wind hit Sam immediately, roaring in his ears and lashing against his body as if a powerful wave had just crashed over him. He fell belly downwards, his body arched and his palms outstretched. He was vaguely aware of the Hercules roaring away into the distance above him, but he didn't concentrate on that. Instead he looked around to check the position of the others. They manoeuvred themselves so that they fell in a circular formation. It was possible to see them all perfectly clearly: the half moon provided plenty of light – it even glowed slightly on the helmets of the unit as they fell. Thirty thousand feet down, he could make out the twinkling of sparsely separated settlements. In a corner of his brain he wondered if any of these would be their target. It was impossible to tell from this height. They would have to wait until they were closer to the ground.

That wouldn't be long.

They hurtled towards the earth, deafened by the rush,

their senses keen with adrenaline. Terminal velocity, the maximum speed they could achieve. Thirty seconds passed.

A minute.

A minute and a half.

Everything was as it should be. Despite himself, Sam felt a surge of wild excitement. A thrill. As his altitude decreased, his view of the landscape below became less extensive; but those bits he could see became clearer. They were freefalling into a widely deserted area. In the distance he thought he saw the headlamps of a vehicle. But it was the only one. From what he could tell at this height, there were very few people around who might possibly notice the unit HALOing in.

The freefall suits of his troop ruffled in the fast-moving air, like a banner being whipped in a gale. Below and in the distance, Sam saw the chutes of the four men who had preceded him burst open. The others were under canopy. They intuitively adjusted the direction of their freefall to get closer to them. Any second now it would be their turn to open.

Four thousand five hundred feet. Cullen was the first to open his chute; the rest of them followed suit immediately. Sam tugged on his rip cord and felt the chute erupt into the air. There was a sharp jolt through his body as his velocity suddenly reduced; the rushing sound eased off and the unit started to float gently towards the earth.

Under canopy, it didn't take long for them to see the band of forested area towards which they were headed. Currently they were a little too far east, so almost with a single mind they changed their course to bring them down safely in the area beyond the trees. Perhaps a mile to the north, Sam saw buildings. Three of them, set in a horseshoe shape.

The training camp.

His eyes narrowed as he gazed at it through the dark visor of his helmet. All thoughts of the thrill of the HALO jump dissolved away. He could think of nothing now but getting back down to earth.

The camp disappeared from his field of vision. All he could see below him now were the trees and the area of flat ground behind them where they were to land – and where the others already had. Unclipping the straps that bound his rucksack to his legs, he allowed the pack to fall to the ground, still attached to him by virtue of a long, tough lanyard rope. As the pack fell to earth, he prepared his body for the impact of landing.

Ten seconds.

Five.

He hit the ground running with that strange sense of regret that always follows a jump. Behind him the chute wafted silently to the ground. He quickly unstrapped the cords of the rucksack from around his legs, then unclipped the whole thing. Pulling off his helmet and removing the mask, he started tugging the chute towards him, bundling it up into a crumpled ball. All around him, the others were doing the same thing. They made hardly any sound.

Sam checked out his surroundings. The moon that had illuminated them in freefall now cast shadows on the ground and gave him surprisingly good vision. He was standing about thirty metres from the tree line in a field of stubble. South of him there appeared to be another field with a crop a good two metres high. Hemp, he reckoned. A lot of it. An acre of that would earn him more than a Regiment salary. Sam turned his back on it as the others started to congregate around him.

'Get into the cover of the trees,' Mac hissed. 'We'll dump our gear there, out of sight.'

The unit hauled their rucksacks onto their backs and ran towards the forest.

It was much darker under the canopy of the trees. No

moonlight for them to see by. They removed their freefall rigs and piled them by a tree. Only then did Mac speak again. 'All right, guys. Listen up. Two units. Jack, Luke, Cullen – you're with Sam. Matt, Steve, Hill – you're with me.'

Craven, Tyler and Cullen moved towards Sam. Mac addressed them as a group. 'Head north through the forest,' he told them. 'Approach the camp from the west. We'll hit it from the south. Let us know on comms when you're in position.' He shot Sam a sharp look.

They all nodded briefly, absorbing their instructions.

It took a minute or two for everyone to engage their comms kit and attach their NV. The moment he brought his goggles over his eyes, Sam felt that the whole forest had been illuminated in the familiar, hazy green. Gnarled tree branches spread out before him like witches' fingers. It was eerily silent, apart from the sound of the men around him preparing themselves. He unclipped his Diemaco from the side of his body, then looked round. Everyone was ready. Sam gestured at Tyler, Craven and Cullen then pointed sharply in a northward direction before starting to run through the forest.

Sam moved quickly but with care. The NV allowed him to see where he was going, but it didn't completely reveal the smaller possible hazards underfoot. As he ran, he scanned the area all around, his senses acute as he kept an eye out for anything suspicious. Behind him he heard the firm, steady footsteps of the other three. They were keeping close, but not *too* close so they didn't present a bunched up target for any unseen enemy.

A patch of open ground – a kind of clearing. Sam upped his pace. He wanted the cover of the trees again. He felt exposed here.

Far too exposed. It was like a sixth sense.

Sam didn't even hear the shot. The weapon that fired the

round must have been suppressed. The first he knew about it was from the sudden, alarmed voice over the comms.

'Man down!'

SOPs kicked in. He instantly threw himself to the ground, a horrible, sickening feeling in the pit of his stomach. The comms was suddenly filled with voices, with panic. He heard Tyler's voice above it all, hissing, in an urgent whisper.

'Craven. Craven's down. Jack, can you hear me? Bollocks! *Craven's fucking down! We're being dicked!*'

Sam crawled round on all fours to look back the way they had run. There was no one standing: Tyler and Cullen had also gone to ground. In the distance, there was a flash of movement. He pulled up his Diemaco so that it was lying on the ground in front of him and aimed into the thick darkness of the trees up ahead.

There was barely any time to think. The figure had taken cover behind a tree, but even now was emerging from its protection and raising his weapon. Sam could see enough to be sure it wasn't one of his troop, and that was all he needed to know.

He fired.

The suppressed round ripped from his Diemaco and the figure up ahead crumpled to the earth.

'*Sit rep, now.*' Mac's voice. Angry. A bit panicked. '*What the hell's going on?*'

'Enemy down,' Sam hissed urgently into the comms. 'Tyler, do you copy?'

'Roger that.' Tyler's voice was tense.

'Cover me. I'm going to make sure I don't need to finish the job.'

Sam pushed himself to his feet and ran across the open ground to where the body of his target was lying. Bending down, he pulled the corpse back into the trees. Then he examined it.

The guy was dead, there was no doubt about that. It looked like Sam's round had hit him directly in the left eye; most of one side of his skull seemed to have exploded. Sam wasn't interested in the hole in his head, however. It was the clothes on his back and the weapon in his fist that caught his attention. The sniper was carrying some variant of the AK-47; an ops waistcoat contained a large quantity of ammo and other weaponry; but what really stood out was not the Kalashnikov or the other bells and whistles – it was the weapon strapped across the dead man's back. Sam had only fired a GM-94 grenade launcher once, but once was enough to know that it was perhaps the most effective weapon he was ever likely to use. This wasn't the kind of toy you expect to come across just anywhere.

In one of the man's ears there was a comms earpiece, much like the one Sam was wearing. It was slightly bloodied as Sam pulled it out and put it to his own ear.

He listened carefully.

It was difficult to tell, but he thought he could discern three separate voices. They weren't speaking English, however. Sam was no linguist, but he recognised the language.

Russian.

He looked down at the corpse again. This was no ordinary soldier. He was too well kitted out; his equipment was too good. Possibilities tumbled through his mind. Private security? Someone with cash to splash, enough to kit out a private army? In the darkness, he found himself shaking his head. He didn't think so. The GM-94 was Russian-made, and standard issue for Russian special forces. The man Sam had just killed was no squaddie. He'd put money on it. But then . . .

'What the fuck are Spetsnaz doing *here*?' he murmured to himself.

'Say again.' Mac's voice over the comms.

Sam quickly refocused himself.

163

'We've got more company,' he said. 'I've nailed the shooter, but he's got a comms system. I've listened in. Estimate three others in the vicinity. How's Craven looking?'

A silence. And then, his voice strained, Tyler spoke.

'Gone,' he said.

A moment of silence in the comms.

'Shit,' Sam hissed as a surge of anger burned through him. How the hell had this happened? They'd only been on the ground five minutes. How the *hell* had it happened?

He didn't get long to think about it. As he looked back across the clearing he saw more movement. 'Tyler, Cullen – you still down?' he demanded.

'Roger that,' they both breathed in unison.

'Stay where you are. I've got a visual on another shooter.'

He raised his Diemaco once more. Looking through the sights he tried not to concentrate on the crumpled mound ahead of him that he knew to be Craven's body. As he fired, the round exploded in the green light of his NV, like some kind of ghostly firework. His target fell immediately to the earth.

'Did I say three others?' he growled. 'Make that two.'

'We're coming up from the south.' Mac's voice sounded as though he was running. 'It sounds like they know where you are. You sure you only heard three others, Sam?'

'Makes sense,' Sam replied tersely. 'Four-man unit. Tyler and Cullen are in open ground. I'm by the tree line. Guys, stay down. I'll keep you covered from here.'

'Wilco,' came the grim reply.

Sam pressed his back against a tree, his weapon raised and ready to fire. His mind was in turmoil. He couldn't make sense of it. These Spetsnaz guys – if indeed that's what they were – seemed to be expecting them. But how? Nobody knew they were coming, did they?

Did they?

He stayed close to the ground. Occasionally over the

164

comms he heard Mac hissing an instruction to Andrews, Davenport and Webb; other than that he could do nothing but scan the surrounding woodland, keeping his NV-enhanced eyes peeled for unexpected movement. Briefly he thought he saw something again; but whatever it was settled into stillness. Sam kept alert, watching over the prostrate forms of Tyler and Cullen, his finger twitching on the trigger, ready to fire at a moment's notice.

All around him, the silence of the night was broken by sudden, unexpected noises: the falling of a twig, the scurrying of an animal. His senses were heightened; every-thing seemed louder than it actually was. He could feel his own heart beat, hear his own breathing. He estimated that the others could be no more than two hundred metres behind them. How were they approaching? Had they spotted their enemy?

It must have been about two minutes before the kills came, and they came in quick succession. Sam heard the muted thud – surprisingly close-by – of one of his unit's suppressed weapons; moments later, he heard another.

'Two men down,' Mac reported. 'Let's hope no one shows up to do a changing of the fucking guard.'

Sam edged back to the Russian's body and listened in again on the bloodied comms earpiece. Nothing. Silence.

'We're clear,' he stated flatly. 'Damn it, what the hell happened there?'

In the clearing, Tyler and Cullen rose slowly from their lying-down position, looking for all the world in the eerie green hue of the night vision like corpses rising from the dead. 'Came out of fucking nowhere,' Tyler replied. From a distance, Sam watched as he went over to where Craven's body was lying. And then, echoing the suspicion that had been buzzing around in Sam's head: 'Almost like they knew we were coming. Jack just caught one. Could have been me.'

As Tyler spoke, the others came into sight, running into the clearing with their weapons raised. Mac spoke, his voice terse. 'Leave Craven there,' he instructed, almost purposefully lacking in emotion. They were still in country; the mission might be going tits up, but it still had to be completed. 'We'll scoop him up when we extract.'

Tyler hesitated. 'They were fucking waiting for us. We need to get out of here. What if the contact's been reported?'

'We're carrying on,' Mac overruled him. 'Get to the edge of the tree line. Matt, Steve, Hill – retrace steps back to original attacking positions. We'll reassess the situation when we've got a view on the camp. Quick, before anybody else decides to join the party.'

Sam looked at his watch. 03.27. They still had time before sunrise, but Tyler was right: they needed to watch their backs. It was never easy leaving the fallen behind; Sam had to break through a barrier of reluctance to make himself do it. But they had to keep moving. And he had to concentrate on the important stuff.

On Jacob.

As he ran towards the tree line, he found himself wondering what would happen if he found one of the guys about to put a bullet in his brother. It was an uncomfortable question and one which he quickly put from his mind.

The tree line, twenty metres ahead. And then, for the first time Sam laid eyes properly on the camp. It would take Mac and his team a couple more minutes to get back into their original positions, so in the meantime he could get his breath and gather his thoughts. Tyler and Cullen joined him, spaced out at ten-metre intervals, while Sam examined the training camp itself.

Just as the aerial map had suggested, there were three buildings. They started about twenty metres away from where Sam was standing. What they had originally been built for, he couldn't tell. They were very simple concrete blocks, long and low, with corrugated iron roofs and rusting metal doors. It was the kind of place you wouldn't look at twice; you'd probably think it was derelict. The buildings surrounded a courtyard, in which there was an old pick-up truck, as well as some oil drums and diesel canisters. Sam observed that one of the buildings was connected to an electricity pylon – this place might have been the arse end of nowhere, but there was power, which meant they could expect to be illuminated.

There was one other thing that caught his attention. In the gap between two of the buildings he saw the smaller, shed-like structure that he had observed on the map back at the briefing. And outside the shed, he noticed with a sharp intake of breath, a dog on a leash lay sleeping.

A vision hit his mind. Jacob, with a black Labrador at his side. He liked dogs more than he liked people, they used to say.

Was he alone, away from the others, in that little shed? Sam didn't know, but it seemed likely.

Mac's voice crackled over the comms. 'You in position?'

'Roger that,' Sam replied.

'Do you have a visual on the truck?'

'Yeah.'

'How far?'

'About twenty-five metres.' He felt his eyes narrowing. In an ideal world, the vehicle needed to be put out of action: in the frenzy that was about to occur, the last thing they wanted to do was have one of their targets making it to the pick-up and getting away. Exploding the tyres from this distance, however, was risky. Their weapons might be suppressed and next to noiseless, but a round going into one of those tyres was going to make a bang . . .

And then, slowly, Sam smiled, despite the events of the last few minutes. It wasn't exactly standard operating procedures, but when the unit was debriefed he could concoct a perfectly reasonable operational excuse for taking out the truck; and the noise could just give Jacob the few seconds warning that he needed.

He raised his weapon, quickly before anyone could instruct him to do otherwise. The moment the tyre burst the unit would move in. Silently. Deadly.

Sam fired. His aim was good. Through the NV he saw the shredded remains of the tyre explode into the air.

A bang. The truck jolted and sank down on one corner.

'*Jesus!*' Tyler hissed over the comms. 'Who was that?'

'Me,' Sam said. 'Don't want anyone doing a runner.'

'You'll wake the whole fucking camp . . .'

'*All right!*' Mac's voice snapped over the comms. 'Shut up, everyone.'

Sam felt a surge of gratitude towards his friend. 'There's a dog tied up to the north-west,' he said quickly. 'Don't want the fucker barking. I'll deal with it before we go in. Then we can hit the buildings.'

A pause.

'My job, Mac,' Sam continued cryptically into the comms.

More silence. And then, 'Roger that.'

Sam nodded with satisfaction. He set his jaw and prepared to skirt around the edge of the camp.

Towards the dog.

Towards the shed.

And towards whatever was inside.

★

He awoke. Like a drowned man unnaturally brought to life, he splashed through the surface tension of his sleep, his senses suddenly alert.

He blinked in the darkness, sitting up in his simple bed and instinctively feeling for the handgun that he always kept by his side. He knew the noises of this place: the occasional screech of an owl, now and then a truck trundling down the nearby road – though these were few and far between. But the bang that had awoken him? That was unusual. And he had come to learn that unusual meant suspicious.

Silently, but quickly, he stood up and pulled on his clothes. To the side of his bed was a window. The mechanism was old and rusted up – just like everything else in this shit hole – and it took him several goes to loosen it.

He opened the window. It was small; but not so small that he couldn't squeeze his way through. He wriggled through the opening, closed it again as best he could from the outside, then pressed his back to the wall and listened.

Listened hard.

His beard itched. He realised he was sweating.

He continued to listen, holding his breath so as to hear better.

Footsteps. He could definitely hear footsteps.

His eyes darted to and fro. He edged along the wall, reaching the corner where he stopped once more and held his breath. Firmly clutching his handgun, he raised it to shoulder height.

It had only ever been a matter of time before this happened. Somewhere deep down he had always suspected. Always suspected that they would send someone after him. But he wasn't going to give them the satisfaction.

Then he went tense.

Footsteps again.

There was someone approaching.

There was someone very close.

★

Sam ran towards the shed. When he was ten metres distant, he raised his weapon, aimed at the sleeping dog and fired.

The suppressed round slammed silently into the animal's body. It jolted, then lay still once more.

He ran up towards the shed. The door was closed. It was a wooden door, not visibly reinforced in any way with a locking system. No need to blow it off and risk a close-range shrapnel wound from the round ricocheting off the door. He shut his eyes and prepared to enter.

He didn't get the chance. When the voice came, it came from nowhere, as did its owner.

'*Drop your weapon!*'

Sam's body tensed up. His head was not turned towards his assailant and he knew that if he made any sudden movement, it would be fatal.

'I don't want to kill you,' the voice hissed. 'But I will if you don't drop the gun.'

Sam's body went hot then cold. He recognised the voice, of course. How could he not?

He lowered his gun, but didn't drop it.

And then he spoke. Quietly. Hoarsely. But firmly and with one hand over his comms mike.

'It's me, Jacob,' he said. 'It's Sam.'

ELEVEN

A pause. It seemed to go on for ever.

'*Drop the fucking weapon,*' Jacob hissed. He nudged the butt of the handgun against Sam's arm.

Slowly, Sam bent down and placed the Diemaco on the floor. He straightened up and removed the NV goggles from his face.

It took a moment for his natural night vision to adjust to the darkness as he turned round to face his assailant. A moment for his brother's features to emerge from the blackness like a Polaroid slowly developing. He wore a scraggly beard and looked older. Leaner. Nothing could disguise those eyes, however – those dark, intense eyes that seemed to look right through you. He wore rough combat trousers, a pale T-shirt and a sturdy khaki jacket. His feet were clad in black leather boots.

'*Sam?*' his brother hissed incredulously. 'What the hell . . .?'

'*You have to get out of here,*' Sam interrupted him. '*Now,* Jacob. There's six other Regiment guys with me and we've got orders to kill everybody here. You included. Jacob, you *have* to go.'

No movement. Mac's voice over the comms: 'Sam, where are you?'

'*They're going to come to find out what's happened to me any second.*'

His brother's eyes were confused. Jacob stared hard at

Sam, almost as though he hadn't heard what his younger brother was saying.

'*Jacob!*'

Jacob blinked, then looked around. He nodded and stepped back as Sam bent down to retrieve his gun. The two brothers looked at each other again. And then Jacob spoke. His voice was low.

'They'll tell you things, Sam,' he said cryptically as he took a couple more steps back, retreating further into the inky night. 'Things about me. Don't forget that you're my brother. Don't believe them.'

'What are you doing here, J.?' Sam asked, words suddenly tumbling out despite the urgent need for his brother to get away quickly. 'What's going on? What are you doing with these people?'

The expression on Jacob's face didn't change. 'Don't let them trick you, Sam,' he whispered. 'It's what they're good at.' Sam felt a sudden pang of loss. He was forcing Jacob away, but all he really wanted was to be with his brother. 'Things aren't what they seem, Sam,' Jacob pressed. 'I *swear* to you they're not what they seem.'

And in an instant, disappearing as swiftly as he had appeared, Jacob's dark features melted away into the night. Sam heard the heavy sound of his brother's footsteps running away, westwards into the forest.

'*Sam!*' It was Mac's voice on the comms. 'Where the hell are you?'

Sam felt himself churning up, but he couldn't allow himself the luxury of hesitation. He quickly pulled his NV goggles on, trying to readjust his mind to the job in hand. His brother had escaped; now he needed to make sure that nobody else did. 'Job done,' he replied. 'I'm on my way back now.'

He hurried round the corner and emerged into the courtyard. The rest of them had advanced. Tyler and Cullen stood on either side of the door to the westernmost building. The others had also taken up their positions, two men to each of the other buildings. Cullen gave him a thumbs-up.

'Mac? Do you copy?' he spoke into the comms.

'Roger that.'

'We're ready.'

A pause. The bloodbath was about to begin.

'Go!' Mac instructed.

Cullen held up three fingers. Two fingers. One finger. With all his force he kicked the door in and instantly they were inside.

The door itself was situated halfway along the building. It opened on to one long room, a dormitory of some description. There were eight beds, all positioned against one wall. By each bed was a low locker, a chair and very little else. The place had the bare, austere feeling of an army barracks. Sam indicated with a quick point of his finger that Cullen and Tyler should take the right-hand side, while he took the left. They split up and went about their work.

There was movement in the dormitory. Nothing much – just a few bodies drowsily stirring. Through the NV goggles, Sam could see a couple of the occupants sitting up in their simple beds, staring blindly into the darkness and groping sleepily. These were the targets he'd have to eliminate first, before they had the chance to start a panic. Sam raised his Diemaco and aimed directly at the head of one of the sluggish figures.

As he prepared to squeeze the trigger, however, an image flashed cross his mind. It was Clare Corbett, sitting at her kitchen table, her face stained with tears of terror as she recounted what she knew. The red-light runners. These young men, targeted and groomed by MI5.

Sam set his jaw. He wasn't paid to think about the rights and wrongs of his orders. He was just paid to carry them out. What was more, if he was to cover his tracks, he had to do so without hesitation. Already he had heard the thump from Cullen's weapon as he eliminated one of the targets.

He fired. The round slammed straight into his target's neck. The young man was thrown back against the wall, by the force of the round. The bullet exited, tearing a huge hole in the flesh through which a neat, sickly pool of blood slowly poured out. He had slipped to the floor and was on his way over to the dark side. By that time, however, Sam's sights were elsewhere. He strode down the room without moving his weapon from the firing position. His second target was also sitting upright before the round hit. Not for long. Numbers three and four were just lying there, asleep. They would never have known what hit them.

He turned and looked at Cullen who was already striding towards the door. 'Then there were none,' he announced into the comms.

Mac's voice came crackling back. 'And the same here,' he stated grimly. 'Job done, gentlemen. Let's do the house-keeping and get the hell out of here.'

★

The unit retraced their footsteps around that silent training camp, checking that the targets were indeed dead – Sigs in hand in case they needed to administer a final, fatal headshot. They went about their work in a kind of grim silence – not out of respect for the guys they had just killed, but out of professional efficiency and because now that the operation was nearing its end, the reality of Craven's death was beginning to sink in. It had happened so quickly. So randomly. It could easily have been any of them. It just happened to be Jack Craven who would be returning home in a body bag. It just happened to be *his* family who would be mourning their loss with scant knowledge about the circumstances of his death. Part of Sam thought, *Fuck it,*

174

there's no room for sentimental bullshit here. People died on ops. They all knew that. They all knew the risk. That didn't make it any easier, though.

Despite all this, Sam couldn't help feeling a faint surge of exhilaration. Jacob had escaped. He'd done what he came here to do. Nobody spoke as they briskly conducted their business, other than to give or acknowledge instructions. Certainly they didn't discuss who had been waiting for them, or why. They just knew they had to get out quickly.

They split up. Davenport and Andrews were despatched to reclaim Craven's body. Webb and Tyler went to retrieve the freefall rigs. Cullen was sent to the road. This was where the Hercules would come in to land, but they needed to ensure that no civilian vehicles would be on that stretch when the plane touched down. Perhaps the dope farmers who inhabited this part of the world would put their hallucinations down to overenthusiastic consumption of their own crop. But perhaps not. The tough little Scot took a supply of stinger spikes with him, sharp metal road blocks that would deflate the tyres of any car that went over them. He would use the spikes to cut off a stretch of road at both ends, while they waited to extract. The dope farmers would no doubt be distinctly miffed by the shredding of their tyres, but it was better than being crushed by the undercarriage of a Hercules.

Sam and Mac remained at the camp. Mac called the air team with instructions to prepare to extract, while Sam went through the buildings yet again with a small but powerful digital camera, taking a visual record of the deceased.

It was a grisly job. During the hit, Sam had not been aware of the rank smell of all these men living together with little in the way of facilities. Now that his senses had more time to absorb such things, he realised just how bad the stink was. But of course, there was another smell for his senses to deal with now. The smell of death. They had not been long dead, but already that familiar stench was leaching pungently into the air.

In all he counted eighteen of them. Eighteen young, British corpses, assassinated by their own government. Many of them had been hit in the face. Their faces had caved inwards from the impact of the round, noses sunk in, mouths collapsed. It was like someone had taken a giant hammer to their skulls. Sam took their pictures anyway. Some of them had been rolled onto their fronts by the force of the rounds. More than once, as he turned their still-warm bodies over, blood gushed out of their wounds like a fizzy drink foaming from a bottle. As they had been expecting, all the faces were Caucasian. White by race, white by death and white by the bleaching effect of the camera's flash as he systematically recorded the gruesome evidence of their night's work. In some corner of his mind he wondered if the dead men really were British, as they'd been led to believe. Why were they being protected by a Spetsnaz unit if that was the case? But on the wall by one of the men he came across a centrefold from a pornographic magazine. The model had her legs wide open and by her head there was some writing. He read enough of it to see that it was English before moving on, quickly, racing from bed to bed like some demonic paparazzo desperate to get to his next subject.

When all the photos were taken, Sam slipped away – checking first to make sure he hadn't been observed – up to the shed. The dead dog lay outside in a pool of blood. Sam ignored it. He took a deep breath, opened the door and stepped inside.

It was a tiny space, just enough for a low camp bed and a few square metres of standing room. Although the bed was unmade, showing all the signs of having been abandoned in a tearing hurry, the rest of the bunk area displayed a military neatness, the few belongings tidily and precisely squared away. Sam looked over his shoulder to check that nobody had entered, then opened a small cabinet by the bed and rummaged inside.

There was very little there. A few clothes – it was difficult to tell what in the gloom – some chocolate and a bottle of water. He found what felt like a small piece of card; pulling it out, he realised it was a photograph. An old one. With a pang he recognised his mother and father in the early years of their marriage. It was surreal, seeing that image of his father out here, miles from home, when in fact he was wasting away in a Hereford hospital. He stuffed it in a pocket. Back in the locker, his fingertips came across something else. Something hard. Rectangular. He pulled it out and examined it. It was a laptop computer. Sam reached into his backpack and pulled out his torch so that he could look closer at it. The thing was well-worn and scuffed, though the case was hard and durable. He gave half a moment's thought to opening it up and seeing what was inside, but he quickly decided against it. If any of the guys found him doing that, they'd start asking questions; and he wasn't sure he wanted to answer them . . .

Sam stuffed the torch and the laptop into his pack, before hurriedly returning to the centre of the camp.

As he jogged back outside, to his surprise, he found himself thinking of Clare Corbett's words. '*Those people at the training camp. Are you really going to kill them, Sam?*' It crossed his mind that he should feel some sort of sympathy for these dead men. Pawns in some game they didn't understand. But he didn't. Or rather, he couldn't. His mind was too preoccupied. There were too many things racing through it. The adrenaline rush of the mission. Craven, dead. The need to extract quickly.

And Jacob. Above all, Jacob. His brother's perplexed, frightened face. His mysterious words. Sam pictured him even now racing away from the camp, not knowing if he was being followed or why the Regiment had been sent to kill him. Not knowing what the future held. It seemed wrong that Jacob should be so close to him and yet so far from Sam's help now. What had Jacob meant? *Things aren't what they seem . . .*

'Damn it,' he whispered to himself as he hurried back to the centre of the courtyard. 'You can say that again.'

Mac was waiting for him, alone. He switched off his comms and indicated that Sam should do the same. 'Well?' he said finally when they knew none of the others could hear them.

'Well what?'

His friend raised an eyebrow. 'Did you find him?'

Sam avoided his eye. 'No,' he lied. He didn't know why. It just felt like the right thing to do.

Mac cast him a level gaze that did nothing to hide his suspicion.

'What?' Sam demanded. He felt himself jutting out his chin, a sudden heat running through his veins. 'Fucking what?'

'Sounded like you went dark for a couple of minutes back there, Sam. Sure you didn't see anything?'

He started squaring up to Mac. 'What the hell are you saying?'

They had barely ever argued before, let alone fought; but Sam was seeing red and for a heated moment he didn't know how long that record would last. If Mac felt threatened, though, he didn't show it. On the contrary. He drew himself up to his full height and stared Sam out.

'I'm not saying anything, Sam. Just remember how much *I'm* risking staying quiet about this, hey? Just remember that.'

Sam didn't reply. His eyes continued to be locked with Sam's for a few further uncomfortable seconds, then he turned and walked away.

Davenport and Andrews were the first to return. They carried Craven's corpse with them in a field stretcher – little more than a body bag with poles along the side for ease of transport. Davenport had Craven's weapon; Andrews his backpack. Moving quickly to the side of the truck where Sam and Mac were waiting, they gently eased Craven's body down to the ground, then straightened themselves back up with the heaviness of men who had been carrying a mental load as well as a physical one.

'It was a clean kill,' Matt Andrews said quietly, the troop medic's black skin shining with sweat in the moonlight. 'He wouldn't even have known what hit him.'

'Suppressed AK-47 round, that's what,' Sam said. With everything else that had happened, he realised he hadn't shared with the others his information about the welcoming party. 'The shooters were Russian. One of the guys I nailed was packing a GM-90.'

Davenport gave a low whistle. 'Serious bit of kit for a stroll through the woods.'

'Yeah,' Andrews added. 'Bit much for shooting pigeons.'

'Spetsnaz?' Mac suggested. He avoided Sam's eye and it was clear that the tension between them had far from dissipated.

'That's my guess.'

An unsettling silence descended upon the four of them as they grappled with the implications, a silence made only deeper by the presence of their dead colleague. When Tyler and Webb returned with the freefall rigs, Mac brought them up to speed. Tyler listened to the news with an expression of increasing bitterness. 'Fucking Russki *bastards!*' he spat, walking away from them before suddenly and violently kicking the body of the pick-up truck. Craven had been his friend, and no amount of training could teach a man how to deal with losing his mate.

There was no time to stand around consoling him,

though. 03.45. Dawn was approaching. 'Get to the road,' Mac ordered. 'The bird's on stand-by. Let's get out of here.'

Nobody argued with that. They gathered up their gear and their fallen colleague and hurried away from the camp, towards the road which was about fifty metres to the north. Cullen was waiting for them, a solitary figure, short and squat. 'You took your fucking time,' he observed, before looking up and down the road and indicating the somewhat rickety-looking telegraph poles that lined both sides. If the Hercules tried to land along this stretch of road, its wings would be damaged by the poles and they'd be walking home. They would have to come down.

'Det cord?' Mac announced. 'Who's got it?'

It was Tyler. From his pack he pulled two reels of what looked for all the world like white washing line. Hang your clothes on this, though, and you'd get a nasty surprise. Tyler threw one of the reels to Sam, who quickly started to unfurl it. On the far side of the road he ran to the closest pole, wound the det cord five times around the wood, then trailed it on to the next pole and repeated the process. Tyler did the same on the other side of the road. They each had enough cord to wrap it around eight telegraph poles; they were widely spaced, however. It would give the Hercules enough space to land.

Sam and Tyler ran back to where the others were waiting for them. Tyler removed two detonators from his pack – small silver tubes, each about the size of a pencil – and a roll of tape. Expertly taping the detonators to the cord, he then fished out his clacker – a small, handheld electrical generator – and a roll of wire. He connected the clacker to the detonator, then turned round and nodded at the rest of them.

The team jogged back to a safe twenty-metre distance. Tyler held up one hand and they prepared themselves for the bang.

The det cord exploded with a ferocious, deafening crack, like a hundred rounds all being fired at the same time. It echoed in the air, an immense clap of thunder, and would have been heard, Sam reckoned, for miles around.

By Jacob, no doubt, wherever he was.

The very instant the noise of the exploding det cord slammed into their eardrums, the telegraph poles toppled, falling away from the road and turning it into a perfectly serviceable runway. Instantly Mac was on the radio, reading out their exact coordinates from his small GPS device and requesting immediate extraction. Then he turned to the men. 'Five minutes!' he shouted. 'Get in position.'

Sam checked his watch. 03.56. Only minutes till dawn. It had been a long, dark night. One of the longest Sam could remember. The blackness, though, was just starting to give way to a faint glimmer of morning. It was only the vaguest hint of daylight, but it was enough to remind Sam of everything that had happened during the preceding hours of darkness. He suddenly felt exhausted, mentally and physically. But flagging now wasn't an option. They were still on the ground and the operation was not yet completed. Not until they were safely back in the belly of the Hercules could he even think of letting the pace drop.

The unit divided into two, three on one side of the road, four on the other. The bird might have their coordinates, and they might have a clear landing space. But there was still something they could do to help guide it safely to earth. Each man removed his torch from his pack. They then lay on the ground, spaced out at regular intervals along either side of the road, and shone the torches upwards. From the air, it would mark their positions as clearly as the lights along an ordinary runway.

Sam lay there uncomfortably in the almost-darkness. They would get scant warning, he knew, about the plane's arrival:

the roar of its engines would only be audible to them when the Hercules had emerged from the dark sky and its wings were practically above them.

He waited. Waiting was always the worst. It somehow felt as though you weren't in control. Five minutes ticked by, excruciatingly slowly.

Sure enough, the boom of the engines was sudden and thunderous. It seemed to come from nowhere. As the dark shadow of the wings passed over them, Sam felt his whole body tremble with the proximity of the aircraft. The landing wheels screeched as they hit firm ground. Sam heard an immediate change in the timbre of the engines as they were thrust into reverse to bring the bird to a sudden, abrupt halt. He pushed himself to his feet, as did the others. Half a mile down the road, the Hercules was already turning. They raced around and gathered up their gear and Craven's body bag, waited for the aircraft to come to a standstill and then rushed towards it. The tailgate was lowered and, with the loadmaster ushering them on with urgent sweeps of his arms, they hurried up into the plane.

Craven's body was strapped to a stretcher bed attached to the side of the plane; the rest of the gear was stowed underneath. As the men prepared for take-off, the tailgate was already closing. The aircraft had barely been on the ground a couple of minutes before it started to retrace its steps, accelerating quickly up the road. Once it was airborne, it started a sudden, steep incline, ferrying the unit speedily away from the location of their op and back to the relative safety — if safety it was — of the base back in Bagram.

And as the Hercules soared into the air, Sam's mind was concentrated on only one thing. It was not the op — that was past history now, water under the bridge; it wasn't the grisly collection of assassinated corpses they'd left in the training camp and on the twiggy floor of the surrounding woods; it wasn't even Craven's death, though he carried with him the same nagging sense of loss and anger that he knew they were all experiencing.

It was this: the image of one man, bearded and dark-eyed, running with fierce desperation through the unfamiliar surroundings of Kazakhstan. His blood would be pumping. Most likely he would be more than a little scared. His mind would be focussed on the road ahead; on surviving; but equally he would be keeping one eye behind him.

Because once somebody has been sent to kill you, you never stop looking over your shoulder.

PART TWO

TWELVE

Run.

Jacob Redman kept that one thought in his mind. It was difficult, because other thoughts were jostling for attention. The Regiment, out there to kill him. To kill all of them. Sam. Jesus, *Sam.* When his brother had appeared, Jacob had thought he was seeing a ghost. What other explanation could there have been for Sam randomly turning up in one of the most obscure corners of central Asia? He didn't know what the noise was that had woken him up; he *did* know that if he was in charge of a Regiment unit like that, nobody would have been allowed to stir until the job was well and truly underway. And they wouldn't be stirring afterwards. No, somebody had made a noise to warn him. It must have been his brother.

He put that thought from his head. *Just keep running. It's all you can do.*

He followed the course of the road, but kept away from it, choosing instead to run along the edge of the high hemp fields where his khaki jacket at least would give him some manner of protection. What he would have given for one of the digital camouflage suits Sam had been wearing. But that wasn't an option. He just had to make do with what he had.

A deafening bang.

Jacob threw himself to the floor, his hands instinctively reaching for his weapon. *What the hell was that?* Explosives of some kind, back towards the camp. The thunderclap echoed across the skies. What were they doing? Blowing the buildings? He shook his head. Why would they do that? They'd just want to be in and out. He was breathing heavily. There was dew on the hemp fields and it soaked his skin.

He pushed himself back up and continued running. He must have put a good mile between himself and the camp. A little slower now: he needed to conserve his energy and by the sound of it he wasn't being followed, at least not closely. After another five-minute run he even allowed himself to stop and catch his breath again. It was as he was standing there, his back to the hemp field that he saw it. It seemed to come from nowhere, appearing in the sky like a UFO. And as it passed, perhaps thirty metres above Jacob's head, the animal roared, a huge, mechanical, whining roar that filled his ears and the skies. Jacob watched it pass, his face impassive. He knew what it was, of course. He'd flown in enough C-130s in his time. Who knows, maybe he'd even flown in that one. A curious mixture of emotions washed over him as he stood there, looking in the direction the plane had been heading. He couldn't see it any more, but he could imagine it turning, its tailgate opening and the men bundling inside. And he knew it would be back. Three minutes? Four?

He was right. The Hercules had barely passed him the first time before its great shadow appeared overhead once more. Jacob looked up as it rose steeply into the sky, ignoring the battering his ears were taking.

'Well done, Sam,' he muttered quietly to himself as once more it disappeared from view. 'Good lad.'

The Regiment had extracted. It meant Jacob was safe. Or at least safer. He certainly didn't want to be anywhere near the buildings when it was discovered that they contained a couple of dozen murdered corpses. People all over the world were adept at putting two and two together to make five; but in these rural backwaters even more so. The hemp farmers who brought them their supplies in return for fistfuls of notes knew his face. He needed to put as much distance between himself and the camp as possible; and he needed to make sure nobody saw him do it. He continued to run.

Night was beginning to turn into morning. He cursed the arrival of daylight. It made it more difficult to stay hidden. The road was badly kept and potholed; on either side, the endless hemp fields, deep green.

The half light became full light. Still he ran. Early morning became mid-morning. Still he ran. Seven miles, he estimated. Eight. The sun started to become hot. Jacob's clothes, which had been damp with the dew, were now soaked with sweat. He needed water, but it was almost midday before he came across the thin trickle of a stream. Every ounce of his being shrieked at him take a few mouthfuls, but he held back. Instead, he followed the trickle upstream for several metres, checking there was nothing in its path to foul the water, before finally, hungrily, swallowing mouthfuls of it down his parched throat. His body gratefully accepted the liquid and he felt revived, like a wilted plant that had just been watered.

It was too hot to run now, so he walked. But he still kept away from the road. He hadn't seen a single vehicle all morning, but it was safer this way. The sooner he could get to a village, the better. To the best of his knowledge the nearest settlement was about thirty klicks along the road from the camp, but he couldn't tell how far he had come. Twenty klicks, perhaps? Twenty-five?

It was mid-afternoon before the village appeared up ahead, shimmering slightly in the warmth. Jacob stopped at a distance, squinting at the settlement for a while before planning his next move. He couldn't stop people noticing him walking into town, with his unkempt, sweaty hair and beard and his dirty clothes. But if he came from this direction, and people started asking questions, he might find them difficult to answer. So he turned away from the road into the surrounding fields, and circumvented the village at a distance of about a mile. It took him an hour to rejoin the road on the other side, but it meant he could enter town from the north, putting any inquisitive villagers off the scent.

It was a poor, featureless place. A network of telegraph poles dominated the sky, criss-crossing over the buildings like a cat's cradle of wires. Below them, the buildings themselves were irregular but simple – breeze-block constructions, most of them, some rendered and painted white, the majority left a bland concrete grey because that was cheaper. They had high-pitched roofs, made mostly of corrugated iron; and shutters, some of which had been painted in bright colours.

The main road bisected the village; in the centre was a junction from which other, smaller roads, little more than dirt tracks, spread out. The ground on the side of the roads and around the buildings was a thick, dusty sand. Aside from a few trees, there was little in the way of greenery.

Jacob attracted plenty of stares as he strode into the village – grizzled male Kazakhstanis mostly, with Mongol-looking faces, weathered skin, old clothes and beaten-up baseball caps embroidered with the names of American cities they would never see. They certainly didn't look friendly, but that, Jacob knew, was the way of villagers the world over. He ignored their stares as he continued into the centre of the village.

He passed stalls on the side of the street. They were small, rickety things manned by small, rickety stallholders. Some sold watermelons, others sold different kinds of fruit. At one there was a pig roasting on a spit. The smell was almost enough to make Jacob swoon, but the look he received from the owner didn't encourage his patronage. It wasn't that Jacob was scared of these people. He just didn't want to make a scene. As far as he could tell, there was only one actual shop. It was distinguished from the other buildings by virtue of a curved frontage and steps leading up to the entrance. Painted on the white, curved wall in bright yellow letters was a sign, but as he didn't read the Kazakh language, Jacob couldn't tell what it said. He stepped inside anyway.

It was gloomy in the shop, and bare. A fat woman sat behind a makeshift counter. She glowered at Jacob as he entered, keeping guard over a tawdry collection of items many of which Jacob could not tell what they were – tins, mostly, with indecipherable writing and pictures of disgusting-looking food. A few wizened vegetables in a couple of crates. Among the junk, however, some familiar packaging jumped out at him: Western chocolate bars and fizzy drinks. He checked in his back pocket – there were a few crumpled notes. Not enough to buy very much, but it would keep him in sugar-rich instant energy for a day or two. He grabbed a couple of handfuls of chocolate and some cans of Coke, then returned to the counter where the woman wordlessly accepted his money.

He was ravenous. On the steps outside he devoured two of the chocolate bars and a can of drink. That made him feel a bit better. The remainder he jammed into the pockets of his trousers and jacket, then he continued to walk around the village.

Still the flat looks came. Flinty and disagreeable. Jacob ignored them. He was busy with other things. Busy looking. There weren't many vehicles and what there were did not inspire much confidence, being mostly tiny, Russian run-arounds. Towards the western edge of the town, however, he saw a dwelling place on one edge of a square that was bigger than most. It had a low wall topped with spiky railings running around the outside and a set of heavy, metal gates. Beyond the wall was a rare patch of green and, unusually, the building itself was two storeys high. Its shutters were painted electric blue. To the right of the wall, but clearly still part of the same compound, was a small garage.

Jacob pulled another can of Coke from his jacket and loitered. This looked a likely place. He sipped nonchalantly from the drink and started to stake it out. Thirty metres away there were children playing in the street with a football. They didn't approach; indeed they cast him the same mistrustful looks that he received from everyone else. But a few of them, he noticed, had a game of kicking the ball close to him, a kind of unspoken dare. Pushing the boundaries. Boys will be boys.

Movement at the front of the house. Two men exited. They were big and wore unfashionable denim jackets that bulged in such a way as to suggest they concealed firearms. Behind them was a much smaller man. He had olive skin, a moustache, and tightly wound black hair. He walked behind the bigger men, but it was obvious that he was in charge. In charge of the men and, in his own mind at least, in charge of everything.

One of the bodyguards opened the gate. The kids stopped playing, grabbing their ball and bunching up together on the far side of the road. They jabbered quietly, but Jacob couldn't understand what they were saying. He just watched as the three men walked towards the garage.

One of the kids, presumably as the result of a dare, took the football and kicked it. The men paid no attention. One of them, though, noticed Jacob, who put his head down and walked quickly away. Only when he reached the corner of the square did he glance round. He saw the garage open to reveal a truck. Nothing fancy, but a sturdy, elderly four-by-four that would suit his purposes perfectly.

He wasn't followed.

On the outskirts of town, far from the road, he took shelter in a ditch. It was, at least, dry and there was nobody about so he didn't worry about being seen. The hot afternoon waned slowly. He took the opportunity to rest and plan the rest of the day's activities. The guy with the two stooges, he surmised, was most probably the local hemp baron. Not the kingpin – his place wasn't nearly flush enough for that; just some kind of middleman who the real drug lords would stamp on in an instant if it suited them, but who until then was content to swan around the town like he owned the place. Jacob knew his type – he'd seen them in all parts of the world where people made their money harvesting narcotics.

It took an age for night to fall; an age during which Jacob could do nothing but wait. And think. In his mind he replayed the events of earlier that morning a thousand times. There was a weird kind of symmetry to what had happened. All his life it had been Jacob looking out for Sam. That was just the way it was – Sam had been the kind of kid that needed looking out for. Constantly. Now the tables had been turned and it was Sam who had saved Jacob's neck.

He felt himself getting angry as he always did when he thought about his family.

The silvery moon rose before it was fully dark. It was already bright, though: it often was in this part of the world. He had watched many of these moons rise and fall. With the onset of full darkness came the stars. Heaven was full of them, amazingly bright. There was very little ambient light in the Chu Valley. It made the sky look like a Christmas card.

It was past midnight when Jacob eased his way out of the ditch. He ate some more chocolate and then began tramping his way back into the village.

The streets were deserted, but the moon was so bright it was almost like midday. He found his way with ease. Having memorised the layout of the network of streets, he avoided the road in which the hemp baron's house was located, coming upon it from a more circuitous route.

In the night air an animal howled.

He stepped gingerly into view of the house. A guard stood at the gates. One of the guys from earlier? Perhaps. From this distance he couldn't tell. He was leaning lazily against the wall, with a rifle in one hand. Jacob could see the orange spot of a cigarette glowing like a firefly in front of his face. He stepped back into the shadows again and considered his options. If he was to proceed, the guard needed to be out of his way. But how was he going to do that? The guy had a good field of vision. It didn't matter how quickly he ran towards him, he'd still be able to raise his rifle and have a go . . .

Jacob retraced his steps. The guard was in position to stop anyone getting into the compound; so the last thing he would expect was for an assailant to be there already. He approached the house from the back. The wall was not high – low enough to scale, certainly. Jacob pulled himself up and held on to the large spiky railings, a little taller than he was, to peer into the compound. All was dark. He heaved himself up. His feet clattered slightly against the metal railings, causing a hidden animal somewhere nearby to scuttle away; but he managed to get one foot in between two of the spikes and push himself over, landing heavily on the ground below.

He kept minutely still for a moment, waiting for the clump of his landing to dissipate and listening for any signal that he might have disturbed someone; but there was nothing, just the recurring howling of the animal in the distance. Jacob got to his feet, grabbed his handgun and crept silently round to the front of the house.

The guard was still there, in front of the gates, and still smoking – Jacob could see the smoke rising above his head. He crept towards the gate, his handgun outstretched. Within seconds he was standing right behind the unsuspecting guard.

He put the gun through the railings and tapped the end of the barrel twice against the man's skull.

The guard dropped his cigarette and spun round. When he saw Jacob he made to grab his own weapon; but Jacob shook his head sharply and instead the man stepped nervously backwards.

The gates were not locked. The gun still pointing at its target, Jacob opened them and stepped outside. The guard couldn't take his eyes off the weapon; so when Jacob delivered a sharp, sudden blow with his free hand into the man's neck, it must have come as a surprise. He crumpled to the floor, unconscious.

Quickly, silently, Jacob closed the gates, strapped the man's rifle – an old Russian-made AK-47 – over his shoulder and dragged the body towards the garage. These doors were not locked either – why bother when there's a security guard on duty? – so they were quickly inside.

Jacob worked with haste. He rifled through the security guard's pockets, finding nothing more useful than a small amount of money, then turned his attention to the truck. There were several canisters of fuel in the garage, so he loaded these into the back along with the AK-47, before taking his place in the driver's seat. No key. That wouldn't be problem.

There were two ways he could start it. A screwdriver driven deep into the ignition with a hammer then turned with some kind of wrench would work; but there was no screwdriver, no hammer and no wrench, and besides, it would create more noise than he wanted to make. Better to hotwire. He pulled the plastic casing away from under the steering column and located the wiring loom, which he ripped out with a firm tug. There were five or six wires here. It was just a matter of finding which ones were hot. He touched two at a time together, methodically, and before long the truck had coughed into life.

Jacob jumped out and opened the garage doors. Seconds later he was away. He drove slowly through the village streets, sensibly, so as not arouse suspicion. But as soon as he was on the main road, he floored it.

Jacob Redman was happy to be getting the hell out of Dodge.

THIRTEEN

The mood in the Hercules was bleak.

No one spoke. They just sat there, all eyes on Craven's bloodied body bag. Sam knew what they were all thinking: that it could have been any of them; that in situations like that, survival is just a fluke; that maybe, if one of them had looked another way or been a bit more on the ball, Craven would still be alive, joking with them in the afterglow of a mission successfully completed. But Craven wasn't going to laugh with anybody ever again. And as they flew south, Sam wondered if the same might be true of himself.

He could feel the tension with Mac. His old friend was avoiding his eye. Sam didn't really blame him. He didn't deserve to be kept in the dark. Why then, was Sam doing it?

The plane shuddered. Just turbulence.

He was doing it, he realised, because he, too, was still in the dark. Jacob might be safe, or safer, but Sam had just as many questions and hardly any answers. And when you don't know what you're talking about, maybe it's best to keep your mouth shut.

He thought of Jacob. Where was he now? Running blindly, no doubt. Keeping hidden. Wondering why the Regiment had been sent to kill him and how many others there were with the same aim . . .

It was fully day by the time the Hercules started losing height. Sam would never have thought it would be a relief to touch down in Afghanistan, but that was exactly how he felt. When the aircraft came to a halt and the tailgate opened once more, sunlight and warmth flooded in. Sam staggered, exhausted, on to the tarmac with his Diemaco slung over his back and the others following in a ragged group.

Members of the squadron were waiting for them. Not everyone, but at least twenty – enough to make it clear that word of Craven's death had preceded them. They stood grim-faced and respectful, not saying anything to the returning soldiers, because they knew there was nothing to say. Sam avoided their gazes. Craven's death wasn't his fault; even if he hadn't had other plans on that mission, the kid would still have bought it. But he couldn't help feeling a twinge of guilt. Keeping things from your mates like that wasn't the Regiment way. Now that it was over, it made him feel bad.

By the entrance to the aircraft hangar where they had first arrived was the spook who had briefed them. He showed no signs of having been up all night. His clothes, despite the already uncomfortable heat, were neat. There were no bags under his eyes. He addressed Sam, because Sam was the first to arrive at the hangar.

'Care to tell me what the hell went on out there?'

Sam stopped. He turned slowly to look at the man.

'What?'

'I said, care to tell me what the hell went on out there?'

Stay calm, Sam told himself. He could feel his blood like lava under his skin. 'I thought,' he replied as mildly as he was able, 'that perhaps you could tell us that. There was a waiting party for us. Russian special forces. A bit of an intelligence fuck-up – I'd say it was *you* that's got the explaining to do.'

A voice from behind. Mac. Quiet. 'Take it easy, Sam.'

But the spook spoke over him. 'Listen to me, soldier . . .'

Something snapped in Sam. Blinded by a sudden rage, he stepped towards the spook before he could even finish speaking, grabbing him by his collar and pushing him roughly against the wall. '*No*,' he hissed. 'You fucking well listen to me, sunshine . . .' The spook weighed nothing; his square glasses fell from his face and his previous look of smug resolve had changed to one of alarm. Sam sneered at him, but as he held the guy up against the wall, the words just seemed to dissolve from his mind, leaving only the anger.

Hands on his shoulders, pulling him back. 'Leave him, Sam.' Mac's voice. Not loud, but firm.

Time stood still. Sam felt the spook trembling. With a contemptuous flick of his hands he allowed the guy to fall. His knees buckled as he hit the ground, but he managed to stay standing. Back on terra firma, however, the anger returned to his face. He opened his mouth to deliver some sort of reprimand; but then Mac was there. Like a father hushing a small child, he put one finger to the spook's lips. 'Tell you what, pal,' he said. 'Do yourself a favour and shut the fuck up, okay?'

The spook looked at Mac, then at Sam, then at the half dozen other burly SAS men that had surrounded him. His face twitched.

'Your flight back to Brize Norton leaves in half an hour.'

Mac nodded with satisfaction. 'Good lad,' he said, making no attempt to avoid being patronising. He turned to Sam. 'Come on, mate,' he said. 'Let's get ready.'

Sam looked down at the floor, suddenly embarrassed about the way he'd been with Mac. 'All right,' he mumbled.

They walked away together. But as they did, the spook called out from behind them, emboldened perhaps by the fact that they were leaving. 'Don't think that's the end of it!' he shouted. 'You'll pay for that!' His voice sounded ridiculously poncy, like the bully in the playground of a posh school.

It just so happened that as the spook called out to them, Craven's body was being wheeled off the Hercules. Sam turned back to the man, but this time he knew he could keep himself under control.

'We already did,' he spat. 'We already did.'

And with that he turned, pleased to be leaving Bagram – and that nob-jockey spook – behind him.

★

He didn't need a sleeping tablet to knock himself out on the return journey. None of the boys in the troop did. He simply hung his hammock on the other side of the plane to where Craven's stretcher was attached and within minutes of being airborne he was asleep. A deep and dreamless sleep, despite the hum of the jet engines and the troubles of the night before.

It was around midday when they stepped out onto the tarmac of Brize Norton. The air was misty and damp – a thousand miles from the clear, dry heat of northern Afghanistan. With a sickening lurch, he saw a regular civilian ambulance parked close to the plane, its blue light flashing silently in the misty air, its rear doors open. That was for Craven; the rest of them were to be transported in the same two white buses that had brought them to the RAF base in the first place. Only this time, there was an addition.

At the foot of the steps leading from the aircraft, an MOD policeman stood counting them all off. He wore a white, open-necked shirt, black body armour and a protective helmet. In his fist there was a Heckler and Koch MP7. He didn't look like he was there to welcome the lads back from holiday.

There were four more of them, all tooled up, all standing in such a formation as to encourage the men straight on to the buses. 'What's with the plate hangers?' one of the guys asked the policeman at the bottom of the stairs as he passed. 'Worried we're going to run riot?'

The policeman remained expressionless. 'Just move on to the bus,' he ordered.

A silence among the men as they were herded by these armed police on to their transports, and not a happy one. As they took their seats, a discontented murmur arose. Sam and Mac sat together. They didn't speak. They didn't need to. They knew something was wrong. They watched through the window as Craven's body was loaded into the ambulance, then driven out of sight at a funereal speed, the vehicle's flashing light like some kind of beacon. But it wasn't the only flashing light they'd be seeing. Once the doors of the buses were closed up, two black police vehicles arrived. Their windows were blacked out, but they, too, had the emergency lights blinking on top. The convoy pulled away, one MOD vehicle at the front, the other at the back.

'Where are we going?' one wag shouted from behind. 'Hereford or Wormwood bloody Scrubbs?'

A smatter of laughter. Sam didn't join in; he glanced at Mac, who returned his look with a raised eyebrow. 'I think our little secret might be out,' he murmured quietly, so as not to be heard.

Sam looked out of the window. More British Army soldiers congregated glumly outside the main terminal building. The sight of the two white buses being escorted off the airfield supplied a welcome diversion for them: they stared as the squadron passed.

They were on the main road before Sam turned to Mac. 'Thanks for your help back at Bagram,' he said quietly. 'That guy – I don't know, he just got to me.'

'Forget about it,' Mac replied lightly. 'I know what you Redmans are like when you see the red mist. Bunch of fucking lunatics. Thought you were going to do a J. on him.'

It was an inappropriate joke, but Sam smiled anyway. 'Yeah,' he replied. 'We should probably try to chill a bit.' He looked around to check nobody else was listening. 'Look,

201

mate, I don't know what all this police stuff is about, but when we get back to base, deny everything, okay. This is my problem. I don't want you taking the rap for it.'

Mac shrugged. 'Whatever you say,' he replied.

'I mean it, Mac.'

'Yeah,' Mac replied. 'I can tell. Look, Sam, I don't know what's going on. You don't want to tell me, fine. But any time you need some extra muscle, you know where to come, right?'

Sam surveyed his friend. 'Yeah,' he replied brusquely. 'Thanks.'

The gates to RAF Credenhill were already open when they arrived – clearly someone had radioed ahead to let them know they were on their way. When they came to a halt in the main courtyard the conversational buzz in Sam's bus – which had fallen to a silence towards the end of the boring drive – started up again. Something was going on here. There were more police vehicles for a start, and quite a number of MOD officers all carrying their MP7s. One of them approached the back of the bus and opened it.

'All right, you lot, out you get, but no moving from the courtyard.'

'What the hell's going on?' It was Davenport and he sounded like he'd had enough.

'You'll find out soon enough. Come on, down you get.'

They de-bussed and started hanging around in groups. A few of the guys lit cigarettes. A lot of them grumbled. They were knackered. They just wanted to get back home and didn't appreciate being treated like a bunch of jailbirds.

Sam stayed to one side. He didn't chat with the others. He didn't smoke with them. Something was coming that involved him. He knew that. He supposed he should be apprehensive, but he wasn't. When you'd faced what he had, it took more than a few MOD coppers to put the wind up you, no matter what sort of hardware they were wielding. But he didn't expect what happened next. None of them did. It was the talk of Credenhill for months to come.

There were stairs leading up to the main headquarters building. A number of figures appeared at the top: two more MOD policemen – they were swarming round this place like flies around shit; two men in suits, one old, one young, who Sam didn't recognise; and Mark Porteus. The CO wore camouflage gear, as always; and the hard features of his scarred face were as proud and uncompromising as always. But everyone fell silent as they saw him, because his arms were in front of him, firmly handcuffed. One of the MOD policemen prodded him with his gun. No one did that to Mark Porteus. Not ever. But Porteus didn't react. He stepped slowly forward, down the stairs. As he walked, his face scanned the crowd, as though he were looking for something or someone in particular. His eyes were narrowed, his forehead creased into a deadly serious expression.

When his eyes fell upon Sam, he stopped.

The look was piercing. It burned through the crowd of soldiers and picked Sam out like a searchlight. It was a look full of meaning. Not anger. Not blame. But meaning nevertheless.

And in that moment, Sam felt all sorts of things slot into place. Clare's article. The phone number. The hooded figure at his door.

Porteus.

It had been him all along. As the CO, *he* would have been in possession of information from the security services that nobody else would have had. *He* would have been in a position to deploy Sam's squadron. And most importantly of all, Porteus knew Jacob. He would have recognised his picture. This was why, when Sam had returned from

203

Helmand Province, the boss had kept his distance; this was why he had stayed away, out of sight. He'd been trying to warn Sam, without it being seen that this was what he was doing.

Now Porteus looked at Sam, his proud face held high. Sam nodded, gently, almost imperceptibly. If you hadn't known what that silent exchange meant, you'd most likely not have seen it happen.

As the rest of the squadron looked on in astonishment, Porteus was once more jabbed in the back by an MP7. If it annoyed him, he didn't let it show. He just allowed himself to be escorted to one of the police vans. Two MOD policemen joined him in the back, the doors were shut and locked and the van was driven away.

The conversation started buzzing again. Still Sam stayed separate from the others. He watched as the younger of the two men on the steps approached Mac. *A word in your ear,* the man's expression seemed to say; once he had Mac's attention, he spoke, though Sam couldn't hear from that distance what he was saying. He'd find out soon enough, he guessed. But before he did, he became uncomfortably aware of somebody watching him. Looking back up the steps, he saw the older man. His grey hair was neatly combed back, his eyebrows were bushy and his face had the deeply lined dignity that only certain old men manage to achieve. He wore a suit and tie and he was looking at Sam with an almost mournful expression.

Sam absorbed that stare, refusing to be intimidated by it. The two men remained locked in a kind of silent conflict until Mac approached.

'Sam,' he muttered under his breath. 'They want to debrief us. The troop, all seven of us that were there.'

Sam didn't even blink.

'*Now*, Sam. Kremlin.'

He nodded vaguely, dragged his eyes from the old man

who seemed in no way uncomfortable about what had just passed between them, and followed his friend.

Sam walked as if in a dream. Behind him, the sound of the others talking. 'Wouldn't have cuffed him if they didn't think he was going to try to leg it,' Tyler was saying.

Davenport didn't agree. 'That, or they wanted to make an example of him. Why pack him into the police van in front of us when it could have been done on the QT?' His voice was full of disdain. 'Chickenshit cuntlickers. Porteus is all right. Have a right scene on their hands if they do the dirty on him.'

A couple of others grunted their agreement.

The two men in suits were waiting for them in the briefing room, as was Jack Whitely. The Ops Officer looked harassed – Sam couldn't tell if their arrival made him more or less nervous. It didn't matter either way. A quiet word from the younger of the two suited men and he left the room, a little red-faced perhaps, but slightly relieved to be away from the tension.

The suits sat in silence. Once they were all in, the old man cleared his throat. 'Gentlemen,' he announced. 'My name is Gabriel Bland.' He nodded towards the younger man. 'This is Toby Brookes.'

Brookes sniffed.

'You'll be debriefed later in the usual way,' Bland announced. 'I just have one question for you.' He looked at each of them in term. 'You will have noticed,' he added, almost apologetically, 'your commanding officer being, ah, escorted from the premises.' His tone might have been apologetic, but the implication wasn't: mess around with me and you'll get the same treatment. There was silence in the room as Brookes handed each of them an A4 photograph.

Sam didn't need to look at it. He knew it would be Jacob. Bland appeared to notice his lack of regard for the document and raised an eyebrow. And so Sam glanced at the picture.

It was different to the one he had seen before in this very briefing room. Older, taken when Jacob was still in the Regiment. Sam avoided looking at Mac; no one else in the room said anything.

Bland cleared his throat theatrically. 'I should like to know,' he said, 'if this individual was one of your targets during your recent expedition.'

Silence.

'Did you kill him?'

Still nothing.

Bland continued to look from one man to the next, a suspicious schoolmaster weeding out the naughty child. But the response remained the same. Nothing but silence.

And then Mac spoke. 'I know this person,' he said. His voice was filled with mock suspicion. 'What's this all about?'

'I'm asking the questions,' Bland replied peevishly.

'Then you'd better ask me,' Sam announced. 'I photographed the dead. And I'm sure you've done your homework and know who this is.'

Sam's challenge hung in the air. Bland surveyed him calmly. 'Very well,' he purred finally. 'The rest of you may leave. Return the pictures to Toby, please. Sergeant Redman – it *is* Sergeant Redman, isn't it? – I wonder if I might ask you to stay here.'

Sam shrugged. The rest of them stood up and quietly left, though there wasn't one of them that didn't look over their shoulders as they did so, obviously wondering what the hell this was all about. They didn't hang around to find out, though, and within a minute Sam was alone with the two spooks.

For a while none of them spoke. Sam remained seated. Bland and Toby were standing; Bland turned and faced the front wall, looking at nothing in particular, while Toby went and stood by the door, out of Sam's sight.

206

'I am just a humble civil servant,' Bland stated finally, still not looking at Sam, 'but I suppose I don't need to tell you that it is the matter of a moment's work for me to have you court-martialled. A short testimony from Detective Inspector Nicola Ledbury and . . .' He turned round and smiled humourlessly. 'And the fragrant Clare Corbett, and I rather think your illustrious career will be brought short by a stint at Her Majesty's pleasure. A *longish* sting, if you get my meaning.'

All of a sudden, Sam's mind was a rush. Nicola, Clare – how the *hell* had this guy caught up with them? Sam hadn't told anyone. He'd been careful.

'Surprised, Sam?' Bland asked. 'Surely not.' He paused for thought. 'I don't want you to think that you're in any way unappreciated, you and your, ah, friends. You have a, ah . . .' He smiled again. 'A *good right fist*. But you didn't honestly imagine . . .' Now he allowed a bit of sharpness in his voice. 'You didn't honestly imagine that you were going to out*think* the Secret Intelligence Service?'

A pause.

'You didn't imagine,' Bland persisted, 'that you would outmanoeuvre MI6, did you, Sam?'

Sam felt the blood rising to his face as Bland sat down next to him. The MI6 man carried with him the faint whiff of aftershave; Sam was immediately aware that he must stink.

'If you're such a bunch of fucking geniuses,' Sam retorted, 'then you don't need to speak to me.'

'Oh, please, Sam. Let's, ah, let's not be unpleasant with each other.' He stood up again. *You're nervous*, Sam thought to himself. *You're trying not to show it, but you are.* 'Miss Corbett told us everything, Sam: that she had foolishly told you the contents of her ill-informed article; about your brother being in the training camp. She was really quite, ah, talkative. So please do me the courtesy of not pretending

207

that you travelled to Kazakhstan without the express intention of compromising the mission. Do me that courtesy, Sam.'

Sam jutted his chin out.

'Was he there, Sam? Did you see him?'

Sam refused to answer and a shadow of frustration passed over Bland's face. 'I would find it quite unpalatable,' he said ominously quietly, 'to have to force this out of you, Sam. But your file tells me that your field investigation techniques are quite specialised. So you know the sort of things we might do to, ah, loosen your tongue.'

The threat hung in the air. Sam took a deep breath. 'All right,' he said quietly. 'All right. I recognised Jacob at the briefing. I went out to stop the guys putting a bullet in him.' He looked directly at Bland. Fiercely. 'Maybe you'd do the same for *your* brother. But Jacob wasn't there. No sign of him. We eliminated the targets and came home. End of fucking story.'

Bland nodded and for a moment he appeared satisfied. He came and sat down again.

'I'm afraid, Sam, I'm not entirely sure that I believe you.'

'Well that's your problem.'

'It is indeed,' Bland murmured. 'It is indeed my problem.' He stared straight ahead. 'You do realise, Sam, that Miss Corbett got quite the wrong end of the stick, don't you?' As he spoke he looked directly at Sam, who couldn't help a flicker of interest registering on his face. Bland feigned surprise. 'Oh,' he muttered. 'Oh, dear. Well, she is a most appealing young lady. I can, ah, I can *quite* understand how you might have fallen for her charms.'

'She was fucking terrified of you,' Sam replied hotly. 'If it *was* you that put the frighteners on her and bumped off that contact of hers.'

'Did I frighten her?' Bland asked. 'Well, yes, I suppose I might have done. It seems to be an occupational hazard.

I would prefer not to. But then I don't have the advantages of your youth and vigour, Sam. I'm afraid I have to be a little more robust to get what I want.'

Sam ignored him. 'I think Clare was telling the truth.'

'No doubt about it,' Bland replied. Sam blinked. 'At least there's no doubt that she believed she was telling the truth. But believing you are right and *being* right, these are two very different things, are they not?'

'You tell me,' Sam replied. His voice was surly, but he couldn't help it.

'I *am* telling you, Sam. Clare Corbett, alas, was misled. It's not her fault, of course. But she was misled nevertheless by her . . .' He struggled to find the phrase. 'By her "red-light runner".'

'You telling me they don't exist?' Sam demanded hotly. 'You telling me that we didn't just eliminate a load of them in Kazakhstan?'

Bland shook his head. 'No,' he replied. 'They exist. Very much so. Intelligence agencies are extremely adept at drawing profiles of people from, oh, an astonishing variety of sources, Sam. It would be an easy job for me to pull up all sorts of information about you, for example, that you wouldn't even imagine we'd be interested in. Which super-markets you shop at, your taste in films, your taste in just about everything. Should we be of a mind to, you under-stand. Clare's red-light runners fitted a very precise profile. The sort of people that someone at least would have a use for.'

'So why are you killing them?' Bland's wordiness, his roundabout way of talking, was beginning to get on Sam's nerves.

'Of course,' Bland replied enigmatically, 'you and I both know that we are called upon to do questionable things in the course of our duty.' As if that explained everything. 'I've learned a lot about your brother in the last few hours, Sam.

A very great deal. He had a most distinguished service record, did he not?'

Sam didn't reply.

'And then, what can we call it? A moment of madness? You were there, weren't you? In Baghdad. You saw it all happen.'

'It was an accident,' Sam seethed. 'Jacob stepped in to . . .' He stopped himself. What was the point? This guy was going to believe what he was going to believe.

'A cover-up,' Bland continued, as though Sam hadn't even spoken. 'Jacob Redman was, ah, cut a deal to avoid embarrassment to the MOD. Everything brushed under the carpet to avoid a scandal, but Jacob to be RTU'd. An embarrassment too far, Sam, wouldn't you say? And so he left the army. Left the country. Cut off all ties. I would say, in circumstances such as this, that a man might become, ah . . .' He searched for a word. 'Bitter?'

'If you're trying to say something,' Sam whispered, 'why don't you just say it?'

'Treason, Sam,' Bland announced with sudden force. 'It's not a terribly fashionable word, is it? Smacks a bit of the Gunpowder Plot, doesn't it? But it's very apt, Sam, for what's going on at the moment. Very apt indeed. I believe Jacob to be guilty of treason, Sam. And if you don't help me find him, then you will be guilty of it too.'

Once more a smile spread across the older man's lined face. Sam shut his eyes and as he did so, his brother's words echoed in his mind. *They'll tell you things, Sam. Things about me. Don't forget that you're my brother. Don't believe them.* And he remembered the red-light runners, butchered in their beds by the Regiment's weapons, and how easily one of those could have been Jacob.

'You're insane,' he told the old man. 'You're totally fucking insane.'

Bland's gaze flickered over to where Toby was standing.

Clearly he didn't like being spoken to like this in front of a subordinate, but if he was angry he managed to keep a check on it.

'What if I were to tell you, Sam, that the red-light runners were being trained not by MI5, but by a foreign intelligence agency?'

'Who?'

'I, ah, I think I might keep that information to myself for the time being, Sam. Though if you think about it, I'm sure you would come to the same conclusion as me.'

'Then why did you kill Clare's contact?'

'We didn't, Sam. We didn't need to. He was, ah, taken care of by the time we reached him.'

'Who by?'

'We don't know.'

'But he told Clare he was working for Five.'

'Indeed he did, Sam. Indeed he did. Because that was what he believed.'

Sam's eyes narrowed as he tried to work out the implications of what Bland was saying.

'You see, Sam,' Bland continued, 'Miss Corbett's red-light runners are exactly what she thought they were. With one difference. They *thought* they were working for MI5. They *thought* they were patriots. But they weren't, Sam. They were stooges. They had been duped.'

His words rang around the room.

'With the red-light runners trained, primed and re-inserted into the UK, their handlers had a secret network of operatives willing to do their bidding. We have no idea how many of them there are out there. Tens? Hundreds? Just waiting to be activated. Just waiting to be given the order.'

As he spoke, he did not take his eyes from Sam.

'Your brother is involved, Sam, in some way. I don't think I need to tell you what sort of threat this poses to the national security. So if you have any information about Jacob, I recommend that you tell me. Now.'

Bland took a step back and put his hands behind his back. There was an air of finality to his movements. He had said his piece. It was up to Sam now.

Slowly, Sam pulled his backpack towards him. Opening it up at the buckles he fished his hand inside. His fingers brushed against the hard contours of the laptop he'd found. He felt his mouth go dry. The last thing he wanted was for that computer to fall into the Firm's hands. The pack was staying with him, no matter what. Next to the machine was the small digital camera which he had used to photograph the deceased. He pulled it out and handed it to Gabriel Bland.

'Pictures,' he said shortly. 'Of everyone we killed. They're your red-light runners. Jacob wasn't with them. Final answer.'

Bland narrowed his eyes as Sam stood up and slung the pack over his shoulder. 'I'd like to be excused,' he demanded brazenly.

Bland appeared to consider that for a moment. You could see the wheels ticking in his mind. Finally, he nodded over at Toby, a short, instructive nod. Returning his attention to Sam, he smiled and held out one arm.

'Please,' he murmured politely, as though he were the maître d' in a fine restaurant ushering his guest to the exit.

Sam gave him an unfriendly look, then turned and left. As he walked back out into the Kremlin he heard, but did not see, Toby closing the door behind him.

★

There was silence in the briefing room. Toby Brookes knew better than to speak out of turn.

He remained by the door, looking at his boss. Bland was

a cold fish, Brookes knew that better than most. Full of fancy words and exquisite manners, but a total shit when he wanted to be, and a temper to match. But he had the ear of the important people – including the chief of the SIS – and was as much a part of the furniture at Legoland as, well, the furniture. As far as Brookes knew, he had no family to speak of. Christ, the bastard never even seemed to go home, and he expected the same of his staff. Brookes had barely seen his wife for two weeks, not since all the business with Clare Corbett erupted. Carry on like this and he wouldn't *have* a wife much longer, but there was no point saying that to Gabriel Bland.

Brookes coughed, not because he needed to, but to remind Bland that he was actually still there. One of his boss's eagle-like eyebrows shot up.

'What do you think, Toby?' he asked quietly. 'I would very much value your opinion.'

Brookes blinked. Bland had never asked his opinion. *Never.* The old man avoided his eye, and in a flash of intuition Brookes realised that he was unsure of himself.

He stuttered.

'You think I am foolish, giving any information at all to a man like Sam Redman.'

'His talents don't lie between the ears, sir, if you understand my meaning.' Instantly, Brookes regretted his comment. He should have flattered the boss. That was what he wanted to hear.

'I most certainly do understand your meaning, Toby. I most certainly do.' Bland's eyes became lost in thought once more. 'Sam Redman is a man who thinks with his emotions, and with his biceps; not his mind, Toby. We've given him enough to be going on with. I predict that he will do whatever it takes to locate his brother. And we *must* locate his brother. That much is clear.'

'Yes, sir,' Brookes agreed obligingly.

Bland nodded his head, then looked directly at Brookes. 'See to it that he is followed. Category one target. Phone taps, trails, the works. Don't concern yourself with legalities – I'll clear it all with the chief. I want our best people on it, Toby. And I *don't* want them to be seen.'

'Yes, sir,' Brookes repeated, before turning to open the door.

'Toby,' Bland called. There was a warning in his voice.

He turned.

'I mean it, Toby. Our *best* people. This will be the making of you.' He smiled, a rather sweet, paternal smile. 'It's a most important operation, Toby. I just want to make sure you fully appreciate and share my sense of urgency.'

Brookes nodded, not knowing if he was expected to speak.

'Good,' Bland said calmly. 'Good. Now then, I suggest we leave this place. I've never liked it much. It smells of men. Most unpleasant. Really most unpleasant.'

And with a sudden speed he walked towards the door. Toby Brookes only just managed to open it in time to let him through.

FOURTEEN

He had driven all day, stopping only to refuel the truck from the canisters of diesel in the back, or to buy fruit from one of the occasional stalls that popped up from nowhere. Whenever he stopped he kept the engine running so that he didn't have to hotwire it again; and he kept the handgun close to his body in case anyone got any clever ideas.

Now it was evening. He was numb with tiredness. The road stretched out ahead of him, wide and empty. This place seemed to go on for ever and with only his sense of direction to guide him, Jacob Redman experienced many moments of doubt. He knew he needed to travel west and slightly north and, unable to read the road signs and in the absence of maps or any proper navigation gear, he had relied on his reading of the sun during the day and the stars at night. But these were not precise measurements. Distances were long in this part of the world and if he went wrong, he could find himself stranded in an unpopulated part of Kazakhstan with no diesel and a dwindling supply of money. The few notes he had stolen from the guard when he took the truck were enough to buy him a little food, but not nearly enough for fuel. There were a limited number of times he could steal from people before getting caught and he *really* didn't want to have to fight his way out of a Kazakh police cell.

Not that there were many people to steal from. In this vast country he could drive for an hour without seeing a soul;

when he did it was frequently just a peasant tending animals in a field. No police, thank God. No army. Not yet.

He glanced at the fuel gauge. Close on empty. He pulled over and jumped down, walking round to the back and opening up. He had kept hold of the empty fuel canisters – four of them, lying on their sides with only the AK-47 for company – on the off chance that he came across a free supply of diesel. But he hadn't. Only one of them had any of that precious, pungent liquid inside. He heaved it out of the back, undid the screwtop and started pouring it into the truck's fuel tank. There was a glugging sound, as though the engine was thirstily drinking the fuel. Before long, the last drops had been squeezed out. The canister clattered as he threw it back into the van; Jacob took his place behind the wheel once more and allowed himself to close his eyes. Just for a minute.

He shook himself awake. 'Damn it,' he hissed, angry at his lack of self-control. There was no time for sleep; and he had wasted fuel while the engine ticked over. He shook his head and pulled out into the road once more.

It was growing dark now. The sky, which had been blue but dotted with cotton-wool clouds, grew orange. He had left the hemp fields of the Chu Valley far behind and now the surrounding countryside was far more flat. Fields of grassland extended into the distance. Soon they would be parched by the fierce summer months. Summer. But Jacob could not expect to see the greens and yellows of England. That thought came to him with a pang and not for the first time he found himself hankering after home. You could be an exile for any amount of time, he realised, but you never fully grew used to it. There were always moments when you wanted the comforts of home and for Jacob this was one of them.

He pushed that thought from his mind, as he had so many times before. He wasn't going home now, or any time soon.

216

A town up ahead. He trundled through. It was indistinguishable from the one where he had picked up the vehicle. A little bigger if anything. On the far side of the outskirts, he pulled over. It was a risk, but he had to check he was on the right track. An elderly man sat outside his house on a low wooden bench. He had the Mongol-looking face indigenous to the region, deeply lined; he wore a winter jumper, despite the fact that it was a warm evening; and he looked at the new arrival with undisguised mistrust. Beside him, tethered to a splintered old post, was a goat. The animal looked a lot sprightlier than its owner.

Jacob had one note left. He pulled it from his back pocket and handed it to the man. The man looked for a moment as though he was going to take great offence, but at the last minute he stretched out a thin, trembling hand and accepted the offer. He secreted the money in the breast pocket of the shirt he was wearing under the jumper, then turned his attention back to Jacob.

'Baikonur?' Jacob asked.

At first the old man appeared not to have heard; at least, if he *had* heard, he pretended not to. So Jacob repeated himself. '*Baikonur?*'

Slowly, the man started to nod. He turned his head looking in the direction Jacob was travelling, then gradually raised his arm and pointed.

'Baikonur,' he said in a grizzled voice. His lips receded in on themselves, in the way only the lips of old men can. He pushed himself heavily to his feet and tottered the couple of metres over to where the goat was tethered. He held out a bony hand and the animal nuzzled his fingertips. Everything about his body language indicated that the conversation was over.

That was fine by Jacob. He'd found out what he wanted. He was on the right track. He rushed back to the truck, took his place once more behind the wheel and drove off. With luck, he would have enough fuel. If not, he'd just have to improvise. That didn't matter. It wasn't the first time. It wouldn't be the last.

He shook his head again and tried to stop his drowsiness from overcoming him.

★

Sam's mind was ablaze.

Everything Bland had said chased its way around his head. Did he believe him? He didn't know. He certainly didn't trust him. And he *certainly* didn't like the way the bastard spoke about his brother. One thing was for sure: there was no way Sam was going to take Gabriel Bland's word for anything.

There were unanswered questions, too. Things that just didn't stack up. As he drove home, he kept reliving those moments in the woods outside the training camp: Craven catching one; the silent corpse of the Spetsnaz soldier. *Were* they Spetsnaz? Whoever they were, it seemed to Sam that they had been expecting the Regiment. Waiting for them. But how was that possible? The operation was top secret, a quick in-and-out job. The only way anyone would have known about the unit's arrival was if they had been told. And if they had been told, that could mean only one thing. A leak. A mole.

What if I were to tell you, Sam, that the red-light runners were being trained not by MI5, but by a foreign intelligence agency? Bland's words popped into Sam's head. If Spetsnaz were being tipped off, everything pointed to the Russians, but that made no difference to Sam. He was being played by the Firm either way. He remembered Porteus, handcuffed and humiliated. He was being punished for tipping Sam off, that much was clear. But why then had Bland let Sam himself go so easily? He was up to something.

218

Manoeuvring. He didn't trust Sam any more than Sam trusted him.

He parked outside the flat. It always felt weird, coming home after an op. Like he was coming back from the office. Today it felt weirder than most other times. He took his rucksack from the back seat. It wasn't regulation to take his gear home with him, but he didn't care. It wasn't like he was going to leave the contents of his bag at RAF Credenhill.

Sam locked himself into the flat and closed the curtains of the front room. Only then did he pull out the laptop computer.

He hadn't had a chance to examine it, so he did so now. It was unremarkable. A little too unremarkable, perhaps: it bore no logo, no brand name. Its metal casing was scuffed and worn: the machine looked like it had received some pretty heavy use. Sam opened it up. Nothing unusual, just a bit of Kazakhstani grit that tumbled from the hinge and fell on to Sam's lap. Some of the keys were worn away so that you could no longer see which letter they displayed; the delete key had come away completely, displaying its plastic skeleton underneath.

Sam found himself breathing heavily. He knew he should switch it on, but for some reason he felt reluctant. Perhaps, he told himself, he didn't want to find out what this machine contained.

He scowled and pressed the power button.

For a second there was nothing. Then a whirr, and an electronic chord pinged around the room. The screen flickered and lit up. It was blue. A blank box in the middle, with a flickering cursor. Next to it: PASSWORD.

Sam blinked. He had no idea what to type. He should have expected this, but he hadn't. Cursing under his breath, he closed the machine down. How was he going to break into it? How the *hell* was he going to break into it? Take it to a shop? No. He couldn't just walk in somewhere and demand that someone he didn't know hack into a computer; especially when he didn't know what the computer contained. And when he went through his list of friends and acquaintances, people who *might* know someone who knew someone – well, they were all Regiment. Hereford was a closed shop. Word got around. No doubt tongues would already be wagging about his interview without coffee with the Firm in the Kremlin meeting room. He didn't want to add fuel to the fire.

He sat in silence. Jesus, he stank worse than a hooker on the blob. He needed to shower. Picking up the laptop, he walked into the bedroom to strip. When he went into the bathroom, he carried the computer with him too. He wasn't going to let it out of his sight. No way.

Half an hour later he was clean and freshly clothed: jeans, a hooded top and his trademark leather jacket replacing the stinking camouflage gear that sat in a heap on the floor. With the laptop under his arm, he left the flat. He realised as he walked outside that he was on tenterhooks, his eyes darting around for anything unexpected. But there was nothing. Sam climbed into his car, put the laptop on the passenger seat and drove off. He didn't know when he had made the decision. He didn't even know for sure that he *had* made it until he hit the motorway heading towards London. His eyes were fixed in the rear-view mirror as much as they were on the road ahead. Sam almost expected to be followed; the fact that he couldn't pick up any trails did nothing to quell his paranoia.

By the time he was approaching Addington Gardens in Acton, evening was beginning to close in. It was with a sense of déjà vu that he parked up in the same road parallel to Clare Corbett's street. Hiding the laptop under his jacket, he sauntered to the corner of the road. Sam didn't feel inclined simply to walk up and knock on the door – that would be making life too easy for anyone performing surveillance on the flat, if indeed that was what they were doing. Instead he loitered on the corner. Clare couldn't stay at home forever. All he had to do was wait.

He glanced at his watch. 18.00 hrs. Darkness fell. 19.00 hrs. Inhabitants of the street left and returned to their homes. Sam couldn't see anyone in the road who looked as if they were keeping watch over Clare's place, but he knew that didn't mean anything. He knew that if he were snooping, he would probably take up position in an upstairs room of one of the houses opposite.

It was just gone seven-thirty when Clare's door opened and she stepped outside. She walked briskly, her head down and her arms, clad in a heavy brown coat, wrapped around her body. She looked small. Sam pulled his hood up and started following from a distance. He only increased his pace once they had both turned on to the main road. Clare didn't dawdle. She wove in and out of the other pedestrians in the half light; Sam had to concentrate so as not to lose her. She came to a halt at a bus stop where a small crowd had congregated. Sam loitered for a few metres behind, keeping well out of sight.

The bus arrived, a long one with a flexible midriff. It was almost full and the windows were steamed up. Sam joined the queue, a couple of places behind Clare; when the moment came to pay his fare he had to scrabble around in his pocket to find change for the impatient driver. By the time he had paid, Clare had taken a seat towards the back. There was a spare place next to it. He put his head down again and approached her.

She was lost in thought, her pale eyes staring through the window, the condensation on which she had wiped away with one hand. She clearly hadn't noticed Sam; he waited for the doors to close and the bus to move off before speaking.

'Clare,' he said softly. 'It's me.'

He felt her body jump and put a reassuring hand on her arm. Never had he seen such alarm in someone's face. Her skin, already limpid, went white; her eyes bulged.

'*Sam!*'

She looked around, as though expecting to see someone else there, but then dragged her attention back to him. She looked frightened now. 'I had to tell them,' she whispered. 'I'm sorry. They threatened me . . .'

In front of them a drunk started to sing. Most of the other passengers looked at their boots.

'Forget about it,' Sam muttered. 'Look, I need your help.' He frowned. 'I didn't know where else to go.'

She shook her head nervously. 'I can't, Sam. I can't have anything more to do with this.'

One of the passengers in front – an old woman with a hard, nosy face – glanced round at them. Clare bowed her head again. 'I just can't,' she repeated.

The bus came to a halt; a few passengers left, others embarked. A harassed woman with two kids jostled towards Sam, staring at him in a way that suggested he give up his seat. He didn't. They sat in silence.

'We need to get off,' Sam said. 'We can't talk here.'

'I can't talk anywhere.' Her voice was shaking. 'You've got to leave me alone.'

His hand was still on her arm. He squeezed it. 'No one's followed me,' he reassured her. 'I took care.'

Clare looked around again. 'How do you know nobody's following *me*?' she demanded.

He couldn't answer that. Instead, he stood up and pulled on her arm. There was a little resistance, but she gave way in the end – not through enthusiasm, he realised, but because she knew she didn't have much choice. They shuffled, arm in arm, to the double doors. Sam could feel her trembling with anxiety.

When the doors opened next, only a couple of people got

out. Sam waited, choosing his moment carefully. Only when he heard the hiss of the doors about to close did he move. He tugged Clare sharply – so sharply that she tripped slightly. The closing doors caught his arm, but they made it on to the street and if anybody had been intending to follow them, they wouldn't be able to now.

The bus drove off just as Clare angrily pulled her arm from Sam's wrist. 'What are you *playing* at?' she raged.

They were in a busy, suburban street just outside a rough-looking pub. A couple of passers-by glanced at them, clearly thinking they were having some kind of domestic. Clare stomped off, but Sam kept with her. They walked in silence for at least a hundred metres. In the end, though, as he knew it would, Clare's curiosity got the better of her. She stopped in the middle of the pavement and looked angrily at him.

'Did you find it? The training camp?'

He nodded.

'And did you . . . the red-light runners . . . did you . . . ?' She seemed unable to formulate the words 'kill them'.

'I found my brother.' Sam sidestepped the question.

Her lips thinned. 'Is he okay?' she asked, a bit calmer now, her Irish lilt a bit softer.

Sam shrugged. 'He got away, if that's what you mean.' He pulled the laptop from under his jacket. 'He left this. I can't get into it, but I think it might have some answers. Seeing as you're looking for some answers too, I thought you might help me with it.'

Clare hesitated. Her eyes narrowed. 'That bastard came to my flat again, Sam. Just waltzed right in. He knew you'd been to see me. God knows how, but I couldn't deny it. How did he know, Sam? Was someone watching you that night?'

'I don't really know. Look, do you know someone who can help us with this?' He grinned. 'Most of my friends would try to open it with an MP5.'

'A what?'

'Never mind. Are you going to help me?'

Clare glanced around, as though searching for a way out. But she didn't run. She looked at him helplessly. 'My sister,' she said in a defeated kind of voice. 'Her son, he's a kind of . . . whizzkid. Nerd, actually. Sits in his room all day with the curtains closed. He could probably . . .'

Her voice trailed off.

'Where do they live?' Sam demanded.

'Not too far from here. We could get a bus.'

'We'll get a cab,' Sam said shortly. 'Come on.'

It was a scant twenty minutes later that Sam was putting a ten-pound note into the hand of a cabbie. They were in a residential street that was almost indistinguishable from the one where Clare lived. Only once the cab driver had driven away did Clare lead Sam towards one of the houses. It was a gentrified-looking place: two stories and an elegant pathway with black and white tiles in a chequer pattern. Clare turned to him. 'His name's Patrick,' she said. 'He's sweet, but he's a bit of a . . . a *teenager*, if you know what I mean. A bit . . . Just go easy on him, that's all.'

'I'll be good as gold,' Sam murmured.

Clare led him up the path and rang on the doorbell, while Sam lurked a metre or two behind her.

It took a minute for anyone to answer. When the door opened, a kid stood in the frame. He was thirteen, maybe a bit older – Sam had no talent for judging such things. His hair was lank and he had whiteheads on his forehead and cheeks. Fuck, the kid had a face like a pepperoni pizza. He stank of BO and sly wanks. He was probably in the middle of a crafty hand-shandy when they had arrived. That was probably why he was in such a foul mood. He looked at Clare about as enthusiastically as he might look at a door-to-door salesman.

'Hi, Patch,' Clare said brightly.

'It's Patrick,' the teenager replied.

'Mum in? Dad?'

He shook his head.

'Mind if we come in?'

Patrick looked over her shoulder at Sam, appearing to measure him up. 'He your boyfriend?'

An awkward pause. From behind, Sam saw her put her fingers lightly to her hair. 'This is Sam,' she replied. 'Can we come in please, Patrick?'

The kid shrugged and stepped aside.

It was warm in the house. Warm and quiet. The kid shut the door and then loitered uncomfortably in the hallway, too gawky to look directly at his aunt or her guest. 'Actually, Patrick,' Clare said, delicately, like she was tiptoeing, 'it's you we came to see. We need some help. Sort of a computer thing.'

Patrick did his best to pretend not to be interested.

From under his jacket, Sam pulled the laptop. 'Forgot the password,' he said. His voice sounded a bit clumsy in his ears. He wasn't used to talking with children.

Patrick looked at the laptop, then up at Sam. 'No one forgets their password,' he said.

'Please, Patrick,' Clare interrupted quickly. 'It would be a real help. Can you get into it?'

Patrick shrugged again. It looked to Sam like this was a default action for him.

'Yeah,' he droned grumpily. 'Probably. Just load the BIOS and repartition the . . .'

'Tell you what, mate,' Sam interrupted him. 'Why don't you just do it?'

'*Sam!*' Clare whispered; at the same time Patrick, looking offended, spoke.

'I'm busy,' he retorted. He turned petulantly and headed towards the stairs.

Clare gave Sam an annoyed look, but he ignored it. He

strode towards the teenager and put a firm hand on his bony shoulder. 'Tell you what, Clare,' he announced. 'Why don't you give me and Patrick a couple of minutes?' Clare looked unsure of herself, but with a meaningful glance from Sam she disappeared along the hallway and into the kitchen. Sam spoke to Patrick in a low whisper. 'Here's the deal,' he said. 'Either I go up into your bedroom and make a quick list of all the websites you've looked at in the past few hours and show them to your aunt, or you stop acting like a twat and help us out.'

Patrick blushed. He looked as though he was searching for a response, but his angry, embarrassed expression got in the way. 'Deal?' Sam asked.

Patrick managed to look, if anything, more surly. 'Deal,' he replied.

Minutes later, the three of them were in his bedroom. It was quite a big room, but still managed to be dingy by virtue of the musty, unwashed smell. Two computers sat next to each other, both of them whirring; Patrick glanced guiltily at them, then up at Sam who had to stop himself from smiling. He and Clare took a seat on the kid's unmade bed, while he took the laptop from them and sat on the floor to open it up.

Patrick's pallid face glowed in the light of the computer screen as his fingers tapped the keyboard deftly and speedily. There was no sound in the room; just the faint clack of the keys. Sam found himself holding his breath. A nervousness at the pit of his stomach.

Time seemed to stand still. He could feel Clare occasionally looking at him. He ignored her.

The clacking stopped. The glow on Patrick's face dimmed and a confused expression came over him.

'What's the matter?' Sam demanded.

Patrick pretended not to hear. He just stared intently at the screen.

And then the light returned, illuminating his acne-ridden face just as it had done before. He smiled, then turned to the two adults sitting on his bed.

'Done it,' he announced.

He tried very hard not to look pleased with himself as he stood up and nonchalantly handed the laptop back to Sam.

FIFTEEN

The screen was blue. A couple of familiar icons shone in the top left-hand corner. One of them was yellow and shaped like a folder. Underneath, in rounded white letters, were the words RED LIGHT RUNNERS.

The two adults exchanged a look.

'What was the password?' Sam asked distractedly.

' "Max",' the kid replied.

Sam's stomach knotted.

'Not a very good password. Should be longer, have a few numbers in it . . .' Patrick looked offended that nobody seemed to be listening to him.

'Let's go,' Sam said, closing down the computer and standing up. As he walked to the door, he was aware of Clare fishing in her bag and pulling out a tenner.

'Give my love to your mum,' she said, handing the note to her nephew. Patrick grunted. He didn't show them out.

Sam didn't speak until they were on the street. 'We need somewhere private,' he said. 'Somewhere to read this. Is there a hotel near?'

Clare shrugged. 'I don't know. Probably.'

They hit the pavement, Clare having to trot in order to keep up with Sam. It didn't take them long to find a hotel – the Abbey Court in a residential road called St James's Gardens, a shabby, converted house with rooms to rent which reeked of curry. They were eyed suspiciously by an immensely fat Pakistani woman who demanded payment for the night in advance and clearly didn't believe the pseudonym that Sam gave off the top of his head. The room itself was far from comfortable. A TV in one corner, a lumpy bed with a floral bedspread in the middle. As a hotel room, it was the pits. For their purposes, it was absolutely fine. They sat together on the edge of the bed as Sam cranked up the computer. Using a single finger he entered the password to be greeted once more by the blue screen. He directed the cursor on to the folder, then double-clicked.

A window opened. It contained more icons, perhaps twenty. Each one was labelled with a name. Sam stared blankly at it. 'What's this?' he asked, more to himself than to Clare.

Her hand brushed against his as her fingers searched out the mouse. She directed the cursor to one of the icons at random, then clicked it. A short pause and a grinding from the laptop's innards. Then a document appeared.

There was a photo at the top, a young man with shoulder-length blonde hair. Beneath the photograph, laid out neatly and stretching far beyond the bottom of the screen so that Clare had to scroll down to see it all, was a startling array of personal information. His name, of course – Paul Harrison – and his address. But also his sexual orientation and a list of known previous girlfriends. His parents' address and telephone number. His national insurance number. A list of three official police cautions. Parking fines. His Tesco Clubcard number. His likes and dislikes. Every car he had ever owned. Every job he had ever had, and the wage he had been paid. A graphic of his signature. His closest acquaintances – their names and addresses. A link to his Facebook profile and a list of all his 'friends'. His credit card numbers and certain purchases that he had made. His bank account numbers and security details. Three e-mail addresses and their passwords. The IP address of his computer and the most popular websites visited from that address. Films he had seen, TV programmes he had watched. Music he listened to.

The list went on. Sam and Clare read it in silence. Neither of them commented out loud on the one word that had screamed out to them more than any other. It was written in brackets just beside the subject's name. It read 'DECEASED'.

Clare got to the end of the document long before Sam and impatiently closed down the window, immediately opening another. A different picture, different details. Still the same ominous label after the name: 'DECEASED'. She browsed through more of them, spending less and less time on each one, until finally she brought up a document that made her catch her breath.

'*Bill,*' she whispered in shock. '*It's Bill.*'

The photograph of Clare's contact stared out at her. He had black skin with patchy, tightly curled stubble and a gappy smile. Like all the others, he was deceased. But they already knew that.

Sam stood up. He didn't know what to say or what to think. Jacob was something to do with these red-light runners, he accepted that. But what? And if they were dead, what did that have to do with his brother?

They'll tell you things, Sam. Things about me. Don't forget that you're my brother. Don't believe them.

But he didn't know what he *should* believe. He stared out of the window. It was beginning to rain and the drops slid down the pane, lit up by the streetlamps beyond.

'Sam.' Clare's voice was unsure of itself. 'I've found something else.'

He turned and approached her.

'Look at this,' she continued, spinning the computer around on her lap so he could see it. 'His e-mails. He's only sent them to one address, each time with one of these documents. There's only one contact here – the person he's sent them to.'

'What's his name?' Sam demanded.

'Alexander Dolohov.'

Sam's brow furrowed. He had never heard the name before. 'Any more details on him?'

She turned the computer back towards her and started fiddling, but as she did she shook her head. 'Nothing,' she murmured. 'His name and his e-mail address. That's all.' She looked up, bright eyed. 'You could e-mail him!'

Sam shook his head. 'No way. If I want to talk to this guy, I'll do it the old-fashioned way.'

'What if he doesn't want to talk to you?'

Sam sniffed. 'I guess I'll just have to turn on the charm.' Clare clearly heard the tone in his voice and didn't reply. Sam looked at her with his eyes narrowed. 'Can you get someone to track him down?' he asked. 'Someone from your paper?'

'I could do it myself,' she said.

Sam shook his head. 'The Firm are on to both of us,' he said. 'If we start sniffing around we'll alert them. Nobody but us knows about this laptop. Let's keep it that way.'

'I could ask someone, I suppose . . .' She sounded uncertain as she pulled out her mobile.

'Not with that. There's a phone downstairs, in reception. If you've got someone you can phone, do it from there.'

Clare appeared to think for a minute. 'All right,' she decided finally and with a heavy sigh. 'All right, I'll do it. Wait there.'

'No,' Sam replied. 'I'll come with you.'

'I'm not going to do a runner you know.'

'I'll come with you.'

She shrugged. 'Whatever.'

They were eyed by the suspicious receptionist as Clare made her call. Sam hovered nearby, just out of earshot as she mumbled privately into the phone to some faceless colleague, then left the number of the hotel. The receptionist was clearly trying hard to listen to the conversation, but Clare was talking too discretely for that. 'It'll take an hour or so,' she told him as she hung up.

Sam nodded. He turned to the receptionist. 'Let us know if we have a call,' he instructed and was repaid with a nondescript gesture. Sam considered being more forceful, but decided against it. 'We'll be in our room,' he said brusquely.

He and Clare left the reception and climbed the stairs back to their room.

Neither of them noticed the man on the other side of the street, an umbrella protecting him from the rain, his eyes firmly fixed on the door of their hotel.

★

They say that the darkest hour comes just before dawn. For the young Kazakh man in a small village in the southern part of that huge country, it came a lot earlier than that. He lay in his bed, fast asleep, blithely unaware that his snoring could have woken the dead. Or even that he was only a squeeze of a trigger away from joining them. The trigger in question belonged to a fully loaded AK-47 and, at that precise moment, the cold steel of the weapon was about to be pressed into the fleshy part of his cheek.

His eyes shot open. He gasped. In the darkness, silhouetted against the silver moon that beamed through his open window, stood a man. He couldn't fully see his face, but he could tell he was big; and he could tell that the man was holding the weapon in one hand. The other was up towards his face, one finger pressed to his lips.

'Shhh . . .' he said quietly.

The young Kazakh man started to tremble. He tugged his thin sheets a bit further up his body, but his assailant pulled them away again revealing him to be naked apart from a pair of rather unfashionable underpants. The stranger bent over, grabbed him by the arm, and pulled him out of bed.

He did not dare shout out. The weapon was pressed into his back now; it hurt his knobbly spine. '*What do you want?*' he whispered in Kazakh, but the man did not appear to understand him. They moved swiftly out of the bedroom, into the only other room of the small house. Through the window he saw – on the forecourt of his small petrol filling station – an old four-by-four truck. The lights were off, but it sounded like the engine was turning over. It was parked right by his single, solitary pump and just beyond the small booth where he took his customers' money near the controls for the pump.

He turned to the gunman. In here he could see his face better. He had dark hair and a scraggly beard. His eyes were narrow and hard. The gunman pointed towards the booth. 'We're going there,' he said. 'You're going to turn the pump on.'

The Kazakh didn't understand his foreign-sounding words. '*I have no money,*' he replied in his own language. '*No money here!*'

His assailant pointed to the booth again. Then, letting go of him for a moment, he mimed the turning of a key. The man nodded quickly, then ran back into his room. He pulled on his trousers and shirt while the gunman surveyed him from the doorway, then removed a bunch of keys from his trouser pocket and held them up. The gunman nodded in satisfaction. 'Open up,' he said, then stepped aside to let him pass.

He was marched, at gunpoint, outside. The gritty ground was painful against the soles of his feet, but he was hurried quickly to the booth anyway. His hands shook and it took a couple of goes to insert the key into the door; but once he managed it, the booth opened easily. Inside he headed straight for the till and flicked it open. '*Look*,' he said, indicating the empty tray, '*nothing!*'

The gunman shook his head darkly, then pointed out towards the pump. Only then did he understand. The guy wanted fuel. For a brief instant he wondered why someone would go to such trouble – such danger – simply for diesel, but he didn't let it worry him for long. Under the counter there was another keyhole. He inserted the relevant key and switched it on. On the forecourt, the faint humming of the pump started up.

The gunman, still pointing the weapon in his direction, urged him outside. They approached the vehicle and, without having to be asked, he started filling the tank. Meanwhile, the gunman opened up the back and dragged out four empty fuel canisters. When the vehicle was full, he moved on to these. The dial on the pump whizzed around and somewhere at the back of his mind the young Kazakh had a vision of simply stuffing hard currency into the canisters. But he said nothing. The presence of the wicked-looking weapon was enough to keep his mind on the job.

His whole body was trembling by the time the fourth canister was filled and returned to the back of the truck.

The gunman raised his weapon. He aimed it at the young man's forehead.

A terrible cold numbness spread through his body. He closed his eyes. '*Please*,' he whispered. '*I have done as you asked.*'

He waited for the sound of the shot.

A bang. It seemed to go straight through him. But it wasn't the gun. He opened his eyes. The gunman was not there. The noise had been only the sound of an exhaust backfiring. He collapsed to his knees in relief, watching, shivering, as the vehicle disappeared into the darkness.

★

234

Sam and Clare sat in their room, surrounded by a bubble of tense silence. The night they had spent together was all but forgotten. They were not two lovers in a hotel room; just two people with a common interest, and common fears.

'There could be more than one Alexander Dolohov, you know,' Clare said.

'Then I'll visit them all.'

'How will you find out which is the right one?'

Sam didn't answer. There were some things she didn't need to know.

Clare stared at him. 'You've found out things that I don't know, haven't you?'

He shrugged. 'Your friendly granddad from MI6 paid me a visit.' He saw Clare shudder slightly. 'They've got a theory.'

'Care to share?'

Sam hesitated. His instinct was to keep everything to himself, but it seemed a bit ridiculous keeping Clare in the dark. 'The red-light runners,' he said. 'The Firm claims they're nothing to do with MI5. That they're being trained up by some foreign agency and led to believe they're working for Five.'

Clare's eyes widened. 'Who?' she asked breathlessly.

'Your man wouldn't say. My guess is the Russians.' His voice went quieter. 'Remind me to ask Dolohov when I catch up with him.'

Clare looked at him intently. 'But Sam, maybe you should just *tell* MI6 what you found on this laptop. I mean, it could be serious.'

Sam shook his head. 'No way.'

'Why not?'

He considered telling her – about the Spetsnaz soldiers surrounding the camp and his suspicions that someone in the Firm had tipped them off about the Regiment's arrival – but he kept quiet. 'It's just not safe,' he muttered inadequately. 'Trust me.'

At that precise moment, there was a knock on the door. Sam and Clare exchanged a look just as a voice called from the other side. 'Phone!'

They hurried downstairs.

Clare took the call almost in silence, the telephone nestled in the crook of her neck as she made notes in a speedy shorthand. She nodded occasionally – pointlessly – and when the conversation was over she uttered a brief word of thanks before replacing the handset. A short nod at Sam and they returned to the privacy of their room.

'Well?'

'Two Alexander Dolohovs,' she said. 'One in Manchester, one in London.'

'Shit,' Sam cursed.

'Not really,' Clare replied. Despite the stress, there was a twinkle in her eye. 'The one in Manchester is three years old.' She scribbled an address on a piece of paper from her notebook, tore it out and handed it to Sam. 'I'd say that was your man.'

Sam read the address. A road in Maida Vale. Flat 3.

'My friend couldn't get much on him. He teaches Russian at a university college in Bloomsbury. I, er, I also asked her to look into a couple of other things.'

Sam raised an eyebrow. She indicated the laptop. 'The red-light runners. I gave her the names of the two latest, er . . . the two who died most recently.'

'And?'

'Accidents. Both of them. A car crash and a, er . . .' She blushed. 'A sort of sex game gone wrong. No suggestion of foul play.' She said this last part brightly, as if it were good news.

'Of course not,' Sam murmured.

They sat in the dim light of the bedside lamp. Rain

pattered hard on the window. Sam tried to connect this new information in his mind, but he still felt like he was doing a crossword without the clues.

'How is your brother involved in all this, Sam?' Clare asked quietly. She was looking wide-eyed at him, as though scared of the answer.

'I don't know,' he replied. 'Maybe he was on to them. Jacob always thought he could do everything by himself.' He set his jaw. 'I'm going to go and see Dolohov.'

'Now?'

'Yeah. Now.'

'I'll come.' She sounded plucky, but nervous.

'No you won't.'

'You can't keep doing this to me, Sam. Bringing me in when it suits you, then discarding me when I've given you everything you want. It's not fair. I'm coming with you.'

Sam felt his face twitch. He stood up and looked out of the window. When he turned round again, his face was in shadow. 'Go home, Clare,' he said softly.

She sat obstinately on the bed. Sam looked back out of the window. 'You asked me earlier if I killed the red-light runners. Do you want to know the truth? They were sleeping when we arrived. I shot them in the neck. I would have aimed for the head, but we were ordered to take their photographs. It's not very easy to recognise someone who's had their face blown away. Take it from me – it happened to some of them.' He turned once more and stepped into the light. Clare was looking at him in horror. 'Shocked, Clare? That's fine. *Be* shocked. It stopped worrying me a long time ago. But let me tell you this. I don't know who this Dolohov guy is. If he's got something to do with your dead red-light runners, though, he's not going to want to talk about it. So it's going to be up to me to persuade him. Still think you want to be part of the party?'

It took a moment for Clare to reply. 'Holy Mother of God, Sam. What are you going to do to him?'

Sam looked at her seriously. 'Do to him? Hopefully nothing. Hopefully he'll sing like a canary.'

'And if he doesn't?'

'If he doesn't, I've been trained to make people talk.'

'You're going to hurt him?'

Sam continued with his dead-eyed stare. 'Yes,' he said quietly. He looked at the door. 'We should leave. There's no point waiting and I don't suppose you fancy spending the night in this shit hole any more than I do.'

SIXTEEN

Sam looked at his watch. 11 p.m. The rain had not let up; in fact it was worse. He was soaked to the skin as he walked along the Maida Vale street lined high with mansion blocks. At this hour and in this weather there was nobody else around. Cars had parked double on the road and lights shone out of those flats whose occupants had not yet gone to bed.

Dolohov's mansion block was just like all the others along this part of the road: rather grand, imposing buildings with elaborately tiled entrances and ornate doors. He walked past the building several times, looking up for any likely entry points. Each floor had a small balcony protruding from the front, but without any equipment they were impossible to scale. He walked to both ends of the terraces, looking for fire stairs that he could use to get up to the roofs; but there were none. With grappling irons and the regular resources of the Regiment, gaining entry would be child's play. By himself it was going to be much more difficult. He cursed under his breath as the rain swelled intensively. There was only one way he could get access to this place and that was through the front door.

The mansion block had a state-of-the-art intercom, which Sam viewed from the pavement. He quickly dismissed the idea of simply ringing Dolohov's flat – he wanted to retain the element of surprise – and so he was left with only one option.

He scoured the pavement for a twig – just a small one. Then he bent down and undid his shoelace. And then he lurked under a nearby tree, and waited.

The rain continued to pour, but it made no difference to Sam. He couldn't get any wetter. He could get colder, though, and he did. He started to shiver. He had been waiting for the best part of an hour when a taxi arrived, its yellow beams lighting up the rain and the road as it stopped right outside the mansion block. A woman emerged; she paid the driver, erected her umbrella and walked briskly up to the mansion block. Sam hurried after her. They reached the door at about the same time.

The woman – she was perhaps in her late fifties and had striking, once-beautiful features – looked at him nervously as she held her key fob up to a panel on the intercom. Around her neck she wore an expensive-looking fox fur, the stuffed paws of the animal still attached. The door clicked open and she pushed it.

'Thanks,' Sam said, filling his voice with gratitude. 'Lousy weather, eh.' He looked down and pretended to see that his bootlace was undone. The woman was inside now; Sam crouched down on the doorstep to do up his lace; as he did so, he dropped the twig against the frame of the door. It went unnoticed by the woman who was shaking down her umbrella. Sam stood up again and smiled at her. She looked uncertainly back at him and cleared her throat.

'I don't mean to be rude,' she said, 'but do you have a key?'

Sam shook his head. 'Staying with a friend,' he explained.

The woman looked unsure of herself. 'I'm sorry,' she said, apologetically. 'It's just, we have this agreement, all of us. Would you mind buzzing up? Can't be too careful . . .'

Sam stepped back immediately and held up his hands. 'Of course,' he said cheerfully. 'Very sensible. No problem.'

The woman let go of the door. It started swinging slowly closed. 'Thank you!' she called. 'So sorry!'

She disappeared from sight.

Sam waited. He didn't want to walk in while she could still see him. The door closed, but did not click shut. The twig had done its work.

He gave it a minute before entering. His clothes dripped on the marble floor of the small lobby. To his right was a metal post cabinet with a locked box for each flat. Flat three bore the words *Professor Alexander Dolohov* in a neat, rounded hand. Sam started to climb the stairs.

The stairwell, warmly carpeted and with a smooth banister, was dark. At each landing was a glowing light button, but Sam didn't press them, so his natural night vision became adjusted to the darkness. There was just one flat on each level. As he approached the third floor, he found his heart was pumping fast. Was it nerves, or was he getting out of condition?

Flat 3. The door was like all the others. Glossy black paint, a shiny brass number and a brass bell. Sam looked at the bottom of the door. A thin strip of light escaped. There was somebody there. He took a deep breath. It would be easy enough to shoot the lock and force his way in, but that would cause alarm in the mansion block. Much better to do it the easy way. He rang the bell.

There was silence. Sam couldn't even tell if the bell had sounded. He rang it again and for a slightly longer time. Still silence.

And then a man's voice, slightly high pitched and with the trace of an accent. 'Who is it?'

Sam sniffed. 'Delivery for Dolohov,' he called. 'They let me in down the bottom.'

A pause. No reply. Sam thought he heard footsteps on the other side of the door and without any warning, the strip of light at the bottom of the door disappeared. The darkness in

241

which Sam stood became a little bit more impenetrable. He felt a surge of adrenaline as he stepped to one side of the door and pressed his back against the wall, feeling for his weapon. His hands were steady, but his breathing was deep and slow. All his senses were on high alert.

Suddenly, silently, the door clicked open, just a few inches. Inside was dark.

Sam's sopping clothes were clammy against his skin as he stood in the blackness, carefully selecting his next move. Whoever was inside, whoever this Dolohov character was, he clearly didn't believe that someone had just turned up to deliver him pizza. But the opening of the door was an invitation of some kind. He just didn't know what to. Edging towards the gap, he held the gun firmly in his right hand, while gently pushing the door further open and peering inside.

It was difficult to make much out in the darkness. There was an entrance hall of sorts, a circular table in the middle and an ornate mirror on the wall, which reflected some kind of ambient light seeping in from a room off to his right. He could see nothing to his left because the door was in the way. The walls were filled with bookshelves.

'Alexander Dolohov?' he called.

No reply.

'I need to speak to you. I'm armed. You might as well show yourself. It'll stop things getting messy.'

Silence.

Sam stepped inside. His eyes flitted around, but he couldn't see anyone. He could make a pretty good guess as to where his target was hiding, though: behind the open door. They always chose the most obvious places. Sam momentarily readjusted the gun in his hand and then, in one swift movement, hooked his left foot around the edge of the door, slammed it shut and pointed his weapon into the space that had just been revealed.

No one was there.

It was at that precise moment that he heard the footsteps again. Swifter this time, and behind him. He turned around quickly, just in time to see the silhouette of a man approaching, some kind of cosh held above his head, ready to use. The man was smaller than Sam, smaller and fatter. But fast. Sam just had time to see the thick, square-rimmed glasses that covered his eyes, before the cosh was brought down on his head with a sudden, brutal crack. Dizziness overwhelmed him. He tried to aim his gun again, but he could feel his knees going. Vaguely, he was aware of the cosh being raised once more; he felt it slam against the side of his face.

And then he fell to the ground. He felt sick, but only for a moment as the darkness seemed to close in on him, and he passed out.

★

When Sam awoke, his head felt crushed and his skin was stinging. A light – a bright one – shone into his face, blinding him and making him squint so hard his eyes were almost shut. How long had he been out? He couldn't tell, but as he touched his fingers to his cheek and felt the wetness of his own blood he realised it couldn't have been that long. His clothes were still soggy.

He was sitting on a hard wooden chair at the end of a long table. The lamp was situated at the other end of the table and behind it sat Sam's attacker. In front of him, lying on the table, was Sam's gun; in the man's podgy hand was another weapon – a GSh-18 pistol. Smaller than more modern hand-guns, but a firm favourite of the Russians. Including the Commie cunt in front of Sam.

'Dolohov?' Sam demanded. His voice was little more than a croak and as he spoke a wave of nausea passed through him.

243

A pause. Sam wished he could see the guy's face properly.

'I think it would be wiser,' Dolohov replied with the elegant precision of man for whom English is not a native language, 'if we concentrate first on who *you* are.'

Sam didn't reply. His mind was working overtime.

'A few . . .' Dolohov sounded like he was searching for the right words. 'A few ground rules. I haven't tied you up, but if you move from that seat, I will shoot you without hesitation. I'm sure I don't need to repeat myself. *Do* I need to repeat myself?'

'Your gaff,' Sam replied, peering harder into the light. 'You do what you want.'

'I intend to.' Dolohov stood up and stepped away from the light, revealing more of his features. He was a small, dumpy little man with a jowly face behind unfashionable spectacles. His thin hair was Brylcreemed and combed into a severe parting. He wore slacks and an open collar under his jumper. The small gun in his hand remained firmly pointed in Sam's direction.

'I consider it unlikely,' Dolohov mused, 'that a man such as yourself, armed with a weapon such as that, is a mere delivery boy. A common thief perhaps, here to rob me for drug money?' An unpleasant smile spread across his face as he shook his head. 'I don't think so.'

Sam refused to let any expression cross his face. 'A university professor,' he countered, 'armed and coshing anyone who turns up at his flat late at night. Doesn't quite add up.'

Dolohov gave him an icy look. 'Self-defence,' he stated.

'Sure.' Sam shrugged. 'But against what?'

'Against interfering idiots like you.' Dolohov took a step closer and Sam could sense his anger. 'I recommend that you tell me who you are and what you want, otherwise our conversation will be very short.'

Dolohov's glasses were slightly crooked on his face. If he

wasn't carrying a weapon, he'd look faintly ridiculous. He took another step towards Sam, as if to underline his seriousness.

Keep coming, Sam thought to himself. *Just keep coming.* His face still hurt, but the nausea was passing. 'I thought we might have a chat,' he goaded his assailant.

'About what?'

'About some e-mails.'

Dolohov's lips thinned. 'What e-mails?'

Sam smiled at him, an intentionally arrogant and infuriating smile. He said nothing.

'*What e-mails?*' Dolohov straightened his arm and took another stride towards Sam.

That was all he needed.

Sam moved quickly. With one hand he grabbed Dolohov's podgy wrist in a crunching grip, pulled himself to his feet and circled his other arm tightly round the man's fat neck. Dolohov fired his gun; the bullet slammed into the back of the chair, knocking it a metre along the floor before it rocked and upturned. Sam squeezed Dolohov's neck, while firmly gripping his gun hand.

'Drop the weapon!' he hissed.

A gasping sound from Dolohov's throat, but the gun stayed where it was. There was a fireplace to Sam's right, surrounded by marble and with a shelf above that housed delicate china figurines. Sam twisted Dolohov's body round, then slammed his wrist against the fireplace. One of the figurines toppled and smashed; the gun, too, fell from Dolohov's hand as he gasped in pain. Sam continued to squeeze his neck. The flesh bulged and the gasping sound from Dolohov's throat grew weaker. Sam had to concentrate. Keep the stranglehold for too long and he'd kill the man, but he just wanted him to lose consciousness. It would give Sam a few precious minutes to prepare for what had to happen next.

245

Dolohov's body started to go limp. Sam held firm. The struggling ceased, so he relaxed his grip; as the man fell to the ground he manoeuvred his arms under Dolohov's armpits and gently lowered him to the floor. Two fingers against his neck. A pulse. Sam nodded with satisfaction.

He had to move quickly. Violence like that affected different people in different ways. He could be out for five minutes or thirty seconds. Sam had to restrain his prisoner before he woke.

Running to the entrance of the room he switched the main light on and took a moment to get his bearings. He was in the room that he had seen leading off the entrance hallway. It was plush. Next to the fire there was a comfortable, intricately upholstered armchair and on the opposite wall an antique chaise longue. At one end of the room were big windows looking out over a long garden far below and the roofs and towers of London beyond. Thick, corded curtains hung on either side. There was art on the walls, rich rugs on the floor and books seemingly everywhere.

Sam approached the long table in the middle of the room. He disconnected the light from its socket, then, with a sharp tug, pulled the flex from the lamp. Returning to the body on the floor, he bent down and pulled Dolohov up, plonking him on the chair which had been positioned behind the lamp. He took the flex and wound it tightly round the man's body, arms and around the back of the chair, before tying it tightly. Dolohov could wake up any second, but he wouldn't be going anywhere in a hurry. It gave Sam a chance to explore the house a bit.

To find the tools he needed.

He drew the curtains first, then made sure the front door was locked from the inside. The little kitchen, which was reached by a thin corridor that led off the main hallway, was modern and scrupulously tidy. An unopened bottle of vodka sat on the side. Sam grabbed it, twisted the top open and took a gulp. The fierce alcohol warmed him immediately as he started to rummage through the kitchen drawers. There were plenty of knives, good sharp ones, but it was the sturdy set of poultry shears that caught his attention. He added them to his stash, then helped himself to a few tea towels that were neatly piled up. Rummaging though a cupboard he found a small culinary blowtorch. His man obviously fancied himself as a chef, but he wouldn't be making brûlées tonight. He found a drawer containing a set of DIY tools for odd jobs – pliers, a hammer, two standard-sized screwdrivers. Sam took the pliers. Walking back into the main room, he placed everything on the table. Then he turned back and surveyed Dolohov, whose head was drooping onto his chest.

In the Regiment they called it field interrogation. Torture by any other name, of course. Earnest politicians denounced it in public, but their special forces were well trained in extracting information by whatever means necessary. Sam had long since lost any squeamishness about the Regiment's methods and he wasn't in the mood to mess about. Was he going to torture an innocent man? He shook his head. The guy in front of him oozed many things. Innocence wasn't one of them. Once you'd done this enough times, you got a feel for these things.

Dolohov stirred. He raised his pale face and looked at Sam with the confused expression of someone waking from a long sleep. It took a few seconds for him to remember what was happening; when he did, he stared at Sam with undisguised hate. His eyes flickered towards the gun on the table, but there was no way he could reach it.

Sam took the bottle of vodka, then approached his captive, raising the bottle to Dolohov's lips.

'Drink?' he offered.

Dolohov turned his head away and muttered something. It sounded like Russian. It also didn't sound very polite.

Sam inclined his head, took a swig, then replaced the bottle on the table. He walked round to the back of Dolohov's chair, bent down and spoke just inches from his ear. 'I'm going to give you one chance,' he whispered, 'to tell me absolutely everything you know. Who you are. What you do. Believe me, Dolohov, you don't want to fuck around.'

A pause. And then Dolohov spoke. 'I teach in a university,' he said. His English accent had slipped. 'And you,' he continued, 'you can go to hell.'

Sam's eyes narrowed. He straightened up and walked back round to Dolohov's front. Taking one of the tea towels, he approached the Russian.

'Open your mouth.'

Dolohov kept his lips clenched firmly shut. Sam raised an eyebrow and, without warning, dealt a massive blow to his ample stomach. The Russian gasped loudly, winded by the punch; his eyes bulged as Sam stuffed the tea towel into his mouth. Dolohov's body seemed to go into spasm as he tried to bend over and gasp for air; but the flex and the cloth in his mouth meant he could do neither.

Sam watched as the Russian gradually got control of his breathing and his body. Then he looked around. In one corner of the room was a stereo system. He switched it on and pressed a button on the CD player. Classical music swelled into the room. Sam adjusted the volume: not so loud that it would disturb the neighbours, but loud enough to muffle any sounds that came from the room.

And only then did he take the poultry shears from the table.

By now, Dolohov's glasses had slipped down his nose. He looked over them, noticing the shears for the first time.

Instinctively he shuffled his chair back a few inches, shaking his head. Sam ignored him and approached.

There was no point making threats. The first rule of field interrogation was to let the person you're questioning know that you're serious. 'Remind me,' he said. 'Which hand was it you were holding that gun in? Left or right?' He furrowed his brow theatrically. 'Left, I think. We'll start with the left.'

Dolohov made some kind of noise and shook his head more vigorously. He was sweating like an altar boy in church. Sam walked round to his left-hand side and felt for the Russian's fingers. They were clenched shut, but it was no great problem to unfurl his trigger finger. More noises – squeals, almost. Sam ignored them. He opened up the blade of the shears before clasping them round the base of Dolohov's fat finger.

And then he squeezed.

The sharp blades slipped easily through the layers of skin and fat, like a warm knife cutting into jelly. Only when they hit the bone did he have to squeeze harder. The blades crunched through, more on account of Sam's force than their sharpness. The finger came away and blood flowed copiously from the fresh wound.

Dolohov's body had started convulsing, his muffled squeals more constant. Sam walked casually to the table, placed the amputated finger in full view of its former owner, then picked up the blowtorch. 'We don't want you bleeding to death,' he told the Russian.

It wouldn't take much to cauterise the wound. The cigarette lighter from a car would do it, but Sam had to use the tools at his disposal. The flame from the blowtorch was a pale blue – you could barely see it – but it would do the job nicely. He approached the still-squealing Dolohov and touched the flame to the bleeding stump of his finger. The wet blood dried brown and a foul, acrid smell hit Sam's nose.

Dolohov's arm stiffened with the pain, but the blood stopped flowing.

He stayed out of Dolohov's sight for a few moments before removing and cauterising a second finger – the little finger, this time, on the right hand. The bone was smaller here; the shears made short work of it. It had the same effect on Dolohov, however. The muffled squeals seemed to go into overdrive and he shook so much Sam thought for a moment that his chair might topple over. He walked round to Dolohov's front, switched the blowtorch off for a second time, then stepped back, before pushing the Russian's glasses back on to his face, opening his mouth as if to say something, then making a pretence of deciding against it.

He took the pliers, grabbed the thumb on the Russian's right hand and held it firm. Sam clasped the thumbnail between the jaws of the plier and squeezed, tightly clamping the nail. Then he pulled. He watched with near total detachment as Dolohov squealed like a pig. Sam had to pull hard to tear the nail off, but after several tugs it was loose and he was finally able to drag it out of its roots, like a dentist loosening a tooth.

Sam walked out of the room and back into the kitchen. He'd give Dolohov a few minutes to sweat it out and worry about what was coming next before going back. In the meantime, he turned on the tap and started washing off the blood that had smeared all over his hands. Pink water ran into the basin. His hands were perfectly steady.

Sam rummaged in a cupboard and found a deep saucepan. He filled it with water, then returned to the main room. Dolohov had passed out. Good. He'd hit his pain barrier and he wouldn't want to do that again. Sam stood in front of him, then threw the cold water over his head. The Russian awoke with a shock. He stared at Sam in horror as Sam picked up the wooden chair that had previously been shot down, then placed it opposite his victim before sitting only inches away from him.

'What shall we do next, Professor Dolohov? Same fingers on the other hands? Or maybe . . .'

He smiled, as if a good idea had just struck him, then looked down at Dolohov's crotch. Dolohov shook his head violently – even more violently than before. An odour drifted towards Sam's nostrils. In a situation like this, guys would often piss or cack themselves. It smelled as though Dolohov, the pussy, had done both.

'You're right,' he said. 'We'll leave that till last. After all, it's only a small one isn't it? Drink?' He reached for the bottle, then yanked the tea towel from Dolohov's mouth. This time Dolohov accepted the drink, a good mouthful of it. It didn't stop his heavy breath from shaking and trembling, though. Not a bit of it. He whispered something in Russian, then addressed Sam.

'You are an animal!' he spat.

''Course I'm not,' Sam replied calmly. 'If I was an animal, I'd have started with your thumbs.' He leaned forward conspiratorially. 'Have you got any idea how difficult it is trying to take your underpants off without any thumbs?'

Dolohov gave him a monstrous look.

'But we'll move on to the thumbs next,' Sam continued, 'unless I get what I want.'

'Untie me.'

'Don't be so fucking stupid, Dolohov. I want to know who you are and what you do. And believe me, my friend, if you say the word "university" again, this is going to be a long fucking night for you.'

SEVENTEEN

'*Ja russkii.*'

Dolohov spoke first in his native language. His eyes were closed, perhaps because of the pain, perhaps because he was scared or perhaps in resignation, because telling the truth was a trial for him. He opened them, then reverted to English. 'I am Russian.'

'I'd got that far.'

The Russian pursed his lips with loathing. 'If you know so much, then I will remain quiet.'

Sam just gave him a steady look. Dolohov couldn't withstand it for long. His flabby face was pale and sweating.

'I work for the Russian government.'

'Spetsnaz?' Sam was almost asking himself.

Dolohov sneered. 'Do I look like a Spetsnaz dog?' he demanded, before shaking his head. '*Federalvoi Sluzhbe Bezopasnosti*. The FSB. My country's security service.' Every word he spoke sounded like an effort, as though he was forcing himself against his better judgement. 'Though when I first came to London, it was known by a different name.'

'Ah . . . the KGB.'

Dolohov looked meaningfully at the bottle of vodka. 'I would like . . .' he started to say.

'Just keep talking, Dolohov.'

The Russian breathed deeply. 'I am a professional,' he whispered. 'You are a professional too, I think.'

'We're not talking about me. Keep going.' The smell of burnt flesh still hung in the air.

'I receive orders from Moscow. There are people who need removing. Terrorists. My job is to remove them.'

He closed his eyes again and appeared to be trying to master the pain. A silence fell across the room. Sam slotted this new information into the jigsaw of his mind. The details of the red-light runners. The word DECEASED ominously printed above them. 'You're a hitman.'

Dolohov didn't open his eyes. 'And what are you?' he replied. 'A church warden?'

'The last two hits you made,' Sam demanded. 'Tell me who they were?'

Only then did Dolohov open his eyes again. He moistened his dry lips with his tongue and, although his face was still racked with pain, Sam thought he noticed a glint in his eye. Enthusiasm? He couldn't tell. 'They are dead,' he said.

Sam stood and picked up the shears. Dolohov shook his head violently. 'Young men,' he started gabbling. 'My job is to make their deaths appear accidental. To stop anyone from investigating them further. The last hit was a car crash. I doctored the engine and made it happen when he was speeding on the motorway. Before that . . .' His cheek twitched. 'Before that, what your doctors call auto-erotic asphyxiation. I made it appear as if my target had . . .'

Dolohov continued to talk, but for a moment Sam lost his concentration. The words matched the information Clare had given him. He knew the Russian was telling the truth. 'So you're the guy that's been bumping off the red-light runners,' he said.

'The what?' Dolohov asked. He managed a half-smile. 'That is what you call them? I call them fools.'

An image flashed through Sam's brain. Kazakhstan. The training camp. The bullets pumping into the bodies of the slumbering kids. The photos of their corpses.

'Talk to me,' Sam demanded. 'Everything you know.'

Dolohov's face reverted to its look of hate. 'You work for the British security services?'

'I work for myself. Spit it out, Dolohov. Now.'

The Russian paused before speaking, almost as if gathering his thoughts. Sam listened in silence to the monologue that followed.

'You call them red-light runners. Perhaps they call *themselves* red-light runners? I do not know why. The truth is that they are just foolish young men, targeted by the FSB. A very particular type of person. A type of person that would be attracted by a particular . . . A particular *lifestyle*. A type of person that enjoys danger. A type of person that is easily misled. As I have already told you: fools. They are approached – I do not know how or by whom – and told that they have been selected for a certain purpose: to work undercover for your MI5.'

'Only they're not working for Five at all,' Sam interrupted thoughtfully. 'They're working for the Russians. But they don't know it.'

Dolohov inclined his head. 'They are taken to a training camp where they are given instruction. Surveillance techniques, the construction of improvised explosive devices, weapons training. When they are returned to this country, my government has a sleeping army. If one of them is caught, they do not know who they are really receiving their instructions from. They will always tell the same story – that they are working for MI5.' He gave Sam a piercing look. 'No matter how many of their fingers you cut off.'

'None of this explains why you've been slotting them, Dolohov. You'd better start sounding convincing.'

A wave of pain passed across the Russian's face again. He spoke with difficulty. 'They are told to keep silent, to tell no one. It is . . .' He searched once more for the correct words. 'It is *drummed into them*. But to be silent is not in their nature.

We know, sooner or later, that they will speak. They are weak and impulsive. They cannot help it. For a year, perhaps, they are able to keep their own counsel. But after that, they start to get sloppy. They are not professionals, like us.' Sloppiness, Sam deduced, was something he could not abide. 'That is when I am called in. They are given twelve months. In that time they may or may not have been useful to our cause, but they are eliminated anyway, then replaced by fresh recruits.'

'Jesus,' Sam whispered. The Russian's casual disrespect for the lives of his victims impressed even him. What Dolohov was telling him had begun to fill in some of the gaps; but there were more questions springing into his mind. Some of them he wanted answers to. Others he wasn't sure he did. Dolohov, though, was flagging. It was obvious. His body had taken punishment and his head was starting to droop. Even so, Sam wasn't in the mood to mollycoddle him.

He reached for the bottle of vodka and held it to Dolohov's lips. The Russian took a gulp, then winced slightly as the alcohol burned his throat. Sam stood then turned and faced the fireplace. A thick silence descended. He contemplated his next question.

'I'm afraid,' Sam said finally, 'that I don't really believe you.'

He turned once more, strode quickly to the table and before Dolohov knew what was happening he had grabbed the shears and was already unfurling one of the Russian's thumbs. Dolohov tried to shout out, but his breathlessness stopped him for a moment. When he eventually managed to speak, it was with more of a sense of terrified urgency than Sam had ever heard before.

'There's more. I can tell you more. *Do not do it again!*'

Sam paused. Dolohov was almost weeping now. Through gritted teeth, the ultimate humiliation. His good English failed him. '*I begging you not do again.*'

'Start talking.' Sam kept the blades of the shears resting against the skin of the Russian's thumb.

Dolohov spoke quickly. 'I do not know everything. They do not *tell* me everything. It is better that way. But I know *some* things. One of them is to be activated. Maybe he already has. A major hit. Political. It will happen soon.'

'Who?'

'I do not know.'

'I don't believe you, Dolohov.' He allowed the blade to slice gently the skin on his thumb.

'*I do not know! I would tell you if I did . . .*' And again his voice collapsed into sobs of helpless terror.

'What's the name of the red–light runner?'

But Dolohov couldn't speak. He just shook his head, desperately, while the sounds of animal fear emerged from his throat.

Sam found himself breathing deeply and sharply. He let the Russian's hand fall, ignoring the trickle of blood that seeped from the small flesh wound. Without a word he walked out of the room. He felt the sudden need to be alone, away from Dolohov. The need to collect his thoughts. The need to decide if he really wanted to ask the question that was on his lips. There was a fire in his blood. Anger. His head was spinning. In some corner of his brain he knew that Dolohov's life was hanging by a thread. Sam Redman was on the edge, barely able to control himself. A nudge in the wrong direction and he would do to the Russian what both of them had done to any number of red–light runners.

He calmed himself. His eyes narrowed and his jaw set. He walked back into the room feeling numb, but somehow purposeful at the same time. Dolohov was slumped, corpse-like. Sam had seen it before – the shock that drained all colour from someone's face. Even his lips were grey. He stood in front of the man and gave him a thunderous look.

'Who gives you the orders?' he asked. 'Who tells you to kill the red-light runners? Who gives you the details?'

Dolohov raised his head and paused as he summoned up the last dregs of his arrogance.

'You really know nothing,' he observed in a weak voice. 'Is our system really so difficult for you to work out?'

Sam didn't hesitate. His body under the control of some force other than his thoughts, he grabbed his handgun from the table and pressed it hard against Dolohov's head.

'*Who?*'

'The same man who trains them,' Dolohov whispered. A trickle of sweat ran down the side of his face. 'British. We never meet.'

'Damn it, Dolohov. What's his name?'

They'll tell you things, Sam. Things about me. Don't forget that you're my brother. Don't believe them.

It was like a dream. Sam heard the words and they were like a trigger firing a weapon. Out of control, he raised his gun hand and slammed his fist against the side of Dolohov's face. The Russian's glasses cracked and flew across the room; the chair in which he was sitting tottered back and fell to the ground, taking its occupant with it.

Sam knelt down and once more pressed the gun against the Russian, this time into the flesh of his neck. '*I don't believe you,*' he hissed. '*Tell me the truth. What's his name?*'

But Dolohov was past lying. He repeated himself slowly and in an exhausted tone of voice. 'His name is Jacob Redman,' he croaked. 'Now I have nothing more to tell you. And if you are going to kill me, I ask that you do it now and you do it quickly.'

★

A bright orange sun rose slowly above the horizon of southern Kazakhstan. The countryside through which Jacob

257

Redman drove his truck was bland. Flat and featureless. Every few miles he would drive past a settlement, but he saw only the occasional shepherd. Now, though, up ahead and in the distance, he saw the bleak sight of Communist-era tower blocks emerging above the horizon – concrete monuments to a time long gone, but they were still inhabited, no doubt. There were cars here on the outskirts, as well as the ever-present goats. Jacob just kept his eyes on the road ahead.

He was getting close now. His journey was nearly at an end.

The road took him past the town and further into the flat landscape. In his rear-view mirror he watched as a military vehicle approached from behind, clad in green and brown camouflage webbing and carrying God only knows what. Jacob allowed the truck to overtake him, but then kept the vehicle in his sights. After all, the chances were that they were heading for the same place.

Gradually, he began to see landmarks, sights that he knew indicated he was indeed on the right path. A control tower in the distance with a satellite receiver spinning slowly on the top. More vehicles – articulated lorries as well as military ones. Brown-grey concrete buildings, austere, unwelcoming constructions that again spoke of this country's Soviet past.

Jacob was tired. He had been driving non-stop, allowing himself ten minutes shut-eye every few hours just so that he could keep going. Now that he was nearing the end, however, he felt a surge of adrenaline. It was no longer a struggle to keep awake. His mind was alert.

A fork in the road. The military vehicle up ahead bore left. Jacob followed. They continued through the drab countryside for several miles before he saw a high, wire boundary fence emerging from the distance. The military truck began slowing down. There were signposts now along the side of the road. Jacob couldn't decode them because they were in

Russian, but he could tell that they were warnings to stay away. He continued driving nevertheless.

They were only metres from the boundary now. A large panel announced their location in austere black letters.

Космодром Байконур

Jacob's Russian was good enough for that. Baikonur Cosmodrome. Built by the Soviets in the mid-Fifties, it was the largest operational space launch facility in the world. The truck ground to a halt. The military vehicle ahead was allowed in, giving Jacob a plain view of the entrance as the truck disappeared into the vast expanse of the cosmodrome. There was a barrier marked with red and white stripes. The boundary fence had rolls of barbed wire on the top that made it look like some kind of concentration camp. There was a lookout post, but it was old and didn't give Jacob the impression of being much used. By the barrier were a number of guards. They wore military uniform and carried the ubiquitous AK-47s. Jacob, in his non-military truck, had clearly raised their suspicions. Two guards approached, their weapons raised.

Jacob put his hands on his head.

The driver's side door was opened. Chatter from the soldiers. Russian. It made no sense to Jacob. A few of them swarmed round the back. It wouldn't take them long to find Jacob's own AK stashed away with the fuel canisters. He needed to be careful not to make any sudden moves. With his hands still on his head he stepped out of the car. There were two AK-47s pointing right at him, and they were just the ones he could see.

And then he spoke. Not in his own language, but using the small amount of Russian at his disposal, the words that he had been practising in preparation for this moment over the past twenty-four hours.

'Menya zovut Jacob Redman. Ya rabotayu v Federalnoi Sluzhbe Bezopasnosti. Ya hocu vstretit s nachalnikom etogo faculteta.'

'My name is Jacob Redman,' he said. 'I am working with the FSB. Take me to the head of this facility.'

PART THREE

EIGHTEEN

Vaziani Airbase. Georgia. Sixty miles from the Russian border.
If anybody had been looking into the dawn sky, they would have seen the lights of the RAF C-17 Globemaster glowing in the distance as it made its approach. But nobody was watching. Aircraft were hardly a curiosity here, either for the Georgian nationals that manned the base or for the small platoon of British troops who kept themselves to themselves, but were not welcomed with much enthusiasm by their hosts.

So it was that the Globemaster, which had made its way from the UK over commercial airline routes – only to stray off piste towards Vaziani at the very end of its journey – was little more than a blip on the air-traffic control screens until it thundered towards the runway, its emissions causing the air all around to wobble and become hazy. As it turned off the runway and started taxiing towards the hangars, it passed an area of bombed-out land, scars of the attack on the base by Russian fighter jets in the late summer of 2008. The attack had not been so bad as to damage the infrastructure of the base itself, and the Globemaster came to a halt without any problems.

The engines had almost wound down to silence by the time three forklift trucks had trundled up to the aircraft. Unusually, though, they were shadowed by two military vehicles. The Georgian airbase staff were unimpressed with the British troops' insistence on accompanying them every

263

step of the way; but the troops themselves had their orders, and that was to make sure they were present at all times during the unloading of the Globemaster's cargo.

It didn't take long. It was a small cargo for such a large plane. Eight cases, each of them about the same size as a small van; wooden, and with the words HUMANITARIAN AID emblazoned on the side in big black letters. Under the watchful eye of both the troops and the loadies from the Globemaster, the forklift operators carefully transported each box into one of the nearby aircraft hangars. When they had completed their task, they left with their vehicles, without even a gruff nod at any of their guests.

The hangar doors were swung shut. It was a huge, cavernous space lit by industrial strip lighting, and in which the voices of the troops echoed and rebounded. They had made the place their own in the weeks that they had been here. In one corner of the hangar were low tables with full ashtrays; a few mattresses were unfurled on the ground; someone had even cadged an old black and white TV set, but it was largely unused. Russian-language TV didn't hold much interest for them.

In the centre of the hangar, just metres from where the crates had been unloaded, stood a man. He was the only person in the place who wasn't in army camouflage gear; instead he wore perfectly ordinary civvies, and not very fashionable ones at that. He was approaching middle age, wore rimless glasses and had a balding head, which he disguised by careful brushing of what remained of his thin hair. The guys called him 'Doc'. Their standard joke was to ask him for remedies for imaginary ailments that they'd made up on the spot – usually some grotesque affliction of the genitals. The Doc took it all in good humour. He had long since given up telling them that the letters after his name were not a medical qualification but a scientific one. After all, there weren't so many jokes to be made about the scientific engineering that was his particular area of expertise.

The Doc held a clipboard with an inventory list. Eight cases. He ticked them off. Then he turned to the nearest three soldiers and waved his pencil vaguely at them. 'Would you mind?' he asked politely.

One of the soldiers grinned at him. 'Don't know what you'd do without us, Doc,' he said good-naturedly. He strode to one corner of the hangar before returning with a large metal crowbar. The wooden crate made a splintering sound as the guys forced it open, revealing its contents.

'That what you ordered, Doc?' None of the soldiers appeared remotely surprised that the contents of the crate, whatever they were, were most decidedly *not* humanitarian aid. There were several long, wide-calibre metal cylinders; there were conical warheads and various other intricate bits of machinery. The Doc ticked these items off on his list before asking for the crate to be sealed once more, while the others were opened and checked.

'Hope *you* know how all this stuff fits together, Doc,' a voice called from behind him. 'Looks like a fucking overblown Meccano set to me.'

The Doc didn't take his eyes from the clipboard. 'Yes,' he said vaguely, before turning round and peering at the soldier over his glasses. 'You might want to put that out,' he said, indicating the cigarette hanging from the soldier's lips.

The soldier blinked, then dropped the cigarette on the floor as if it were suddenly red hot. He ground it out with his foot.

The Doc nodded with approval, then turned back to his clipboard with a faint, unnoticed smile. A cigarette, of course, would cause no damage whatsoever to the components that had just been delivered. But the guys were keen enough to take the mickey out of him. He didn't see why he shouldn't have a bit of fun of his own.

He continued with his inventory. It took the best part of an hour to check all eight cases, but at the end of that time he was satisfied that everything was present and correct. He cleared his throat and issued his polite instruction.

'All right,' he called to the assembled company. 'Everything's here. You can load the cases up and move them on. And please, be gentle with them. You might all have the heart and soul of Spanish baggage handlers, but we really don't want to be throwing these things around too much, now do we?'

★

You'll be sent a package. It will contain everything you need. Only open it when you're alone. Don't let anybody else see what's in it. The abrupt instructions of his handler, the dark-featured former soldier who had trained Jamie Spillane and the others in Kazakhstan, had scarcely left his head since he had called a few days ago.

The package had arrived two days later. Jamie Spillane didn't know who had sent it, but he decided not to think about that too much. The landlady who owned the bedsit where he was staying had been unable to disguise her interest in the box. She brought it up to his room and stood in the doorway for far too long a time after she had placed it in his hands and received a curt word of thanks from Jamie, who had been forced to shut the door in her face. Nosy bitch.

He had looked at the package for a good long time before opening it: half because he was waiting for the landlady to piss off, half because he was nervous. It just sat there on the bed in its tightly wound brown packing tape and neatly typed label. Jamie smoked a cigarette, locked his door from the inside and paced the room before he even attempted to open it.

It took a while. His chewed nails were not up to the task of unpeeling the packing tape. He was forced instead to use a key from the bunch in his pocket to tear into the tape and open up the box. The contents were cushioned in a roll of protective plastic, the type that as a kid he had liked to pop between his fingers. Jamie discarded it without so much as a squeeze and stared for a moment at the contents inside.

He removed the camera first. It was heavy. Chunky. Not a lightweight little gizmo for taking random snaps, but a serious piece of kit. Included in the box was a telephoto lens. It took Jamie a while to work out how to fit it to the body of the camera, but once he had managed it he was pleased with the result. He took the camera to the small window which looked out over the street and into the attic rooms beyond. While he had been looking out the previous night, he could have sworn some chick had been undressing in one of those windows. It was too far to be seen and enjoyed with the naked eye, but now that he had a bit of help . . .

She wasn't there. He sniffed, then pulled down the blind and dumped the camera on to his bed. Only then did he turn his attention back to the box. It wasn't as deep as it had looked from the outside and his hands were trembling with excitement as he unpacked the compartment at the bottom. Excitement and a little apprehension. As he pulled out the small, black handgun, his mind flashed back to the training camp. *If you need a weapon, it will be supplied to you. Don't fuck things up by trying to get hold of one yourself. People will just start asking questions.*

He liked the way it felt in his hand. A Colt. He felt pleased with himself for recognising it. He aimed it towards the door and discharged a silent, imaginary bullet. Then another. And then, laying the handgun on the bed next to the camera, he removed the final item from the package: a box of rounds.

Only then did he go about choosing a hiding place for his new toys . . .

And now, two days later, he was making use of one of them.

He had arrived in Russell Gardens, West London, at 6.30 a.m., the earliest the Underground would allow. He could have taken a cab, of course, but that would not have been secure. *Don't let anybody know where you are or what you're doing.* Much better to take advantage of the anonymity of the Tube. The building he wanted, couched between the relative bustle of Kensington High Street and the Holland Park roundabout, was totally unremarkable. Had it not been for a small plaque by the door which read *Embassy of Georgia to the United Kingdom of Great Britain and Northern Ireland* it would have been impossible to say what function it served. Jamie loitered, but not too close. He couldn't *see* any CCTV, but that didn't mean there wasn't any. Anyway, he didn't need to be too close. That was what the telephoto lens was for, after all.

It was cold in the early morning, so Jamie was pleased with the hooded top he wore underneath his coat. It kept him warm as well as going some way to concealing his face. Even so, he had to stamp his feet as he waited. *They arrive between eight and ten in the morning.* It meant he could be waiting for some time. Jamie didn't mind. Quite the opposite. He was excited. His fingertips tingled. He was looking forward to executing the first part of his assignment. He thought about the people who were always so quick to think the worst of him. Mum. Dad. Even Kelly. If they could only see him now. His mouth was dry with the thrill of it.

He took a seat on a bench on the opposite side of the road, making sure that he had a clear view of the embassy. Removing his mobile phone, he started fiddling with it to blend into the background. Just some kid obsessed with texting, people would think. He continued to wait. Now and then he would put one hand into his pocket. The Colt was there and he would grip it. It felt good.

No more than twenty-five metres to the main entrance, he calculated. It would be fine.

He waited some more.

In the event, it was just after nine when a car pulled up outside the embassy. It was chauffeur driven, but it wasn't a particularly grand or impressive vehicle – a bog-standard Renault Laguna. Its hazard lights flashed as it double parked, while the chauffeur stepped out and opened the back door. Two men emerged. They were both rather fat, one clearly older than the other. As they squeezed through the parked cars, on to the pavement and up to the steps of the embassy, it was the older man who took the lead, walking with a kind of brusque impatience. The second man followed several steps behind. His gait was a little less ostentatious and he carried in his right hand a quite ordinary-looking briefcase.

Jamie raised his camera, zoomed in and started to snap. He managed to take a substantial burst of photographs before the younger of the two men stopped, turned and looked behind him. Through the zoom of the camera, Jamie saw that the man was staring straight at him.

He felt his blood freeze. He lowered the camera and instinctively pulled his hood down. *If they see you, don't panic. Just walk away. They'll assume you're the Press.* He turned heel and walked to the end of the road. Adrenaline surged through him. Any moment now, he thought to himself, I'm going to feel a hand on my shoulder. They're following me.

He upped his pace.

Jamie turned the corner, into the busy main street. He ran across the road, ignoring the beeps from the cars, which had to brake and swerve to avoid him. On the opposite pavement he stopped and looked back.

No one.

He grinned as he felt a sudden exhilaration. It had gone well. He put his hand over the screen at the back of the camera and flicked through the images he had taken. They were good. He'd got what he wanted. That evening, having changed his clothes and therefore his appearance, he would repeat his performance, this time outside the Georgian Orthodox Church further west of here, where he had been told these two men worshipped regularly. From a randomly chosen Internet café he would e-mail the best of his photographs to the address he had been given.

And then he would lie low and wait. Wait for another package, and for the opportunity to carry out the second part of his instructions.

*

Dolohov's wounds were bad. He kept asking for vodka, but Sam refused to give him any. He needed to use the alcohol to keep the stumps disinfected, a rough and ready way of stopping his captive from developing fever, but the best he could come up with. Dolohov managed not to scream when he plunged the wounds into a bowl of vodka, but that was more out of exhaustion, Sam sensed, than bravery. He found codeine in the bathroom cabinet and kept the Russian dosed up on that. It was hardly going to remove the pain, but it would take the edge off for as long as the supply lasted.

They sat in silence, Dolohov still restrained by the electrical flex. It was clear that the Russian knew how close he had come to death. When he had uttered Jacob's name, a madness had come over Sam. He knew what people looked like when they thought they were about to die. Dolohov had that look.

But Sam had calmed himself at the last moment. And he

had done his best to keep calm during the slow hours before morning. Apart from during Sam's painful make-shift medical attentions, the two of them had sat in silence, Dolohov obviously trying to manage the pain and Sam trying to manage the implications of what he had just learned.

After Bland had collared him and spun him the MI6 line, Sam had simply not believed him. There were too many things that just didn't add up and Jacob's parting words had never been far from the front of his mind. But Dolohov had no reason to lie to him. On the contrary, he had every reason to tell the truth. What was more, Dolohov did not know Sam's name. He did not know his relationship to Jacob. Bland might have been playing mind games; Dolohov almost certainly wasn't.

And then there was the evidence of the laptop. It was Jacob's – at least, it had been taken from Jacob's things – and he *had* e-mailed details of the dead red-light runners to someone. Whichever way he looked at it, Dolohov's story stacked up.

Except for one thing. If the Russian was telling him the truth, his brother was no longer the man he once knew. He had become someone else.

Sam turned to the big windows at the end of the room and parted the curtains. The low, crisp sun of dawn shot in. Sam winced, but did not move the curtains. The morning sky was red and scudded with lean pink clouds. There was a chorus of birdsong. In Kazakhstan it would be later in the day, but the same sun would be shining down. Shining down on Jacob. What would his brother be doing now?

What the *hell* would his brother be doing?

Treason. It's not a terribly fashionable word is it? Bland's voice was as clear in Sam's head as if he were actually there. *I would say, in circumstances such as this, that a man might become bitter.*

Sam found himself having to control his anger again.

They'll tell you things, Sam. Things about me. Don't forget that you're my brother. Don't believe them.

How could he forget that? How could he believe them? Jacob *was* his brother. He deserved the benefit of the doubt. But he also had some explaining to do. For a moment, Sam considered contacting Bland again, telling him what he knew. But he put that thought from his mind. The memory of the Spetsnaz troops in Kazakhstan, of Craven's death, was still fresh. Nobody had yet explained to him with any degree of satisfaction how the Russians knew they were coming. The Regiment had been expected and in Sam's book that meant one thing: a tip-off. Go singing to MI6 and the chances were that every word of his conversation would end up on a transcript roll somewhere in Moscow. He shook his head as he continued to look out at the night sky.

Sam needed to see Jacob. Face to face. To ask him the questions that needed asking. His brother deserved that at the very least. And mole or no mole, he needed to do it without the interference of MI6. They would be heavy handed in their questioning. They would more than likely torture him to get the truth. They would do to Jacob what Sam had done to Dolohov, or something like. And he wasn't prepared to let that happen.

He turned to Dolohov.

'Can you contact him?' he asked abruptly.

Dolohov, bleary eyed, raised his head. Jesus, he looked like shit. 'Who?' he demanded.

'Jacob Redman.'

Momentarily, a wily look crossed Dolohov's face. It disappeared as soon as it had arrived, to be replaced by that sombre expression; it did not, however, go unnoticed by Sam.

'Yes,' Dolohov replied. 'I can contact him.'

'How?'

'By e-mail.'

Sam nodded. He thought for a while longer before speaking again. 'Do you often contact him?' he asked.

Dolohov gave him a contemptuous look, as though it were a stupid question. 'It has never happened yet.'

'But if you asked for a meeting, would he come?'

Dolohov shrugged. 'I don't know. He could be anywhere in the world.' A pause. 'But yes, I think he would come. I am a man of a certain importance.'

Sam approached the chair. 'I'm going to untie you,' he said. 'I've got your gun and mine. One of them will be pointing in your direction all the time.'

The Russian sneered.

'I mean it, Dolohov. You won't even be able to take a shit without me being there. Just in case you had any plans to play silly buggers.'

'To play what?'

'Just do what you're told, Dolohov. If you want to make it through the day, that is.' Sam walked round to the back of the chair and untied the flex. It fell from around Dolohov's body. The Russian raised his arms and for the first time looked at his hands. They were a mess. The skin was stained and smeared with blood and the stumps where his fingers used to be glistened painfully. Dolohov looked bilious.

'Count yourself lucky you didn't go the way of the red-light runners, Dolohov,' Sam told him, pointing his gun nonchalantly in the Russian's direction. 'But there's still time, so let's not fuck around. Where's your computer?'

Dolohov looked towards the main doors of the room, out on to the hallway. 'In my bedroom,' he said.

'Get moving.'

The Russian pushed himself weakly to his feet. He was unable to walk in a straight line as he staggered out of the room with Sam following behind – close, but not too close. The guy was a trained assassin, after all.

The bedroom was large and high-ceilinged. It was dominated by a big iron bed with an elegant patchwork quilt. There was a fireplace in this room, too; and next to it, against the wall, a large oak desk with a laptop computer neatly placed upon it.

'Sit down,' Sam instructed. 'Open up the computer.' Dolohov did as he was told. Sam paused as a thought hit him. 'If you send e-mail from here, is it secure? Can anyone tap in?'

Dolohov shook his head. 'Of course not. I have a virtual private network. I can communicate with Moscow, or anyone, without the risk of my communications being intercepted.' He placed his wounded hands flat on the table. 'I assume from your question,' he said shrewdly, 'that you are not involved with the security services.'

Sam remained dead-eyed. He put his gun against the back of his captive's head. 'Just do what you're told, Dolohov. Write it now. Request a meeting. As soon as possible.'

He watched as Dolohov slowly and painfully used one of his remaining fingers to type a message. With each stroke of the keyboard he winced, leaving a moist trail of red where the stumps brushed against it. The message was short and to the point. MEETING NEEDED. URGENT. REVERT WITH TIME AND PLACE. DOLOHOV. The Russian slid one finger over the mouse pad, inserted an e-mail address into the address field, then directed the cursor towards the send button.

'Stop,' Sam said.

Dolohov froze.

'Put your hands on the table. Both of them.'

Sam removed the gun from the back of Dolohov's head, walked round to his side and pressed the weapon against the

274

back of the Russian's right hand. Dolohov looked up at him in horror.

'You think I'm stupid?' Sam growled.

'What do you mean?' Dolohov's voice was little more than a breath.

'I think you might have forgotten something,' Sam pressed; and from the way Dolohov jutted out his jaw involuntarily, he could tell his suspicion was on the money. Dolohov would have some way of raising a distress signal in a situation like this. A phrase to be inserted into any communication or, more likely, a phrase to be omitted. 'Are you going to alter that message so that it doesn't raise any alarms?' Sam demanded. 'Or are you and I going to start talking about how useful your thumbs are again?' He pressed the gun down harder. 'It's up to you, Dolohov. But I think you know I'm not fucking around.'

A pause. And then, slowly, Dolohov's free hand slid once more to the keyboard. At the beginning of the e-mail he typed an extra sentence: ALL IS WELL AT THE UNIVERSITY. His breath was shaking as he waited for further instruction from Sam.

Sam gave it a few seconds. Then he raised the gun and put it to the side of Dolohov's head. 'I don't believe you,' he said, his voice grim.

Dolohov's body slumped. He opened his mouth to speak, but no words came. Either he was a brilliant actor, or Sam had scared all the remnants of duplicity out of him.

'All right,' he said. 'Send the thing.'

It looked to Sam as if it took all of Dolohov's energy to raise his hand again. But he did it and with what looked like a superhuman effort, he moved the cursor once more to the send button.

And then he clicked. The window disappeared. The e-mail was sent.

It could be an hour before they received a reply. It could be a day. It could be a week. All they could do now was wait.

NINETEEN

FSB Headquarters. Moscow.
In the era of Communism, the huge, austere yellow-brick building on Lubyanka Square had housed not only the offices of the KGB, but also their prison. Many people who came to the attention of the secret police could expect to end up in this building, where torture and forced inter-rogation were commonplace. Not far from the centre of Moscow, it served as a constant reminder that the state would accept no dissent. Now, however, its reputation was less severe. It was still an administrative building, and no doubt it harboured many ghosts for those Muscovites who still remembered those dark days, but people could now walk past it without feeling a nervous chill that was nothing to do with the weather. Without feeling that the building itself was watching them.

Jacob Redman, emerging from the car that had been waiting on the tarmac for him at the airport, looked up at it. The car's windows were tinted, so he squinted as the bright daylight hit his eyes. He'd managed to get some much needed shut-eye on the plane that had transported him directly from Baikonur to Moscow, under the watchful eye of the two Russian soldiers that had accompanied him. Even now they were escorting him from the car up to the main entrance of the building that now housed part of the FSB's offices. Jacob walked briskly and with purpose. The heels of his shoes echoed on the hard floor of the cavernous entrance hall, which still bore signatures of its past – a lack of natural light and a kind of facelessness that hid the terrible things that had once gone on here. A suited official recognised him immediately and, with a nod first at Jacob and then at the two soldiers – an indication they were no longer required – he led the Englishman silently up three flights of stairs, along a corridor, which Jacob knew looked like every other corridor in this building, until they reached a door. The suit knocked, then held the door open and Jacob walked in. The door was closed tactfully behind him.

It was a large office, more comfortable than might perhaps have been expected given the basic nature of the rest of the building, but hardly luxurious. Thin carpet tiles on the floor. A leather sofa, but old. And a functional desk in the centre of the room, behind which sat a man. Nikolai Surov was a thin, sallow-faced man with sharp eyes and perfectly white hair. It was impossible to judge his age. Fifty? Sixty? Seventy? Any of these were possible. He was reading a report of some description; as Jacob entered, he raised his eyes. There was no expression in them, but that was usual. Jacob had met the director of the FSB enough times to know that he played his cards very close to his chest.

Surov indicated a chair on the opposite side of the desk. 'Sit down,' he said. His English was thickly accented, but very good. Jacob took a seat as Surov laid his report on the table and gazed at him with his inscrutable eyes.

'We had not expected to see you in Moscow for a long time,' Surov said finally.

'Thanks for the warm welcome.'

His sarcasm was lost on the director. 'They did not offer you a shower and some clean clothes at Baikonur?'

Jacob was unshaven and dirty. 'I guess they must have forgotten their manners. They told you what happened at the training camp?'

Surov nodded. 'How can you be sure it was the SAS?'

'I recognise their handwriting.' He hadn't mentioned Sam in his report. There were some things the man sitting opposite him *didn't* need to know. 'What happened to your Spetsnaz boys who were supposed to be keeping watch in case something like this happened?'

'Dead,' the director said shortly. 'Along with all the recruits. Your former colleagues did their work well.'

Jacob remained stony-faced. 'I told you a four-man unit wouldn't be enough.'

The director appeared not to hear. He sat silently for nearly a minute before he spoke again. 'Your agent in London . . .' He scanned his desk for another piece of paper. 'Jamie Spillane?' His rendition of the name, couched as it was in his thick Russian accent, made it almost unrecognisable.

Jacob nodded.

'He has been activated. We have supplied him with what he needs. You are sure he is . . .' Surov's eyes narrowed. 'You are sure he is fitted for the task?'

'As well as any of them,' Jacob said shortly.

'He will be discreet?'

Jacob shrugged. 'Who knows? As discreet as any of them can be. Once you hand him over to the Georgians, he can be as indiscreet as he likes.'

'And you are confident he believes he is working for MI5?'

'He has no reason not to.'

'Good. This is a very important operation for the continuing security of the Russian people. There will be a medal for you.'

'I'm not interested in medals. Just the money.'

Surov nodded. 'There will be that, of course. The assassination will be the last operation for your students. Now that the British know what is happening, I am

279

ordering the immediate elimination of all unactivated agents in the field.' He smiled. 'All except Jamie Spillane, of course.'

Jacob remained expressionless. 'Sounds like Dolohov's going to be busy.'

Again Surov nodded. 'Dolohov. Yes. We need to speak about Dolohov. You have received a communication from him.' For a split second Surov's eyes showed signs of amusement at Jacob's flicker of surprise. 'You did not know that we monitor your e-mails? Of course we do.'

'Of course,' Jacob replied flatly. 'What does Dolohov want?'

'To meet you.'

Jacob raised an eyebrow in suspicion. 'Bit of a coincidence?'

'It is worrying. We can rest assured that Dolohov does not know the details of the Georgian operation. But it is unusual for him to make any contact with us at all.'

'Any distress signals?'

'On the contrary, he included his identification code with the message. It's definitely from Dolohov.'

'Don't be so sure,' Jacob replied. 'If *I* wanted to get him to do what I said, I've got a few tricks up my sleeve.'

The director looked perplexed. 'Tricks up your sleeve?' he asked before shaking his head in momentary annoyance at his lack of understanding. 'There is,' he said, once he had regained his composure, 'every possibility that Dolohov has been compromised.'

'Then you need to take him out,' Jacob said. 'Now.'

Surov's eyes narrowed. He put his arms in front of him and pressed his fingertips together. 'Dolohov is a valued agent,' he said. 'He has worked for this service – and the service that preceded it – for many, many years. Even before glasnost and perestroika.' He smiled. '*Especially* before glasnost and perestroika. In the days of the old regime, he was a most committed patriot. That is not a quality you value highly, I know . . .'

Jacob gave him a dark look. 'Patriotism's a two-way street, Surov.'

'Dolohov performed many . . .' He inclined his head. 'Many *operations*.'

'Perhaps he just likes killing people.'

'Perhaps,' Surov acknowledged. 'But he continues to be of great use to us even now. If he has truly been compromised, then yes, I would agree that action needs to be taken. But we owe him the courtesy of finding out. As you say, patriotism is a two-way street.'

'Fine,' Jacob said shortly. 'Good luck.'

The director looked at him meaningfully. 'Dolohov is an unusually skilled operator,' he continued. 'If he has requested a meeting with you, then a meeting with you is the only thing that will satisfy him. Anything else will scare him off. The Georgian operation will reach its conclusion in five days' time. And with the end of your operations in Kazakhstan, it would seem that you are available to us for other purposes. Assuming, that is, that you remain committed to helping us?'

Jacob looked away for a moment. He felt the muscles in his face tense up. 'What do you want me to do?'

Surov didn't take his eyes from him. 'Go to England,' he said. 'Determine whether Dolohov has been compromised. If not, speak to him. If he has, in that case you know what to do.'

'So much for your two-way patriotism,' Jacob muttered.

The FSB director answered immediately. 'We are at least giving him a chance. That is more than the British government ever did for you, is it not?'

Jacob stood up. Already his mind was turning over.

Getting to England would not be child's play. He didn't want to risk a fake Russian passport with UK immigration. If the alert had gone out about him, his likeness would have been distributed to all the ports of entry. No. He'd have to do something different. Get entry to another country using false papers and make his own arrangements from there.'

'Can you get me to France?' he asked the director.

'Of course,' Surov said mildly.

'Then tell Dolohov I'll meet him. Three days from now. 10 p.m. The statue of Eros in Piccadilly.' He stood up and made to leave.

'Sit down, please.' A hint of steel in Surov's voice.

Jacob hesitated, then retook his seat.

'You have not been to the UK for some time.'

'Six years.'

'Many things change in six years. We informed you of your mother's death. You were wise enough to stay away, not to let sentiment cloud your judgement.'

Jacob remained silent.

'You will continue to do the same, I hope.'

Again, silence.

'Your father is unwell,' Surov said. Jacob could sense he was waiting for a reaction; he gave him none. Surov handed him a photograph: a bleak-looking building with lots of cars parked outside. Jacob thought he recognised it. 'Very unwell. He is in residential care here. I am telling you this in case you feel the urge to go asking questions. The urge to hunt him out. You do not need me to tell you that this would be a very bad idea.'

Jacob put the photograph back down on the table. 'He's dead to me,' he told the Russian.

Surov reclaimed the picture. 'Good,' he said. 'Very good. We will supply you with a passport and tickets to France within the hour. You need money? We will arrange it. You will be on the next flight out. Is there anything else you need from me?'

Jacob shook his head. 'Nothing else,' he said, before turning and leaving the director of the FSB alone with his thoughts.

★

Jacob Redman had not been gone more than a minute when there was another knock on the door of the office of Nikolai Surov. '*Prikhoditye,*' the director intoned. '*Come in.*'

The man who entered was a good deal younger than Surov. He wore a neat but inexpensive suit, though the tidiness of his clothes was more than offset by the unruliness of his hair. He had sharp eyes and an unsmiling face. Surov indicated that he should sit down, but the younger man preferred to stand.

'You were listening, Ivan?'

Ivan nodded. 'Of course.'

Surov raised an eyebrow to encourage Ivan to continue speaking.

'I do not trust Jacob Redman,' Ivan said. 'I have never made a secret of that.'

Surov inclined his head. 'Of course not,' he accepted. 'But then, you do not trust anybody. That's why you are good at your job.'

If Ivan took Surov's comment as a compliment, there was no indication of it on his stony face. 'I have a friend,' he said. 'He got himself a new woman. She left her husband for him. And now she is cheating on my friend. I asked him if he was surprised. He said, "Not really."'

Ivan had earned the right to speak his mind, in Surov's view. He had a natural aptitude for intelligence work and was running networks all over the world that were of paramount importance to the FSB. One day, Surov knew, if politics didn't get in the way, Ivan would be running the service.

'That's a charming parable, Ivan,' he said with a half-smile. 'I suppose it has some sort of relevance to our discussion.'

Finally Ivan took a seat. 'Jacob Redman betrayed his country. That makes him untrustworthy by definition.'

Surov pressed his fingertips together. 'That is one way of looking at things,' he conceded. 'But there are others. Jacob Redman is, I think, more complicated than you imagine.' He stood up and started to pace the room. 'Your friend's lover,' he asked. 'The one who is cheating on him. I wonder what her former husband thinks of her?'

No reply from Ivan.

'He hates her, I would imagine. Perhaps he wishes her dead, I don't know. Make no mistake, Ivan. Jacob Redman hates his country. He served them well, but he was badly treated. Humiliated. Oh, I do not blame them – the British, I mean. Some things are more important than the embarrassment of a soldier, no matter how good he is. But the British made a dangerous enemy in him. Outcast by his country and outcast, too, by his family. Jacob Redman is clever and he is ruthless. His only allegiance now is to the money we pay him.' Surov stopped pacing and looked directly at Ivan. 'People find it very hard to question their allegiance to money. And you cannot deny that Jacob Redman has proved his worth to us many times over.'

'In my opinion,' Ivan replied gruffly, 'that only means he has good cover.' He changed the subject. 'You would really have Dolohov eliminated?'

Surov did not allow any emotion to cross his face. 'If he has been compromised, I see no other option. I would regret it deeply, but he has too much information that we do not want falling into the hands of the British.'

'The Georgian operation?'

'No. He knows something is planned, but not who, or when. Certainly he does not know it so soon.'

'And Redman? It is one of his recruits that is preparing the assassination; but does Redman himself know why we are ordering it?'

'Of course not,' Surov replied. 'The British have a phrase: never let the right hand know what the left is doing. It is important always to remember that in our work.' He smiled again. 'But you know all this, Ivan. You don't need me to remind *you* of the basics.'

On one wall of Surov's office was a map of the world. He approached it and, for a long moment, found himself staring at the thin line that marked the Russian–Georgian border. When he spoke again, it was almost to himself. 'The Kremlin will not permit the British to interfere with affairs so close to our border. They are fools to try. The operation will occur in five days' time.' He smiled. The twenty-sixth of May. Georgian Independence Day. A celebration for these people.

He turned back to Ivan. There was a glint in his eye now. 'This will be Redman's last operation for us,' he announced suddenly. 'He has served us well, but there comes a point when people like him start to have an inflated sense of their own importance to us. I will let him deal with Dolohov and after that, Ivan, you may dispatch one of your people to deal with him however you see fit. That should put your mind at rest, should it not?'

Ivan nodded.

'Good,' said Surov. 'See to it that Redman has everything he needs. And keep me informed of any developments. I want to know exactly what's going on with Dolohov. And the Georgian operation must not fail, Ivan. It's too important to our security for that.'

Silently, Surov took his seat once more and picked up the papers he had been reading before Jacob arrived. Ivan understood that the meeting was over. He stood up, and left without a word.

TWENTY

Time was passing painfully slowly. Sam had kept the curtains shut everywhere in the flat, so when day turned into night it was barely noticeable.

Dolohov was crucial to Sam's plans. But he was fading on account of his wounded hands, so Sam did his best to patch the Russian up. The codeine tablets had run out, but he found clean gauze and tape; he tied Dolohov to the chair once more before applying it, and he allowed the Russian a little alcohol at regular intervals to keep the shock and the pain at bay. He found bread in the kitchen, and cold meat. There was tinned food too – stews and soups, thick Eastern European stuff. Sam didn't want to stay here any longer than he had to, but he needed to wait for a response and he was prepared to dig in for as long as that took.

Dolohov slept sitting down. Sam allowed himself the occasional bout of shut-eye too – he hadn't slept since the flight back from Bagram and was feeling it – but not before checking that the Russian was firmly tied to the chair. He kept both handguns on him at all times. Dolohov was exhausted and in pain, but he was a sneaky little bastard and Sam didn't trust him not to have a go.

Every hour, he checked Dolohov's computer. And every hour he came away disappointed.

Dawn arrived. Sam awoke from a half-drowse with a shock. His hands automatically reached for his weapons and he looked around him, momentarily confused. Then he saw Dolohov, bound and nodding, and he remembered where he was. The tension he had been living with over the past few days returned. He stood up and walked to the bedroom where he checked the computer. His heart gave a little lurch.

A message had come through.

For a moment something stopped him clicking on it. An unwillingness to receive yet more confirmation that Jacob was involved in things Sam didn't understand. But the moment passed. He was grim-faced and suddenly alert as he brought the message up on to the screen.

There was no greeting. No pleasantries. Just a time and a place.

WEDNESDAY. 22.00 HRS. EROS. PICCADILLY.

Sam absorbed the information. Then, unwilling to leave Dolohov alone for more than a few minutes at a time, he returned to the main room.

The Russian stirred as he entered. He looked blearily up at Sam, distaste and contempt carved into the lines of his face. His eyes followed Sam across the room as he sat opposite Dolohov, grabbed the vodka bottle and gave the Russian a swig.

'Any plans for Wednesday night?' he asked once his captive had taken a mouthful of alcohol.

Dolohov looked confused.

'Statue of Eros, 10 p.m. You and Jacob Redman. Looks like you've got a date, my friend. Looks like you've got a date.'

★

Gabriel Bland paced. He didn't want to seem on edge in front of Toby Brookes, his subordinate, but he couldn't help it.

288

Brookes looked tired. As though he hadn't slept in days, which was probably true. Running a surveillance team was often as arduous for the pen-pushers as it was for the men on the ground. But that didn't make Bland inclined to go easy on him. Quite the contrary. He needed to know that the heat was on. 'How long have they been in there?' he demanded.

Brookes repeated the information he had given Bland on an almost hourly basis over the past day or so. 'Redman arrived there about midnight on Saturday, May 21. Our man followed him there from the Abbey Court Hotel in Hanwell, where he'd holed up with Clare Corbett for two hours.' He looked at his watch. 'It's 9 a.m. now, May 22. So I make it thirty-three hours.'

'And you're sure he's still in there?'

'We have an SBS team monitoring every exit to the building, just as you ordered, sir. Unless he can walk through walls, Redman hasn't moved out of that place.'

'Clare Corbett?'

'Back home, sir. Hasn't left. Three telephone calls, all from her mother.'

'And this Dolohov individual in Maida Vale?' Bland pressed. 'Have they come up with anything at all about him? Any reason why Redman might suddenly find him such captivating company?'

'Nothing, sir. He teaches Russian at a London University college in Bloomsbury; been living here for thirty years and keeps himself to himself. Lily white, sir. Penchant for Tolstoy, if his library record's anything to go by. Not even a parking ticket to his name.'

Bland scowled. 'Nobody's that clean,' he said. Toby nodded politely in agreement.

The older man turned and look out of his office window over the skyline of London. What was Redman playing at? This long period of silence, of disappearance, was disconcerting. Redman was up to something; Bland just didn't know what.

'The SBS unit. They're on standby? Ready to go in?'

'We just have to give them the word, sir. We can have Redman and Dolohov in custody in minutes.'

Bland breathed out deeply. In the absence of the SAS – he'd learned his lesson in terms of sending them in after their own – their sister regiment was the next best thing. But it was a hard call to make. He had to keep his eye on the most important things. Strip away what was not relevant. He was gambling on Redman making contact with his brother. It was crucial that Bland got his hands on Jacob, to turn him upside down, shake him and see what fell out. Maybe he should just stick to his instinct that, eventually, Sam Redman would lead them to Jacob.

He closed his eyes. In this job, he had learned, there were two kinds of doubts. The big ones, about the rights and wrongs of what he had to do. They were the ones to ignore. But the little doubts, the little nagging ones . . . Something was going on in that Maida Vale flat. Something was afoot. Gabriel Bland needed to know – he decided at that moment – what it was. And he needed to know now.

He turned to Toby.

'Send them in,' he said. 'Immediately. I want to sweat them both today. I want to know what's going on.'

Toby nodded and made for the door.

'And Toby?'

'Yes, sir?'

'Make sure they know who Sam Redman is. Make sure they know he's SAS. He's not going to come quietly.'

Toby nodded his head, as quiet and unflappable as always. 'We'll bring them in safely, sir. I'll see to it personally.'

The younger man left. Gabriel Bland continued to pace the office, those little doubts darting around his mind.

★

09.30 hrs. Sam had rummaged through Dolohov's cupboards and found a shoulder bag which he had filled with the remainder of the food from the fridge, another bottle of vodka and some more gauze for the wounds. Now that they had an RV time and place, there was no reason to stay here. In fact, it would be stupid to do so. Anybody could come knocking – innocently or otherwise – and that could be a disaster. They needed to stay anonymous.

'We're leaving,' he announced once the bag was packed.

'Where?' Dolohov breathed.

'Somewhere safe.'

'Safe for you, or safe for me?'

'Just safe,' Sam muttered. He would find a hotel, pay for it with cash. Sit it out with Dolohov until the RV time. 'You got a car?' he asked.

Dolohov nodded.

'Where are the keys?'

'In the kitchen. There is a . . .'

A sound.

'*Shut up!*' Sam hissed. He pulled his gun just as his eyes flickered to the closed curtains. 'Did you hear that?'

Dolohov scowled at him. 'I heard nothing.'

But all Sam's senses were suddenly alive: his eyes were narrowed and his hearing acute. He backed away from Dolohov, towards the fireplace, then started edging over to the window. It was probably nothing – a bird fluttering against the glass – but he wasn't going to take the risk.

Silence. Unnatural silence. It seemed to ring in Sam's head. His mouth went dry.

Gun at the ready, he held his breath and waited. Waited for the silence to settle down. Waited for his paranoia to pass.

It didn't.

Far from it.

The noises seemed to come from all directions at once. An explosion from the door; a thumping from the bedroom. And here, the room in which they were standing, the shattering of glass. Dolohov shouted in sudden surprise and fear; there was movement behind the curtains. Sam fell to a crouching position, pointing his gun in the direction of the curtains and waiting for a figure to show itself.

Voices. Muffled. 'Hit the ground! *Hit the fucking ground! NOW!*'

An object flying through the air. A sudden bang and a blinding white light. Sam had discharged enough flashbangs in his time, so it was hardly a fresh experience; but they were always a shock when you weren't expecting them. He cursed and shook his head, trying to reorientate himself after his senses had gone to pot.

But by that time it was too late.

A boot against the side of his face. He fell to the floor and felt another boot pressed heavily against the wrist of his gun hand, grinding it into the rug. He struggled blindly, scrambling to stand, but at that very moment he felt the cold steel of a gun barrel pressed against the side of his head. His vision returned. He was being held at gunpoint by a balaclava'd man with an ops waistcoat and an M16.

'*Don't . . . make . . . a . . . fucking . . . mistake,*' a low voice growled, pronouncing each word clearly. '*We know you're Regiment. We've got you covered.*'

Sam froze. He counted two other guys with their M16s trained on him. A third was untying Dolohov, and he knew there would be more in other parts of the flat, checking there was nobody else there, securing the entrances and exits. Multi-room entry. Textbook stuff.

'Drop your weapon.'

Sam released his fingers and allowed the gun to fall from his hand.

'Flat on the floor,' he was ordered. 'Hands behind your back. You know the drill. Do it. Now. *Do it fucking now!*'

Sam had no option. These guys weren't trained to fuck around, they were wound up like tightly coiled springs and they'd nail him if he so much as put a fingertip out of place. He did as he was told – slowly, so they wouldn't think he was making any sudden movements.

'Flat's clear,' another voice announced. 'Cuff them both.'

His head against the floor, Sam could see nothing but the feet of the unit. A moment later, he felt a set of Plasticuffs being firmly attached around his wrists, tight so that they dug into his skin.

'Jesus.' A muffled voice from near where Dolohov was sitting. 'What the fuck's this sicko been doing?'

Sam was pulled roughly to his feet. M16s all around pointing at him. Two of the guys were looking at Dolohov's hands.

Dolohov spoke. Desperation in his voice. 'He has held me captive for two nights. He has tortured me. He is insane. You have to take me to a hosp–'

'Shut up, Boris, or we'll finish the fucking job for him.'

'Just cuff him and get them both in the van.' The instruction came from a guy with a Geordie accent, standing in the entrance to the room, clearly the unit leader. He pointed at Sam. 'Any shit from you, my friend, and we'll start making holes. Got it?'

Sam jutted his chin out and didn't reply. A fist in his stomach. He doubled over, winded. '*Got it?*'

'Got it,' he gasped. He nodded and glanced over at Dolohov, who was having his own wrists bound behind his back. The Russian gave him an evil look, as though he was enjoying seeing Sam get a dose of his own medicine. He didn't get much chance to enjoy it: he was pushed by one of the unit towards the hallway. Dolohov almost fell; at the last minute he regained his balance, but he looked a mess as he staggered towards the door.

Sam was nudged by the barrel of a gun in the same direction. He walked.

'Regiment?' he asked grimly.

'You taking the piss?' a voice hissed. 'Now shut the fuck up and keep walking.' He sounded insulted. Sam guessed it was the SBS. Always walking round with a chip on their shoulders about the SAS, always feeling they're somehow the superior service and angered by the glory the Regiment boys got.

'Who the fuck sent you?' No reply. Sam was bundled down the stairs. Every synapse in his brain hunted for a way out; but four men had their guns trained on him and there was nothing he could do. As they stepped out of the mansion block, he saw a woman and recognised the fox fur round her neck. To say she looked shocked was an understatement. 'What on *earth* . . . ?' she started to say; but she was ignored as the unit pushed Sam past her and on to the pavement.

Two plain white Ford Transits awaited them, the stock-in-trade of a special forces pick-up team, double parked against the other residential traffic in the street. Sam was forced into the back of one of them. All the seats had been ripped out to make a big open space in the rear. Two men were already up front and as Sam was pushed onto the hard metal floor of the van, he heard the engine rev.

'Move up front,' a voice instructed. Sam shuffled along the metal floor and ended up with his back against the front seats. There were four SBS guys in the back with him now – Dolohov was clearly being transported in the other van. One of them slammed the door shut and the van screeched out into the road.

It had been a neat pick-up, Sam had to give them that. He watched as the guys pulled off their balaclavas. Sam had worked alongside the SBS any number of times, but he didn't recognise these men with their dishevelled hair and, he couldn't help thinking, smug faces. It would be the talk of the town at SBS HQ in Poole that they'd been sent in to lift a Regiment guy. Sam did his best not to think about that. He kept his mind calm and, almost by reflex, started to check what assets he had at his disposal. Each of the SBS men wore ops waistcoats with flashbangs and fragmentation grenades. Their weapons were lowered – it would be stupid to discharge them in the back of the vehicle unless absolutely necessary. Rounds could easily ricochet off the metallic sides of the van and mistakes could always happen in a moving vehicle. But all this was academic. With his hands cuffed behind his back he was as good as useless.

The van stopped and started through the streets of London. Behind him, fixed to the back of the chair against which he was pressed, there was something sticking upwards. He didn't know what it was – a rivet of some kind, perhaps there to stop the front seats from sliding too far back on their runners.

'Looks like the Firm want you off the street pretty bad,' one of the guys piped up. 'You must have been a very naughty boy.'

Sam sniffed. Keep them talking, he told himself. Keep them distracted. 'I've had my moments,' he said.

'What did the Russki do? Shag your missus?'

'Caught her giving him a rusty trombone,' he said with a forced grin. 'I told him he was lucky I didn't cut his dick off.' He looked around him. 'So, where are we going? Don't tell me: curry and a few beers followed by a strip club?'

'All right, you lot,' one of the SBS men announced. He had blonde hair and Sam thought he recognised the voice as being that of the unit commander. 'Let's all shut the fuck up. You'll find out where we're going when we get there.'

Sam smiled at him. It took all his effort. 'Suppose there's no chance of stopping for a slash, then.'

By now, Sam had deduced that the rivet behind him was just small enough to slide between his Plasticuffs and his wrists. He did it slowly, so nobody could see what was going on. And then they sat in silence.

The driver was skilled, Sam could tell that. SF trained. He weaved in and out of the traffic, causing plenty of horns to beep as he cut up angry commuters. It still took him a long time, though, to get up any kind of proper speed. Half an hour, maybe? Sam knew he had to bide his time, wait for his moment. He imagined they were on the outskirts of London by now.

He tried to work it all out. Damn it, he'd been careful not to pick up any trail. Maybe he'd been too preoccupied to take the right precautions; or maybe the Firm had put so many spooks on him that he didn't stand a chance. He cursed himself, and as he did so the sallow features of Gabriel Bland rose in his mind. This was his gig, that much was clear. He wanted to get his hands on Jacob, and with Dolohov in his possession he now had the means to do it. Sam closed his eyes. He had given the Russian details of the RV. Now *that* was stupid. It meant that Bland and his goons would be there to welcome Jacob the moment he arrived at Piccadilly Circus; Sam wasn't going to let that happen.

'So we off to Poole?' he asked. 'I could do with a dip.'

His attempt to cajole information about their destination was met with silence. Where were they headed? SBS HQ? Hereford? Somewhere else? He did his best to stay calm. To look subdued. If he was going to get himself out of this mess, the first thing he needed to do was lull his guards into a false sense of security. Sam hung his head on his chest and closed his eyes. He wanted to look tired. Defeated. The Plasticuffs were still wrapped around the metal rivet. It would take a hell of a pull to split them. It might not even work. But he had to try. Wherever he was being taken was bound to be a hell of a sight more difficult to break out of than a moving van. He just had to wait for the right moment.

It took a while to come.

The van was moving steadily. Not too fast, but steadily. That was good. It would be better if he could see out of a window, check the surroundings. But that was not possible. He waited, breathing deeply, preparing himself for the manoeuvre that he had planned out in his head.

He waited.

'Looks like someone had a late night,' one of the unit said in mock-motherly tones. A couple of the others laughed.

He waited some more.

The van swerved, slowing down into a bend. The SBS men leant into the curve, their balance momentarily precarious. Now or fucking never, Sam told himself. He tugged his hands away from the attachment; the Plasticuffs dug into his skin. This was going to hurt. It didn't matter. He had to do it.

Now.

He yanked his wrists with all his strength.

It was the plastic digging into his flesh that he felt first. Cutting it. He ignored the stinging sensation. The muscles in his arms burned as he continued to pull. And then, with a sudden snap, the Plasticuffs broke.

For a moment, no one seemed to know what was happening. Sam hurled himself towards the nearest guard and grabbed a flashbang from his ops waistcoat before throwing it to the back of the van. Confusion. He shut his eyes and – as he prepared for the noise – jumped to his feet, spinning round so he was facing forward.

Impact. White light against the inside of his eyelids before he opened them again. He was deafened and slightly disorientated, but he reckoned he had the advantage. Ten seconds before the others were back to full capability. He had to work fast. With brute force he pressed the driver's head flat against the steering wheel. The horn beeped loudly.

Shouting all around. With his free hand – bloodied from the deep cut on his wrist – he reached down and unclipped the seat belts of both front passengers. He grabbed the steering wheel; and only then did he check the road.

They were in a country lane. Long. Straight. Just them and an area of woodland on either side. He felt hands on his shoulders. '*Get on the fucking floor!*' a voice shouted. '*Get on the fucking floor, now!*'

Sam ignored the instruction. He twisted the steering wheel sharply, towards the forest on the right-hand side. A tree fifteen metres away: he headed towards it. In the rear-view mirror he saw a jumble of bodies. The sudden change in the vehicle's direction had knocked his guards off balance. The guy in the passenger seat put one hand in his face and grabbed his arms, trying to push him away from the driver. But Sam held firm. He continued to drive the van straight towards the forest, then braced himself firmly against the driver's seat, waiting for impact.

When it came, it sent a vicious shockwave through his whole body. He jolted harshly and painfully. The hand came away from his face, but not willingly; it only moved because its owner had moved too.

The windscreen shattered. Blood and glass as his assailant's head slammed into it. The four-man unit in the back lurched forwards in a confused mess. But they wouldn't stay confused for long. Sam threw himself forwards, past the bloodied face of the guy in the passenger seat and headlong through the shattered windscreen. Shards of glass needled his skin, but he did what he could to ignore them as he slid down the steep, crumpled bonnet of the Transit and hit the ground to one side of the tree they'd crashed into.

Shouts behind him. Orders barked. He couldn't hesitate for a single second. Sam powered himself up to his feet and ran. Hot blood from his cut-up face pumped into his eyes, half-blinding him. Still he ran with all the force in his body.

There was a copse of trees up ahead. Ten metres. If he could make it there in the few seconds before the others were out of the van, he had chance. He sprinted, half-expecting to feel a bullet slam into him. But he didn't, and he just kept running.

The urgency of the chase surged through him. The SBS guys could be one metre behind or fifty, he just didn't know and he wasn't going to slow down to find out.

The forest passed by in a blur. Sam didn't know where the hell he was or where the hell he was going. He only knew he had to run. If the unit got him in their sights, they'd open fire; an M16 round slamming into his back and it would be game over.

He weaved and threaded randomly through the trees. Under different circumstances he'd have taken more care, covered his tracks. But he couldn't do that now. The only thing he had on his side was whatever speed he could muster.

And if that speed failed him now, it would be end of story . . .

TWENTY-ONE

Jacob's flight – a charter that carried about thirty Russians, but which had been put in the air, he suspected, especially for him – had landed in Marseilles earlier that morning. He entered the country using his false identity of Mr Edward Rucker, an IT contractor, without difficulty; and within half an hour of landing, Mr Rucker had hired himself a Laguna and a GPS navigator from the AVIS office just opposite the terminal building. He had paid the extra few euros to waive his damage excess, even though he knew he would never be returning the vehicle. A man stealing a hired motor doesn't pay any more for it than he has to – it was just a way of diverting suspicion.

From the airport he drove to the outskirts of Marseilles, a concrete mess of low-rent high-rises. Gangs of kids – North African, mostly – hung around in groups, smoking and drinking. Jacob navigated the streets swiftly. Surov's man had given him the name and address of a contact round here and he wanted to get the meet over and done with.

He pulled up outside one of the concrete towers, pocketed the GPS and stepped out into the humid exterior before locking the doors and glancing skywards. Thirteenth floor. A bastard to break out of in an emergency. He made his way into the building. The lift was broken and the stairwell, covered in graffiti, smelled of piss and spices. He trotted up hurriedly, aware of some voices down below that hadn't been there when he entered. Had he attracted attention from the dealers and the drunks? Probably. But it didn't matter. He could handle them.

The entrance to Flat 207 was the fifth in a long line of doors along an external corridor. The paint was peeling away. Jacob banged a fist against it and then stepped to one side. He waited tensely.

A voice from the other side.

'*Oui?*' A man. Gruff. Unfriendly.

'Edward Rucker,' Jacob called. '*Vous m'attendez. Je veux acheter quelques trucs.*'

Another pause. The door clicked open slightly. Jacob gave it a moment, then used his foot to open the door further. He peered in. Gloom. No noise from inside.

He stepped over the threshold.

As his eyes grew used to the dimness, he saw there was someone standing in another doorway at the end of the corridor. Black skin. Patchy stubble and a scarred face. As soon as their eyes met the man disappeared into the room, leaving Jacob to shut the door behind him and follow.

It stank in the flat, a mixture of marijuana and sweat. As Jacob entered, his mind instantly catalogued what was there. Thin, frayed curtains against the windows. Yellowing walls. A bare light bulb hanging from the ceiling by a flex and a woman, mixed race, crouched in the corner. Asleep? High? Impossible to say. Upturned milk crates – chairs, Jacob supposed. A sofa, threadbare. Several flight cases. None of them open. The man stood in front of them. He wore a brightly coloured woollen top, but his face was a lot less friendly. He scowled at Jacob.

'English?' he asked in a heavily accented voice before taking a drag on a roughly rolled cigarette.

Jacob nodded.

'What is it you want?'

Jacob looked at the flight cases. 'Open them,' he instructed.

The man's lip curled. He raised one finger and shook it. 'Show me your money first, *mon ami.*'

Jacob gave him a flat look. 'Forget it,' he said, before turning to leave. Instantly the man was all over him, pulling him back into the room. He stank intensely of body odour. Jacob swatted him away, but stayed. The man, suddenly faintly obsequious, scurried back to the flight cases without another word.

Even Jacob was impressed by their contents. Assault rifles, sub-machine guns, handguns. Rocket-launcher attachments, tear-gas canisters and grenades. One of the flight cases was filled with boxes of rounds of all types. As weapons stashes went, it was a good one.

'Who do you get this shit from?' Jacob asked. The man just smiled, revealing an incomplete set of teeth. He didn't answer. He did, however, step aside to let Jacob examine the merchandise. Jacob knew what he was after and it was no surprise that his attention was immediately caught by one weapon in particular. It was a suppressed Armalite AR30, a sleek bolt-action weapon with a twenty-six-inch barrel. 'Serial numbers ground off?' he demanded.

'Of course,' the man replied, as if slightly insulted. 'I show you how to use it?' He sounded excited by the prospect.

Jacob shook his head and rested the weapon carefully on the floor. 'Shut up and let me look.'

From another case he selected a bipod and a telescopic sight, before turning his attention to the handguns. There were eight or nine to choose from; he felt most comfortable with a Sig 226, a Regiment stalwart. He added this to his stash, then examined the rounds. 7.82s for the Armalite. Enough to go through body armour and still make a fucking big hole. They came in sleek boxes of ten, about twice the size of a cigarette packet. The AR30 had a five-round magazine. Jacob took two boxes. Twenty rounds. Enough for a test fire to zero the weapon in; and enough for the op. 'Match rounds,' the dealer said. 'Very good, very . . .' He fished for a word. 'Accurate.'

A box of .357s for the Sig and Jacob was done. He turned round to the seedy arms dealer. 'How much?'

The guy looked like he was plucking a figure out of thin air. 'Three thousand,' he rasped, before flashing another of his unpleasant grins. He folded his arms.

Jacob knew he was being ripped off, but he didn't care. He pulled out his wallet, peeled off the notes and threw them dismissively on to the couch. 'I need a bag,' he said.

The dealer scooped up the money. In the corner the woman stirred. She looked over at them, bored, before seeming to notice Jacob. Something lit up in her face. '*Salut* . . .' she said, pathetically trying to make her rasping, addled voice sound seductive. She patted down her clothes and found a cigarette. '*As-tu du feu?*'

Jacob turned away. 'The bag,' he repeated. He didn't want to stay in this dump any longer than he had to. The dealer disappeared to find something, while Jacob stripped down the Armalite. Minutes later he was walking back down the stairwell, the dealer's insincere '*Enchanté*' ringing in his ears and the weapons stashed in an old canvas holdall. On the ground floor, some youths had congregated. They had a lairiness about them, and gave Jacob the eye; but they soon noticed the canvas bag and backed off. Clearly they knew why strangers arrived in this building, and what they were carrying when they left.

Jacob stowed the weapons in the boot of the Laguna, climbed into the driving seat and got the hell out of there. He had a long journey ahead of him and he needed to get started.

★

Gabriel Bland walked quickly, Toby Brookes trotting behind.

Bland had never been to this interrogation centre, a deserted farmhouse in the middle of the Hampshire country-side. It had a well-protected basement where matters were discussed that would never make it on to *The Archers*. Better all round for him not to visit, though he had made use of plenty of the information that had been extracted here by various means – some of them legal, others decidedly not. Today, however, he had no time for coyness.

'I want to know everything he's said,' Bland told Brookes as they walked through the farmyard, past a faceless security guard and into the house proper. 'Miss nothing out, Toby.'

'Redman broke into his house, sir. Tortured him.'

Bland stopped and looked at Brookes, his eyes flashing dangerously. When he spoke, it was in an emphatic whisper. '*How*, Toby?'

Brookes glanced at the security guard, clearly embarrassed by his boss's rebuke. 'Removed his fingers, sir. Two of them.'

Bland showed no sign of shock.

'Seems like Dolohov sang like a canary, sir. Still singing. I guess he doesn't have the stomach for any more interrogation. That and the fact that we've hinted that if he plays ball, we won't send him back to Moscow.'

Bland didn't bother to remark on how unlikely *that* was. 'Go on,' he instructed, allowing Brookes to lead the way through the farmhouse kitchen and down a set of cellar steps into the basement. He listened as Brookes detailed what he knew about Dolohov, an intricate story of assassinations and intrigue, with Jacob Redman at the heart of things. The meeting at Piccadilly Circus two days from now.

They walked down a long corridor with a concrete floor and uniform doors on either side. 'One other thing, sir,' said Brookes. 'Dolohov told Sam Redman that he thinks one of the red-light runners has been activated to carry out a hit. Major political figure. No details on who or when, but we'll get our inquisitors to sweat it out of him.'

Bland stopped in his tracks for a second time. He blinked and looked at Brookes – who sensed that he had once again said the wrong thing – with evident exasperation. 'Why didn't you tell me this before?'

Brookes kept quiet, like a schoolboy receiving a telling off.

'Listen carefully.' Bland pronounced his words slowly, as if to a child. 'I want increased security for all members of the Cabinet. Special forces bodyguard assigned to the PM. Alert COBRA and tell them we take this threat extremely seriously. Level 1. Cross reference this information with any other intelligence chatter. Have you got that, Toby, or do I need to repeat myself?'

'No, sir. Now, sir?'

'Show me where he is first.'

They walked to the end of the corridor, then turned right. On their left-hand side a pane of glass looked into a room. Next to it was a door above which a red light was illuminated. 'One-way glass, sir. He can't see you.'

Bland nodded and Brookes disappeared to make the calls, leaving his boss alone to stare into the room. It was sparse. Just a table and two chairs. At one of them sat a man. His head nodded, as though he kept falling asleep and awakening himself at the last moment; his hands were palm down on the table. They were heavily bandaged.

Brookes returned, a little red-faced and out of breath. 'All done, sir.'

'Good,' Bland replied. His previous frustration had left

him and now he felt strangely pensive. 'Do you believe him, Toby?'

Toby Brookes hesitated.

'I, ah . . . I only ask,' Bland continued, 'because he gave you a great deal of information in a very short amount of time and with almost no, ah . . . persuasion. Does that not strike you as odd?'

'Redman cut two of his fingers off, sir. Cauterised the wounds with a blow torch. Tore off a fingernail. God knows what else he threatened. If someone did that to me, I don't think I'd be in the mood to play games.'

'Indeed not,' Bland murmured, still not taking his eyes of Dolohov. 'Indeed not.' His voice trailed off. 'To think,' he resumed suddenly, 'this man has been working under our very noses for all these years.'

'He hardly looks like an assassin, sir.'

Bland nodded slowly. 'You're too young to remember the Cold War, Toby. It was a lesson well learned in those days that the person you were looking for was likely to be the last person you expected. The char ladies. The postman.' He narrowed his eyes. 'The Cold War is supposed to be a distant memory,' he said. 'But you know, Toby? Sometimes I wonder. Sometimes I really do wonder.'

'Yes, sir,' Brookes said, obviously uncomfortable with his boss's moment of reflection, looking like he didn't know whether to stay or go.

They continued to stand in silence, still looking at the nodding foreigner.

'I find myself,' Bland mused, 'in the curious position of having to readjust my opinion of Sam Redman. If it weren't for him, we'd still be groping in the dark. Speaking of which . . .' He looked hopefully at Brookes.

Brookes shook his head. 'No sign of him, sir. The SBS made chase, but he got away. We've got eyes out in Hereford and Clare Corbett is still being trailed, but I don't hold out much hope. He just seemed to vanish.'

'Nobody just vanishes, Toby,' said Bland angrily. 'I think we can safely say where he will be in two nights' time.'

'Piccadilly Circus, sir?'

'Piccadilly Circus, sir. Along with Mr Dolohov, ourselves and, of course, Jacob Redman. It sounds to me like quite a party.' He continued to gaze through the one-way glass at Dolohov.

'Yes, sir.'

'Jacob Redman has to enter the country somehow. No doubt he will have a false passport. You are sure that his photograph has been disseminated to all the ports?'

'Quite sure, sir.'

Bland sniffed. 'Then let's hope our immigration officials are feeling alert.' He bit his lower lip. 'I think I'd like to have a little chat with our friend Dolohov, as he's feeling so compliant. I've been playing cat and mouse with the FSB for some time now. I'm absolutely positive that we'll find plenty to talk about, aren't you? And in the meantime, Toby . . .'

'Yes, sir?'

'In the meantime, I want to make sure everything is done to catch up with these infuriating brothers. They are running rings round us and it's becoming embarrassing, not to mention dangerous. Find Sam Redman, Toby. And I want his brother the moment he sets foot on UK soil.'

★

It took ten hours hard driving up the autoroute to reach the bland flatness of northern France. At one point Jacob took a detour and drove off into the middle of nowhere. In a deserted field, far from any sign of habitation, he test-fired the Armalite, zeroing it in to his eye. Thanks to the suppressor, the weapon barely even disturbed the birds in the trees. Back on the autoroute, he paid for his petrol and tolls with cash; when he pulled off the motorway into some faceless French town to buy a sturdy rucksack, a high-quality windproof Goretex jacket and waterproof trousers from a camping shop, plus a pair of heavy-duty lopping shears from a DIY place, he paid cash for them too. It raised an eyebrow or two in the camping shop, but that was better than leaving an electronic trail with Edward Rucker's credit cards, no matter how safe he believed the identity to be.

Night had fallen by the time he started seeing signposts for Boulogne. He eased off the accelerator. Nothing was going to happen before midnight. He had a few hours to kill.

He headed for the centre of town. Parking up outside a small *épicerie* he bought bananas and chocolate for energy, as well as water. Not much. Just enough to see him through till morning. Back in the vehicle he ate ravenously, sank a litre of water, then drove off. He followed signs for the marina and it only took him minutes to arrive.

There were hundreds of boats here. Yachts, motorboats, some of them old, some of them expensively new. Jacob parked up, shoved his hands in his pockets and – with the air of a tourist enjoying a late evening walk, while ogling at the pastimes of the idle rich – he headed down into the throng of vessels. The salty air was filled with the sound of halyards clattering against their masts – a good sound because it meant there was a decent wind; lights glowed from a nearby clubhouse, reflecting on the shimmering water; there were very few people about and those that were nodded at Jacob in a friendly, comradely way. He felt relieved that he had cleaned himself up before leaving Moscow. Had he looked a state among these well-heeled boat owners, he'd have stuck out; but in his Goretex he felt he fitted right in. He nodded back. In another life and under other circumstances, this would have all the hallmarks of a relaxing holiday stroll.

Nothing could have been further from the truth.

The boardwalks extended a good fifty metres out into the bay. Jacob sauntered along them, but as he did he examined each vessel he passed. There were plenty of expensive yachts moored here – sleek, white beasts that were no doubt more comfortable inside than most people's homes. They were no good to Jacob. Too difficult to steal. He needed something small, but robust. Something with an outboard, but also with sails – the chances of there being enough fuel on board were small and he didn't want to alert himself to the port authorities by carrying canisters of diesel around when he was an unknown face.

Ignoring a sign warning members of the public off continuing along the boardwalk and stepping over a metal chain acting as a feeble cordon, Jacob eventually found his baby. It was the polar opposite to the grand yachts he had seen elsewhere: an Enterprise, the kind of thing a kid could sail in the right conditions. The chances of this vessel having been fitted with some kind of tracking device by a wealthy, paranoid owner were slim. But as far as he could tell, it looked seaworthy, and Jacob had a better chance of handling this vessel than something bigger and more complicated. Most importantly, the boat was already rigged, the sail tied to the boom and protected from the elements by a thick blue canvas. The centreboard lay in the hull, as did the rudder and tiller; and there was a small outboard motor. This little boat was far from glamorous, but it was well suited to Jacob's needs.

He turned, strolled back along the boardwalk and returned to his car. A quick look at his watch: 22.38 hrs. He would wait till 01.00 when there were fewer people to see him go about his business. Then he would make his move.

He sat. He thought about the journey to come. It would

be tough. Maybe he should have done it another way. Travelled under the tunnel with the illegal immigrants. Paid a lorry driver to hide him in the back of his vehicle. He shook his head. No. Too dangerous to leave things to the incompetence of others. He needed to get entry into the UK by himself. By sea was the only method.

And then? What?

He thought about Sam and the urgent look on his face.

He thought about Sam.

Time passed.

A knock on the window. Jacob tensed. He looked out. A policeman. '*Défense de stationner ici.*' No parking. He looked at his watch. Gone midnight. No point arousing anyone's suspicion for the sake of a good parking spot. He nodded at the cop and started the engine. Round the corner he found a better place to park. No streetlights.

He continued to wait.

12.58. Jacob stepped outside with his rucksack containing the hired GPS unit, the garden lopping shears and a bottle of water. Opening the boot his hands groped for the weapons bag. It was heavy. He felt the muscles in his arm tense as he lifted it from the boot and locked the car. The bag firmly in his hand, he walked back towards the marina.

The halyards were still tinkling, but there was nobody around now. A reassuring breeze carried the sound of a car ferry from nearby Calais. Jacob stepped confidently along the boardwalk until he reached his boat. He stashed his gear in the hull, then took the lopping shears and went to work on the small chain that moored the boat to the pier. They cut through the metal without much problem. The boat was free in under a minute.

Jacob started the outboard motor with a tug of the starter cord; it purred easily into life. The boat nudged its neighbour as he moved it out, but before long he was heading inconspicuously towards the port entrance. Two green lights up ahead indicated that the exit was clear. Jacob held his course and directed the vessel out into open sea. It was suddenly much colder here and Jacob was glad of his wet-weather gear. Bringing the boat momentarily to a halt, he grabbed his rucksack and pulled out the GPS unit, before altering the scale on the screen so that the coastlines of both France and England were visible and he himself was a small green dot between the two. Forward throttle and he was heading north again.

There were no lights on the boat, but even if there had been he wouldn't have turned them on, preferring to benefit from the cover of darkness. The swell of the sea itself was illuminated only by the ripple of the moonlight; in the distance he could see the glow of cross-channel ferries and other fishing traffic. He concentrated on keeping clear of them and heading as straight as possible into the impenetrable darkness of the ocean and towards the south coast of England.

The fuel lasted for half an hour before the engine spluttered and stopped, leaving the vessel to bob impotently in the middle of the sea. The swell was bigger here; Jacob's clothes were wet from the spray as it lapped against the side. The GPS indicated he'd travelled a third of the distance in that time. More than he'd hoped; but now it was time to sail. It had been a long time since the Regiment had given him his Yachtmaster training and it had come in handy a few times since then. Never in a million years would he have thought he'd use his knowledge for purposes such as this; but times had changed and Jacob had changed with them.

His fingers were cold out here. Cold and numb. He detached the outboard motor and pulled it into the boat. Untying the canvas from round the boom was a slow business. When it was off he folded it neatly and stowed it in the hull, weighted down under the weapons bag, then turned his attention to the main sail. It was wound tightly round the boom and tied with a sturdy cord. Jacob unwound it carefully: a rip in the main sail and it would be a long swim back to Boulogne. He pulled on the halyard and his fingers felt for the cleat, a small metallic U with a screw that closed up the open end. His cold fingers grappled with that tiny screw; once it was finally off, he threaded the cleat through the ring at the top of the mainsail, reattached the screw and prepared to hoist the sail.

Jacob felt for the wind. He was square to it. The moment he hoisted the sail it would billow up and the vessel would start moving. He needed to prepare everything before that happened. He attached the rudder to the back of the boat, fixed the tiller then slid the centreboard through the hull. A quick check of the weapons bag, which he stowed underneath a bench at the fore end of the boat; then a good swig of water. He relieved himself over the side, checked everything was okay with his GPS, then prepared to sail.

He tugged hard on the halyard and braced himself. The sail slid easily up the mast and started flapping in the wind. Grabbing the mainsheet – a thick rope that was now flapping around in the hull – he tugged. The sail billowed and filled with wind. Almost immediately he felt a crash of spray as the boat lurched forward and slammed into the swell of the sea. With his other hand he grabbed the tiller and held the rudder square to the vessel. The GPS was in his lap. The boat had turned slightly to the west, so he pulled the tiller and readjusted the sail so that he was heading north.

He was already soaked, so the spray didn't bother him. It was cold out here at sea, but he was concentrating too much on manoeuvring the boat to feel uncomfortable. He needed to keep the thing steady. He needed to keep her on course. He needed to keep her upright.

Jacob Redman put all other thoughts from his head as he set his jaw and his course. With nothing around him but darkness, it was impossible to sense how quickly he was moving. A fair rate, he deduced, from the sound of the wind screaming in the sails and the tilt of the boat. Occasionally there was a gust; whenever that happened, Jacob spilled some wind by letting out the mainsheet a little until the gust had passed. He kept half an eye on the GPS unit. Slowly the little green dot grew closer to the northern shoreline.

He kept a careful track of time, knowing how easy it was to lose a sense of such things at sea. 02.00 passed.

03.00.

04.00.

And then the sky started glowing with a faint pink light. Morning. And with it, in the distance, the sight that Jacob had been waiting for.

Land.

The wind was behind him now, urging him onwards. The tiredness that he felt from being awake for nearly twenty-four hours fell away as Jacob looked carefully towards the shore, his eyes searching for unpopulated areas and deserted stretches of beach. Only when he was a couple of hundred metres out did he see a likely target. He adjusted his course and started tacking towards it.

His body was aching with cold and tiredness. Exhaustion. It took all his effort, as he approached this rocky inlet, to lean forward and pull the centreboard, first halfway and then, when he was only a few metres out, fully up. The boat wobbled precariously; Jacob braced himself just as she slammed on to the pebble-strewn shore. The wind was still screaming in the full sails; he crawled to the centre of the boat and tugged the halyard down, bringing the sail with it.

All of a sudden the noise stopped. He was surrounded by an almost silence. Just the lapping of the waves and the calling of a seagull. Without giving himself a moment to rest, however, he grabbed the weapons bag and his rucksack, then climbed out of the boat.

And for the first time in six long years, Jacob Redman stepped out on to English soil.

TWENTY-TWO

May 23. 07.45 hrs. Mac was at home. At home, and glad that his wife Rebecca had let him back after his recent misdemeanours. Not before time. The atmosphere back at base was horrible. Porteus's departure had caused a weird air of mistrust among the men. Moreover, word of how Sam had been asked to stay behind with the men from the Firm had got around. It didn't take the guys a great deal of head scratching to work out that the two events were related and, as everyone knew, Mac was Sam's closest mate in the Regiment. They went way back. He could barely show his face without someone trying to pump him for information. Truth was, Sam had gone off the radar. Mac had tried to call him any number of times; he'd even gone round to his flat. He felt half-worried, half-angry. There was no doubt about it: Sam Redman had some explaining to do.

Back home, nobody knew anything of this, and so it was that he found himself at the breakfast table of the unimposing two-up two-down in Hereford, listening to the chink of his kids' spoons against their cereal bowls, while nursing a cup of coffee and a hangover. Rebecca, sitting in her dressing gown with her long hair mussed, cast him an occasional kittenish look. Amazing what a night of drunken passion could do. He smiled at her.

'Are you back for ever now, Dad?' asked Jess, his nine-year-old daughter.

Mac smiled at her. Not for the first time he felt a pang of

guilt about his less than perfect parenting skills. ''Course I am, love,' he said.

'Except for when you go away to kill baddies,' Huck butted in, his mouth still half full of Weetabix. Huck was seven, and although he knew nothing of the SAS, the fact that his dad was a soldier with lots of guns had caught his imagination. 'How many baddies did you kill last time, Dad? Loads, I bet.'

'*Huck!*' Rebecca admonished him. 'Stop asking your father silly questions and eat your breakfast. You're going to be late for school.'

'*You're* not even dressed,' Jess observed sulkily.

Rebecca opened her mouth to deliver another reprimand, but Mac gave her a subtle shake of the head. 'I'll take them,' he said.

'Yeah!' Huck cried. He jumped down from the table and rushed to find his school things.

It was just gone eight-thirty when the kids were ready. Mac pulled on his jacket, kissed Rebecca on the cheek and led them outside. It was a ten-minute walk and he hoped the fresh air would clear his head.

He didn't even make it out of the front garden before he stopped.

The figure standing on the other side of the street, leaning against a lamppost, looked like a ghost. Mac's sharp eyes saw that his face was cut up; his eyes were haunted.

'*Sam,*' he said under his breath.

Sam said nothing. He didn't even move. He just continued to stare.

'Come on, Dad!' Huck shouted. He was out of the gate now, his schoolbag slung over his shoulder. Jess was kicking her heels.

Mac looked over at Sam. 'Wait there.' He mouthed the words silently and pointed a finger to emphasise what he was saying. '*Wait there!*'

Sam nodded.

The walk to school was a brisk one. Huck talked nine to the dozen, but barely received a response from his dad – just a ruffling of the hair at the school gates, and a kiss on the cheek for a slightly embarrassed Jess. They sloped off into the playground and Mac ran back home. As he turned on to his street, however, and looked over at the lamppost, he saw that Sam was no longer there.

'Fuck's sake,' he said under his breath.

'Language, language.' A voice from behind.

Mac spun round. Sam, right behind him.

'Jesus, Sam. What happened to your face?' Close up he could see just how bad it was. The skin was sliced and splintered, all the way from the top of his forehead to the bottom of his neck. A couple of the larger cuts had been closed up with steri-tape, but the treatment had a distinctly homemade feel about it. Sam touched his fingers to his face; as he did so, Mac noticed that his wrists were also deeply cut.

'Head-butted a windscreen,' Sam said. 'Long story.'

'You'd better come back to mine,' Mac replied. 'Becky's good at this stuff. She can patch you up a bit better.'

Sam shook his head. 'Let's walk.'

They headed to a nearby park. Mums with kids played at the swings, but the two men took a seat on a park bench at a good distance from them. Sam looked like something from a horror movie, after all. They sat in silence for a moment. Mac deduced that Sam would speak when he was ready.

'Jacob was there,' he said finally. 'In Kazakhstan. I warned him off.'

Mac took a deep breath and nodded. It wasn't a total surprise, but it took a certain effort to dampen down his anger with his old friend. 'That what you told the Firm?' he asked.

Sam shook his head.

'They believe you?'

'No. Listen, Mac. All sort of shit's gone down since then. I need to know I can trust you to keep it to yourself.'

'Fucking hell, mate. Everyone's asking questions.'

'Can I trust you?'

Mac closed his eyes. 'Yeah,' he said quietly. 'Course you can.'

Sam gazed into the middle distance and then he started to speak – quickly, as if the words were painful for him. Mac listened in rapt attention as his story unfolded: Porteus's letter, the red-light runners, seeing J. Then Sam described his interview with the Firm – how Bland had called his bluff about going out to rescue Jacob and how Sam had denied everything. He told Mac about the laptop, Dolohov, escaping from the SBS. And, finally, the meet.

'When is it?'

'Tomorrow night. Piccadilly Circus. The Firm will be there, Mac. Dolohov knew the time and place. And they're hardly going to give J. the benefit of the doubt.'

Mac took a deep breath. 'Mate,' he said. 'I don't want you to take this the wrong way, but J.'s got a lot of questions to answer.' He lowered his voice. 'Are you sure he's not in cahoots with the Russkis? He was treated like shit you know . . .'

Instantly Sam lost his temper. 'You think I don't fucking know that?' He slammed his wounded hand against the arm of the park bench.

'I'm just saying,' Mac flared. And then, more quietly, 'I'm just *saying*, all right?'

Sam was breathing heavily to regain his composure. He stood up and started walking. Mac walked with him. 'These red-light runners,' he said, his voice clipped. 'You know what? They don't sound so different from me when I was a kid. If it wasn't for Jacob, I'd still be like that. It was him that put me on the right track, you know? Not my parents – they'd washed their fucking hands of me. Not my

318

friends – they were a bunch of shitkickers. It was Jacob.'
He stopped and looked intensely at Mac. 'I don't know
what Jacob's up to,' he said. 'I just don't fucking know.
Half of me thinks he's working for the FSB, some kind of
gun for hire. Half of me thinks there's got to be more to it
than that. I'm not going to know until I ask him, Mac. Face
to face. If the Firm get their hands on him, that'll never
happen. You know what those bastards are like, Mac –
they'll make what I did with Dolohov look like a tickle
under the armpits.'

Mac stared at his old friend. He could feel his anger and
his confusion, like heat from an oven. And somehow – he
wasn't quite sure how – he knew what was coming.

'I need help, Mac. At the RV. The place is going to be
crawling with spooks and ham-fisted coppers. I need another
set of eyes. I need a weapon. I can't ask anyone else, Mac. I
can't *trust* anyone else.'

Mac looked down to the ground. He felt torn – torn
between his loyalty to Sam and . . . And what? Had Jacob
turned? Was he a traitor? It seemed impossible; and yet . . .

He sighed, then looked back up at his friend. 'You
remember Baghdad?' he asked quietly.

''Course.'

'Before it happened, during that raid. We could have been
goners if Jacob hadn't turned up.'

Sam nodded.

'Do you remember what he said, when you two crazy
fuckers were persuading me we could take the house by
ourselves?'

Sam narrowed his eyes.

' "You're a long time looking at the lid." I've never
forgotten that. Thought about it a lot.'

'It was something he used to say.'

Mac took another deep breath and looked over Sam's
shoulder, into the distance. He could just make out the back

of his house from here. He allowed himself a moment of silence.

'All right,' he said finally. 'Count me in. What do you want me to do?'

★

In a small bedsit in North London, a young man sat alone. Two more anonymous packages had arrived. Jamie Spillane once again took the precaution of locking his door before opening them. He needn't really have bothered, for the contents of the first package would have been quite uninteresting to the casual observer. Just a briefcase. Not even a new one. This was brown and scuffed. The casual observer, however, would not have understood its relevance. They would not have realised that this briefcase was an exact copy of the one Jamie Spillane had taken such pains to photograph. He had e-mailed the images from an Internet café to a perfectly unremarkable and innocent-looking e-mail address; and now it had arrived, each mark and scratch perfectly replicated. He set it to one side on the bed and turned his attention to the second package.

It was well sealed. He struggled to get it open. Once he did, he removed the contents gingerly. A mobile phone, brand new, with a sticker on its back detailing its number. Jamie placed the phone gently on the briefcase, then removed another object. A wire, with a jack plug at one end and two metal prongs at the other. The sort of thing that, if you found it lying at the bottom of a drawer, you'd probably throw away. A set of lock picks and a tension wrench.

The package was still not empty. There was one item left. He closed up the box and slid it under his bed. Then, after a few moments reflection, he pulled it out again. There would be something slightly uncomfortable, he decided, about sleeping above a stash of high explosive. He stashed it in the corner of his room, draped a jumper over it, then stowed the mobile phone and lock picks in the briefcase and placed it back in its box.

Jamie Spillane often wondered where these items came from. *Don't worry about that*, he'd been told. *It's better you don't know.* Still, he did wonder. It was lonely work, doing this by himself. But if the job went well and MI5 saw that he was a good asset for them, maybe they'd find more for him to do. He smiled at the thought.

Three days now. May 26. It had to be that day. Jamie didn't know why, but his instructions had been quite specific. Before then he still had things to do. Preparations to make. They weren't straightforward, but he was trained for this. Everything had gone well so far and he saw no reason to think that it wouldn't continue to do so.

Jamie found his mouth going dry with excitement at the very thought.

★

Evening fell. Jacob Redman looked out on to the streets of North London.

He had bought himself jeans and a couple of shirts from a charity shop in a bland town somewhere on the south coast. From a greetings card shop he had bought a roll of bright red ribbon, the kind used for wrapping gifts – though Jacob had something very different in mind. By now he had stashed the weapons in his rucksack, which he didn't let go of as he travelled by train into Victoria. He checked into a Travelodge near the station, where he stowed the rucksack under his bed and allowed himself a couple of hours' sleep. His body ached from the strains of the night crossing; but when he awoke and showered he felt invigorated. Leaving the weapons where they were, he headed out of the hotel and into the Underground. Victoria line to Green Park;

Piccadilly Line to Manor House. Then a 20 minute walk. Now, as the light was failing, he found himself at the seedier end of Stamford Hill. He was stalking something and he knew this would be a fertile hunting ground.

He sat in the warmth of a café on the corner of a huge crossroads. The roads were busy – commuters coming home from work – but he knew they would soon calm down. That was when he would take to the streets. He sipped on his coffee slowly, closing his eyes as the caffeine surged through his veins, and carefully going through in his mind everything that was supposed to happen in the next twenty-four hours. It had to go smoothly. It *had* to. He had seen the suspicion in Surov's eyes. He knew that if anything went wrong, he'd be dodging the FSB's hitmen for the rest of his life.

He continued to wait.

Jacob was kicked out of the café just before 9 p.m. He didn't make a fuss. Instead he took to the streets again. He walked down a main road that headed west from the crossroads, then left into a network of residential streets. A number of them were dead ends, with signs declaring them to be NO ENTRY between the hours of ten and six. To enable the residents to get a decent night's sleep without the noise of cars? Jacob knew better. The NO ENTRY signs were intended to dissuade kerb crawlers. Hookers were rife in this part of town. Get rid of the punters and you get rid of the problem – that was the theory. It didn't work. As the clock ticked towards 10 p.m., the women started to appear, as though drawn to the moon and the stars.

Their attention was attracted by Jacob – a lone man, clearly giving them the eye. 'Looking for a bit of business?' one of them asked – a hefty girl, perhaps in her late twenties, the veins on her legs visible beneath her short skirt. Jacob bowed his head and walked on. She wouldn't do. Not nearly. It didn't seem to bother her – she took a bored drag on her cigarette and waited for another fish to bite.

Jacob wouldn't be rushed. Each hooker he passed, standing sentry on their own street corners, he eyed up. He looked lascivious, no doubt, but he didn't care. They were too old, too small, too fat, too thin. But after about half an hour of searching, he saw one girl who looked like she might fit the bill. She was tall — about as tall as Jacob — and had short dark hair. She was comfortably in her forties and nobody could say she was pretty. As Jacob eyed her up and down, she addressed him. 'Looking for a trick, darling?'

Jacob looked around, checking that he wasn't being watched. He moved closer to the girl. She stank of cigarettes, but her eyes seemed sharp enough; sharp enough to make him believe she wasn't a junkie.

'Yeah,' Jacob replied. 'Kind of.' He flashed her a smile. 'Something a bit different.'

That didn't seem to surprise her. 'Different is more expensive, love. Money up front, too.'

Jacob pulled out his wallet. As the hooker looked greedily on, he pulled out four fifty-pound notes and put them firmly into her outstretched hands. 'Must be proper different,' she muttered as she tucked the money away into her clothes. 'Where we going?'

Jacob shook his head. 'Not tonight,' he said. 'Be here tomorrow, you'll get the same again, plus a decent tip if you do well.'

Her eyes narrowed. 'What exactly you got in mind, love? Us girls have got to be careful, you know.'

Jacob smiled again. Friendly. Reassuring. 'Just an appointment with a friend of mine,' he said. 'Nothing kinky. Likes a bit of dressing up. Bit of role play. You don't mind that, do you?'

The hooker shrugged. 'Four hundred smackers,' she said,

'I'll dress up like Orville the bleedin' duck. What time you want me?'

'Eight o'clock,' Jacob replied. 'Don't be late. If you're late, I'll have to get one of your friends to join us.'

And with that he turned away, leaving the girl to reflect on her good luck, and hoping she'd stay sober enough to keep their rendezvous the following evening. In the meantime he had another job to do. He felt in his jacket for the roll of red ribbon, then started heading back towards the Underground where he jumped on a train for Piccadilly.

There were preparations to be made, and he had to make them well in advance.

★

May 24.

Sam hadn't been able to stay in Hereford for any longer than was necessary. It wasn't safe there. Too many eyes. The Firm would have his house under surveillance, that much was sure; and Credenhill was out of bounds. Much better to get out of the city and back up to London. Even there he would attract the attention of passers-by with his cut-up face. He had suppressed the desire to go and see Clare – no doubt they'd be scoping her place out too – so he'd bought himself a hooded top to conceal his features as best he could, then laid low in the small room of the Heathrow Holiday Inn, where he hoped he'd be able to merge into the background.

Mac arrived at 12.30. One look at him told Sam he hadn't slept. He dumped a bag on the bed. It contained two Browning Hi-Power pistols with a box of 9 mm rounds and a couple of ops waistcoats to conceal the weapons and ammo. 'Best I could do,' he said shortly. Sam didn't know where he'd got the gear and he didn't bother to ask. He strapped on the waistcoat and loaded the Browning. It made him feel a lot better.

'What time's the RV?' Mac asked when they were tooled up.

'22.00,' Sam replied. 'The Firm will have shooters in place already, though.'

'Damn right,' Mac agreed. He looked serious. 'The place is going to be crawling with them, Sam. If they get their sights on J. before we can pick him up . . .'

Sam shook his head. 'They won't shoot to kill.'

'How do you know?'

'They'll have pumped Dolohov for everything he knows. He'll have told them about the hit this red-light runner's going to make. If they think J. knows something about that, he'll be no good to them dead.'

'Wounded is fine, though,' Mac said. 'I think we can expect them to engage him.'

'Which is why we've got to scope him out first. But we can't just hang out around Eros. The Firm will be expecting me to turn up. We have to keep hidden until the last moment.

Mac's eyes narrowed. 'Not *we*,' he said. '*You*.'

Sam furrowed his eyebrows.

'Think about it,' Mac urged. 'They might be expecting you, but they'll never be expecting *me*. I can probably stand right next to Dolohov and get away with it.'

Sam didn't like the sound of it. It would be putting his friend right in the line of fire. But it was almost as if Mac knew what he was thinking. 'Fuck's sake, Sam, I've done worse. And I'll have the advantage. I'll just look like some tourist feeding the pigeons. I know the Firm are morons, but even they won't want to start shooting up innocent civilians.'

'Yeah,' Sam agreed. 'Much better to leave that sort of thing to us.'

'You're not going soft on me, are you, mate?'

Sam put the thought of the red-light runners in Kazakhstan from his mind. 'No. Course not. All right, Mac. You wait by the statue. There's a newsstand on the north corner of Piccadilly. I'll stay there. When Jacob approaches Dolohov . . . *If* Jacob approaches Dolohov . . .'

'Yeah?'

'You know the building that used to be a record shop?'

'Tower Records?'

'The newsstand is just outside it. The moment you ID Jacob, you hold up five fingers. I'll put a round into the front window of the shop. Should cause quite a bang. Glass will shatter. I reckon that'll be enough to distract everyone's attention, don't you?'

Mac nodded and pulled at what remained of his right ear.

'Think it'll give you enough time to warn J. – to get him away?' Sam asked.

'Yeah,' Mac nodded. 'But what about you?'

'I'll be all right.'

'The Firm might think you're Jacob, making a distraction. You might get some incoming.'

'You got a better idea?' Sam snapped.

A pause. 'No, Sam,' Mac replied. 'I haven't got a better idea. We'll do it your way.'

And without another word, Mac turned his back on his friend and started fiddling with the straps on his ops waistcoat. Sam couldn't help thinking that he was tying them tighter than they really needed to be.

TWENTY-THREE

Piccadilly Circus

It looked like just another night. The huge neon billboards flashed high overhead: an advert for *The X Factor*. Then the weather: dry but overcast. The date: May 24. And then the time: 9.50 p.m. On the corner of Shaftesbury Avenue a man with a guitar sang old pop songs, but was mostly ignored by the passers-by. The air was filled with the smell of fried onions; buses and cars swung round the roundabout, dodged by half-drunk pedestrians. Japanese tourists, looking at everything through the lens of a camera. There was a lot of pissed totty out on the streets, tarts dressed in mini-skirts shorter than the average belt, belching, stubbing out fags in the road and screaming at nothing in particular. On their flanks stalked hordes of horny, Brylcreemed blokes trying to look hard in their fake Ralph Lauren tops and identical black shoes. They were burping and swigging from alcopop bottles, ready for a fight, gasping for a shag. Just another night in London town.

Toby Brookes sat in the back of a black cab at the north end of Lower Regent Street. The windows were not blacked out, but were heavily tinted. Opposite him sat an MI6 field agent, a much older man, whose work name was Gillespie. Gillespie would be giving orders to the surveillance and pick-up team; Brookes would be giving orders to Gillespie.

'Dolohov's in place,' the field agent said.

Just then there was a knock on the window. Brookes looked out to see a policeman indicating that he should roll it down. 'Not the best place to park, sir,' the copper said. Brookes didn't reply. He just held up some ID. The policeman's eyes widened. 'Sorry to disturb, sir,' he said, much more quietly, before turning and walking away.

Brookes glanced out of the window of the cab. He could just make out the figure of the Russian on the west side of Eros, facing south towards Brookes's cab. He wore a big overcoat and his wounded hands were plunged into the pockets. He barely moved. Dolohov knew he was being surveyed from every possible angle; that there was enough firepower aimed in his direction to take out everyone milling about on the steps around the statue: the group of eight or nine schoolchildren posing for a photograph; the couple snogging; the guy with half his ear missing, sitting a couple of metres away slowly munching on a burger.

Brookes's stomach twisted. Bland was furious that it had come to this. Not furious in a loud, explosive way, but in that calm, wordless manner that was so much more threatening. But what else could he have done? Sam Redman had gone dark; Jacob Redman had not been picked up at any of the ports. They didn't have any other hands to play. If it all went pear-shaped tonight, Brookes could expect to leave the table. Hell, he could expect to leave the casino.

Gillespie put two fingers to his earpiece. 'All units ready,' he told Brookes. Then he smiled. 'Don't worry, son. We've been here before. It'll be a walk in the park.'

'Just keep your mind on the job.'

Gillespie inclined his head. He obviously didn't like taking orders from someone younger.

'I mean it, Gillespie. If this doesn't go like clockwork you'll be drawing your pension before midnight.'

And so will I, he thought to himself. He dug his fingertips into the palms of his clammy hands and went through everything in his head. Piccadilly Circus was surrounded by rooftop snipers. All the watchers had been supplied with the target's likeness. The moment Jacob Redman approached Dolohov, they'd move in. Ten vehicles were on standby – black cabs, white vans, sports cars, nothing suspicious. They would block off each of the six exits to the Circus, while an armed response unit of fifteen men closed in on the statue of Eros. Instructions: shoot to wound, not to kill.

Christ. If that wasn't enough, nothing would be. Redman was only one man, after all.

Brookes looked at his watch: 21.54.

Six minutes to go.

He stared out of the window, and waited.

★

21. 55.

Mac swallowed the last mouthful of his burger. It was cold. He'd spent too long eating it. Crunching up the packaging he dropped it on the floor. Some kid gave him a hard stare, but he ignored it and lit a Marlboro Light. He wasn't a regular smoker, but it gave him a reason to be sitting alone, here on the steps of the statue of Eros.

Two metres away from the man Sam had called Dolohov.

He did not look directly at the short fat man, but even from the corner of his eye Mac could tell that Dolohov was nervous. He was standing too still for a man who was at his ease. The Russian had his hands deep in his pockets. Mac allowed himself a smile. He knew why *that* was.

Mac checked his watch: 21.56. He took another unwanted drag on his cigarette. Across the road, leaning up against the window of what used to be Tower Records, but which was now closed down, its windows misted from the inside, he saw Sam, hooded to stop people gazing at his cut-up face. If anyone looked at him too closely, they'd think from his face that he was just some drunk, his scars a residue from a fight. As disguises went, it wasn't a bad one.

Mac looked about, as casually as he could. There were probably thirty people milling around the statue of Eros, tourists mostly. He didn't know why they felt the need to be there. His eyes scoured the late-night crowds spilling into Piccadilly Circus from Regent Street. Hundreds of people. This place was like a jam jar. The people were like wasps. They swarmed to it.

It had been six years since he last saw Jacob, but Mac felt confident that he would recognise him. The dark hair. The serious eyes. His stomach turned. Nerves. Nothing to do with the operation. He could handle that. But seeing J. again. Especially when he had so many questions to answer.

And if Mac was nervous, what the hell was Sam feeling?

He took a last drag on his cigarette before stamping it out on the ground. Dolohov hadn't moved.

He wanted to look at his watch again, but stopped himself. Clockwatching would make him look suspicious. And anyway, Jacob would come when he came.

It was only a matter of minutes now.

The neon billboards flickered on the edge of Mac's vision.

He lit another Marlboro Light, and waited.

★

Sam held a copy of *Nuts* magazine in front of him as he leaned against the shop window. Plenty of naked flesh on the pages, but had anyone asked him what he was reading, he wouldn't have been able to say. His eyes didn't even brush the text or pictures in front of him. In the distance, on the other side of the statue, a neon digital clock counted down the seconds.

21.57.

Dolohov was in position. It had almost been a relief to see him – it meant at least that Jacob had not yet fallen into the Firm's hands. But Sam's mouth was dry, his blood hot with anticipation. He double-checked Mac: there he was, lighting another cigarette. That was two, now. He cursed under his breath. Two cigarettes in two minutes. Damn it, Mac *looked* like a guy waiting for something to happen.

He breathed deeply. He kept watching. His fingers felt for the Browning strapped into his ops waistcoat under-neath his loose, hooded top. It was comforting to have it there.

21.58.

His brain burned with concentration, with the strain of trying to stop the crowds morph into one impenetrable blur. He looked for evidence of the Firm, but saw nothing suspicious. That figured. Unmarked cars, plain-clothed agents – they'd have pulled out all the stops to make sure they looked like part of the scenery.

21.59.

Mac had finished his second cigarette. He was blowing into his hands as if to warm them. But it wasn't cold. Or maybe Sam was sweating for other reasons. His eyes darted around. He could taste the anticipation. His brother was here somewhere. He had to be.

Damn it, Jacob. Where are you? Where in the name of . . . ?

Sam's breath caught in his throat.

Everything around him – the noise of the cars, the chattering of the people – dissolved into silence. The world went by in slow motion.

Someone was approaching Dolohov.

In the distance the neon clock announced the time: 22.00 hrs.

Sam could only see the figure sideways on. He wore a black raincoat. Long. Down to his knees. It had a hood, pulled up to cover his head. Dark glasses. He stepped confidently. He was five metres away from Dolohov.

Everything happened so quickly; and yet, in Sam's mind, so painfully slowly.

Dolohov looked up, recognition in his face. He knew he was being approached.

From two metres away Mac took a step towards the Russian. As he did so, he looked across the road and directly at Sam. Sam waited for the signal. Five fingers. But Mac was hesitating. Dark glasses and a hood – they stopped him from giving a positive ID. He looked unsure. Sam's hands slipped into his top, ready to pull out his Browning. Ready to defend Jacob from whatever was to come.

A bendy bus blocked Sam's vision for three or four seconds. He cursed. When the bus slipped out of view the figure was only a metre from Dolohov; and Mac was looking at Sam in panic. Fuck it, thought Sam. We need the diversion. *Now!* He put his hand to his gun.

But before he could spin round to blast out the shop window, he stopped. For three reasons.

The first, a screeching of tyres. Vehicles everywhere. A crunch as two cars hit each other. Men sprinting across the road and towards the island. Weapons being pulled.

And the second, a sudden, twisting realisation that something was wrong. The figure, dressed in black. It was the same height as Jacob. Almost the same build. But something wasn't right. The gait? The slope of the shoulders? Sam didn't know what, but he did know one thing.

The figure in black wasn't his brother.

It was a dummy. A decoy.

The third reason, that was something he should have seen. Something he should have noticed. It had been right there staring him in the face all the time, after all. It was a small thing. Just a length of red ribbon, tied to a lamppost to the right of Eros and fluttering in the wind.

A sickening feeling in his stomach. He knew what the ribbon was, of course. A wind marker. There to make sure a sniper knew exactly what kind of breezes he was up against.

'*Mac!*' he screamed at the top of his voice. '*Shooter!*' But too late. Mac had already realised something was wrong. He stepped back, then looked over at Sam as if to say, 'What the hell do I do now?'

But Sam couldn't answer. He didn't have the time. All he could do was watch what happened . . .

★

21.57.

From the roof of the former record store, Jacob Redman looked down on to the statue of Eros. By his feet there was a dead body.

It had been dead for ten minutes and blood still flowed from its head wound. The corpse's comms set was now fitted to Jacob's head, and it was Jacob who responded into the microphone every two minutes, when the sniper unit's commander checked that all was okay. And when the commander had reminded them that if Jacob Redman was positively ID'd they should shoot to wound, he had replied with a curt 'Roger that.'

Through the telescopic sight attached to his Armalite, he viewed the red ribbon. It fluttered slightly to the south-east. A steady wind. Gentle. But enough to swerve a round off-course. He redirected his aim towards Dolohov, then moved it fractionally to the left. Experience told him that this would be a direct hit.

The Russian appeared frozen. Fear? Jacob didn't care. It made it easier for him to keep his target in his sights.

Earlier in the evening he'd visited the hooker again. Another two hundred quid in cash and the promise of a third payment once the job was done. In the back of his mind there was a niggling worry that she wouldn't show. He suppressed it. Jacob had seen the way the girl's eyes had lit up at the prospect of more cash.

Money. Sometimes it was the only thing you could trust. She'd be there.

21.58.

It had been straightforward getting up here. An external staircase – a fire exit – leading down into a small alley off one of the mews streets between Piccadilly and Regent Street. If you didn't know these places were there, you'd never notice them; but Jacob had been party to enough rooftop stake-outs to know how to gain access.

He kept his gun trained on Dolohov.

21.59.

He had told her to be on time. Not a minute early, not a minute late. They had synchronised their watches. Jacob pulled away from the telescopic sight and looked down with the naked eye. An ordinary London scene. No sign of spooks or police of any kind. Maybe there weren't any. Maybe Dolohov was clean. Safe. Uncompromised. If that was the case the girl would lead him away to the RV point. If not . . .

Jacob put his eye back to the telescopic sight.

Only seconds to go.

His hand was steady, his breathing regular.

22.00.

He saw her, bang on time.

Dolohov looked up. His eyes narrowed, a look of bemuse-ment. He had realised something was wrong. Another figure came into his field of view. For a split second Jacob thought he recognised him, but his attention was too focussed on other things to give his brain any time to work it out.

Too focussed on Dolohov.

And too focussed on the sudden flurry of activity that was occurring around him.

Cars storming up on to kerbsides all around. Men running towards Dolohov from every side. A net closing.

Surov's question had been answered. The Russian was compromised. It didn't take a genius to work that out. Jacob knew what he had to do.

His first shot was accurate. It slammed into Dolohov's skull, even as the muffled crack from the suppressed firearm dissolved into the hubbub of the city. A flash of red as the fat man toppled, but by that time Jacob had already moved his sights towards the girl. She had opened her mouth. A scream, though he couldn't hear it up on the rooftop.

There was no hesitation. No quickening of the pulse. The girl could identify him. She would talk. She had to go the same way as the Russian.

He fired. Once more his aim was true. One side of her head exploded, spattering the man who had grabbed her at that very moment before she too fell dead to the floor.

Chaos down below. Jacob surveyed it briefly through his telescopic sights. Terrified pedestrians, running from the scene and screaming. A flood of men pulling their weapons, surrounding the dead bodies like a ring of steel. They aimed their firearms outwards; but none of them aimed upwards.

None of them except one.

He knew exactly where the shots had come from; he was looking directly up, though he didn't bother aiming his handgun, because he no doubt realised he didn't have the range. It was the man Jacob had thought he recognised. And now that he had him in his sights, he realised why.

'*Mac.*'

Mac continued to look up.

Jacob almost felt as if he was staring his old friend in the eye.

★

The ground was covered in bits of pulverised brain and bone. The air filled with screams, partygoers and pissheads who'd just been given a nasty dose of reality. Mac tried to ignore them all. He looked up to the rooftop above Sam. That was where the shots had come from, no doubt about it, and now he thought he saw a flash of movement. All around him was chaos. Men barked contradictory orders at the horrified pedestrians and each other alike. A black cab with tinted windows pulled up and two ashen-faced guys jumped out. They started shouting too, but their voices were lost in the melee.

On the other side of the street, Sam had frozen. Mac slipped away from the pandemonium around him and ran across the road to where his friend was standing. 'Shooter on the roof!' he shouted. 'He has to come down on Piccadilly or Regent Street. You take one, I'll take the other.'

'Did you see him?' Sam's face, despite the cuts, was grey.

Mac shook his head. 'I saw a figure, that's all. Too far to ID.' In the distance, the sound of sirens. '*Move, Sam*. I'll take Piccadilly, you take Regent.'

Sam nodded and in an instant they parted.

Mac sprinted. Word that something was up had clearly spread quickly – pedestrians were flocking towards Piccadilly Circus and he was running against the tide. As he ran, he took in everyone around him. None of them were Jacob.

Thirty metres. Forty metres. Fifty. To his right, a mews. He turned into it, then stopped a moment. To his right

336

again, an alleyway between two shops. Narrow. Dark. Big metal bins and a rear loading-bay entrance to one of the shops on Piccadilly. At one end, a tall, spiral metal staircase. Mac gripped his weapon. Without any more hesitation, he ran towards the steps and started to climb. He looked upwards and pointed his gun in that direction too, half expecting to see the shooter descending at any moment. He tried to go quietly, but that was impossible, not at speed. His footsteps made the metal of the staircase echo and ring.

The roof onto which he emerged was perhaps thirty metres by thirty. At one end, heading towards Piccadilly Circus, was a low wall and a gap; then an almost identical roof beyond, and another one beyond that. Around the edges were disused chimney pots, brick turrets with vast television aerials and more low walls. Good cover for anyone who needed it.

It was quiet up here. The noise of the traffic and sirens from down below was audible, but faint. Looking around he saw nobody. The sound of traffic and sirens drifted upwards; but they were somehow disjointed. He felt as if he was in another world.

Mac gripped his Browning. He held his gun hand out and stepped forward, his eyes narrow.

'Jacob!' he called. His voice echoed.

Jacob.

Jacob.

He stepped forward again, checking left, checking right, moving ahead. His senses were alive. As sharp as glass. But he never even heard the footsteps behind him.

'Drop the gun, Mac.' And as he heard the words, he felt hard metal against the back of his head. He closed his eyes. He didn't need to turn round to see who it was. The voice was instantly recognisable.

'I said drop it.'

Mac let the weapon fall from his hands.

'Walk.' Jacob's voice was clipped. 'Now.'

Mac stepped forwards. Ten paces. Fifteen.

'Hands on your head.'

He did as he was told. And then, slowly, he turned round.

Jacob looked older. Older than he should have done. His dark eyes were darker, his face more intense. His handgun didn't falter in its direction: it was aimed directly at Mac's head. A silence as the two men looked at each other.

'A long way from Baghdad, J.,' Mac said.

No reply.

'I was there,' Mac continued. 'In Kazakhstan. Sam risked a lot to warn you. Me too. Reckon we deserve to be told what's going on.'

Still no reply. Mac lowered his hands from his head. *Keep talking,* Mac told himself. *Keep talking.*

'I don't think anyone's going to be mourning Dolohov. Not from what Sam said.'

'Where is he?' Jacob demanded.

'Close,' Mac replied. 'He'll be here any moment.'

'He should have stayed away. Both of you should have stayed away.' Jacob sounded unsure of himself. It wasn't like him. Mac couldn't remember ever having seen doubt in his friend's eyes; but he saw it now.

He stepped forwards. 'Put the gun down, J.,' he said. 'You're not going to shoot me any more than you're going to shoot your brother.'

'Don't move.'

Mac ignored him and continued to walk slowly.

'You're not going to shoot me,' he repeated. 'What's going on, Jacob? Put the gun down and talk to me.'

But Jacob didn't put the gun down. And he didn't talk to Mac. Not any more. His lip curled. Almost as though he was just an observer to the scene; it crossed Mac's mind that it was an expression of pure anger and dislike.

The first shot from Jacob's handgun slammed into Mac's right shoulder. It felt like a heavy punch at first, and he fell to the ground as a hot wetness seeped into his clothes. Fuck. The round hadn't exited. He could feel the bullet lodged in his shoulder. It felt like someone turning a slow, sharp knife into his muscle. He could even feel how hot the round was. He looked up. Jacob was there, staring down.

'Cocksucker!' Mac spat. 'We fucking saved your bacon . . .'

'You should have stayed away, Mac,' he said as he stretched out his gun arm again and aimed it at his old friend's skull.

Mac shook his head, desperately, violently. But he knew he was properly cunted. He thought of his wife, Rebecca. He thought of Jess and little Huck. He opened his mouth to speak, but words wouldn't come.

'*You should have fucking stayed away.*'

Mac Howden didn't hear the shot that killed him. The bullet entered his head before he even had a chance. Nor, as he fell to the ground with one side of his head shot away, and miniature fountains of blood spraying upwards, did he see the look on the face of his killer.

A grim look. A horrified look. A wild-eyed look. A look of utter, brutal self-loathing. The look of a man covered in bits of another man's brain tissue and blood.

The look of a man who could not believe what he had just done.

★

Sam ran along Regent Street, his gun in his fist. He collided with two men – big, burly and drunk. They wore jeans and football shirts, sporting joke orange beards. They yelled obscenities at him in broad Scottish accents and pushed him in the chest. Sam didn't even bother to warn them. He whacked the gun against the side of one man's face, which softened into an angry red welt. The other man he kneed in the groin before continuing to run.

His mind burned with impossible thoughts. He tried to keep his focus, to look for somewhere to access the rooftops. But he had run a hundred metres. Two hundred. He turned left, but found himself lost in a complex of side streets between Regent Street and Piccadilly. His blood raced with urgency. Like in a childhood dream he felt he couldn't run fast enough.

He was on Piccadilly now, running east. Finally, to his left, he saw a small mews road. He ducked into it. To his right an alleyway, and a set of metal fire-exit stairs running up. Sweat poured from him, but he didn't slow down. Three steps at a time. Four. He hurtled up, stopping to catch his breath only when he was on the roof.

He looked around, his gun at the ready. With a sense of nauseous anticipation he almost expected Jacob to be there. Half-formulated phrases buzzed around his brain. He felt a curious mixture of excitement and blind anger.

But Jacob wasn't there. He was nowhere to be seen. As he stared out over the rooftops, however, Sam became aware of something else. Firmly gripping his gun, he stepped forward until he was standing right by the body.

Sam didn't need to check it was dead. The face was unrecognisable, just a shredded, bloodied pulp. He knew it was Mac, though. He recognised the clothes and even if he hadn't . . . He just knew.

Time stood still.

Sam bent down. He stared at the damaged corpse of his friend. His blood turned to ice in his veins. He couldn't move.

They'll tell you things, Sam. Things about me. Don't forget that you're my brother. Don't believe them. What had sounded before like a warning now sounded nothing but a deceit.

'Jesus, Mac,' he whispered. And then, with a sudden outburst of violence. '*Jesus!*'

He stood up and looked around for something to kick, something to punch. There was nothing and so Sam found his arms flailing uselessly in the air, like some animal twitching violently in its death throes. He heard a voice. It was a hollow, hoarse scream.

'*NO!*'

Only when the scream had echoed away into nothing did Sam realise it had come from his own throat.

He looked around helplessly, as if by searching on this lonely rooftop he could do something about the terrible events that were unfolding. But there was nothing to do and his eyes fell on the body of his friend, unnervingly still in the way only corpses can be. As he looked he heard Mac's voice in his head, repeating Jacob's words:

You're a long time looking at the lid, Sam.

Blood was still seeping from his friend's wounds. It oozed up against the sole of his foot.

You're a long time looking at the lid.

Sam stepped back. And as he did so, he realised the whole world had changed. That *he* had changed. Jacob had always made him feel like a kid. The younger brother, always looking up. Respectful. In awe.

Not any more. Things were different, he saw that now. He stretched himself to his full height and jutted his jaw at Mac. 'He's not going to get away with it, Mac,' he said, his voice still raw from the scream. 'I fucking *promise* you, he's not going to get away with it.'

Sam drank in the sight of Mac's body – the last time, he knew, he would ever see him – then turned his back. It was wrong to be leaving his corpse here, but he had no other choice.

Not if he was going to do what he needed to do.

Not if he was going to avenge his friend's death.

Not if he was going to find his brother and put a stop to this, once and for all.

TWENTY-FOUR

Toby Brookes's voice was strained and emotional. Gabriel Bland had to press his confounded mobile phone hard into his ear in order to hear him above the sound of shouting and sirens. With each piece of news he found his fury doubling. Dolohov dead. Another civilian casualty and all this in front of a city full of witnesses. Worst of all, no sign of Redman – of *either* Redman. No leads, no nothing.

When Brookes had finished telling him everything, he was silent for a moment. 'I, ah . . . I suppose I don't need to tell you,' he said eventually, 'that you are in a very, very grave situation, Toby.'

'I've just seen two people shot.'

'I don't believe I need that statistic repeating.'

A pause. And then Brookes again, angrier than Bland had ever heard him: 'Fuck this! Just . . . just *fuck this*!' A click, and the line went dead.

Bland stood in his office with the phone to his ear for a good while after Brookes's voice disappeared. Brookes had cracked. That much was clear. Bland couldn't let that distract him. There were more important things at stake than a young man who couldn't take the pace. He had the unnerving sensation of everything unravelling around him. His breath came in deep, nervous lungfuls. Then, suddenly, with an uncharacteristic burst of violence, he hurled his phone against the window of his office, which looked out over London. The toughened glass of the window was entirely unharmed; the phone, however, shattered. He stormed to his desk and buzzed through to his assistant. 'I need to speak to the chief,' he said. 'Now.'

And what a conversation it was going to be. This was turning into the biggest balls-up the service had seen for years. They could issue all the DA notices they wanted, but with so many witnesses to the shootings it was probably all over the Internet already. And things were going to get worse. A major hit, Dolohov had said. Political. Jacob Redman was their only link. Without him they were blind men in a dark room. If things were bad now, they were going to get a whole lot worse.

Gabriel Bland headed towards the door, steeling himself for the encounter to come. It promised to be ugly. He knew that if anyone was going to take the rap, it would have to be him.

Five minutes later, the Chief of MI6 was staring up at him with a look of blank astonishment.

Bland had never appreciated the experience of taking orders from someone his junior. He had seen the service's chiefs come and go. He had disapproved of none of them quite so much as this one, with his ridiculous ideas of making the service more 'open' – interviews with the media and advertising for posts on the Internet. This obsession with image, however, was just a distraction from the nitty gritty of their day-to-day work.

But right now, Bland had to put all that from his mind as he stood in front of his boss, who could quite clearly see an early retirement looming. 'Who's your agent on the ground?' he demanded.

'Toby Brookes, sir.'

'Fire him. Fuck-ups don't come bigger than this, you know. I've already got the PM asking me why he can't take a leak without one of our guys looking over his shoulder. Now you're telling me our only lead is missing

344

and our collateral's dead on the ground at Piccadilly Circus.'

'Yes.'

The Chief banged his hand on the desk. The coffee that was sitting there sloshed out of its cup. 'Our analysts are crying into their files,' he fumed. 'None of them can tell me why the Russians would order a hit on one of our politicians. Things are frosty with Moscow, but there's no *point* to it. Nothing to be gained.'

Bland cleared his throat. 'The Russians are a law to themselves, sir,' he said. 'Especially after Litvinenko . . .'

The Chief's face hardened at the memory of the former Russian spy assassinated on British soil – another big embarrassment for the service. 'That's what happens when you put a former KGB hood in charge of the fucking country, Gabriel,' he said, neatly batting the implied criticism away. 'Moscow's a liability at the moment. God knows what they're trying to do.' He frowned. 'These Redman brothers. They're our only chance of getting some sort of clue as to what's happening. Where the *hell* are they?'

Bland didn't reply. He had nothing to say.

The Chief gave him a dark look. 'Listen to me carefully,' he said. 'You've got every asset this agency can throw at it. Find them, Gabriel. And when you've found them, do whatever it takes to get everything they know. *Whatever it takes,* Gabriel. I'm sure you understand what I mean. No comeback.'

Bland nodded, his eyes dead. 'I understand, sir.'

'Good. Now get the hell out of my sight. I don't want to hear from you unless it's to tell me that you've got one or other of those bastards in custody. And if *you* haven't done it within twenty-four hours, I'll find someone more capable who can.'

★

In another part of London, far away from the bloodshed of Piccadilly and the panic at MI6 – and completely oblivious to both – Jamie Spillane was breaking into a house.

It was a small house. In order to make his way up to the back door, the young man had climbed through several adjacent gardens. His fingers were splintered from climbing up and down wooden fences – he felt slightly foolish for not having worn any gloves and made a mental note to do so in the future – and the contents of his rucksack jutted uncomfortably into his back.

There was a small patio outside the back door. It was a bit of a shit heap – bags of rubbish, an old barbecue, a rusty bike. The paintwork on the door was peeling and the wooden frames of the two external windows were rotting away. Each window was covered from the inside by a blind, and the glass of the back door was mottled and frosted. The young man couldn't see which room he would be entering. He looked at his watch. A quarter to one. Silence from the house and no lights from the upstairs windows. The occupier was fast asleep.

He felt inside his jacket pocket. The lock picks and tension wrench were there. The young man licked his lips and bent down to the lock. As he prepared to insert the picks, he gently tried the door handle.

It moved. He pushed the door open. Nobody had thought to lock it. He shrugged slightly and mastered a little twinge of disappointment as he realised he had rather been looking forward to picking the lock, to using one of the skills he had learned.

No matter. He quietly stepped inside and shut the door behind him, then stood perfectly still for a few seconds while his eyes adjusted to the darkness.

He was in a kitchen. It smelled of food that he didn't recognise and imagined he wouldn't find very good to eat. There were dirty plates in the sink and most of the work surface in this small room was crowded. How strange, he thought to himself, that someone working in an embassy should live in such squalor. An archway led into another room. A street light from the front window illuminated it. There was a thick carpet in here, and a tiny table at one end, pressed against the window – one of those that looked out on to the back garden. At the other end, a two-seater sofa in front of a television, with a coffee table in between the two.

A creak. He jumped.

Beyond the sofa was a door, closed, that he assumed led upstairs. He found himself staring at it, half-expecting someone to burst through. But no one came. The creak was just that, he realised – the joists of the house relaxing. Still, his breath came in deep bursts. His skin felt hot and cold at the same time. He dragged his eyes away from the door and looked at the object lying on the coffee table.

The object he was looking for. The brown briefcase.

He forced his muscles into movement, removing his rucksack from over his shoulder and starting to undo it. His fingers were shaking slightly; it seemed to take an age to unbuckle the straps. The more he hurried, the slower he seemed to go, but eventually he got it open. Next he pulled out the replica suitcase and opened it. The original case contained a few papers. He flicked through a few of them. They were written in an alphabet he couldn't understand, but as he scanned through, his eyes fell upon the words *Kakha Beridze* in English lettering. He nodded with satisfaction. There was also a pen clipped to the interior and a used paper napkin, crumpled and stained where its owner had wiped their mouth. The young man meticulously removed each of these objects and transferred them to the replica case. He then rifled through the original to check there was nothing he had missed. It was empty, apart from a few crumbs, which he carefully picked up and dropped into the replica. Then he closed both cases, placing the replica back on the table in exactly the same position that the original had been and stuffing the original into his rucksack.

The young man stood up. As he did so, his attention was caught by something he hadn't noticed before. A picture on the wall. In the foreground a meadow, green and dotted with little yellow flowers; behind that, a line of snow-capped peaks. The sky, deep blue and dotted with puffy white clouds. Below the picture, in bright, tacky writing, the words *Beautiful Georgia*.

He looked at that picture. Not for the first time, he wondered why he was being asked to do this. He was not into politics and he struggled every time he tried to work out the consequences of this operation. But, as he had done so many times before, he let it go. He was just a small piece in the bigger intelligence jigsaw, he knew that. Maybe if he did his job well, if he proved he could be trusted . . . well then, maybe something else would come his way.

Hoisting the rucksack over his shoulder, he stepped back towards the kitchen. On the table at the end of the room, something caught his eye. A wallet. He approached it and saw several notes peeking out.

Somewhat unnecessarily he looked over his shoulder. It would be so easy to steal the contents of that wallet. Just a couple of notes. Who would notice? He struggled with himself. *Whatever you do, don't be tempted to steal anything. It'll raise suspicion. You mustn't do anything to give away the fact that you've been there.*

He took a deep breath. The temptation was difficult to control, but he managed it. Just. He stepped through to the kitchen, then out into the back garden, closing the door quietly behind him. Squeezing his splintered hand open and closed, he prepared to scale the garden fences again. He allowed himself a brief smile. It had gone well. In an hour he would be back home and then there was just one more part of the operation to complete.

And *that* would be the easy bit.

★

Sam sat in the unwelcoming surroundings of his hotel room. He looked numbly at the bag Mac had brought with him. How long would it be before they found his body? Hours? Days? Weeks? Every impulse urged him to go to Mac's family, explain to his wife what had happened. But he couldn't do that. He was a wanted man. Rebecca was going to have to suffer her husband's unexplained absence a bit longer until she heard the news that would turn her world upside down. It sickened him to think about it.

And it sickened him to think about his brother. He didn't doubt that Jacob was the shooter. The whole scenario had his fingerprints all over it. The ribbon. The decoy. It was the way his mind worked. Sam knew that better than anybody.

And better than anybody he knew what a mess he'd made of things. He should never have got Mac involved. Dolohov's death was just the beginning. Jacob's red-light runners were planning something. Something big, but he didn't know what and he was no closer to finding out. Go to the Firm now and they'd stick him in the deepest hole they had. They'd be panicking. They'd know they had to find Jacob and they'd know Sam was their only link. Half the fucking service would be out there looking for him. Anywhere they thought he might be – his flat in Hereford, Clare's place. And of course, he couldn't show his face at SAS headquarters. His passport would be flagged and his mobile phone bugged.

All this because of his brother.

Jacob's dark features flashed before his eyes. *Jacob was a real soldier*, his dad had said.

'We're all real soldiers.' Sam muttered out loud the reply he had given his father. We're all real soldiers, and sometimes we do things we're not proud of. He thought of the red-light runners in Kazakhstan, turned from unknowing stooges to cold corpses at the squeeze of a trigger. In the darkness of the night, when it was just Sam and his conscience, he knew he would be haunted by those young men. He was a soldier, but he wasn't without feeling.

Jacob was a real soldier.

Was Jacob proud of what he had done? Was his own conscience pricked? Was he without feeling? Could he kill one of his closest friends and not be haunted by it for the rest of his days? Or was he too far gone for that?

Sam felt himself sneering at the thought, the anger welling up in him once more. Half of him wanted to see his brother; the other half didn't know what he'd do when he caught up with him.

He looked over at Mac's bag once more. Solitary. Ownerless.

Jacob was a real soldier.

His dad's voice echoed in his head.

Sam stopped. His brow furrowed. Through the fog of his tired mind he remembered the last time he had seen his father. It had only been a few days ago, but it seemed like half a lifetime. Fragments of that conversation seemed to float in the air around him.

Jacob was a real soldier.

You know what those bastards are like. Jacob was an embarrassment to them. We both know how easy it is to get rid of people who are an embarrassment.

He always looked out for you, Sam.

You talk about him like he's dead.

If your brother was still alive, what's the one thing he'd do if he knew I was cooped up in this shit hole, pissing into a pipe and wasting away to a fucking skeleton? What's the one thing he'd do?

Sam hadn't answered. He hadn't had the heart. He knew too well that nothing would have kept Jacob away.

Nothing would have kept Jacob away . . .

Nothing would have kept Jacob away . . .

And suddenly, in that dingy hotel room, it was crystal clear what Sam had to do. He looked at his watch: 3 a.m. The night was slipping away. He only had one chance to catch up with Jacob. If he missed that, he knew, without any doubt, he would never see his brother again.

His ops waistcoat was on the bed. He strapped it to his torso, secreted the Browning pistol into it, then covered himself with his hooded top. He looked around the room. Nothing to take. Just Mac's bag, and he didn't need anything from that. It would only slow him down. He left it there as he slipped out of the room and surreptitiously left the hotel. In the hotel car park, he felt as though a million eyes were watching him. He ignored them. They were imaginary. *Kill the paranoia, Sam. You haven't time for it.* He started examining the cars on offer. Nothing modern, he told himself. Nothing with an alarm or immobiliser. Get your collar felt by the Old Bill now and you'll have some serious explaining to do.

He walked. He kept alert.

It was an old Fiesta that caught his eye. A dent on one side, with rust creeping round it. A shabby, unkempt interior. Sam looked around to check that he was alone. Nothing. Nobody. He walked round to the passenger's side where, with a sharp jerk of his elbow, he smashed the window in. The glass shattered onto the passenger seat. Leaning in, he stretched out to open the driver's door, then walked round and climbed in.

The vehicle belonged to a woman or a short-arsed man – he had to move the seat fully back in order to sit properly. His fingers groped for the panel under the steering wheel and, with a sharp tug, he pulled it off. With both hands he felt for the wires underneath; in less than a minute he had hotwired the engine into life.

Another time check: 03.15. Assuming the car's owner awoke no earlier than six, Sam had three hours. It was enough. In three hours' time he would be long gone.

In three hours' time he would be back in Hereford.

TWENTY-FIVE

Hereford, May 25. 04.55.

Max Redman awoke.

His room was dim, almost dark, with the morning light just beginning to bleach the air. As always happened, it was the confusion that hit him first. Where was he? What *was* this place? And then the pain. The dull, insidious ache that weakened his thin limbs and reminded him, with a shock that never grew less brutal through familiarity, that he was imprisoned — both by his illness and by the four walls that surrounded him.

He groaned, then lay there listening to his own rasping breath. It was only gradually, and with a creeping sense of unease, that he realised he wasn't alone.

With difficulty, he moved his head to one side. A figure by the door. The old man couldn't make out who it was. He squinted, but it was no good and he felt the anxiety of the infirm.

'Who's that?' he asked, his aggressive voice neutered by his weakness. 'It's too early for breakfast. I'm not fucking hungry.' Deep down, though, he knew it wasn't someone bringing him food. He struggled to stretch his thin arm out for the control that would move his hospital bed into a sitting-up position. His fingers touched it, but it slipped from his grasp. He swore and tried again. By that time, however, the figure was moving. Stepping towards him. And the closer it got, the clearer its features became.

Max Redman's weak limbs became weaker. His breath rasped all the more. The figure stood by his bedside and looked down. Neither man said anything.

It was Max that broke the silence. 'My God, Jacob,' he breathed. 'What's happened?'

His son's face was ravaged. There were deep, dark bags under his eyes and a frown on his forehead that reminded Max of when Jacob was a little boy and had been scolded. But his eyes themselves had the thousand-yard stare, that look of numb shock that Max knew from the battlefield.

Jacob didn't reply. He just continued to look down on his father.

For a brief, irrational moment, Max wondered if he was being visited by a ghost; he wondered if his own eyes looked as haunted as his son's. Max Redman was not a man who was easily scared; but he felt fear now, creeping down his spine and making his extremities tingle and burn. If this wasn't a ghost, why would Jacob not speak?

'What's happened?' he repeated. His voice sounded unsure. Max would never have been anything other than dominant in conversations with his sons, but now the tables had turned. He was frightened of Jacob. It took courage for him to stretch out his hand towards his son's, an unprecedented gesture of timid affection. Their skin touched.

And then, slowly, like a man in church preparing to pray, Jacob lowered himself to his knees. He looked to the floor and allowed his father to place his thin hands on his head. They stayed like that, father and son, for nearly a minute. They might have stayed longer, had they not both been disturbed by the faint sound of wheels screeching in the car park outside. Jacob stood quickly. His eyes had narrowed, but his face had lost none of that troubled expression. He walked backwards until he was halfway across the room and his face was once more shrouded by the half light. Then he turned and walked to the door.

'Your mother couldn't live without you, Jacob,' Max said. Jacob stopped, but didn't turn round. His father's difficult breathing filled the room. 'Neither of us could live without you.'

A thousand thoughts suddenly emerged in Max's mind, like the dead rising from their graves. A thousand emotions. A thousand apologies. But he didn't have the energy to speak any more, even if he had had the skill to articulate them. And so they went unsaid, lost in the dark silence between the father and his son.

Max closed his eyes. He heard the door click open, then fall quietly shut. When he opened his eyes again, Jacob was gone.

★

It was precisely three minutes past five when Sam's stolen Fiesta screamed into the car park of his father's care home. There were barely any other vehicles there, just those belonging to the night staff. He stopped at an angle across two parking spaces and sprinted towards the building.

The receptionist on duty looked startled as he burst in. The man shouted something, but whatever it was didn't register in Sam's mind as he hurried past, along the corridors that smelled of disinfectant as he followed the familiar route to his dad's room. As he ran, he put his hand under his hooded top and loosened the Browning that was nestled in his ops waistcoat. A strange sense of calm fell over him, an other-worldliness. He didn't know quite what would happen when he reached the room, but with an almost emotionless detachment he knew he would be ready for it.

His father's door. Closed, just like every other one along the corridor. He paused briefly, pulled out the Browning and, weapon at the ready, opened it slightly.

No sound. He kicked it open further and stepped inside.

His father was lying there, just where he always was. The bed was flat, the curtains closed. But Max's eyes were wide open. Sam pointed his gun quickly to all four corners of the room. There was just the two of them, so he approached his father's bedside.

Max's face was grey. Tired. His eyes were red and the rough skin on his face was dabbed with moisture. Sam had never seen his father cry. Not even when Mum had died. It didn't happen. There was no doubt about it, though. Max Redman had been crying and Sam knew why.

'Where is he?' he demanded.

Max stared at his younger son. He looked like he was struggling to control his emotions. 'Why the piece?' he asked, his eyes flickering to Sam's gun.

Sam grabbed the control for the hospital bed. It seemed to move in slow motion, to take half a lifetime to bring Max upright. When finally his father was in a sitting position, Sam spoke again. 'I know he's been here, Dad. Where's he gone? What did he say?'

Like a petulant child, Max pursed his pale lips.

'Damn it, Dad! It's important.'

Max's chest rattled as he breathed. 'Is he in trouble?' he asked, before collapsing into a fit of coughing. As the fit subsided, he closed his eyes. 'He looked like something had happened.'

The image of Mac's dead body flashed across Sam's mind, like a hot iron branding the skin of a live animal. He felt the muscles in his face tightening involuntarily, giving away his emotions. Max's eyes narrowed. He might be old and sick, Sam thought, but he wasn't stupid. His father looked away resolutely.

Sam took a deep breath. He couldn't tell his father the truth. It would kill him. But he had to know what had passed between Max and Jacob. He had to know what his brother had said. 'Listen, Dad.' His voice low, urgent. 'I don't know what he told you, but yes, he's in trouble. I can help him, Dad. I can get him to safety. But I've got to know where he is. If I don't find him, someone else will.'

A noise outside the door. Commotion.

Max's face hardened. He refused to talk. It was all Sam could do to stop himself grabbing his father's nightclothes in his fist through frustration. 'For God's sake, Dad! For once in your life don't be so fucking stubborn. Jacob's not the golden boy you think he is.'

'Stay out of it, Sam,' Max replied, wheezing as he spoke. 'It's nothing to do with you.' More coughing. 'All right, so Jacob came to see me. What's wrong with a son wanting to visit his parents?'

As Max said those words, two things happened. In a sudden flash of insight, Sam knew where Jacob would have gone. And just as that thought hit him, the door burst open. 'That's him!' a breathless voice said. Sam spun round. In the corridor he saw the receptionist he had so abruptly ignored on his way in; and in front of him, entering the room, was a security guard – broad shouldered, grim-faced and rushing towards him.

Sam acted on auto-pilot. A violent kick in the groin and the security guard doubled over. Seconds later, Sam had one of his arms crooked around the man's neck and his Browning pressed up against his head. Sam pulled him into the corridor.

'Get in the room!' he shouted at the receptionist. '*Get in the fucking room or I'll kill him!*' The frightened receptionist did as he was told. As Sam stepped backwards he heard his dad shouting weakly. '*Stop him. He won't do anything.*' But the receptionist was too terrified.

'Don't make a fucking mistake,' Sam told his hostage, 'and you won't get hurt.' He hustled him along the corridor and down the stairs. They echoed noisily, but it was early and nobody else was awake. The guard was crying with fear.

Sam just ignored it. They hurried through the reception area. By now the receptionist could have called the police. Sam didn't have any time to lose.

Outside the building, he dragged the guard halfway to the car, then stopped. 'Get on the ground,' he instructed. The guard, frozen with fear, did nothing. '*Get on the fucking ground!*' He pushed him down and the guard hugged the tarmac. 'Move an inch and I'll fucking kill you,' Sam told him, before sprinting to the car. He was sweating profusely despite the early-morning chill, as the car coughed into life. Speeding from the car park, he looked in the mirror; the guard was still prostrate on the ground.

All notions of care and secrecy had evaporated from Sam's mind. He drove furiously, screeching round corners and ignoring red lights. The few cars that were on the road at this early hour swerved away from him; horns blasted then faded away. Sam ignored them all. He knew the road he had to take, even though he hadn't driven it for four years.

The graveyard was surrounded by black iron railings topped with spikes. Sam's Fiesta came to a halt just outside the entrance, two wheels up on the kerb. He grabbed the gun that had been sitting on the passenger seat, jumped out and sprinted in among the graves. It was a large cemetery; as Sam ran among the stones, images of the last time he was here flashed in his mind like punches. The coffin being lowered into the ground; a small group of people standing around, barely protected from the biting cold; Sam himself standing next to his father; and the absence of one person keenly felt by everyone there.

What's wrong with a son wanting to visit his parents?

Jacob was there, just as Sam knew he would be. He stood on the unkempt grass in front of the simple tombstone, his shoulders hunched and his head bowed, his back towards his brother. Sam halted some thirty metres away. He caught his breath and extended his gun hand. And then he walked forward.

He didn't expect Jacob not to hear him; he just wanted to be prepared when his brother turned round. Sam was barely ten metres away when he did.

Sam stopped. Jacob also held a gun. Both brothers faced each other and Sam couldn't take his eyes from Jacob's face. He looked like he was wearing a mask – a mask of anxiety and hate. He didn't appear at all surprised to see Sam.

'Long way from Kazakhstan, Sam,' he drawled.

An unnatural silence surrounded them.

'Is that what you said to Mac?' Sam asked. 'Before you killed him.'

Jacob's face wrenched itself into an agonised expression. His hand, Sam noticed, started to shake. 'Mac got in the way,' he said. 'It was his own fault.' Sam didn't reply, so Jacob repeated his words, as though trying to persuade himself that it was true. 'It was his own fault.'

'You know that's not true, Jacob.'

Now it was the older brother's turn to be silent.

'Mac was helping me. Helping *you*, actually. Trying to stop the Firm from sticking a bullet in you.'

'I didn't need your help.'

'Clearly not.'

They stood.

'You should have been here four years ago, J.,' Sam said. 'When we buried Mum. You should have been here.'

Those dark eyes bored into him. 'She wouldn't have missed me. Not her, or the old man.'

'You're wrong.'

Jacob snorted with contempt.

'Jesus, J. What the hell's happened to you?'

'You should put the gun down, Sam. You're not going to shoot me.'

Sam looked meaningfully at Jacob's own weapon. His brother shrugged, then stowed it inside his jacket. Sam lowered his gun arm, but he kept the weapon in his hand. 'I'm waiting for you to tell me that I've got it all wrong, J. That you didn't kill Mac. That your red-light runners . . .'

Jacob interrupted him sharply. 'How did you know about them?' Then, almost as soon as the words left his mouth, he nodded in understanding. 'Dolohov,' he said.

'We had a little chat.'

'Good for you. I'm going to leave now, Sam. Why don't you go back to the old man's bedside. Talk about what great soldiers you both are.'

Sam's eyes narrowed. 'You honestly reckon *that's* what he thinks?'

Jacob didn't reply.

'Since you went dark, he's talked about no one but you. I mean it, J. I can't spend five minutes in his fucking presence without hearing how much better you are than me. Or *were*. He thought you were dead, J., because you never came to see him.' Sam looked over at the grave. 'Mum too. If you hadn't left, she wouldn't have given up.'

Jacob's lips had thinned. 'Shut up,' he said quietly.

'No, Jacob. You don't know what I've been through to catch up with you.' He found himself breathing deeply, trying to keep his anger under control. 'Mac had two children, you know. Cute kids. I don't suppose you thought about that when you plugged him.'

'It was his own fault,' Jacob half-shouted, repeating his mantra.

'And Rebecca, too. Wonder how she's going to cope? You know, Mac risked a hell of a lot in Kazakhstan to stop the Regiment nailing one of their own. And in the end *you* nailed *him*.'

'Fuck the Regiment!' Jacob flared. 'I stopped being one of them the day they kicked me out.'

'And then you felt a burning desire to work for the Russians, is that right?'

'I felt a burning desire to work for whoever paid me,' Jacob retorted. 'And don't try to tell me it's anything different to what you do. We kill people for money, Sam. At the end of the day it doesn't matter which people, or whose money.'

It doesn't matter which people. Mac on the roof, blood oozing from his fresh, fatal wound.

Sam felt like he was in the control of some other force, as though his limbs weren't even doing his own bidding. He strode towards Jacob, who didn't move from that spot in front of their mother's grave. He raised his gun hand. Some tiny part of his mind observed that Jacob barely moved to defend himself, and he wondered why just as he brought the hard metal of the gun down forcefully on the side of Jacob's face. A crack – the breaking of bone – and a sudden welt of blood. Jacob staggered, then drew himself up to face Sam.

The two brothers stood, damaged face to damaged face, eyeball to eyeball.

'Feel better, Sam?' Jacob whispered. His words were arrogant; but his eyes were disturbed.

Fury still burned through Sam's veins. He pressed the Browning against the side of Jacob's head. 'You're going to tell me about the hit,' he said.

Jacob jutted his chin out, but didn't say anything.

'Dolohov told me one of the red-light runners is planning a hit,' Sam persisted. 'He didn't know where or when. You're going to tell me who it is, Jacob, otherwise I swear to God I'll kill you.'

The two brothers stared at each other. Then, slowly, Jacob stepped backwards. In the background Sam heard the sound of sirens. Somewhere deep down he supposed it should worry him; but it didn't.

'You won't kill me, Sam,' Jacob said. A calmness appeared to have descended over him. 'I'm your brother.'

He turned his back on Sam and started walking away. No hurry. In fact, there was a slowness to his gait. A heaviness.

The sirens grew louder.

Sam's body went cold. Once more he felt himself in the grip of some other power, as though he were a puppet being controlled by invisible strings from above. He raised his gun hand.

'You're not my brother,' he heard himself say.

Jacob stopped. He was five or six metres away now. When he turned again, there was an animal expression in his eyes.

The brothers stared at each other.

And then, Jacob came at him.

It happened so quickly. Jacob launched himself at Sam with his arms outstretched, going for his throat. It was a clumsy movement, the result of rage, not training. But Jacob was a big guy, and the impact knocked Sam backwards. He fell to the ground and Jacob fell on top of him with the barrel of Sam's gun awkwardly pressed into the hard flesh of his stomach. The elbow of Sam's gun hand crashed against the grass.

Sam never felt his trigger finger move. He heard the shot, though. It rang out across the graveyard, scaring the birds in the trees and causing them to rise up in flocks. He pushed Jacob away from him, but already he was spattered with the blood that had exploded from his brother's stomach.

'Jesus, J.,' he whispered. And then louder: '*Jesus!*'

Jacob lay on his back. His breaths were short and irregular. Blood flowed from his abdomen.

His body was shaking and his skin was white. He looked up at Sam and for the first time ever, Sam saw fear in his brother's eyes. Jacob started to say something, but all that came out was a weak cough and a trickle of blood that spilled over his lower lip.

Another cough and another gush of blood. In the distance, the sirens became louder and suddenly stopped. The crying of the disturbed birds dissolved into nothing and silence surrounded them.

Jacob closed his eyes. His skin became a greyer shade of pale and Sam knew what *that* meant.

'Dad never forgot about you, Jacob,' he breathed. 'Not for a single second of a single day.' Jacob winced and Sam sensed it was nothing to do with the pain. It was as if that one fact was too much for him to bear.

His chest started to rattle.

'You have to tell me,' Sam urged. 'Tell me what you've set up. Who's the target, Jacob? Who do the Russians want dead?'

The sound of shouting from the edges of the cemetery. Sam looked over his shoulder. Movement in the distance. He turned back to his brother. 'For Mac's sake, Jacob. And for Dad's. If he thought you were a traitor, it would ruin the rest of what life he has left . . .'

Jacob's eyes were rolling in their sockets. Fresh blood spewed from his mouth. He choked on it as he spoke. 'You can't stop it. It's in motion.'

'*Who?*' Sam urged. '*Just tell me who?*'

The shouting grew louder. Half of Sam wanted to shake his dying brother; the other half wanted to hug him. '*Who?*'

A pause. It lasted forever. When Jacob spoke again, his voice was so weak Sam had to strain to hear it. 'Beridze . . .' he said.

He heaved again.

'Kakha Beridze.' Sam wasn't sure he'd heard correctly. The words were meaningless to him. A deep breath from his brother. Jacob gained control of his vision and stared him straight in the eye. 'His assistant . . . tomorrow night . . .' His body jerked, as though an electric shock had passed through it. On the edge of his consciousness, Sam became aware that he was surrounded. A harsh voice shouted at him. *'Drop your weapon and put your hands on your head.'* Sam ignored them. He grabbed his brother's arm. 'Don't tell him,' Jacob whispered, and Sam knew what he meant. 'For God's sake, Sam, don't tell him . . .'

Jacob struggled to draw another breath, but it stopped suddenly. There was a horrific silence. And then, with a gruesome, aching slowness, the sound of his lungs deflating. Jacob's eyes glazed over; his body stopped shaking and relaxed on to the grass like ice beginning to melt.

Sam stared at him in lone shock.

'Drop your weapon and put your hands on your head. You're surrounded by armed police.'

He was numb. Out of the corner of his eye he saw his mother's tombstone. He felt as though her eyes were upon him.

'This is your last warning. Drop your weapon and put your hands on your head. If you do not drop your weapon, we will shoot.'

Slowly, Sam laid the Browning on Jacob's chest. He raised his arms in the air and placed them, fingers clasped together, on his head. Before he knew it, he became aware of three flak-jacketed police officers with MP5s trained directly at him. He barely gave them a second glance; Sam could not take his eyes off the body of the brother he had just killed.

He spoke. His voice sounded separate from his body. Monotone. Emotionless.

'You need to contact MI6,' he said. 'Gabriel Bland. Tell him that Sam Redman has some information for him.'

The armed response unit closed in. With their black body armour and grim faces, they looked for all the world like an army of shadows gathering round his brother's corpse.

TWENTY-SIX

The cell in the basement of the Hereford police station was tiny. A single bunk with a thin mattress and a yellow-and-brown-stained toilet without any seat were all the comfort it offered, but that didn't matter to Sam Redman. There were no comforts that would ease what he felt inside.

He sat on the edge of the bed, staring at the yellowing wall opposite. How long he had been in there he couldn't have said. An hour? A day? They were both equally likely. His head was filled with ghosts. Memories of his brother when they were kids, which were unavoidably chased away by the one image that he knew would haunt him for the rest of his life. The image of Jacob, motionless on that cemetery ground, dead by Sam's hand. It didn't feel like it could possibly be true.

A policeman brought in some food. Sam didn't even look at it. 'Where's Bland?' Sam demanded. The policeman — a young guy — gave him a look of contempt. He didn't answer.

Sam continued to stare. Continued to think. He supposed he should weep, but tears wouldn't come. Perhaps he didn't deserve them. Every now and then his guilt would be replaced by something else. Anger. Anger at his brother. Anger so deep and so hot that it felt as if it would consume him. And with it a desire — no, a need — to put everything right. He couldn't undo everything Jacob had done, but if he could stop things getting worse, maybe the anger would go. Or at least subside.

The peephole of the cell door opened. 'I'm not talking to you,' he called. 'I'll only speak to Gabriel Bland.'

The peephole slid shut, then the door opened. A familiar voice. 'Leave us alone.'

Sam turned to look at his visitor. He was accompanied by the young police officer. 'I should stay, sir. He's dangerous . . .'

'I shan't repeat myself,' Bland said. He stared at the policeman.

'No, sir,' the young officer said, withering under the heat of his gaze. Bland stepped inside and waited for the sound of the door locking.

'Hello, Sam,' he said when they were alone.

'Where is he?' Sam demanded. Bland raised an eyebrow. 'Jacob. His body. What have you done with it?'

'It's, ah . . . It's dealt with. I'm sure you can understand that we don't want any more dead bodies cropping up in public places.' A pause. 'You've, ah . . . You've been busy since we last met, Sam.'

Sam ignored his visitor's obtuse comment. 'Dolohov told you about the hit?'

Bland's face gave nothing away. 'Mr Dolohov told us lots of things, Sam. He was extraordinarily talkative. It, ah . . . It seems that a few hours with you can loosen a man's tongue.' He raised an eyebrow. 'Either that, or silence it forever.'

Sam looked away.

'I, ah . . . I understand you have some information for me,' Bland continued. 'I trust this is true and isn't just a way of trying to wriggle your way out of . . .'

'Shut up, Bland!' Sam snapped. 'Just shut up and listen to me!' He rose to his feet and noticed that the MI6 man flinched slightly. 'Jacob gave me a name before he died.'

Bland nodded slowly, his sharp eyes wary. 'And?'

'And before I tell you who it is, I want some assurances.'

An insincere smile spread across Bland's face. 'I hardly think you're in a position . . .'

Sam gave him a stony look. 'Fine,' he said. 'Throw the book at me.'

An awkward silence filled the cell. It was broken by Bland.

'What would these assurances be?'

Sam sniffed. 'Number one, Mark Porteus back in charge. Number two, your heavies leave Clare Corbett the fuck alone. Number three, Mac Howden's family get properly looked after – no bullshit with the insurances, they get the full payout. And number four . . .' He drew a deep breath. 'Number four, not a word about my brother's death leaks to anyone.'

'Ashamed, Sam?' Bland asked mildly.

'No,' Sam lied. 'I don't give a shit what you or anyone else thinks. But if my father finds out that Jacob's dead . . .' He hesitated. 'And how . . .' His voice trailed away.

Bland surveyed him with dead, emotionless eyes. 'I'm sure those things could be arranged,' he said quietly.

Sam scowled. He didn't trust the Firm and he didn't trust Bland. But at some point he was going to have to trust someone and he'd run out of options. 'Kakha Beridze,' he said quietly. 'I don't know who the hell he is, but Jacob mentioned his assistant. And the words "tomorrow night".'

Bland nodded, absorbing the information. 'Anything else?' he asked.

'It's all I know.'

Bland turned and knocked on the inside of the door.

'Wait,' Sam said, and the MI6 man turned. 'In Kazakhstan, at the training camp. Spetsnaz were waiting for us. They could only have known we were there if one of your lot tipped them off.'

The door opened and the young policeman appeared. Bland looked as if he was going to say something, but instead

367

he marched out. 'Be careful who you tell!' Sam shouted after him. And then, even though the door was shut and locked, he repeated himself. 'You've got a mole! Be careful who you tell!'

His voice echoed around the cell. He kicked the bed in frustration, then sat down to wonder if he'd done the right thing.

*

Somehow, Sam slept. It wasn't a refreshing sleep. The bunk was hard and his dreams were haunted. When he awoke in that windowless room he was confused. No sense of time or place. He pissed in the rank bog, then scowled when it wouldn't flush. Then he went back to sitting on the bed. Waiting. He didn't know what for.

The door opened. Two police officers entered and cuffed his hands behind his back. Sam didn't bother to struggle. He could sense their hatred – the hatred of a policeman for a murderer – but he could also tell they had been instructed not to talk to him about the events of the past few hours. 'What time is it?' he demanded.

'Time for you to fuck off out of it,' one of the officers replied.

He was roughly led out of the cell, along an institutional corridor and up some steps. At the main entrance to the police station he drew stares from members of the public: whether that was to do with the cuts on his face, the hand-cuffs or the armoured police van with flashing siren that was parked just outside, he didn't know. And he didn't care. On the wall there was a clock that told the time and date: 18.38, May 25. Sam was wordlessly escorted into the back of the van, then left alone as the doors were shut. He was encased in steel and there was no way to get out, even if he wanted to.

The journey was long and uncomfortable. Sam endured it sitting in the corner of the van, ignoring the bruising jolts that bumped through his body, and brooding on everything that had happened. An idle corner of his mind wondered where he was being taken, but he didn't really care much about that either. He'd find out soon enough.

Having driven at speed for a couple of hours, the van began to stop and start. City driving. He felt it going down a long ramp, then coming to a halt. The doors opened and an armed escort of four men awaited him.

'Where am I?' he demanded, but he received no reply. Just a flick of an MP5 telling him to get out. He was in some sort of subterranean car park, the kind that echoed when you walked. He was taken through a guarded door, along a network of corridors and finally into a room. It was sparse: a table, chairs bolted to the floor, strip lighting and a black window – one-way glass, he presumed. The door was locked and once more he was left alone.

This time, however, he didn't have to wait long. The door opened and two men marched in. One of them was Gabriel Bland. He looked tired. Much more tired than he had been earlier that day. Haggard, almost. With him was a small man. Thick glasses. Dumpy. He was short of breath, had sweat on his wide forehead and carried a thick file. The door was locked behind them and the two men sat down opposite Sam.

'Thank you for joining us, Sam,' Bland said without a hint of irony. He closed his eyes and smoothed his eyebrows with one hand. As he did so, he continued to speak. 'This is Julien Batten. One of our analysts.'

'Where am I?' Sam asked.

Bland's eyes popped open. 'Didn't they tell you? MI6 headquarters. You didn't think we were going to leave you in a Hereford police station, did you?'

Sam shrugged.

'Julien's been processing the, ah . . . the information you gave us. I wanted you to hear his conclusions directly from him.'

Sam couldn't understand what was going on. Bland sounded worried, but he was talking to him like an old and trusted friend. He kept quiet.

'Carry on, Julien,' Bland instructed.

The bespectacled man cleared his throat. 'I hardly need say this falls under the auspices of the Official Secrets . . .'

'Just get on with it,' snapped Bland.

The analyst readjusted his glasses before carrying on. 'Kakha Beridze,' he said, pulling a photograph from his file. 'Georgian ambassador to London. His personal assistant, Gigo Tsiklauri. Beridze's been two years in the job. Hardline anti-Russian, but a good relationship with Number 10.'

'I'm very happy for him,' Sam retorted, before turning to Bland. 'Why are you telling me this?'

'Just listen,' Bland told him.

'Ordinarily, we would have put Beridze low on anyone's list of assassination targets,' Batten continued. 'But the information we have about the FSB's activities in Kazakhstan puts a rather different light on things.'

The memory of Kazakhstan forced Sam's stomach into a knot. He kept listening.

'We've constructed a scenario,' the analyst continued. He waved one hand in the air. 'Just a theory, you understand. Beridze is assassinated by a young man who believes he is working for MI5. The Russians feed this information to the Georgians. Maybe they even deliver the assassin. Clearly it will create a major diplomatic incident between the UK and Georgia.'

Sam scowled. 'So what?' he said. 'Nothing the men in suits can't sort out.'

Bland interrupted. 'I'm, ah . . . I'm afraid it's a little bit

370

more complicated than that, Sam.' He stood up and, seemingly oblivious to the fact that he had asked the sweating analyst to explain what was going on, continued talking. 'For the past nine months,' he said, 'the British military has been constructing a missile launch facility on Georgian territory. The materials are covertly flown in under the guise of humanitarian aid for those Georgian nationals displaced by Russia's military intervention in their country. The Georgian government is happy to help us. With the Russians on their doorstep, they, ah . . . they need all the friends they can get. As for us . . .' He looked sharply at Sam. 'As for us, we *really* need that missile base.'

Sam shook his head. 'I don't understand. You're never going to launch a missile strike on Russia.' He ignored the analyst, who was frowning impatiently.

'No, Sam. Not the Russians. Our conflict with them remains strictly, ah . . . cold.' He drew a deep breath. 'Iran.'

Sam blinked. He didn't understand.

'We've known for some time that their nuclear enrichment programme has been ongoing, despite their occasional claims to have halted it. They're a long way down the line to becoming a nuclear power.'

'Weeks away,' the analyst butted in, and this time he received no reprimand from Bland.

'The Americans know this, of course,' Bland continued. 'They talk a good line about peaceful diplomatic relations with Iran, but believe me, the moment the Iranians become a threat, we'll see a US military surge in that part of the world.' He paused. 'Where the Americans go, the British follow. But we can't afford another war in the Middle East. Georgia is the closest, safest friendly territory we have to Iranian soil. It's only the threat of our missile launch capabilities in that area that's keeping the Iranians at bay. If the Georgians think that MI5 have assassinated their top man in the UK, we can kiss goodbye to the facility.'

Bland paused, then sat down again. 'If that happens, Sam, the Iranians *will* complete their nuclear programme. The Americans *will* invade and we *will* be dragged into it.' Beside him, the analyst was nodding in agreement, his skin even sweatier now than when he had entered. 'We don't need another war in the Middle East, Sam. But if your brother's little plan comes to fruition, that's what we're going to end up with.'

At the mention of Jacob, the familiar conflict of emotions burned through Sam's blood. 'Jacob wouldn't . . .'

Bland interrupted. 'I, ah . . . I rather doubt Jacob Redman was even aware of the wider implications of his actions, Sam. The FSB have put a lot of time and effort into this. I think it unlikely that they would have entrusted him with any more information than he needed.'

A silence fell over the room. It was Sam that broke it. 'I still don't understand why the Russians would want another war in the Middle East.'

The analyst replied. 'The Russians want to avoid a British military facility on their doorstep. War in the Middle East is a happy sideline for them. It keeps the West's hands full, while they pursue aggressive military policies on their own doorstep.'

'In short,' Bland concluded with stinging understatement, 'the assassination of the Georgian ambassador would be a disaster.' He fixed Sam with a meaningful stare. 'It's a shame,' he said, 'that we are unable to speak to your brother about this.'

Sam felt like he had been stung. 'What's the problem?' He knew he was being obtuse, but he couldn't help it. 'You know who, you know when. You can stop it happening. And even if the red-light runner gets lucky, you just tell the Georgians the truth.'

'And if you were the Georgians, Sam, would *you* believe the truth?'

Sam looked away. 'I've done what I can,' he said stubbornly. 'I've told you everything Jacob gave me. It's up to you now.'

Bland surveyed him calmly. Then, without any warning, he stood up and left the room. The sweaty analyst avoided Sam's eye, choosing instead to burrow himself in his file. When Bland returned he had another man with him. The newcomer silently walked up to Sam, undid his handcuffs, then respectfully left the room.

Sam rubbed his wrists. It felt good to be free.

'I'm going to put my cards on the table, Sam,' the older man said. 'I hope you're listening carefully.'

Sam gave him no indication that he was.

'The FSB has run rings around this service. I, ah . . . I don't think it's an exaggeration to say that's largely due to your brother. And what's more, I've underestimated you. You've been one step ahead of us all the way. It would be foolish of me not to acknowledge that.'

Bland let that sink in before he continued. 'Kakha Beridze is due at a function tomorrow evening. A dinner. May 26. Georgian Independence Day, to add insult to injury. Two hundred guests. It's been planned for months. I think we might safely say that this is where the assassination attempt is to take place, don't you?'

Sam nodded, despite himself.

Bland didn't take his eyes off him. 'You know how your brother thinks, Sam. You were on ops with him in the Regiment for years. How would he pull it off?'

'I don't know. With two hundred people there, any number of ways. The guy's a sitting duck.'

'Think, Sam. I don't need to impress upon you how important it is.'

'I don't know, all right?'

Bland nodded thoughtfully, then stood up. He paced a little, before stopping by the one-way window, his back to

Sam. 'Just at the moment,' he said, 'as we speak, Clare Corbett is being taken into custody. We have all sorts of powers to detain her under the Prevention of Terrorism Act, but ah . . . frankly we don't really need them. Mark Porteus, of course, is at Her Majesty's Pleasure, and it really won't take long for our friends in blue to construct a murder charge for you that will earn you a life sentence. Just think of the effect that will have on your father.'

He turned round and smiled thinly at Sam. 'Oh,' he added, 'and I, ah . . . I suppose it barely needs to be said that we have DNA evidence that puts you at the scene of Mac Howden's death. I wonder what his family will think when they learn about *that* . . . ?'

It was as if something had snapped inside Sam. He jumped to his feet and, in two big strides, he approached Bland, grabbing the older man by the scruff of his neck and thrusting him up against the glass. '*You fucking dare . . .*' he hissed, ignoring the shouts of help he heard from the frightened analyst behind him. '*You fucking dare and I swear I'll kill you!*'

Bland looked down on him. His thin body was light and he was clearly alarmed, but he said nothing. He just stared. And then the sound of the door opening. Men with guns. 'Put him down!'

Sam hurled Bland to one side. The old man stumbled, but did not fall. He turned to the guards. 'Get out,' he ordered. Then, seeing that he needed to repeat himself, he shouted: 'GET OUT!' He looked at the analyst. 'You too.' The little man didn't need telling twice.

Only when they were alone did Bland speak again, his eyes tough and determined as the two of them stood barely metres apart, warriors in some kind of duel. 'If you think for one minute, Redman, that I won't do whatever it takes to stop our national security from being compromised, think again.'

Sam stared him down, his breath short and angry.

'I need to get inside the head of this assassin,' the older man continued. 'You're the only person I know who can do it. Work with me and I'll put you in charge of the operation. But I'm telling you, Sam – if Beridze gets killed tomorrow night, I'll do all those things and more.'

Silence. Sam felt nothing but hatred and frustration. Yet he knew when he was in a corner. He closed his eyes and did his best to calm down. Only then did he speak.

'Cancel the event,' he said. 'You could put an entire fucking squadron in there – Jacob would know how to get past them.'

Bland nodded. 'Go on,' he said.

'Put him in a safe house. Regiment guard. His assistant too.' He looked over at the glass. 'Nobody in the Firm's to know where it is.'

'Why the hell not?' Bland demanded.

'I told you,' Sam said. 'When we hit the training camp, we were expected. Spetsnaz. Where else would the information have come from other than inside the Firm? For all I know, the mole could be you.'

Bland's lips thinned. 'There's no mole, Sam. You're seeing shadows. Spetsnaz were there as a precautionary measure, not because they'd been tipped off.'

But Sam didn't want to hear it. 'You want to do this my way, then we'll do it my way. If not, you might as well put me back in that police van. I've lost a brother, a friend and a colleague in the last few days and I'm not going to lose any more. Truth is I don't even know if I can trust *you*, but I don't really have much choice.' He jutted out his chin. 'I want the same team that hit the training camp. What's left of them, at least.' He counted them off on his fingers. 'Tyler, Cullen, Andrews, Davenport and Webb. They were there when Craven died.'

'I didn't have you down as the sentimental type, Sam.'

'I'm not. If this hit is connected to Craven's death, they'll want to make sure it doesn't happen. That makes them the best men for the job. That's my bottom line, Bland. Take it or leave it.'

Bland fell silent. He looked at Sam for what felt like an age, his head nodding gently and his body swaying slightly like a snake.

'All right, Sam,' he said finally. 'You've got yourself a deal. But please don't think I'm bluffing. If Kakha Beridze dies, you're going down. And I promise you – you'll take the people you care about down with you.'

TWENTY-SEVEN

The Georgian Embassy, London. May 26.
Kakha Beridze stared across the desk. He was plump and heavy set, with thick, badger-like hair. He had a thick, dense moustache, the kind that always seems so popular amongst dodgy Eastern European men, and his fat fingers were adorned with gold rings. If he truly had any diplomatic skills, they had deserted him: the Georgian ambassador to London was clearly furious to have been woken up at 3 a.m. by two insistent MI6 spooks. He was furious at having been dragged into the distinctly shabby embassy, and furious at the implacable way in which he was being spoken to by Gabriel Bland.

'Impossible,' he said in his almost impenetrable accent. 'The event has been organised for many months now. I am entertaining Georgian nationals from all over this country. I will not cancel it.'

Bland sat at the opposite side of Beridze's desk. Sam stood behind him, grim and silent. Occasionally, Beridze would glance up at him. His presence clearly made the Georgian nervous. To Beridze's side stood another man, also plump, but younger. He bent down and whispered something into Beridze's ear. The ambassador brushed him off and turned his attention back to Bland. 'Impossible,' he repeated.

Even though he couldn't see Bland's face, Sam could imagine the thin smile on his lips as he spoke. 'It would be perfectly possible,' the older man said, 'for us to be, ah . . .

heavy-handed in order to stop the event from taking place, Mr Beridze. But I thought it would be more politic for us to give you the opportunity to make your excuses.'

Beridze blinked.

'A security threat, you say? What manner of security threat? I demand not to be kept in the dark about this . . .'

'I have no intention of keeping you in the dark, Mr Beridze.' He paused. 'We have very good intelligence that an attempt will be made on your life tonight. Not only on your life, but on that of your, ah . . . assistant.' He held a hand up to the man standing by the ambassador who gave no reaction – he clearly didn't understand what was going on.

'Intelligence?' the ambassador scoffed. 'What sort of intelligence?'

'Good intelligence. From a reliable source.'

Beridze licked his lips. 'Then we will employ security,' he announced. 'Everyone to be searched before they enter. Bags, clothes . . .'

A silence. 'Sam?' Bland addressed him without turning round. 'Off the top of your head, perhaps you could suggest one way of infiltrating Mr Beridze's event, despite such, ah . . . *extensive* precautions.'

Sam sniffed. 'Pen gun,' he said. '.22 calibre. Looks like a biro. Realistic. No one would know what it really was until the target was down.'

Beridze shifted in his seat a little uncomfortably.

'You see, Mr Beridze, Sam is a professional. He has an imaginative way of looking at these things and I'm sure he could come up with any number of, ah . . . variations on the theme. Of course, the person sent to assassinate you will also be a professional. Have I made my point?'

Beridze scowled. 'I will not be bullied.'

'Sam.' Bland continued almost as if the ambassador had said nothing. 'Perhaps you could escort Mr Beridze and his assistant off the premises.'

Beridze stood up, his eyes full of fury. 'I hope I do not need to remind you, Mr Bland, that you are technically on Georgian territory. I will not be spoken to like that in my own embassy.'

Bland stood too. 'Mr Beridze, if you refuse to listen to what I have to say, then there will be a new ambassador in this embassy very soon. To be quite frank with you, that would be a matter of supreme indifference to me. But if you are the subject of an assassination attempt, the implications would be wider than you could possibly know. Your refusal to do as I ask puts the security of this country at risk. I have a number of legal means at my disposal to force you to do what I'm suggesting, which will be embarrassing for you and awkward for our two countries. I would rather not resort to these, but one way or another you *will* be going with this man to a place of my choosing. The manner of your departure is up to you.'

Beridze's heavy eyebrows became furrowed and he tried, without success, to hide his fury. Bland's words, though, had clearly sunk in. The ambassador turned to his assistant and delivered a curt instruction in his native language before returning his attention to Bland. 'I am not happy about this,' he said. 'You may be sure that complaints will be made to the relevant authorities.'

'No doubt they will be in touch with me if it seems appropriate,' Bland murmured, and for a moment Sam felt a creeping respect for him. 'Sam has a car waiting outside,' he continued. 'I suggest we meet you there in, what, ten minutes?'

Beridze gave him a dark look. 'Ten minutes,' he agreed.

*

Together Sam and Bland walked back out on to the street. It was quiet here. Ominously quiet. Sam looked around for a hidden pair of eyes, but the only ones he saw belonged to an urban fox that stared at them from the middle of the road. They stood under the light of a yellow lamp, waiting for the two Georgians to join them. 'It's a mistake for me not to have MI6 coordinating this,' Bland scowled as they stood by the kerb.

'Forget it, Bland,' Sam said, just as the MI6 man's phone rang. He answered it, listened intently, then hung up. 'Hereford. Your unit is already at the safe house.'

'Right,' Sam nodded. He would never have admitted it to Bland, but it felt good to be active again. Good to have something to occupy his mind. Good to forget about the events of the previous day.

The fox sprinted suddenly away. Sam saw Bland jump. The old man was nervous. He had good reason. Sam remained silent.

The Georgians appeared, wearing coats that were too heavy for the time of year. Beridze's assistant carried his briefcase, but the ambassador carried nothing other than a pair of leather gloves. They wordlessly approached and joined them under the yellow light, where Beridze's badger-like hair look almost golden.

'Give me your phones,' Sam demanded.

'Absolutely not,' Beridze replied.

Sam was in no mood to argue. He grabbed the ambassador by the coat and pushed him up against the car. 'Give me your fucking phone!' he repeated.

The startled man plunged his hand into his pocket and pulled out a thin mobile. Sam grabbed it and turned to the assistant. 'You too,' he said. The assistant plonked his bags on the ground and quickly relinquished his handset. Once Sam had them both, he bent down and dropped each one through a drain cover in the gutter. 'Just in case you were thinking of telling anyone where we're going,' he told the startled Georgians. 'Get in the car. Now.'

The two men hurried into the back seat, leaving Sam and Bland alone in the lamplight. They exchanged no words, but the tension between them was drawn on their faces. Sam turned and headed to the driver's side of the car. He was opening the door when he heard Bland's voice.

'Sam.'

'What?'

'Keep them alive.'

Sam shot him a look, nodded, then climbed into the car. He started the engine and drove off without even a glance at the two frightened Georgians sitting in the seat behind him, and leaving Gabriel Bland alone in the yellow light of the lamp.

★

Sam drove carefully through the London night, checking his mirrors as often as he looked at the road ahead. The head-lamps of every car, unnaturally bright as they flashed across his vision, were beacons: a potential trail. At the Holland Park roundabout he completed four full circuits, checking that no one was following. It wouldn't drop a skilful trail – there could be a number of cars following, one waiting at each exit for him; but if he *was* being followed by more than one vehicle it would stretch their resources.

On the Westway he took the fast lane, veering quickly off the road at the Paddington turn-off and slicing his way through residential streets, before turning back onto the Westway and heading further up into town, past Euston and King's Cross, then up to the heart of North London. Having memorised the location of the safe house back at MI6 HQ, Sam drove almost on autopilot.

'Where are you taking us?' Beridze and his assistant had remained silent for the entire journey, just giving Sam ashen-faced glances in the rear-view mirror.

'Somewhere safe,' Sam snapped.

Beridze didn't look convinced. His assistant jabbered something in their own language, but he was cut short by his boss. They continued to drive in silence.

There was more rubbish than there were pedestrians along the Seven Sisters Road. He kept driving. They weren't far now and he would feel better once there were walls around him.

The safe house was in a side street off the main drag of Tottenham Hale, but Sam didn't stop nearby. He drove instead into the large car park by the Tube station. As he turned off the engine and the car lights, Beridze spoke again. 'Where are we?'

'Shut up.' Sam looked around for any sign of another car coming to a halt, but there was nothing. He glanced over his shoulder and pointed at Beridze's assistant. 'Does he speak English?'

'Badly,' Beridze replied.

'I want you both to get out. When I say "walk", you walk. When I say "stop", you stop. Tell him.'

Beridze translated. His assistant gave a nervous nod and the three men got out of the car.

Sam felt naked without a weapon. His skin prickled as he looked around, scanning the area for signs of anything suspicious. Beridze's assistant held his briefcase close to his chest as he looked anxiously around; both men were peculiarly out of place in these bleak, suburban surroundings. As though they were a long way from home.

'Walk,' Sam told them. He pointed back towards the main road. 'That way.'

The two Georgians shuffled off. Sam took the rear, constantly checking around him. At the main road he made them wait, like an anxious parent, until there really were no cars – a road 'accident', he knew, was the easiest way to carry out a hit. When the road was clear he hustled them across.

'How far?' the ambassador asked, already out of breath.

'Keep walking,' Sam told him.

They arrived at the safe house in a couple of minutes. To look at it, you wouldn't think it was anything special, just another in a long line of run-down, three-storey terraced houses. The windows were obscured with net curtains and there were no lights on inside. Further down the street there was an unmarked white van. Sam nodded. 'We're here,' he said.

The three men stood in the street. 'Well?' Beridze asked, his voice sharp with impatience. 'What now?'

'We wait to be let in.'

'But nobody knows we are here.'

'Oh, they know,' Sam replied. And at just that moment the front door clicked open. Sam pushed past the two Georgians, opened the door a little further and peered inside. Darkness. 'It's me,' he called quietly. 'Sam.'

A pause. And then from the silence emerged a figure. Tall, wide-shouldered, a weapon in his hand and a comms earpiece over one ear. Sam recognised the hook nose and the heavy eyebrows, of course. Steve Davenport. 'Morning all. Got some packages to deliver, then?' His voice was flat; immediately Sam picked up on a sense of unease, as if his SAS mate was less than pleased to see him.

'Special fucking delivery,' Sam replied. He turned round to the Georgians. 'All right, you two. Get inside.'

The door was closed and they headed upstairs in near darkness. On the first-floor landing Sam saw a strip of light underneath one of the doors. Davenport opened it and they filed inside.

It was a sparse, unwelcoming room, but then Sam hadn't been expecting the Ritz. A good safe house needed to be basic and free of furniture – the more stuff there was in it, the harder it would be to tell if the place had been tampered with. There was one window in this room, but it was blocked off by a large sheet of black tarpaulin in order to stop any light escaping from a single bulb that hung from the ceiling. A steel flight case of weapons was propped up against one wall, and sitting cross-legged in a corner, packet of cigarettes in front of him and one in his mouth, was Luke Tyler, Craven's Cockney friend and the one who had taken his death the worst. He took a deep drag on his cigarette. 'Welcome to the party,' he drawled. 'These the strippers?'

Beridze looked incensed; Sam just ignored it. 'Where are the others?'

'Cullen's upstairs watching the garden. Means he has to stand on the shitter, but he's got a mouth like a toilet, so he's probably at home. Webb's up there watching the front and Andrews is on the ground floor doing the same.' Tyler took another drag on his cigarette, without taking his eye off Sam. 'Think he saw the milkman earlier on. Nearly shat himself.'

Beridze looked from one man to the other. Even though English wasn't his first language he was clearly picking up on the tension in the room. Sam looked down at Tyler. 'Get to your fucking feet, Luke,' he said. And when the younger man had done so: 'You got a problem, spit it out.'

Tyler dropped his cigarette onto the bare floorboards and stubbed it out with his boot. 'Lot of rumours going around, Sam. Plenty of us want to know what your chat with the spooks after the Kazakhstan job was about.' He set his jaw and stared at Sam.

The accusation hung in the air.

Tyler deserved to know the truth. They all did. But that meant telling them about Jacob and Sam couldn't bring himself to do that. He walked over to the weapons stash and, almost absent-mindedly, picked up a Sig. 'Get the others,' he said.

'What do you mean?'

'Cullen, Andrews, Webb. Get them.'

'They're on stag.'

'It doesn't matter. Get them now.'

Tyler shrugged, then disappeared. Two minutes later the others filed silently in, all of them wearing NV goggles up on their foreheads and with comms earpieces on one side of their heads. Only when they were all assembled did Sam speak. 'Sounds to me like Hereford's turned into a WI meeting.' He looked at each of them in turn. Tyler, lairy and aggressive. Webb, a vicious fire in his eyes. Cullen, his lips pursed in an expression of mistrust. Andrews, his black skin glowing despite the early morning chill, his face calm but watchful. And Davenport, older than the others, but no less wary.

'Craven's dead,' Sam continued. 'You think I know something about it that you don't. Well you're wrong. You really think the Firm are going to confide in me?' He let that thought sink in before he dropped the bombshell. 'Mac's dead too.'

The men looked at each other. Someone hissed the word 'shit', but Sam didn't see who it was.

'Shot,' he continued. 'Point blank. Night before last. Mac was my best friend. So while you're all throwing your toys out of your pram, you might want to give that some thought.'

The men looked a bit less sure of themselves. 'What's the craic?' Cullen asked. 'What the hell happened to him?'

'The Firm haven't told me much. Just that he fell foul of the Russians. Like Craven.' He pointed at Beridze. 'And just like our man here will, if the FSB get their way.' The unit looked towards the Georgian. At the mention of so many deaths, the ambassador had grown a little paler. Sam wondered how much he should tell them – about the missile base and the Iranians. Nothing, he decided. All that meant very little to these guys. Craven and Mac were dead and they wanted to pay someone back for it. Sometimes it paid to keep things simple. And sometimes it paid not to tell the whole truth.

'They're sending someone,' he continued. 'Tonight, we think.' He looked them each in the eye. 'Someone good. I asked for you lot because I knew you'd want this chance.'

A thick silence in the room. The two Georgians shuffled nervously.

'Who knows we're here?' Davenport asked.

'The Firm,' Sam replied. 'No one else.'

Davenport glanced over at the Georgians. 'Our friends didn't tell anyone?'

Sam shook his head.

'Then the chances are we've sidestepped the hit, that no one'll come.'

Sam was about to answer, but Tyler got there first. 'Unless the same person who tipped off Spetsnaz decides to shoot his mouth off about where we are. That what you're thinking, Sam?'

Sam didn't know what he was thinking. Bland's words kept coming back to him. *There's no mole, Sam. You're seeing shadows.* Jesus, he thought to himself. I probably am. It would make sense for Spetsnaz to have been guarding the FSB's little secret in Kazakhstan. With a flash of insight he suspected he'd been wrong. But mole or no mole, one thing was sure: if this hit had Jacob's fingerprints on it, things would be complicated. Very fucking complicated. It was a dark thought, but Sam couldn't shake it.

'Someone will come,' he said, somehow very sure that he was right. One glance at the men and he knew they took him at his word. And one look at the Georgians did the same. 'All right,' he said. 'Back to your positions and keep your fucking eyes open. These bastards have already nailed two of ours. Let's make sure they don't make it a third, hey?'

Daylight came, and with it the ability to walk around the house without alerting anyone outside to their presence. Sam was glad to leave Beridze and his assistant under Davenport's protection to check the place out. It ticked all the boxes. Exits at the front and the back in case they needed to leave in a hurry – there was a gate at the bottom of the garden and from behind the net curtains in the top-floor toilet he could see an alleyway winding back round on to the street. All the exits could be clearly surveyed from the watch points where the men stood guard with their sniper rifles pointing directly at the windows. Sam's pep talk had done the trick – they were alert and watchful. Even Tyler's previous sarcasm had been replaced by a crisp tension. These men were like loaded weapons, ready to be discharged at any second.

Back in the main room, Beridze was sitting on the bare floor while his assistant propped his abundant backside on his briefcase. 'I demand that you find me a chair,' Beridze instructed when Sam walked back in.

'I'm not a furniture removal man.'

'*I am the Georgian ambassador . . .*' Beridze flared, but he was interrupted by Sam.

'If tonight's festivities don't go the way we want them to, Beridze, you won't need a chair. You'll need a box. Now shut the fuck up and let us get on with our job of keeping you alive.'

Beridze scowled at him, but he fell silent.

10.00 hrs. They ate chocolate and drank sugary Coke from the stores the unit had brought with them – and which Beridze, from the look on his face, found distasteful – and waited. Sam attached his own comms, then continued to wait. Long stretches of silence filled the house, broken only by the occasional cough from one of the guys over the comms and the incessant barking of a dog nearby. Sam knew that the buildings on either side of the safe house would be empty, so whenever the silence was disturbed by some indistinguishable noise, everyone jumped. As morning became afternoon, even Beridze had stopped his brusque comments. Something had changed in him. Tiredness? Or had the fear notched up a level as evening approached?

Sam looked over at the ambassador. It was probably a bit of both.

He crouched opposite the two Georgians, his back leaning against the wall as he turned the Sig round in his fingers. The fear, he realised, was rising in him too. Not fear of a fight. Far from it. But a different kind of fear. He felt there was something on the periphery of his vision. Off to one side. And when he tried to turn his mind to see it, it slipped away again. He closed his eyes and tried to zero in.

'Something wrong, Sam?' Davenport asked. Sam opened his eyes to see his colleague checking him out.

He shook his head. 'Nothing,' he said.

But it wasn't true. The shadow on the edge of his vision was there. He knew he should be able to see it, but he couldn't.

All the entrances and exits were covered. He had the cream of the crop guarding the Georgians. But despite all that, despite everything, Sam Redman couldn't help thinking he was missing something.

★

14.20 hrs.

Jamie Spillane wasn't far away. He paced the streets, the faint nausea of excitement churning inside. He kept one hand in his pocket and, with his fingertips, turned the fifty-

388

pence piece that he was carrying over and over. It was stupid, he knew, but like a kid making sure he had his lunch money, Jamie had been holding on to this coin for the last two days. He liked to know that everything was arranged as it should be.

As he walked, his mind replayed his instructions. *21.00 hrs. Do nothing till then.*

How many times had he performed the calculation in his head, just to be sure? 21.00 hrs: that was nine o'clock in the evening. He looked at his watch. Half-past two. The intervening hours seemed like days, an impossible bridge to cross before he could finally complete his operation.

Make sure your face is hidden. Wear a hood, a balaclava, something like that.

'Roger that,' Jamie had replied, attempting to sound military.

Make sure you know where you're going. Work out your route in advance.

Jamie had known his route for days. An anxious father-to-be, plotting the fastest way to the hospital, couldn't have been more fastidious.

He walked faster. On the other side of the street he heard somebody shout at him: 'Wanker!' He ignored it. He didn't need a kerbside brawl to get his kicks any more. He had something else. Something better.

Looking at his watch again, he saw that it was only two thirty-five. He bit his lip, turned and then headed back to his bedsit, where he would wait out the remaining hours. His fingertips continued to roll the fifty-pence piece round in his pocket. Faster and faster. It dug into his skin.

How amazing, he thought to himself, that you can kill a man using just a coin . . .

★

18.30 hrs.

It grew dark. Sam visited each of the observation posts. The men had reattached their NV goggles. They were like statues in the gloom and about as talkative as they watched out of their windows.

'It could happen at any time,' Sam told each of them. And from each of them he got only a brief nod in return.

Back in the main room, Beridze was pacing. He gave Sam an irritated look as he entered, then muttered something under his breath. His wide-eyed assistant remained crouched on the floor.

Silence in the room. The incessant barking of the dog outside.

And at the edge of Sam's mind, the shadows that wouldn't go away.

He tried to concentrate. To remain professional. But his mind wandered, no matter how much he tried to steer it back on course. He thought of his father. At that very moment Max would be lying frail in his bed, perhaps reliving old glories in his head, perhaps rejoicing in the son that had come back to life. *Jacob was a real soldier,* he heard the old man saying. *If it wasn't for your brother, God knows where you'd have ended up.*

'Movement!' Hill's voice on the comms. Sam stood up quickly, pointing his gun towards the door. He sensed Davenport training his M16 at the black tarpaulin that covered the window.

'What is it?' Beridze whispered. Sam heard the two men shuffle into a corner. '*What is it?*'

Neither SAS man moved.

A breathless few seconds. And then, over comms: 'It's nothing.'

Sam lowered his gun, but only slowly. 'False alarm,' he stated. He looked at his watch. 18.56. Beridze spat something in his own language. Sam felt like doing the same. The shadow on the edge of his mind grew darker, but no more distinct.

If it wasn't for your brother, God knows where you'd have ended up.

★

20.15 hrs.

Jamie Spillane had put his hooded top on fifteen minutes ago and spent the intervening time looking at himself in the cloudy mirror. The hood hung over the top of his face by a good couple of inches. In the dark, he satisfied himself, it would be almost impossible to make out his features.

Keep your face hidden. CCTV cameras are hard to spot.

He walked over to his bed. From under the mattress he pulled one of the boxes that had been supplied to him. Inside was the small, black handgun. He placed it in the pocket of his hooded top. Back in front of the mirror, he noticed that it bulged slightly; but no one would know what it was. He smiled to himself. It felt good carrying a weapon. He liked it.

20.19. Forty-one minutes to go. It would only take him ten to get there, but he didn't want to be late. He tugged the hood one final time down over his face, then left his tiny bedsit, making very sure to lock the door behind him as he went.

★

Sam paced.

He'd lost count of the times he had walked through the darkness of the safe house, checking each observation point and receiving nothing but curt responses from the watchful guys. They could sense he was on edge. That much was clear.

391

Back in the main room, the two Georgians were arguing. About what, Sam didn't know. Their voices sounded harsh and guttural. Davenport was looking at them like they were mad; when they saw Sam, however, they quietened down.

'Anything?' Davenport asked.

Sam shook his head. 'Not yet.'

'This is ridiculous,' the ambassador announced. 'Nobody knows where we are. How can *anybody* find us?'

Neither of the SAS men replied. But Sam could tell from the look Davenport gave him that he was thinking a similar thing.

And maybe he was right.

Sam looked at his watch. 20.36. Damn it, he didn't even know what he was waiting for.

Thoughts collided in his brain. He tried to organise them. Jacob had told him to stay away. *You can't stop it. It's in motion.*

Think, Sam, he told himself. *Just think.*

Davenport was looking at him again. So were the Georgians.

His brother wouldn't let this fail. Sam knew him too well. He was clever. Just because he was dead – and the very thought twisted inside him – it didn't mean he hadn't trained his red-light runners to think like him.

You can't stop it. It's in motion.

Sam tried to think what he himself would do. But as he stood in that room, his mind was suddenly flooded with other things: images of his brother. As a kid, playing. As a young man, joining up and persuading Sam to do the same.

A fizzing sound. Davenport had opened a can of Coke. He downed it, looking at Sam over the can as he did so.

Sam blinked. Then he stared. Not at Davenport, but at the can of Coke.

The shadow on the edge of his memory had suddenly grown more distinct.

He saw Jacob again; but this time it was in Iraq, six years ago. The day when it all went wrong.

Suddenly Sam was in the Al-Mansour district of Baghdad again. He, Jacob and Mac were preparing to storm a house, to apprehend a wanted Ba'athist. Their tout had dropped a tracking device outside the house in question, hidden in an old fizzy drink can, so they knew where it was. But they needed a diversion. Something to distract the guards while they raided the building.

Standing in that room, with Davenport and the Georgians, Sam heard his dead brother's voice as clearly as if he was right there with them. Tense. A bit self-satisfied. The very words he had spoken that day so long ago.

I gave the Coke can a bit of extra sugar.

They'd needed a diversion outside the house. Thanks to Jacob's forward planning, there was an improvised explosive device already there.

An IED, already there.

'Jesus,' he breathed. 'We're fucking sitting on it.'

Davenport looked alarmed. 'What's wrong, Sam?' But Sam didn't answer. His eyes had fallen on Beridze's assistant, Gigo. Jacob had mentioned him, but why? Bland's analyst had assumed he was a target, like the ambassador. But he was a nobody. Why would they target him?

Like a balloon being burst, the shadow on the edge of his vision disappeared and Sam saw clearly. *His assistant.* Jacob had been trying to tell Sam something. At the moment of his death, he'd been trying to warn him. *The assistant was the shooter.* He strode over to the younger of the two Georgians and with one tug of his clothes yanked him to his feet before pressing him against the wall.

'Where is it?' he shouted. 'Where's your fucking weapon?' He pressed the gun up against the man's head.

Gigo's eyes bulged. He tried to speak, but was mute with fear.

From behind him, Davenport's voice. 'For fuck's sake, Sam, what are you doing?'

Sam hurled the assistant into the middle of the room. 'Take your clothes off,' he said. Then, over his shoulder at the boss, *'Tell him to take his fucking clothes off!'*

Davenport started to say something, but Sam waved his handgun in his colleague's direction. 'Shut up,' he said.

Commotion over the comms. 'What's going on?' Sam didn't answer.

Gigo was stripping, slowly because of his shaking body. 'Hurry up,' Sam barked at him. He went a bit faster, then stood wearing nothing but his underpants, a pair of gartered socks and a humiliated, incensed expression. He was fat, with a hairy stomach. But there was no concealed weapon.

'What the hell's going on, Sam?' Davenport demanded. Sam's breath came in short, nervous gasps. He looked around. He was missing something. *Damn it, he was missing something.*

And then his eyes fell upon the briefcase, still on the floor where Gigo had been using it as a seat. He felt a cold sickness oozing through his body. 'Open it,' he told the stunned assistant. *'Open it!'*

Gigo walked over to the briefcase, unable to keep his eyes from Sam's gun. He bent down and fumbled with the clasps. When it was open, he stood back.

Sam approached. It looked perfectly ordinary: a few papers inside, nothing more. Gingerly, he picked it up and upturned it. The papers wafted to the floor like autumn leaves, leaving him with nothing more than an empty box.

'You need to calm down, Sam.' Davenport's voice. Tense. Urgent.

Sam looked back at the assistant. His expression was still horrified. But confused too. Gigo obviously didn't know what the hell was going on.

'You sure this is his briefcase?' he demanded of the ambassador.

'Of course it is his briefcase,' the ambassador replied. 'For God's sake, what is . . . ?'

He didn't finish his sentence. He just watched as Sam ran to the weapons cache, pulled out a knife, then cut into the lining of the briefcase. Two slashes, then he dropped the knife and started using his hands.

I gave the Coke can some extra sugar.

Moments later, the extra sugar was revealed.

A thick penetrating silence. Sam held the briefcase in his hands. He stared at it.

Taped to the inside shell of the case was a mobile phone. It was on, but it had been tampered with. From the back of the handset led a wire, connected to several blocks of plastic explosive. A bomb, and a remote detonator.

The world slowed down. He turned to Davenport, whose wide eyes showed that he quite clearly knew what he was looking at. Davenport's voice: *'Jesus, it could blow at any second!'*

And then Sam yelled.

'GET OUT! GET OUT OF THE FUCKING HOUSE! EVERYONE . . . NOW . . . GET OUT!'

★

20.59 hrs.

Jamie Spillane waited outside the phone booth, his head bowed and his features obscured by his hooded top. Booths like this were scarce in these days of mobile phones and he had scouted out this one days before. And he had been here earlier. Twice. To check it was operational and that nobody had vandalised it.

He looked at his watch. It was time.

Stepping into the booth, he pulled from one pocket his

fifty-pence piece and from another a slip of paper. On it, he had scrawled the number of the mobile phone which he had used to create the detonator. The one inside the replica briefcase he had swapped over just a couple of nights before. Vaguely he wondered where it was now. Near? Far? He shrugged. It didn't matter to him. He just kept thinking of his instructions. *This is an important job for the British government. Don't get clever. Don't start improvising. Just do what I've told you and everything will run smoothly.*

He felt a little tremor of excitement as he stepped into the booth. He thought of Kelly, and how she hadn't believed him. He thought of his mum and dad, and how little they thought of him. It brought a small sneer to his lips and a heat to his blood.

He picked up the handset, waited for the dialling tone, then pressed the fifty pence into the slot.

And then he punched in the number . . .

★

'GET OUT! GET OUT OF THE FUCKING HOUSE! EVERYONE . . . NOW . . . GET OUT!'

Davenport was already moving, but the two Georgians were frozen with shock. Sam suppressed his urge to hurl the briefcase away, instead laying it softly on the floor. Then he put the gun to Beridze's head. *'Get out!'* he repeated and pushed the ambassador to the door. His alarmed assistant tried to start putting his clothes back on, but Davenport grabbed the semi-naked man, lifted him from his feet and threw him towards the door.

Chaos over the comms. The rest of the unit were talking over each other. 'Just get the fuck out of here!' Sam bellowed over the top. 'This whole fucking place is going to blow!'

They were on the landing, then the stairs. Beridze tripped;

he fell headlong down the steps, ending up in heap on the hallway. Sam launched himself down, covering the entire staircase in two big jumps. At the bottom he didn't bother to stop and see if the Georgian ambassador was injured; he just picked the heavy man up, his strength increased by adrenaline, and dragged him to the door. It was locked. Sam fired at the lock, emptying the chamber of his Sig with a succession of blasts that tore the air in two as they splintered and split the door open. It was a fucking hair-raising manoeuvre, because if the round hit the lock at the wrong angle it could ricochet off the metal and back into the discharger's face, and Sam would be properly fucked. But he had only a split second to act. Then two solid kicks and he was out, the bruised and terrified Beridze was with him.

Gigo came next, rushed out by Davenport and his M16. Sam was briefly aware of Tyler's features, but he didn't stop to count the rest of the unit into the street. There were pedestrians in the road – only a few, but too many. '*Run!*' he yelled at Beridze. '*Fucking run!*' And then he waved his Sig in the direction of the pedestrians. '*Get away from this house. Now!*'

The terrified members of the public didn't need telling twice: they joined the waddling ambassador and ran away from Sam.

More shouting over the comms before a voice shouted, 'Clear!' He turned round to see the rest of the unit sprinting the opposite way down the road. 'We're clear!'

Sam jumped over the bonnet of a parked car and hurled himself onto the other side, landing heavily on the tarmac, but protected by the metal shell of the vehicle.

He felt the force of the blast almost before he heard it, like a hot, dry wind that scorched his hair and made him grind his face into the ground. And then the sound of the explosion, a flat, deep thump that blew out the windows of the safe house and rocked the car.

A wave of cordite-bleached fog followed, like a giant, thick burnt cloud passing over them. Sam held his breath and closed his eyes, but thick, hot dust filled his nostrils and singed his eyes. He accidentally inhaled and coughed till he was red in the face. It was like he'd smoked fifty tabs in a row.

Shrapnel showered onto the ground.

Then silence.

It didn't last long. From either end of the street, the sound of shouting. Panicked members of the public. Doors opposite the safe house opened. Alarmed residents spilled into the streets. In the distance, sirens.

Sam pushed himself to his feet. His whole body ached. Squinting, he looked down the road and saw Beridze. The Georgian ambassador to London was open-mouthed and shocked. But he was alive, and that was all that mattered.

Then, over the comms, a voice. One of the unit, he didn't know who. 'Mission accomplished,' it said. 'Mission *fucking* accomplished. Christ, Sam. Try and make it a bit closer next time, will you?'

Sam drew a deep breath. 'Yeah,' he replied. His voice was dry and croaking. 'Yeah. I'll see what I can do.'

And with that, he ripped the comms earpiece from his head and threw it to the ground. He didn't give the safe house a second look. He just walked down the road, gun in hand, and as he walked he had the unnerving sensation that two ghosts were walking alongside.

Sam Redman didn't try to shake that feeling. He didn't try to run from those spectres. He knew they would be with him for a long time to come.

He carried on walking, past Beridze, past the curious, alarmed members of the public: a brooding, solitary figure.

A man who knew how lucky he was not to be a ghost himself.

★

Barely a mile away, Jamie Spillane replaced the handset. He had only heard a single ringing tone before the line had been cut off. And he knew what that meant.

The operation had been a success. *He* had been a success. His limbs were trembling with the thrill of it all. Now that he had shown what he was capable of, maybe he would be asked to do it again. Maybe his country would call on him once more. The idea made him shiver with excitement.

Jamie Spillane turned, walked out of the phone booth and made for home, smiling broadly as he went.

EPILOGUE

Two days later.
Gabriel Bland had slept well for the first time in weeks.

When word had come that there had been an explosion in the safe house, he had been paralysed with an icy sickness. Toby Brookes, newly demoted from field work, had been the unfortunate messenger and he had been shot down by an alarmed Bland. 'Find out what's happened. Now!'

Gradually, though, more information had filtered in. No casualties. Beridze alive. All of the SAS team accounted for, except one.

'Who?' Bland had demanded of his timid subordinate.

'Redman, sir. The unit said he made it out alive, but there's no sign of him. I've got eyes ready to search for him, sir. I can put out the word.'

Bland considered this for a moment. 'No,' he said. He looked out of the window of his office. 'No. Let him be, for now.'

Toby had seemed wrong-footed, but he knew not to argue.

'Claire Corbett. Is she still in custody?'

'Yes, sir.'

'Release her.'

Toby looked confused. 'But sir, we haven't questioned . . .'

'Release her.'

'Yes, sir.'

'And I want a representative of the service to visit Mac

400

Howden's wife. She's to be told her husband died as a result of enemy fire in the service of his country. No more, no less. Understood?'

'Understood, sir.'

'Then get on with it.'

Toby had nodded and slipped away, leaving Bland with his own to-do list. The reinstatement of Mark Porteus at SAS HQ would take some clever talking, but Bland was certain he would be able to manage it.

Which left Sam Redman.

Even now, two days later, Bland didn't know what to do with him. The SAS man's face — with its lacerated skin and flat, hard eyes — rose in Bland's mind. He experienced a rare moment of empathy. Redman had endured more in the last few days than most men would ever be able to cope with, and Bland included himself in that. What would he be feeling? What would he be *doing*? Where *was* he? Bland was momentarily tempted to call Toby in to the office, to get him to set the eyes out on Sam after all, just to satisfy his own curiosity. But he didn't. After all, he told himself, if anyone had earned a bit of slack, it was Sam Redman.

Bland sighed. The world, he thought to himself, seemed to be getting more and more complicated. Maybe he was growing too old for the game; he didn't know. In front of him was a document: a DA notice restricting the story of a fatal shooting in a Hereford churchyard some days previously. Bland took a fountain pen, signed it, then stood up and left the room.

He might have slept well, but he was tired. The sort of tiredness that mere sleep would not ease. He needed some time away from all this.

A holiday, Gabriel Bland thought to himself, would do him some good.

★

Max Redman stared at the television set. He hadn't seemed to notice that his son had entered the room. The news programme he was watching blared breathlessly about an explosion the previous night in North London. A terrorist attack, government sources were saying. No casualties, they were pleased to announce. One look at Max, though, and Sam could tell none of this meant anything to him. He was having, as the doctors called it, a 'bad day'.

Not that Sam had *seen* the doctors. After what had happened last time he was here he felt quite sure his continued presence on the premises would not be tolerated. Bland might have been able to smooth things over with Hereford police, but it didn't mean he'd be welcome back here. That was why he had slipped in the back way; and that was why Max was going to have to get used to seeing an awful lot less of him.

'Dad,' he said. Then a bit louder. 'Dad.'

Max turned. There was a look of momentary confusion on his face, as though he didn't know who was talking to him. But then the synapses seemed to click.

'Didn't think you'd be coming back here,' Max said.

Sam shrugged. He walked to his father's bedside and looked at the television. The screen was filled with images of the destroyed safe house, cordoned off and surrounded by armed police.

'Fucking ragheads,' Max muttered. 'They're everywhere. Look at this shit.' He wheezed and then coughed, as if in protest against what he was watching on the screen.

'Yeah,' Sam murmured. He didn't trust himself to say more.

A silence passed between father and son, a silence more meaningful than any Sam had ever known. It was awkward, but he didn't want it to end. He knew what his father's next question would be.

'Did you see him?'

'Yes,' Sam said. 'I saw him.'

'Where was he?'

'The churchyard, Dad. Mum's grave.'

Max's lips thinned and he nodded. His gaze hadn't moved from the screen, but it was obvious he wasn't really watching any more.

'Well?' Max's voice cracked.

'We spoke.'

'You didn't tell me *why* you had to see him.'

Sam felt the skin on his face tightening. 'He's my brother. Why wouldn't I?'

Max seemed to accept that.

'What did he say?'

It was all Sam could do to keep his voice level. 'He said he had to go away, Dad. For a long time. He didn't know how long.'

His father didn't react. He just lay there, motionless.

'I have to go, Dad.'

No reply. Sam looked at his dad's thin face. For the first time ever, he saw Jacob's features there. Older, certainly. Weaker. But Jacob's features. He allowed himself a few seconds to drink them in, then turned to the door.

'Sam?'

He stopped and looked round at his father. There was a fearful look in his eyes, as though he was scared of the question he was about to ask. 'Will I see him again?'

The two men looked at each other and the question filled the air.

But Sam couldn't bring himself to answer. He turned his back on his father and left the room, closing the door quietly behind him.

ONE OF THE MOST TALKED ABOUT STORIES OF COURAGE AND SURVIVAL IN MODERN WARFARE

Of the eight members who set off on the Bravo Two Zero mission in Iraq, only one escaped capture. This is his story.

Dropped behind enemy lines, Chris Ryan and seven fellow soldiers set off on a 200 mile trek across hostile terrain, each man heavily laden with equipment and weaponry. Struggling through unexpected sub-zero temperatures, they soon encountered enemy troops. They then fought against enormous odds in an engagement in which Chris Ryan was separated from his comrades but battled through.

Only two others remained with Chris, one dying of hypothermia and one who was then captured in an Iraqi ambush. The most remarkable part remained – Chris's long lone journey across the desert into Syria under heavy pursuit.

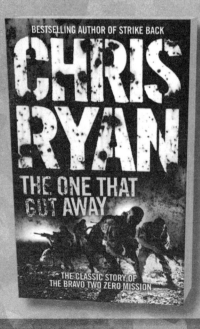

COLLECT THE
FULL CLIP OF BESTSELLING
CHRIS RYAN
NOVELS

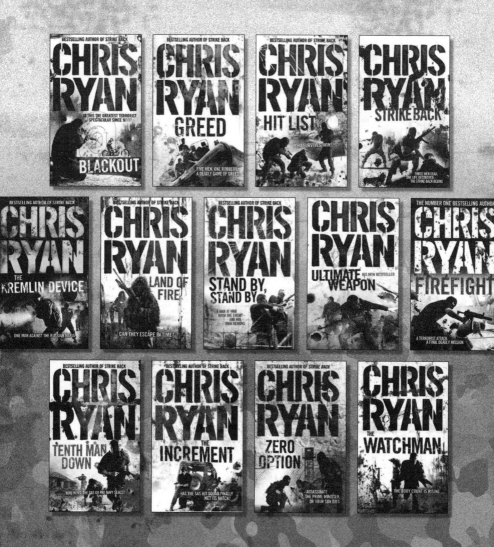

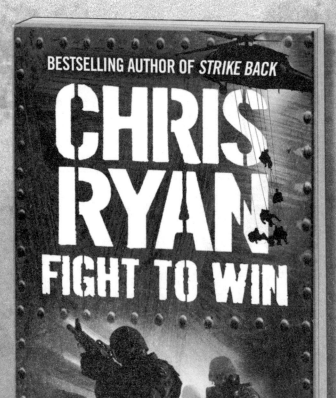